TOUGH
IS NOT ENOUGH

HOW A KAYAK JOURNEY ACROSS
THREE CONTINENTS CHANGED A
CLIMATE WARRIOR

STEVE POSSELT

First published in 2019 by Ebono Institute
74 Prince St, Annerley, Qld
Copyright © Kayak4earth Pty Ltd 2019

A catalogue record for this book is available from the National Library of Australia

Designed and typeset in 11pt Source Sans Pro by Clark & Mackay, Brisbane, Australia

Cover design by Graphiti Design, Lismore Australia

TOUGH
IS NOT ENOUGH

"Yep, Steve is tough alright, but tender too. . . He is a man with heart, a man who cares deeply and gets out there and talks the talk and walks the walk. . . even in a kayak.

"As we fear for our, and our childrens' future, as our planet spins out of control by humans' stupidity and greed, when you feel helpless, faced with the idiocy and blindness of the powerful, the politicians, the people next bloody door – when you try, yet know it's not enough to save our planet– read Steve's book.

"No one has all the answers, and although we mightn't have Steve's stamina, guts and stubbornness... we can nonetheless feel inspired to do our bit as Steve helps us believe in each other, and perhaps in our own way, become a climate warrior and help make a difference."

Di Morrissey AM, author

"Paddling up a flooded Mississippi was a huge kayaking feat but there is much more. Steve's mastery of the conditions and his descriptions of the water will have every paddler enthralled."

Phil Jones, CEO Paddle Australia

"I had no idea the effect reminding Steve that he might not make it to Paris would have on him, but Steve triumphed. When climate change seems so gloomy and you don't know where to turn, follow Steve's lead. We need to keep moving in the right direction."

Senator Bob Brown (retired)

"Reading this book you might reasonably assume Steve is mad. What he did is not mad, though, given the lives of future generations will be vastly affected by the decisions we make now as a global community. Engineers are known for their solid use of facts and their persistence and resilience – that's Steve in a nutshell and I applaud his leadership on this most critical issue."

Peter McIntyre CEO, Engineers Australia

CONTENTS

ACKNOWLEDGEMENTS

To the many people who supported me and the trips, a huge thank you. Without you the trip would not have happened. Some of you embraced the task, some of you struggled. You all tried, you all did your best.

As much as anything, this book is the story of my journey of learning how to work with people. I formed some bonds that will last forever. We had some great adventures together that we will never forget.

Some people donated money, in all $7,000. You are listed at the back of the book. None of this was requested, you just did it. That was amazingly generous and every dollar received boosted my morale and touched my heart.

Michelle Irwin drew the maps and would not accept any money but she must accept my gratitude. She was easy to work with, very competent, and helpful.

The maps are based on Google Maps and Google and any other information providers are identified on each map. We have also referred to products that have protected trademarks. PowerPoint™, GoPro™, Lego®, Velcro® and Skype™ are the trademarks of their respective companies and protected by law. These companies have not sponsored, authorised or endorsed this book.

The photographs were taken by the support crew, or me, and the copyright belongs to Kayak4Eearth.

FOREWORD

You are about to embark on a journey with a very determined and focused man.

Steve Posselt thinks that cycling from Memphis, in the southern United States, to the Atlantic on a $150 Walmart bike is simply a practical response to being unable to paddle up the Mississippi in full flood from the Gulf of Mexico to Chicago. Give it half a day's thought, get a mate in Australia to draw a line on the map, head off to Walmart and buy a bike, and off we go. "Normal."

Some people describe Steve Posselt as a stubborn bastard, but that is a bit cruel before he has even had a chance to introduce himself.

The reason for introducing him at all is that, like many determined and focused individuals, Steve has some trouble recognizing certain aspects of his own character. This does not mean that Steve lacks passion. His presentations are charged with it. He reserves that passion, though, for his causes, not for practical problems … like having to fight for your life.

For many, emotionally charged hours, the editorial team and Steve's nearest and dearest grilled him to introduce you to the women he loved, the friends who supported him, the darkest hours and the moments of exaltation.

As a result of that effort, you are able to speculate on how those moments might have made Steve feel, but you won't get much emotional detail from him. "Shit happens and you move on." You will love Steve Posselt, though, like we all do, because he is driven to succeed – not because he wants to be rich or climb the highest mountain, or paddle the longest river, but – because he cares.

He thinks he is lucky to be alive, we are all lucky to have been born on this beautiful planet. He also thinks that it is shameful that we fail to appreciate that beauty and, even worse, that we wilfully destroy it, in our rush to survive.

He does not expect us to applaud as he paddles past our door, he does not want us to line up and shake his hand in thanks, he does not even really care if we acknowledge the effort he has made on our behalf. All he wants is for us to think about what we are doing and to stop causing harm to the environment.

Geoff Ebbs, publisher

PROLOGUE

My brother reckons I am fearless.
He is wrong. I know fear.
It is what you do with that fear that makes the difference.

Dragging and paddling my kayak down the Murray Darling in 2007 I learned the truth about Australia's rivers, but I learned so much more. At age 54 I had proved to myself, that I was tough enough. In July 2006 the orthopaedic surgeon said my chest and shoulder injuries were horrific. Six months later I paddled 50 kilometres down the mid-Brisbane river and four months after that I set off on a 3,000-kilometre journey from Brisbane to Adelaide with my wheeled kayak. My right hand still could not reach anywhere near my left shoulder, but I was doing what I said I would do. The monkey was off my back. Finally, I was satisfied with myself.

Huge seas off the Australian coast did not faze me. Burning feet from searing temperatures in Australia were just a part of the struggle. Fog in the Gulf of Mexico and freezing winds in New Orleans provided the introduction to the United States. Day after day of drenching rain while dragging the kayak around more than a hundred locks in England, a bouncy trip across the English Channel and a chilly screech down the French coast added excitement to the adventure. That was the physical journey to Paris.

If only that had been all there was.

Before we move into the story, it will help if I explain how these trips work.

My kayak has fold-up wheels. They are on aluminium frames with stainless steel fittings. Although they make it heavier, they are essential to traverse land and they can be easily removed with the tools I carry in the kayak.

My kayak is plastic. This is important because polyethylene is very strong and allows the kayak to be dragged over rocks, dropped off dam walls and generally abused without breaking. It does, however, bend out of shape, especially when it gets hot.

Paddling the kayak, hour after hour, day after day, means that you flex your core muscles about every second for a very long time. You are also sitting with your feet outstretched to the rudder pedals. It is necessary to change position and paddle-stroke technique regularly. Your heels rest on the bottom of the kayak with the balls of your feet on the rudder pedals. You need to move them a lot otherwise the points of contact get blisters. Lift your feet a bit, steer with your big toes, straighten and bend the knees, lean forwards and make big, long strokes, then increase the rate and lean back, lifting your bum off the seat. You need to do everything possible to vary position and stroke to avoid problems with muscles and skin.

Then there is the sail. It helps with changing positions. It works downwind, across the wind and very slightly into the wind. All experienced paddlers understand that it is the paddle and your instinct that keep you upright. The sail is mounted near the front of the kayak, with control lines back to the cockpit to raise and lower the mast and let the sail in and out. It all gets cleated off so that both hands can be used to paddle.

To drag the kayak long distances an aluminium harness connects to the front wheel. The frame steers the wheel and a Velcro® brand strip fastens a stiff canvas harness securely to my waist.

The trips are organized so that I paddle or drag the kayak all the way from point A to point B, say from Parliament House, Canberra, to the Opera House in Sydney. I map out the route and work out how much ground I can cover each day. I then organise base camps as close as possible to the start and end points of each day's journey, but spaced so that I do not have to move base camp every day. I have a support crew that picks me up at the end of the day to drive me to the base camp and help with the media, the blogging, the cooking and the preparations for the following day. That way, I am able to paddle (or walk) the entire length of the journey, but I do not have to carry my food and bed and communications equipment while I am paddling.

When the support crew is working well, I paddle during the day and in the evening have time and energy to work on the blog and upload photos. It takes quite a while to write the blog, downsize photos and then upload them onto the web site, so the support crew usually cooks the evening meal while I do this. By 8.00pm I am usually asleep. The recovery during the night is critical. When you have to get up the next morning and do it all again one's body must regenerate overnight. It is also important to train one's internal body; the morning is the time to get the toilet job over and done with so that there is no urge out on the water. Peeing is fine for blokes as long as the pee bottle has a decent-sized opening.

Because the purpose of the trips is to promote a cause, it is important to blog as often as possible. Sometimes the support crew will contact me during the day and sometimes I might not see them for a number of days. On those occasions I do not use a base camp, I simply sleep wherever I stop paddling for the night. In those cases I will often not get to blog every night. There are plenty of those occasions along the Mississippi River in this book.

Sometimes, those parts of the trip seemed easier. With no blogging responsibilities, just getting from one point to another and taking a few photos, it is more fun. It is more of an adventure and less complicated. The challenge of combining an adventure with awareness-raising – of dealing with people and politics and advocating a world view – is one of the central themes of this book.

I have established my own rules so that I can complete the trips in the shortest possible time. Once on my way I am very focused on progress, stick to my schedule and do not like to be held up. Sometimes that means I will paddle a section backwards, starting where I planned to finish for the night and ending up where I was going to start for the day. I still cover the same ground, but if it helps solve a logistical problem, I will go backwards over one section. Sometimes I might even miss a section to fit in with support crew arrangements and then come back and do that section later. This really bothers me, but it is sometimes necessary.

I usually pick a trip or a route that has not been done before. This makes it more interesting for me and hopefully, for you as well. For instance, plenty of people have paddled from Brisbane to Sydney, but my route was unique. With wheels on the kayak and knowledge of how inland waterways linked, even when there were strong headwinds at sea I could continue by using an inland route.

I hope that lesson and my long experience as an adventurer and climate warrior can help all of us address the 'wicked problem' of climate change and motivate our friends, relatives and neighbours to make the changes we need to make to provide a decent future for our children and grandchildren.

Steve Posselt, 2019 – three and a half years after COP 21 in Paris

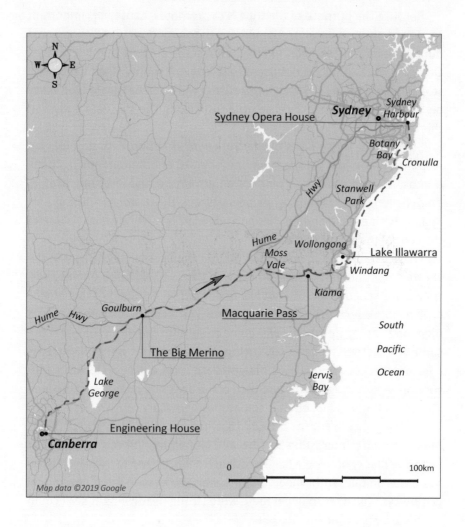

PART 1

AUSTRALIA

CHAPTER 1

WHY

"You do realise that all your life has been about water, don't you?" That was my daughter, Amanda, telling me something about myself. I had to think about it before I agreed. It had just never occurred to me.

She was right, of course, all the way back to Nanna and the watering system for her chooks. Nanna lived with us in our house in Grafton, situated on the banks of the mighty Clarence River in northern New South Wales. Dad had put a dripping tap in the chook pen with an old battery casing underneath so there would always be water for the chooks. When I was old enough to turn the tap on, I could create a river down past the mulberry tree – all the way to the duck pond. The river turned the dirt into mud, which could be massaged into bridges, dams, docks and superhighways. Well, that's what it looked like to me after a few hours of diligent construction.

I spent years on these projects, all of them temporary, washed away in a flood caused by a bucket of water, ready for a brand new construction. When I graduated to building cubby houses in the mulberry tree, they too were temporary. No sooner had I shown Mum what a great construction I had completed, than it would come down to be replaced by a bigger, grander treehouse.

Although I was a timid little boy, too afraid to play cricket with anything but a tennis ball, I loved adrenalin. The highest branch on a tree was always my climbing goal. The faster the adults pushed the billycart down the hill so I could rocket through the gate with millimetres to spare, the better. Mum reckoned I was lucky to get through childhood, but then again she reckoned I was lucky to get to age 40. Now I'm 65 she's astounded. I think there is a good reason that I have made it this far, but let's see what you think after you read this story.

When I went to high school, we moved a few kilometres to a house just half a block from the mighty Clarence River. It didn't have a mulberry tree and the chook pen Dad built was comparatively tiny. I learned to sail on the river with my mate Dougie Palmer, who owned a VJ sailing dinghy. VJs were an exciting boat, for the time, with sliding planks that you pushed out to sit on, feet just reaching back to the hull. We would scream across the river in the nor'easters, back and forth, almost touching the bridge pylons, just keeping from tipping over. The river was more than just a place to sail. When we weren't kicking a footy around we were on the river, in the river or beside the river. One day we were paddling big Malibu surfboards upwind so we could stand up and be blown back to the sailing club. Short boards were just around the corner, but these were the original behemoths, over three metres long.

We were about 14 at the time and swapping stories about life when Dougie remarked, "Do you reckon we are really lucky with all this?"

"Yep," I replied, "Couldn't think of a better place to grow up."

Having travelled around the world a few times and added more than half a century of experience, I still think that.

Despite the distractions of the river, I did well at school until we moved to Port Macquarie – a seaside town three hours' drive south – for my final year at high school. A new school, girls, beer and surf; it is a wonder that I passed any subjects at all. I was lucky to scrape through the year with just enough marks to get into civil engineering. I studied my engineering degree part-time while working for the Sydney Water Board.

In the early 1960s I had watched big machinery dig the drains on the Clarence River floodplain. These excited me, but there was more. I wanted to know how water moved. The drains were a part of that and so were dams, which would be even more fun to build. I was going to become a civil engineer. Water, earth, concrete, steel and timber; I wanted to know about it all.

University was six years of very hard work. I met Warren in the first year and I will introduce him to you, later. Both of us believe they taught us to be workaholics. I have an ancestral, Protestant work-ethic and they brought this out in me big time. One night, less than a year into marriage, I was up late making calculations about dams for a dam engineering assignment. My wife Carol was in bed waiting for me. She waited until midnight. I went to bed at 4.00am. At 6.30am I was back at my desk. No wonder Carol was concerned that she had made the wrong choice.

After my first kayak trip in 2007 – over 3,000 kilometres from Brisbane to Adelaide with one third of that dragging the bloody thing because it was the Millennium Drought – Carol told me that it was difficult to live with someone who isn't normal. Perhaps she meant not normal in many ways. I don't know. We had been together for over three decades so there had been plenty of time to assess.

Maybe this example highlights our differences. While I was way out on a road the other side of Wilcannia, a small and isolated town in Western New South Wales, I was being interviewed by ABC Radio Broken Hill. The kayak was bouncing and clattering behind me. The interviewer held a small recorder between us.

"Got any more trips planned after this one, Steve?" he asked.

"Nope."

"That was a bit quick. You sure?"

"Maybe."

"C'mon, telling a few people in Broken Hill won't matter."

"Well, I have this half an idea that I would like to paddle the length of North America, say Hudson Bay to the Gulf of Mexico."

No harm in saying that, eh? Except radio programs are podcast and Carol could find them. A couple of days later:

"I heard you on the radio, when did you think you might tell me about that?"

"Ummm. Errr. Ummm."

"Well if you do that, you needn't think I'll be here when you get back."

I sort of dodged that bullet by ignoring it completely and went on to do a few thousand kilometres up and down rivers in three Australian states and a 1,000km paddle down the coast. She reckoned that she had forgiven one trip as a mid-life crisis, even supported it, but five? I guess she had a point but I'm a stubborn bastard.

The kayaking had started as a form of exercise, relaxation from stress; paddling from home to work, a water equipment manufacturing business that we owned, just down the river. The business was doing well but starting and growing it had taken its toll. A part of me loved the feeling of success but another part was wary. That watchful part understood that money was not the most important thing in life and there was a lot more to learn about the world. Besides, the stress was affecting my health. Aspiring to work just a 60-hour week and never even getting close was no way to live. Paddling was one way to relieve that stress.

Importantly for the technical background to these kayak journeys, both our house and the business were nearly a kilometre from the river. My kayak had to be wheeled at both ends of the journey.

The wheels also fitted with a plan that was forming in the back of my mind. I was getting ready to sell up the business and take off on a kayak adventure.

I had known a little about climate change since the 1990s and had organised a seminar about it for the Australian Water Association. Then Tim Flannery's *The Weathermakers* hit the bookshelves. Flash bang! I got it!

"This is really bad shit," I reasoned. "We have to change and we have to change fast." Like most new activists I thought that getting the message out was all that was needed to drive change.

I was going to paddle to Adelaide and I was going to help build awareness about climate change. From that moment on, the idea of promoting awareness of climate change and the thought of a kayak journey were intimately intertwined in my brain. Perhaps that's not quite normal, but it was perfectly rational to me.

It seemed to me that people are interested in adventures. I certainly didn't fear death and I was pretty determined, so I thought that I could use trips no-one else had done as a platform to explain what I had learned about climate change. Maybe the trips could even inspire others to act.

I had some personal reasons for wanting an adventure. My right shoulder, along with a lot of the right side of my upper body, had been seriously damaged when I crashed my motorcycle on sand in Central Australia during a motorcycle adventure. Yet again, I had proved my mother's predictions wrong, surviving an accident 3,000 kilometres from home that shattered my body so much that I could not lie down for five weeks. Luck was on my side and I lived. Every day, I recognised that I owed the world because I was still alive. It is a powerful driver, you know,

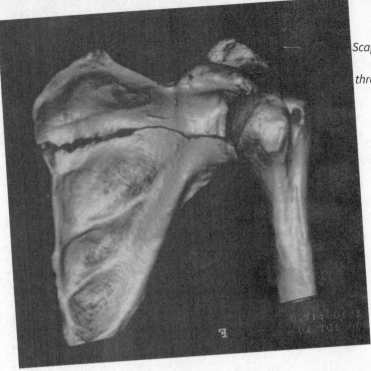

*Scapula fractured
and displaced
through shoulder
joint*

escaping death. I wanted to enjoy the adventure, prove to myself that I was tough and do something to express my gratitude for the fact that I was alive.

To get to Adelaide, I had to drag the kayak over a mountain range. Most people pull things with a harness using their shoulders, but that wouldn't work on a busted shoulder, so we devised a waist harness with aluminium braces connected to the front wheel. Eventually it worked a treat. I was ready for anything – water, no water, mountains, dirt roads, whatever.

There were many wonderful people we met on that trip, including one who would become especially important. Vikki Uhlmann, a friend with similar environmental convictions, had organized a climate change seminar as I went through Ipswich, just west of Brisbane. She was having trouble with a bloke called David Hood who wanted to present his version of climate change – 'Al Gore Plus More'. He was dogmatic that he needed more than the 30 minutes we could offer. He wanted more than an hour, in fact. He was a pushy bastard too, so Vikki handed him over to me. In the end we negotiated something he could live with. So began a remarkable friendship with Hoody. He is outspoken, sometimes confronting, takes no prisoners and is very passionate, but he is rational; promoting science, not

Drying Darling – First trip 2007

belief. Hoody went on to be president of Engineers Australia in 2012 and continues his work energetically. Oh yes, he still is a pushy bastard.

Whenever you absent yourself from society, it is easy to look objectively at it from the outside, to see the madness. I had embarked on a trip about climate change and had learned so much more about the land, the water and the people. I found it hard to return to the status quo, earning money, running my business, supporting my family. Carol and I divorced after 36 years. We probably agree now that it should have happened sooner, given our differences, but we were married very young and thought it would be forever. Besides, I didn't have the guts to hurt her by leaving. Now I wonder if I hurt her more by staying.

I reckoned people who got divorced had failed. Maybe I was too stubborn, too proud, too much of a smart arse, or maybe just too weak to take the plunge.

I kept weaving between life as an engineer and climate activism involving short kayak journeys of up to 1,000 kilometres each. When I was alone in my kayak, I was able to see the world for what it was and clearly imagine how we might build a sustainable future. Back in the real world I was challenged and frustrated by society's deliberate ignoring of scientific warnings. Like most people, though, I was trapped by the stark reality of surviving. The divorce, a near failure on a new business venture, and an underlying feeling of ineptitude as a climate activist … all these forces combined to subjugate my spirit and drive.

Every day I continued to try to make my life count. Our second daughter, Amanda, gave birth to Billy. Then Heidi, my eldest daughter, followed up with Max. Three years later Amanda delivered Josh, and Heidi brought Ayla into the world. In what seemed to me to be a moment of madness – looking on as a grandparent with some experience raising children – Amanda then had Lachy. Three boys in such a short time, no rest in between, no pacing, no staggering the responsibilities. What on earth was Amanda thinking?

Each grandchild made me feel more protective.

In 2005 it had seemed like the world would change its attitude to climate change, though there was always the chance it would ignore the warnings and would head down the destructive path. By 2011 the latter seemed more likely every passing day and the former an ever fainter hope. It was as if we were sliding down a tin roof, the guttering just metres away and then a fatal drop to the ground. Some of us are trying to stop the slide, clawing at the paint with fingernails starting to bleed; others, oblivious to the future, are simply enjoying the excitement of the slide.

My commitment is simple. One day, the world will be in the hands of my children and grandchildren and I will have received my redundancy notice. I want to be able to look into their eyes and say, "Sorry guys, I gave it my best shot. Now it is your turn." To do that, I need to set an example. No excuses. That's what I decided in 2005 and I have not changed that commitment in the least. I have learned a lot, though, about how hard it is to actually do that.

Down the Darling River, I had proved to myself that I could overcome a very serious injury and that I was tough enough to satisfy my own standards. No more did I need to do that.

"Perfect," I reasoned, "let's paddle from the Arctic to the Gulf of Mexico and use that as a platform to educate about climate change." I never even questioned the connection between the question and the mission.

At a Sustainable Engineering committee meeting in 2012 I announced my plan. Hoody was present and his effervescence overflowed.

"I'm coming," he announced proudly.

"Fantastic. We have a year to get it together," I excitedly replied.

"I thought it was two years. Can't possibly do it next year."

And so I decided to delay. It would give me more time to get the money together, allow more preparation and in turn provide for a more effective trip. I discussed this a couple of months later with Geoff Ebbs, editor of my first book *Cry Me a River* and a good mate since the time he played support crew across Victoria in 2009. Geoff asked, "Isn't Paris in 2015?"

"Yeah, I guess so."

"Paris" meant COP21, the Conference of the Parties to the United Nations Framework Convention on Climate Change, starting late November 2015.

"Guess I'm paddling to Paris then," I quipped.

Since 2007, I had dreamed of an adventure from the top of North America to the bottom. That was a huge trip in itself. Now I would be paddling a lot further and the focus would be on climate change education. I changed my plans for what I thought was more important, a cause that is much bigger than me.

With the decision made, logistics could follow. There was absolutely no doubt in my mind, nor Geoff's for that matter, that I was paddling to Paris. There were just a few minor details to sort out.

First task was to decide when. That was easy, just work back from the Paris COP21 date, keep the North American leg and start in Canberra. Oops, seasons don't work. Gotta be in the Arctic area in summer because ice doesn't really work with kayaks. To get to Paris via North America I would have to paddle upstream, up the Mississippi River system. How hard could that be? I had already paddled up the Brisbane and Goulburn rivers. Sure, the rapids had been a bit of a bugger, but there wouldn't be any on the Mississippi.

Geoff asked, "What if your timing is out and there is a flood? You know you tried to paddle the Darling in a drought."

"Can't see a real problem there. They don't last forever and anyway water spreads out. There has to be an edge somewhere and the current out there will be fine." So observed the adventurer with confidence.

Next step was to decide the route and a trip name. Being an honorary member of the Ballina Knitting Nannas Against Gas (that's coal seam gas and fracking), I asked the Nannas for help. The Nannas are my heroes: they are brave, tenacious and act for their grandchildren; willing to do whatever it takes to stop the world being destroyed. I had learned a lot about older women, if I'm allowed use that term. When I was on the Lower Murray, I asked a group of lake protectors why they were nearly all older women. Their response?

"You blokes and your testosterone are too blinkered. You are hell bent on proving yourselves. Successful providers don't take time to see the obvious. Future generations need a healthy environment in all respects. It is up to us to provide that nurturing because you guys won't do it."

That made sense. It was logical and I think I understood. The conversations were a bit emotional but I didn't understand how threatening these ladies could be. The New South Wales government understood. They changed the law so that the fines for women protecting future lives were bigger than the fines for the companies perpetrating the criminal acts against the existing environmental laws. The government is prepared to lock up Knitting Nannas to protect the rights of companies to rape and pillage the land.

Luckily, the Nannas are also a lot of fun and, before I sold my yacht to add to the funds for the trip, we formed the Nanna Navy. About 25 of them would come aboard with their placards, yellow and black knitted scarves, hats and clothes, and we would set off down the river to terrorise Ballina with their chanting and whistle blowing. A couple of blokes were declared 'honorary Nannas' and I count myself privileged to be one of those. One of the younger Nannas, Evie, came up with 'Connecting Climate Chaos' to describe how the trip would link areas where extreme events had occurred, events outside previously known parameters. These areas would encompass Canberra, Sydney, the Gulf of Mexico, New York, the United Kingdom and France. All I had to do was paddle or drag the kayak to each of these places and be in Paris for COP21 by November 2015.

So that was to be the trip, maybe not so easy but surely not that hard. It would involve walking from Canberra to the Pacific Ocean, paddling up to Sydney and then flying to the United States. The US leg would be from the Gulf of Mexico, up the Mississippi and up through Canada to the Arctic waters, and somehow take in New York. The European leg would be a quick dash across England, across the English Channel, down the coast a bit, then turn left and paddle up the Seine to Paris.

Sounds easy when you say it like that.

Louise, Evie's mate, designed the Kayak4Earth logo incorporating the words, Connecting Climate Chaos. We had a banner made and lots of T-shirts produced using her artwork. The rest was just boring logistics. All was go until Hoody couldn't come after all, due to tragic family circumstances. Geoff wasn't interested, even though I offered to pay off some debts that were worrying him. I tried for months to find a replacement. It would have been nice to have someone who could do some filming as well, but try as I might, no-one would make the commitment even with a free trip around the world on offer. That's my perspective, of course. Maybe they were not convinced that turning up in the middle of redneck county with a kayak was going to convince people to change their attitude to global warming. Maybe they had their own dreams and visions. All I knew was that I had committed to go and I was going. I would find someone who cared enough about the climate to go on a year-long adventure across three continents; I just had to try harder.

Hoody still helped where he could. As a Climate Reality Project leader, he had been trained by Al Gore, which gave him contacts in the United States. I decided to upgrade my presentation skills and in June 2014 I also became a Climate Reality Project leader at a three-day training session in Melbourne. We badgered poor old Mario in the US office, who fed us contacts along the North American route and who, like us, had high hopes of getting good exposure to promote what we called the climate emergency.

Life was good. I worked for a bit of money, restored my 39-foot yacht, bought a motorbike, made plans for the big trip and settled into what would be a temporary life. What the trip would bring I had no idea. Would I simply just come back and resume? Probably not. Too many things happen on a year-long adventure. One big concern was my two-year-old relationship with Lea.

I had met Lea in October 2012, beginning a romance that rapidly developed into a serious relationship. I had advised her straight up that I was going to do a big trip involving many months and paddling the whole of the length of North America. For the first year she was keen to come.

"You beauty," I thought, "Finally, someone I love who is interested in the trip."

A bit over a year later, she announced she wasn't coming. What to do? I reckoned that I was in love, and I would have loved to have my partner on the trip, to share whatever ups and downs that might bring. The logical part of my brain said, "Break up and try again, we really are too different." I was torn, as a practical engineer with logical thought processes and being a romantic, enjoying life for what it was. In the end, Lea's advice seemed most practical, not to think of the future but to live each day for what it is. After six months I had reconciled with that. I would live for now, then I would go on the trip with an open mind even though I knew that a major expedition changes you forever. I was very unclear about the long-term prospects for our relationship and more than a little bit concerned about how I would find a support crew to make the trip possible.

Restoring the boat was a fun distraction and a two-year labour of love; very satisfying, but hugely expensive. In the end I had to sell up at 50% of the financial input. A good mate reckoned it was money well spent, as I could have blown that much on divorce recovery therapy. I'm not so sure, but there is a 40-year-old boat out there continuing to make international voyages and that is satisfying to know indeed.

During the two years' boat restoration I got to know my neighbour, Klaas, on the marina at Ballina.

In mid-2014, he and his dog Wolfie wandered down the wharf to my boat while I was engrossed in sanding the deck. He appeared in front of me, holding a handkerchief on his forehead, trying to stem the bleeding.

"What happened, Klaas?"

"I got into a bit of trouble at the boat ramp near the sailing club."

"Yes?"

"Well there was this bloke there who had left his shoes near the fish washing tub. I was washing sand off my feet and Wolfie sniffed this bloke's shoes. He kicked at Wolfie, so I told him not to kick my dog. He said he would kick my dog if he liked, and stood right in my face. What was I supposed to do? I leaned forward quickly with my head, and he started bleeding and yelling, but eventually he went away cursing me."

I was disappointed in Klaas, and told him so. "Klaas! I would have expected a bit better from you, mate. Surely at your age you can get your timing right to do a decent head butt. Let this be a lesson to you. Either get it right or give up, because you're too old."

Served him right for telling me he was 83 when I knew he was only 82.

Klaas was available to come on the trip, the only person who had expressed an interest even after a two-year search, and he had the right attitude. Most people told me he was too old, but I thought differently. He was worldly, having arrived in Australia from Holland in 1952, the year I was born, but had returned to New York, London and Europe many times.

He enjoyed a drink or three most days but he was tough and still had all of his considerable faculties.

He had written a book about his life that was an incredible yarn, brutally honest, and written in his own indomitable style, so I expected that he would make the connection between going on the adventure and documenting it. Most of the people who had previously played the role of support crew had said they enjoyed it. It wasn't fun – because they were often pushed, sometimes to their limit – but most overcame the challenges and came away with countless rewarding memories.

When I asked him if he wanted to come, Klaas took a few days to answer. He was shy, very unlike his usual self, when he said, "I can't afford it."

"You don't have to pay, mate," I replied. "It would be nice if you could use your pension to help with food and anything you want to drink, but the rest is on me." I thought it was a good idea to get the drink bill sorted out up front, given his appetite for whiskey.

His shoulders straightened. He smiled, "Count me in then."

And so the support crew was selected.

I wrote in my diary that we would see tough times, that there would be lots of troubles, that we had no idea what they would be, but we would sort them out as they appeared. Two tough, old blokes having an adventure to put many other adventures in the shade. It wouldn't be easy but the old bastards, mates together, would do it. Ah, confidence, what a wonderful thing.

CHAPTER 2

LEARNING TO WALK

The morning of 15 January 2015 dawned clear and very hot in Canberra, Australia's national capital, which is a bit like Washington DC in a sheep paddock. At 11.00am, after the usual well-wishing speeches to a small crowd accompanied by the local TV station and a newspaper journalist, I set off from Engineering House, home of Engineers Australia, dragging my reserve orange kayak, the first one we fitted with wheels. The route was past Parliament House for some photos, across the bridge over Lake Burley Griffin, through Canberra City and then a long drag out of town to the north.

Engineers Australia was a key player in helping deliver my message. As a member for more than forty years and a Fellow of the Institution I wanted the gravitas of my own professional organization to anchor my trip. The first part of my argument was that we need to accept we have a major, existential threat from man-made climate change. That shouldn't be too hard, given that every climate scientist in the world says so. To be fair, I guess we should say that it isn't every scientist, just 97% of them.

Leaving engineering house (Canberra)

Then, of course, there is NASA, the US Defence Department, Australia's CSIRO and every organization on the planet that accepts science. The fact that some media organizations and governments do not accept their work is the subject of a different, quite disturbing area of study.

The second step I outlined to the engineers present was to decide to do something about it. Again, this seems a lot harder than one would expect. We have not achieved this second stage in any significant way despite having had evidence for decades. Who would have expected people to oppose scientific facts to protect their commercial interests? Not me, but you live and learn.

The third part was the relatively easy bit. You just get the engineers of the world to fix it. Everything required to do that is already known. No new technology is required. Even better, as the world progresses down its path, new technologies will arrive at ever-increasing rates, just as they have in the rapid evolution of computers.

I have spent a dozen years stuck between the first step, raising awareness, and the final step, implementing the solutions. Part of my mission on this journey was to break out of the vicious circle of arguing about the evidence and move forward to action.

One example of the way vested interests twist the truth is the shrill cries from the doubters who say, "You can't store enough electricity." The

21

truth is we have been using pumped storage to store vast quantities of electricity since the 1890s. That is longer than anyone on earth has been alive. All the term means is that when you have spare electricity, you pump water up a hill. When you want it back, you let the water run down again. This was greatly improved in the 1930s with the introduction of reversible turbines. Using electricity to create hydrogen from water is a possible storage mechanism of the future and, again, the technology is already here.

Another term used by the deniers to twist the truth is 'baseload power' or the latest variation, 'cheap, reliable, baseload power'. They imply that the term means enough power to keep the lights on. Unfortunately for their argument, cheap reliable storage such as pumped hydro or hydrogen means that any source of power could fit this use of 'baseload'. The real dirty secret, though, is that the term baseload was manufactured to mean the power produced by a coal-fired power station running at minimum capacity. Because it takes days to fire up a coal powered generator, this power would go to waste each night unless a use could be found for it. The power industry in the 1960s created off-peak pricing to use this amount of power at night. Now they pretend that we need this amount of power to keep the lights on.

This is basic stuff really, but when it is misused over and over again in propaganda from the coal industry, it is pretty effective in masking the real arguments. Those real arguments are that renewables are cheaper than coal, that electricity distribution is very complex, such that even a 100MW battery can make a huge difference to reliability, and that power is simply power. The real problem is the political support for coal and the consequent failure to invest in smart distribution.

Acute pain drew my thoughts back to the present as I hauled my kayak along the Federal Highway. My feet felt like they were melting, the black road was the hottest surface around but I had no choice except to keep walking. This was the route out of Canberra, over the mountains to the sea and eventually to Paris on the other side of the world. I had forgotten how hard it is to drag a kayak long distances, and this was a long, long hill to climb. To stop the kayak from jerking, I take some of the load with my arms. First I put them behind me and hold the harness frame, then they get tired so I hold the frame at my side until my arms cramp up, then I shift my arms to the back again. About then a knee will falter, my back hurts and, as if on cue, the pain in my feet chimes in. After about a dozen or so of these cycles I start to dream about the top of the hill.

The top.

At last!

I speed up, the pain disappears (except in the feet) and I am on a roll. Then there is the descent and the knees complain, the back chimes in, and it's time to stop for a drink.

And so it went for 22 kilometres until I called it a day at an off ramp. "Not a lot of distance," I thought, "but at least it is a start."

It had been a strain to even start on the scheduled date.

A few days before the trip, Klaas' eldest son committed suicide at the age of 52. The news was devastating for him.

"Why didn't he turn to me?" Klaas cried. "Why, why, why?"

I felt his pain but I had no words of comfort, nothing I could offer. Friends advised me that Klaas would have significant grief problems and I needed to be especially aware and sensitive. I admit that is not my forte but I did try my best. His pain was palpable. As they say, no parent should have to bury their child. There wasn't anything I could do except be there for him. I couldn't even do that properly, there were so many logistical considerations.

With the main kayak on a ship to Houston and me having to be there in February to collect it, delaying the trip was not an option, even if it had been possible to reschedule all the other people and components.

Klaas was at the funeral in Sydney and would join me in a few days. Hopefully the more he could get into the spirit of the trip, the less likely he would be to succumb to uncontrollable grief. Was that right? Who knows. You just do your best under the circumstances and I don't think anyone has the right answers.

You can't drag a kayak and drive at the same time, so Hoody had offered to drive my support vehicle, a ute, out from Canberra and get a lift back with his son. That way I could drag the kayak from Canberra to the ute. The next day I would be on my own. A ute, a kayak with wheels, and me. Paris seemed a long way away.

Now, watching the sun dip below the horizon from underneath the tarp I was filled with sadness, with little energy left. My camp was just a plastic tarp strung from the roof racks on the ute to the ground. I investigated the large blisters on my heels. Next were my running shoes that had been destroyed by the heat and the extra forces exerted from dragging my load. You would think that with four significant kayaking journeys behind me that I would at least get this trip's start right, but unfortunately not. For kayak hauling my training back in Lismore had been up and down a steep hill. All of this was wearing standard running shoes, each pair half worn in for the start of this big trip. That seemed perfect to avoid the dreaded blisters. Wrong. I needed thick soles and two pairs of socks at least to insulate my feet from the hot pavement.

Dinner was a beer and a cold can of Irish stew, which was sitting rather uncomfortably in my stomach. This was a momentous day, the first night on a very long journey with so many adventures about to unfold, but my mate Klaas wasn't there. He wasn't there for probably the worst reason possible. My image of two tough old blokes showing the world a thing or two seemed a little faded. Luckily, melancholia doesn't last long when you are absolutely exhausted and sleep took over within minutes. Hoody woke me just after dark when he rang to say that the WIN TV coverage was excellent – a very positive close to a somewhat challenging day.

My exertions during the day gave me back spasms during the night and my heels hurt. It's difficult sleeping on your back while keeping your heels off the ground. Perhaps a mattress would have been better but hey, aren't adventurers supposed to be tough? I awoke feeling better than when I went to sleep, so that had to be good, and was away at 7.00am. After my first trip, I always made sure I had plenty of spare shoes for the walking sections. My running shoes for the day were size 10, as opposed to the size 9 I normally wore, and I was wearing thick socks for heat insulation. This little black duck wasn't going to be caught again on a trip where his feet swelled but his shoes didn't. I learned that lesson in 2007 going from Brisbane to Adelaide with more than 1,000 kilometres of the river dry as a bone. Having dealt with my feet, the next challenge was the ute. It would just have to stay where it was until an opportunity arose to fetch it. With the kayak in tow and the highway beckoning, I was off.

I wasn't sure of the elevations in this area, but I seemed to keep climbing a lot, which put significant stress on the top of my legs. Luckily it sorted itself after 15 kilometres when I went down the hill towards Lake

First camp

George and onto the flat. The blisters got worse, of course, especially where my previous-day shoes had fallen apart the day before, and the overall pain worsened. I had forgotten how much this stuff hurt! The big disappointment was that I felt like I was falling to bits and had only covered 40 kilometres, less than 20% of the distance to the coast, and a tiny fraction of the distance to Paris.

Down beside Lake George around noon, it was time to implement my Leapfrog Plan to retrieve the ute. In the rest area beside the lake, which was mainly grass because the lake comes and goes, I met a bloke called Chris. He had stopped for lunch on his way from Sydney to Canberra and offered to take me back to my ute. I parked the kayak next to the sandwich van where the attendant agreed to watch it for me, and we zipped back the 20 kilometres to the ute. Within half an hour I motored back into the rest area to harness up and was heading north on foot again in the heat. Maybe I should have rested longer. I only lasted eight kilometres on the next leg before I could walk no more. It was only 3.30pm but there was nothing left in my tank. It was a relief that the Leapfrog Plan was working, but my goal had been to walk about 35 kilometres per day, and it was now clear I had set that goal with a younger body in mind.

At the time my Leapfrog Plan seemed quite logical. I was going to Paris and it needed to be done without any time wasting. My support team (Klaas) was not available, but I had to drag a kayak and move the ute. There was no other option. Many people see the absurdity of this back-and-forth situation, but I thought it was a normal response. Maybe it was yet another illustration of what my ex-wife Carol meant when she said that I wasn't normal.

Maybe it was frustration with progress or maybe it was pain, but camped by Lake George I was thinking about the issues which made me angry during the day. My anger was directed at politicians; you know, those people we elect to lead us. Without mentioning names, these guys are any of the following: intellectual lightweights, in the pockets of the fossil fuel industry, or intellectual cowards. Most likely it is the last two but global corporations with a vested interest in maintaining economic growth powered by fossil fuels, population growth and endless consumption seem to hold the political reins.

A tough person looks at the situation, gets the best professional advice possible and then acts on it. Is it a coincidence that most of the destroyers and climate deniers are blokes; that one in particular calls blokes with a social conscience 'girly men'? This is particularly offensive, as Arnie (Schwarzenegger), to whom this is usually attributed, is a staunch supporter of climate action. I think the deniers need to grow some balls, man up, accept the undeniable facts about climate change, and take Australia on a path to solving the problem. Either that or get out and let someone tough enough take over. The big question is whether we care enough and are brave enough to force them to act against the interests of their corporate masters. I have no idea, but they are currently hell-bent on delivering a full-blown catastrophe.

Back in 2008 a group of wonderful people from the Save the Mary River Group, in south east Queensland, convinced me to do a paddle for their cause, utilizing the profile I had gained from the Brisbane to Adelaide journey. After countless emails and phone calls I reluctantly agreed, and what a good decision that was. The trip worked. My efforts inspired many to keep up the fight, a fight that they eventually won. I will forever be grateful to those people for opening my mind to the capacity to create change through grass roots action. It was that sort of action that I wanted to see on a global basis and there seemed to be a big gap between that dream and my current circumstances.

2007 was also a year of epiphany in my water-passionate mind. Dam design had been my favourite subject at university. Controlling water for the betterment of humanity had to be a noble task and my work involved lots of big, fun construction work. I was learning differently, though. Decades of ingrained beliefs were being trashed. The cost of dams to the environment is huge. The United States removed 900 dams between 1990 and 2015. Dams prevent valuable sediments from being deposited on floodplains, they usually interfere significantly with fish passage, and they change the flooding regime of rivers and estuaries which can be critical to fish breeding. Shallow dams, such as the one proposed on the Mary River, are even worse, contributing to greenhouse emissions with the rise and fall of water, causing growth and decay of vegetation.

The then Premier of Queensland, Peter Beattie, had hurriedly chosen to dam the Mary River as part of a solution to his 'Armageddon' water crisis and coined the term 'essential infrastructure' to block any resistance. His plan worked so well in Brisbane that only TV Channel 7 and radio 4BC would run any stories on the dam. There were articles critical of the project all the time in the regional media just north of Brisbane, but in Brisbane itself even the ABC rejected news items passed down from up north. As a consequence, the people of Brisbane had no idea about the issue. I lost some naivety and started to understand media manipulation and censorship in Australia.

There was also a deeper, more sinister, and frightening aspect to the proposed dam. The Wivenhoe Dam was completed in 1985 for both the supply of water to Brisbane and to mitigate floods in that city. At the time, a sign at the dam proudly declared it was sufficient to keep Brisbane in water until 2010. The expectation was that new supplies would need to be on-line by about that time. Lead times are long for water infrastructure, so planning is required well in advance. Like, maybe, a decade or two. By various means of smartarsery, the intervening governments convinced themselves, and the voting public, that all was fine. The water industry was suggesting it wasn't. Premier Beattie said he was unconcerned and that if 'Armageddon' happened he was prepared. Well, we had the Millennium Drought and Pete declared in 2007 that Armageddon had arrived. He had two decades of warnings from professional advisers.

I imagine Premier Pete standing on the road and being told, "Mr Premier, there is a giant tortoise coming down the road."

No response, no action.

"Hey Mr Premier, there is a giant tortoise coming, you had better get off the road."

Still no response, no action.

"Mr Premier, you are about to get run over."

"Holy shit! I've just been run over by a tortoise. How the fuck did that happen?"

Sound familiar? We are in the same place, again. How many people are going to say in a couple of decades, "Why weren't we told the truth about climate change?"

And so my mind wandered. It didn't occur to me until later, but all of my lapses into anger happened at the start of trips and on walking legs. Kayaking doesn't set me off like that.

I woke myself up a few times during the night with my moaning. Pain was becoming a struggle. Maybe it was just that I had forgotten how hard it was to haul a kayak on foot, I thought the next day, but I didn't seem to be doing too well this time around. By lunch time I needed a sleep. I crawled behind some pine trees beside the road and slept on the soft pine needles, leaving the kayak in front of the tree.

Something woke me; there were two young blokes ready to take the kayak.

"Bugger, looks like someone is gonna get hurt here," I thought as I lumbered into action. "Probably me."

I did have an advantage, though. Unlike me, there wasn't much chance they would fight to the death. With my usual diplomacy I enquired as to the situation.

"What the fuck do ya think you're doin'?"

Looking down, I saw they had already thrown out my dried fruit and nut mix. Maybe a 62 year old just aroused from a deep sleep is more threatening than I realised. Maybe I just looked frail and vulnerable, but they backed away. Their excuse was they thought it had fallen off a truck.

"Sure," I growled. "It is sitting there on its wheels with a harness out the front, just like it crashed off a moving vehicle."

They beat a hasty retreat to their cab, no doubt very keen to avoid this old maniac who seemed keen on dismembering them. Had they been quieter, I could have woken to a very nasty surprise indeed. It was a good lesson.

The rest of the day was uneventful, just slogging away along the highway until finding a place to hide the kayak and hitchhike back to collect the ute.

The funeral for Dirk, Klaas' son, was over. It was time to set up camp in Goulburn and head for Sydney to collect my mate. No more leap-frogging and hitchhiking.

I picked Klaas up from the airport where I met his son Nick, who was heading back to Austin, Texas, where we would base ourselves to buy the RV and get ready for the North American leg. Nick is a smart cookie, CEO of a vitamin company, as well as being a lovely bloke. He looks like a Texan from the movies – tall and fit looking, so he fits in and has lived there many years. Klaas gave Nick a large bag to take to the United States for him, so Klaas would only need carry-on luggage when he flew over in February, a week before me.

Klaas and I headed back to Goulburn where I wanted to test a theory postulated by Warren. As I mention in Chapter 1, Warren and I had studied engineering together in the seventies and intermittently stayed in touch. He was almost at the end of his engineering career, a career he loved. In that way he was just like me. His penchant was geology, which I was hopeless at, and I returned the favour in hydraulics. I couldn't figure out why the other guys struggled with it. I loved the subject. Fast forward to this day and age: Warren reckoned we were getting old and had slowed down, and that this would show in my kayak-hauling walking pace. Despite my protestations, I was concerned that he might have a point. Feeling on top of the world with my support crew, and striding out along the highway at maybe 5km/hr, I counted my steps. Top speed was 113 steps per minute. Can't be right, I thought, so I tried harder. Next minute it was 112 steps. On my web site kayak4earth.com is a video of the song 'Down By the Water', by my mate Dennis Nattrass. It is based on my 2009 all-day-walking-pace of 122 steps per minute. I remember that because Dennis spent ages watching footage and muttering 122 while my other mates and I were drinking beer. Having established my walking rhythm, he went home at midnight to write his song to that beat.

"Something to think about here," I thought. Perhaps, heaven forbid, Warren was right. "Better not tell him, though," I thought. He is pretty quick and might come back with a clever riposte I would be unable to counter. I remember a geology excursion. Warren was chipping away at a rock in his hand for reasons obvious only to him and the lecturer. Something was amiss.

"Jesus Christ," Warren cursed.

"Yes," replied Don, the resident smartarse.

"Shut up Son," retorted Warren, as he continued to investigate his rock. He is quick, is Warren.

A good laugh made me feel slightly better that day, unfortunately at Klaas' expense. When he jumped in the car to come and photograph me passing the Big Merino outside Goulburn, he learned a valuable lesson in timing. It is much better to untie the wall of the gazebo from the ute before you drive away, rather than after.

That night, camped in the Moss Vale caravan park, Klaas and I talked about my recent trip to the Great Barrier Reef. I needed to tell him the story about what I had learned so that he too could answer questions if asked when we were overseas. Understanding the twin threats of acidifying oceans and coral bleaching had been an integral part of my education for the trip. We also discussed the role of marketing in promoting these messages. Klaas knew about my relationship with Lea, but not much about her son Connor. I must have been pleased to have an ear, because I ended up reliving the whole trip.

At just 21 Connor was doing very well in a marketing company called Menatwork Comms based in Sydney. He had plenty of media contacts and marketing skills, and reckoned he was keen to be involved in promoting the journey to Paris. We agreed that for me to do a trip up to the Great Barrier Reef would be an excellent learning experience and a foray into what might lie ahead. We also planned on him coming over to New Orleans for a couple of weeks at the start of the United States leg, and since marketing was all either phone or internet, the rest could be done from anywhere. He would just need to experience the United States to be able to properly assist while I was over there.

As well as learning about the reef, Connor and I decided to promote the upcoming trip to Paris by displaying the kayak at the Townsville Port celebrations and wherever we could get media interest. How could I achieve that using the least amount of fuel possible? Take the motorbike, of course! People tow small trailers behind motorbikes, so why not tow a kayak? Still active in the engineering design world, I had the skills to get what I wanted from a trailer manufacturer. To save weight, the design was just two wheels and a long beam fitted to the axle. There were no springs. With a person at each end we could lift it above our heads. The freedom of a motorbike combined with the freedom of a kayak, and the fun and the thrills that both could provide, while still using much less fuel than a four-wheeled vehicle, seemed a pretty good package.

It was 1,800 kilometres to Townsville, the furthest point north on my Great Barrier Reef journey. Following a truck on the isolated highway north of Rockhampton, the searing heat was oppressive. Underneath my jacket, the sweat ran into my jeans, all the way down my bum. As the road straightened ahead and disappeared into the shimmering distance, I opened the throttle and blasted the big motorbike into clear air. The trailer followed obediently but the handlebars wobbled from the turbulence as the rig surged past the truck. Backing off, I looked at the speedo as it dropped through 170km/hr. Not bad. It wasn't legal, of course, but I could forgive a few wobbles of the bike under those circumstances. It was a great rig and I was having the time of my life.

At a tourist operators' meeting at Airlie Beach on the way up to Townsville I was shocked at what the industry leaders said. For the previous few years they had been quietly lobbying government about the

The bike rig. (Airlie Beach, North Queensland)

disastrous state of the reef while at the same time pretending to the public that everything was fine, because they are totally dependent on tourists coming to their businesses. Now they had changed tack. Government was not listening and over half of the reef south of Cooktown had died in less than 30 years.

Let that sink in; half went in one generation.

Why? Partly to provide ports to export coal that, when burnt, causes ocean acidification and warms the water; both effects that kill coral. More immediately, though, dredging releases sediment that migrates hundreds of kilometres, gradually reducing visibility and stressing coral so that shocks such as high temperature events have devastating consequences.

What is absolutely terrifying, though, is that governments have no interest in saving the reef if it affects coal exports. In fact, they actively pursue policies that will destroy more. Some pay lip-service to reef care, one party even got elected on that basis, but immediately it formed government it showed its true colours and backed new coal mines and expanded port facilities. It is difficult not to despair when you know they are destroying the reef for short-term political gain.

Back in 2005 I was the convener for Ozwater, a large conference and trade show held in Queensland every twelve years. It seemed that as it came to Queensland, rather than Brisbane or the Gold Coast, North Queensland should be involved as well, so we held part of the conference in Townsville. There I had met Dr Virginia Chadwick, Chair of the Great Barrier Reef Marine Park Authority. She was one tough lady and a straight shooter. Her mission, she told me, was to try to halt the acceleration of the degradation of the reef.

"Run that by me again," I said, trying to recover from my shock.

"I want to halt the acceleration of the degradation of the reef," Virginia said.

Bloody hell! The degradation had been accelerating for more than a decade and some people did not even accept that it had been degraded.

But then, at the same conference, Ian Hamilton, local engineer and Chair of NQ Water, reckoned that Virginia was an alarmist, that everything was fine and we could get on with more dredging without a care in the world.

Virginia died from cancer in 2009. As far as I know Ian is still around. History will judge the players but the evidence is very clear. Virginia clearly knew her stuff.

The Federal Liberal Party's Environment Minister at the time of the reef foray, Greg Hunt, (known in some circles as The Little Hunt) proudly announced on his web site that "all references to 'in-danger' have been completely removed" from the World Heritage Committee. "This is great news for Australia. It's great news for Queensland. And it's great news for the Great Barrier Reef." WTF, it is more than half dead mate! You can't save one of the world's largest living organisms by censoring a report.

The reef is doomed unless we urgently reverse climate change and I can't see that happening. It seemed to us to be an important message that should be honestly expressed during the journey.

I was pleased that I had managed to share those observations with Klaas. He should have no trouble with conveying that, I said to myself as I snuggled into my sleeping bag. It seemed to be pretty simple and obvious to anyone, except maybe some politicians ... and the media ... and the people who believed the media. Oh, and those people who did not want to give up using fossil fuels.

I fell asleep.

Klaas' blog: *Hi everyone, so far so good. About time I put my bit in. So here goes.*

We camp somewhere and Steve hauls his kayak 28–30 kilometres down the road, phones me and I pick him up, take him back to the campsite, feed and water him and early night. Next morning, break camp, drive to where he finished the day before, drop him off to start his day's walking and I look for a camp site and put up the tent and unload the gear, do the food shopping, prepare dinner and pick him up when he is ready.

Steve is like a man possessed. He is a 'True Believer' and totally dedicated to his mission. He is fanatical in that he insists on walking every inch of the way. While taking him to where I picked him up the day before, I missed the spot. It was pouring down rain and he did not notice the spot either. He insisted on turning back. I said, "Do yourself a favour mate, nobody will know." His answer was, "I would." That showed me what an honest man he is, and I have great respect for him, both for his honesty and his will to complete this physical marathon, walking and paddling half way around the globe to highlight the results of global warming. He is outspoken and has unwavering views. I don't always agree with some of those, but as Voltaire said long ago "I may not agree with your viewpoint but will defend to the last your right to express them."

CHAPTER 3

ADVENTURE TRAINING

There was a mountain to negotiate, where the Great Dividing Range towers above the Pacific Ocean, and a tricky, narrow and very steep Macquarie Pass to descend, before getting to the sea, but we adventurers tackle that stuff with ease. No, that's not quite right. But despite multiple tyre and bearing changes on the kayak, we made it. With great relief, I completed the walking leg from Canberra at a creek feeding into Lake Illawarra, which connects to the ocean south of Wollongong.

I put my kayak in the water and set off for the ocean in earnest on 26 January, Australia Day weekend. Low cloud pressed down, the thick warm air stifling any physical activity. Connor, working the phones back in Sydney, had a bit of luck with media, but most TV crews were more interested in the beach and a few drinks on this holiday weekend. Lake Illawarra was like a mirror, smooth as glass except for an occasional puff of nor'easter caressing the surface every now and then. I couldn't figure out what the weather would do but was concerned that we would get a bit of a blow later in the day. Where I come from, oppressive mornings usually get blown away in the afternoon by a nor'easter. For now it was pleasant paddling to Windang, where I would stop for lunch then tackle the bar to the open sea, but a couple of guys gave me a bum steer on which way to go around an island near Windang, so I did a bit of knuckle pushing and walking, just like I had on the Darling River eight years earlier when it was nearly dry. Klaas was waiting at Windang, where we grabbed a hamburger, before I set off for the entrance into the sea. Just before I reached open water, a police boat was hanging around keeping an eye on the holiday makers. The water police were young (of course) and reckoned, despite my misgivings, that the forecast was for winds easing.

A strong incoming tide provided a battle at the bar, plus the 8–10 knots nor'easter blew straight in my face, just for good measure. Within an hour, I was battling the wind about two kilometres offshore, straight-lining for the next headland. The water police passed me about a kilometre closer to the beach with the wind blowing 12–15 knots and waves building. I wondered which day they meant that the wind would ease. It built to about 18 knots with lots of white water while I bashed on past the islands off Port Kembla. There were some tall pines to aim for after that, but before long what appeared to be a lighthouse nudged out of the horizon. I chanced getting tipped out of the kayak with a quick phone call to Klaas to let him know where I was, then it was back to avoiding the breakers. I wasn't sure how far it was to Wollongong, but reckoned that it was its lighthouse I could see and near where Klaas would be.

It was a hard slog, dodging those breaking waves. The kayak bounced down the back of waves with crunching thumps, the paddles swished noisily as they thrashed at the big chop, and the broken waves passed by with a crash and roar. It wasn't the quiet paddle that I had been hoping for. Wet, busy, noisy and requiring lots of concentration, it was a good reminder of what the Pacific Ocean is like. Never, ever, take it for granted. I pulled into Wollongong Harbour about 4.00pm where I beached the kayak, but it took about two minutes for my knees to respond enough to climb out of it. Klaas was relieved to see me and I was bloody glad that paddle was over.

> **Klaas' blog:** Hi all. This bloke Steve is unbelievable. Walks all the way from Canberra, hops into the kayak, (falls in the drink, ha ha) and then paddles across Lake Illawarra, out to sea and to Wollongong. I am waiting at the harbour and thought he had 'bought it' (ie, had a nasty accident). At 4pm I decided he was lost, and started to ring the water police when he rang me that he was safe. Boo …

With Klaas before we started

The next day's paddle, from Wollongong to Stanwell Park, was uneventful but my mate did have a few things to say.

Klaas' blog: *His majesty in his usual form paddled from Wollongong to Stanwell Park and requested me to be there at around noon to receive him coming in through the surf with me heroically grabbing the front handle so he would not slide back in with the wash. I spend two hours in 38 degrees heat watching the ocean, getting totally dehydrated and mumbling incoherently "Where is the stupid bastard?" when he appeared out of nowhere and said, "Where the fuck were you?" He [had] sneaked in around the corner on the opposite side of the beach, of course, so he could capsize and look pathetic. I'm now for several cold beers. Cheers.*

It costs a lot of money for a GoPro and all the accessories that go with it. I had bought one before my investigatory trip to the Great Barrier Reef. By now I reckoned it was high time I started to use it on the water. Unfortunately, I could not get it to turn on even when connected to the charger. I wasn't sure if it was me or the camera. This had also happened when it was new, which I had resolved with Lismore Camera House where I bought it, and decided again it must be me.

News from the United States wasn't good. The kayak for that leg was now not due into Houston until 18 February and the transport company wanted extra payments. This was my main yellow kayak, the one that had done all of the other trips. The kayak I was using for the Australian leg was my original orange one that I had used to experiment with different wheel arrangements. I had sent the yellow kayak, paddle, clothes and boxes of *Cry Me a River* books to Houston back in December. Klaas had also put a bag of clothes into the crate. We would have been in a lot of trouble without Klaas's son, Nick. He was a godsend and, with his guidance and assistance, everything got sorted out.

Expecting a big day paddling up past the Royal National Park, I took precautions; gloves over taped-up hands, paddle tied to front of kayak, all equipment checked. We arrived at Stanwell Park at 7.00am to find big seas. My chances of breaking out off the beach were about fifty-fifty, so we waited two hours for the surf club blokes to arrive in case I needed them to pick up the pieces that might get strewn along the beach. They suggested we try launching from Coalcliff which I hadn't thought of. It was a few kilometres south and I had paddled past it the day before. Armed with this local knowledge we set off.

Some surfers were out on the southern end of Coalcliff Beach and it looked like there might be a bit of a rip running out near the rocks that could assist my paddle out. I was a lot more comfortable with this scene than the beach break at Stanwell Park. Klaas stayed up on the hill to take photos and a bloke called Rob said he would help me get into the water. To stop water coming over the cockpit rim and into the kayak when I'm on the sand and knuckle pushing into to the water, I need to get into a plastic cover called the skirt. The skirt is worn like a vest, and connects the paddler intimately to the kayak. I also need someone at the front of the kayak to hold the nose into the waves, otherwise it gets washed up onto the sand and I get stuck sideways on the beach, unable to get into the waves. Rob was really good at juggling all these variables, and we agreed on when it was time to go.

The kayak slid out, over rocks lurking just under the water, and I bided my time riding over the small broken waves next to the short, rock peninsula. Bugger, the rudder would not turn. It was stuck and the foot pedals would not move. I really did not fancy my chances of a successful

U-turn. With a big kick on the pedal, it suddenly came loose. Sand had been caught in the mechanism. What a relief. Looking back, Rob was waving his arms above his head that I took as a signal to go. When you are low in the water, you can't see very far ahead because the waves block your view. I bit the bullet and took off at full speed. Cresting a one metre high wave it was immediately evident that I had perhaps mistaken his signal. It really meant, "Oh shit!" At least three big waves, well over two metres high, were on their way in. The surfers started paddling seawards to keep out of trouble and with luck get to a good take-off point for a big ride. I headed for the broadest, green bit I could find and crashed over a steep lip just beside the break. Luckily, the kayak still had momentum as I raced seawards and repeated the effort. The next one was touch and go. It looked like I would make it, but that was by no means certain. I crashed through the lip with the front four metres of the kayak in the air, white water just to the right and also three metres to the left. After that, I was through, over the next one before it peaked. I paddled out another 100 metres, turned north and waved to Klaas to signal all was good.

Klaas got some long-range shots with the 300mm lens. I have since shown him how to focus, but can't say that I am keen on repeating that performance just for the camera. I was lucky to make it through. To have not made it would have been messy, to say the least. He then drove to Cronulla to write his blog and wait for me to get there.

Klaas' blog: *Now I know you are mad, Stevie boy. Bloody two metre waves bashing the beach and you wanted to launch a kayak. I proffered the suggestion you might wait one or two days. But no, you had the bit between your teeth. All the fellows on the hill where I was filming reckoned you would never make it. I was among them and you made me eat my words. You crazy bastard, my hat off to you. That is, if you make it all the way to Cronulla.*

After turning left to follow the coastline up to Sydney, the wind was over my right shoulder, although the swell was coming square onto my right side. It was comfortable for an hour or so. Some great runners would send me scooting along, sometimes up a wave and down the back. Top speed registered on the GPS was 16.8km/hr. I defy anyone to pick a runner just by looking. I certainly can't. It's a matter of feeling when the run is on and then using it. One of the best paddles I have had was with just two other paddlers in an OC4 outrigger at Ballina. There was none of the usual, "Here comes one!" spouted by people who think they can see something coming. We all just felt it and went with the lifts. An OC4 is a four-person outrigger canoe. With only three in it, it was faster than the six people in the OC6 that we were paddling with, purely because of timing and working the waves. Analyse, by all means, I say, but *feel*. Feeling is the secret.

The wind came round to side-on and then it got really wet and messy. Swells were about two metres high, which looks like a mountain from a kayak, but there were other peaks that were like one metre high anthills dotted all over them. On top of this, the odd breaker would come through from the side at chest height. It took a lot of feathering with the right paddle blade to counter the white water and stay upright. Of course, all of this wave action fills the kayak up with water even though the spray skirt is supposed to keep it out. Water runs down inside the lifejacket and any other opening it can find. I had to stop, remove the spray skirt and bail every 20 minutes or so, but did manage to make them drinks and pee stops too, albeit very quick ones. With the spray skirt off things are very exposed, so you need to minimise any time without it in place.

There were no other boats out. Who would be that crazy? The Royal National Park runs for 25 kilometres along the shore where the escarpment meets the sea. From Stanwell Park there are no inhabited beaches, but after about seven kilometres there are a few sand beaches that you can walk down to from the escarpment. The cliffs are rugged and over 100 metres high. It is impossible to land a kayak or a person at their base when the seas are rough. The wind picked up and things got very bumpy indeed. There was no chance now for niceties like using the pee bottle, it was just do it and ignore the consequences. It's just a bit like peeing in a wetsuit, I suppose.

The cliffs don't run in a straight line, and I wanted to stop heading north east, being buffeted by the wind and spray. Every time I began to pass the last cliff in my line of sight, I would hope that the next one would be set back a bit, meaning I could start tracking more northerly. After about four or five disappointments, the coastline did turn in and the wind went back to coming over my right shoulder, but it was still too scary to lift the skirt except for the briefest of bailing flurries.

A commercial airliner materialized in the clouds ahead, so I knew Sydney airport was not too far away, which meant Cronulla was even closer. Kurnell, the beach north of Cronulla, was just visible between rain squalls, but it took ages to find Cronulla tucked in well to the left. I came round the corner inside a low rock island and rode the edge of the waves with the wind thrusting from behind. One small sailing boat was in the bay, plus a couple of motor cruisers, but it wasn't really the weather to be cavorting on the water despite the holiday. Eventually the wind was deflected by the hills, the waves subsided and I started to relax.

At no stage had I been anxious or really concerned about my safety, although I had been apprehensive about my chances of getting out through the break at Stanwell Park, which I had abandoned for my launch from Coalcliff Beach. That said, that day's kayak trip was something much better in the past than the present. Not too many people would enjoy being pummelled towards a 100-metre high lee shore by two metre breaking waves in winds blasting the tops off waves. It was a cold, wet and miserable wait for Klaas on the beach in the bay next to the Cronulla railway station. Man, was I glad to finally see him and get to a hot shower.

An Illawarra Mercury article about me had sparked a few morons on Twitter to condemn the trip. The stupidity and nastiness of some people is like a cancer in our society. It has always been the case, but when you sacrifice most of what you've got to help bring about awareness of what all scientists are saying, it is a bit disturbing to see that shit. I decided I was just being a sook and needed to brush off that sort of thing. Politicians cop it all the time and I believe journos do too. Adventurers (this one anyway) are not strong when the challenges are different to their goal of getting from A to B. On a brighter note, I had not had an angry moment for a few days. It seems like I was right about those angry periods. They occur only near the start of my trips and only on the walking legs, never the paddling sections.

The forecast got worse every time we looked. Swells were predicted to be four metres. That's fine if you are well out to sea and just going up and down, but waves like that smash kayaks to bits when they break near the shore. When I was young we used to live for such swells. Way back then I rode a surfboard. Now I was a 62 year old in a kayak and hopefully much wiser. Discretion prevailed and we put the wheels on for a short trek to bypass paddling around through the entrance into Botany Bay. Jacqueline arrived in the teeming rain to watch the wet paddle from Kurnell across Botany Bay to La Perouse. About my age, she is the sister of a very good

40

friend of mine. We had met at an environmental conference after her brother introduced us by email. Apparently my trip was interesting enough to write about for her post-graduate environmental degree, so she pushed me for details. I gave her what I could, but there were a lot of unknowns. I wasn't sure why she had come to Sydney, though I did find her quite attractive.

For the paddle into La Perouse on the northern side of Botany Bay, Klaas gave me instructions about which side of Bare Island to go. Luckily Jacqueline figured out that his instructions were to come in on the seaward side of Bare Island, when in fact I needed to head for the shelter of Frenchman's Beach. Standing on the rocks, she managed to redirect me by phone just in time to correct the error. Into the shelter of the beach, I folded the wheels down and then walked the 17 kilometres up to Rushcutters Bay on Sydney Harbour. Jacqueline and Klaas arrived in the ute just as I got there, and the Cruising Yacht Club of Australia kindly allowed me to store the kayak on their hard-stand. I guess you could say that we came in the back way. That didn't matter to the yacht club, though. We were a visiting boat and they looked after us. That is what boaties do.

We needed to stay in Sydney and Jacqueline just stayed with us. I had never talked to her about what should happen, but an adventurer is not a monk so when it became apparent that she was planning to stay with me, not us, so to speak, that seemed just fine. We booked a motel together. My very clear memory is that I carefully explained that under no circumstances was I interested in a relationship. I know what trips take. I know that at the end you might be a bit different person. I knew that to get to Paris I would need every ounce of energy and focus that I had.

That said, one can always find additional reserves of energy when required. I was off on an adventure to the other side of the world and free to do whatever adventurers do. Perhaps already I was a legend in my own mind. We made good use of the motel bed and I slept very, very well.

Saturday started with just a few nerves. This was the day of my paddle from Rushcutters Bay to the wharf at the Sydney Opera House. There would be lots of supporters but no media, apart from a mention on ABC national radio. This trip was about climate change. The media's explanation for their absence which they gave to Connor was that they were 'over' climate change. It had all been covered and their audiences were not interested. That was understandable, not OK or even acceptable, but understandable. It's an indication of the scale of the problem we face in changing society's understanding when even an existential threat is not newsworthy.

I guess it is just not easy to get people to come along, even though Al Gore had crafted a very powerful message. The Australian Conservation Foundation, which had organized his training program that I attended, ran a comprehensive article in their Climate Reality newsletter. I had hoped people from that class would use the trip to piggy-back with their presentations, but that hope was in vain. Not one climate reality leader from that class, and there were many in Sydney, showed the slightest interest in my trip. Why, I wondered? I thought I'd joined a team and, in a team, everyone helps everyone. But hey, I was excited and the Australian leg of my trip was nearly done, albeit with a bit of pain. In a couple of weeks I would be in a different country with new challenges, different media and meeting new friends.

Before starting the paddle across Sydney Harbour to the Opera House, we had to drive to the airport to pick up Anne, Klaas' girlfriend, who had decided to fly down to meet Klaas for the Opera House welcome. There is a small, waiting carpark at Sydney airport, so Jacqueline and I waited in the ute while Klaas went off to fetch Anne. We had timed things perfectly and he came into view after only about 10 minutes. Anne was with him, but so was someone else. Shit! It was Lea. This was just a wee bit awkward. I welcomed Lea and Anne and the three women climbed into the back seat. Klaas climbed into the passenger seat but had a problem with his eyes. He didn't know where to look or what to do. In the end he looked at me and shrugged. I was sure I detected the hint of a smile, or maybe it was a grimace. There was no warning he could have given, nothing he could have done. He knew his mate was in a spot and he was sympathetic. And what a spot it was.

Lea had come down from Lismore for two days to be at the Opera House when I paddled in. She and Connor had cooked up the surprise. Surprise? I was astonished. For two years I had worked on the basis that Lea didn't want to be part of the trip and here she was. Of course, it was great to see her but I was confused. Mentally I was on the trip, for better or for worse, and being consumed by it. Not to mention, of course, what had happened the previous night.

Greeting Bob Brown (Sydney Opera House wharf)

Some of the crowd on the wharf (Sydney)

I focused the conversation on the plans for the day and, with the assistance of Jacqueline playing the part of interested support crew, all was well, sort of, more or less. I had dodged a bullet for now.

After setting off from the Cruising Yacht Club where I had left the kayak, I decided to wait near the point opposite the landing wharf at the Sydney Opera House. Being on the water focused my mind back on the trip, but my peace and quiet lasted less than two minutes before the navy turfed me out of there on grounds of national security. I paddled over to Fort Denison waiting for Connor to call me. The call came almost on time and I headed in. As the shape of the wharf grew, the crowd became evident with a sea of blue shirts, our blue shirts! Good-onya Klaas, you must have sold a lot. What a salesman! I pulled in and threw Klaas the rope as pre-arranged and then stepped up the ladder to a throng of people, many of whom were familiar.

I almost missed Ian Dunlop in the crowd. A humble, unassuming figure in a white hat, but a true rattler of corporate cages at the very highest level, he had come to see me. It is blokes like him that inspire me. An original member of The Club of Rome, he knows only too well the earth's limits to growth. He has badgered the BHP board and, arguably, made them understand something of the risks that climate change poses to its business. Ian was an international oil, gas and coal industry executive, chairman of the Australian Coal Association and chief executive of the Australian Institute of Company Directors and, as I said, he had come to see me.

The Nannas were there too and stood out in their yellow and black. They gave me a very small gift to take for good luck, knitted of course. And the irrepressible Hoody spoke as usual. As I absorbed the friendships and the many, many faces, I tried to thank everyone and then fell silent. Bob Brown, my hero and retired leader of the Greens, grabbed the hiatus. He made an absolutely brilliant speech. I was truly humbled and, at the same time, proud and a tiny bit choked up. Hopefully I hid that bit enough to fool everyone. Real adventurers don't cry.

One thing that Bob Brown had said was "even if you don't make it to Paris ..."

"What? That ain't gonna happen," I thought immediately.

What he said continued to bounce around in my head a lot over the next few months. I was going to make it, Bob. One way or another I would make it to Paris.

PART 2

ALONE IN THE U.S.A.

CHAPTER 4

HELLO STARS AND STRIPES

The difficult walking leg from Canberra to Lake Illawarra was over and the mighty Pacific Ocean had provided a serious training run to Sydney. I felt like an adventurer for the first time, even though I had many trips under my belt. These had ranged from 500 kilometre to more than 3,000 kilometre journeys, but this one was to be longer than all of them put together, and across four countries. In a way I felt free. There were no detailed plans, except the specific goal of getting to Paris via the United States and England. Who knew what lay ahead.

It was a shame that Sydney media lost interest as soon as they found out the trip was about climate change but, apart from that, the Australian leg had been a success. Saying goodbye had been hard, though. The grandkids would be a year older next time we met. My three-year relationship with Lea was either suspended or terminated, but we would stay in touch. All I knew was that I was headed to a great unknown. Assets had been sold and there was just enough in the bank for the trip. I loved the fact that some Aussies had donated via the web site without even being asked.

Klaas had flown over to the United States a few days before me, while I tied up loose ends, like getting rid of my ute. I also stopped at Auckland for two days to go caving with a friend. Carolyn is a Canadian, single, fit and pretty tough. In a previous life, she had left her partner in bed while she went downstairs to see if it really was a bear that had broken into their home. We had arranged a cave tour which involved abseiling, an underground flying fox, and an underground stream on inflatable tubes.

Carolyn had booked the caving tour and I had booked the motel. Two rooms – that's what the brochure said. Sure was two rooms; a bedroom and a living room. It was a very big bed admittedly, but it was only one bed. My friend looked at me accusingly, but it was an honest mistake. Truly. I might have fantasized about a romantic interlude, but I was not going to force the situation and embarrass myself by only booking one bed. There was nothing we could do, so I suggested we have a hot spa which was just outside the room in a secluded area. That relaxed the caving muscles and, after an excellent dinner, it was time for bed. I agreed to stay over on my side, a little reluctantly, and she slept on the edge of her side. Even that was too much, though, and the next morning I found her on the floor in the living room. Not such a legend after all, eh?

Auckland had been interesting and great fun, but hardly a resounding, romantic success. I flew to Austin, Texas, where Klaas and Nick picked me up and we plunged into frantic activity. My reverie on the plane had been all too brief. Give me burnt feet, legs that can only shuffle, lee shores with waves crashing over me and the cliffs, pouring rain, searing heat and toxic mud. They were easy compared to the problems of collecting the kayak and fitting out the expedition for the US leg. Despite the blind alleys, the obstacles, the bloody systems, and the intransigence of American bureaucracy, we were ready.

There was one major problem, however. Klaas was not himself. His father and brother had both suffered dementia and now Klaas was exhibiting similar signs. I wasn't sure what it was, but we could pass the same place half a dozen times and he still wouldn't know where we were. He had been arguing with Nick, but I think that's par for the course with Klaas. Sometimes he was fine, but in his present state he was not up to the support role that I had envisaged, and indeed needed, if we were to pull this trip off.

This was very hard; Klaas was my mate. He still is. The death of his eldest son had caused something terrible to happen to his brain. It wasn't dementia, although I initially thought it might be. There were bits of his brain functioning just fine, but some bits, and a lot of the processing connections, seemed to just switch off. Klaas is a terrific bloke, generous of spirit and a great companion, and I somehow knew this would be temporary. The answer Nick and I came up with was to bring his girlfriend, Anne, over to be with him. She was 10 years younger and quite fit. A few people criticized me for putting Klaas through all of this and thought that I should have sent him home. That was easy to say if you had not spent two years trying to put together a support crew and come up with one person. Besides, we were mates, and we were bloody well sticking together. He had promised to support me and I had promised to take him to Paris. We had a running joke that I had brought him over as bear insurance. I could outrun him, so the bear could eat him while I got away. Klaas reckoned he would just play dead and the bear would eat me.

Klaas is good with words and continued to write blogs for the web site.

Klaas' blog: *Hi all. Been in the US now over two weeks. Spending some quality time bonding and getting to know Son Number two again who has been here two decades. I am in Austin, Texas, and the weather is all over the place. When I arrived it was around 20°C and sunny. Then four days of cold and then lovely sunny, shorts and T-shirt weather and today it is back down to 3°C. The Yanks are strange people. They drive on the wrong side of the road, all light switches work the opposite way and the toilets swoosh from the bottom. On the whole, the Texans are very friendly but they talk 'funny'. That drawl is unmistakable.*

Steve in the meantime is his usual self, like a can of worms that can't sit still and relax for more than three seconds, and spends hours on the internet chasing this that and other. However, it is all coming together and the expedition now sprouts a Ford Expedition 5.4-litre 4WD Yank tank nine seater, and a 29-foot caravan ('travel trailer' in Yank talk). It has all the gadgets, like press a button and the lounge room slides out. Hopefully tomorrow we pick up the kayak in Houston, but it is not there yet. It had been delayed in transit and Steve has the heebie jeebies about it. That is all from me for now.

During that first week while juggling logistics I wrote to a friend back in Brisbane:

"This is a very lonely business. I have yet to find anyone who understands. I crave for that, to have a partner who wants to do the same thing, to be part of the team, to experience all of this together, and to come out at the other end savouring the shared experiences and hopefully the reward of satisfactory completion.

Klaas gets it, but he is 83 and at present ill-equipped to deal with the complexities of the task. He does very well for his age, sending emails and searching the internet, but social media, the GPS, the new country's rules and internet banking are all very challenging for him.

I guess I hope for too much, though. People tell me it is my dream, my trip. Maybe they are right; maybe I have just not met the right people. Whatever, all I can do is push on. The word 'ruthless' does not sit well with me, but maybe I am. When I decided to do this I knew what it would do to me, but I overestimated my ability to explain it to others. Many have said that I don't explain myself well, but I thought I did. My ego tells me I can take complex scientific and engineering concepts and explain them simply. It usually works, so maybe the problem is that emotional issues are beyond my ability to explain.

To me it is simple. To take a kayak 8,000 kilometres through different countries on a finite timeframe, through difficult physical experiences, through all the challenges that get thrown up, requires a singularity of mind. Does this mean I am not a good man? I don't know, but I do try to be – at every level. It is distressing when I don't achieve that, but there isn't much more I can do.

A great many people support what I am doing. Well meaning, good people. To them I am grateful, very, very grateful. Some have contributed money, some have helped. The trip is under-resourced but it is what it is. We are very lucky to have Connor and Menatwork Comms for the publicity side. Without them no-one would know about the trip, so it would not achieve its objectives. It is impossible to raise awareness of a secret."

At the time I was struggling to make sense of everything, maybe even to understand myself. Despite trying desperately for three years, I had been unable to find anyone with complementary skills who could come on the trip. It needed someone who could film, someone who could chase media while I paddled, someone who could look after day-to-day operations, like sorting out phone and internet failures, and someone who was passionate about the cause. I didn't even have someone who could help get my GoPro to work, but here we were and I had to make it happen no matter what.

Why was I not inspiring people? At the time I assumed it must be that they did not care about the issue as much as I did, or I had not explained my mission well enough. Maybe I was caught between the idea of the adventurer who follows his own dream, come hell or high water, and the desire to be an effective change agent. It hadn't even occurred to me that there might be a difference. Some very raw emotional experiences were on the horizon. The physical aspects would be easy compared with that. Klaas was certainly not equipped to identify the problem, counsel me and find a way through the labyrinth.

Mario, whom I mentioned in Chapter 1, is a senior Al Gore organizer in the United States and was helping with contacts on the trip. Hoody and I had skyped Mario to discuss Climate Reality Project's support about a year before the start. We thought we could work with local leaders as I travelled up the Mississippi. I would get to meet with them where we would swap ideas and inspirations, maybe even set up a couple of public gigs to talk about the issue. Hoody even talked about getting Big Al to do a send-off in New Orleans. I knew that wouldn't happen, but we would have Connor there and he was a media expert.

Enough navel gazing; the kayak and our gear had arrived. We headed off to a Houston warehouse to collect it. Talk about a cat on a hot tin roof. It would have had nothing on me as I pranced around waiting at the door until I actually saw the crate on a forklift high up over the other boxes, over 100 metres down the warehouse. It eventually reached us, the forklift pushing the crate along the concrete. Half an hour later we were gone after unloading all the heavy stuff and having the aluminium crate lifted onto the roof racks. There was a little damage and almost everything had been taken apart. I don't think they opened the plastic bags with Klaas' clothes in them, even though the duty on his old underpants was 26%.

With the kayak ready, we just needed to finalise our living quarters. At nine metres long and three tonnes dry weight, the travel trailer was huge by Aussie standards, so the towing gear was pretty serious. Like nearly all the US vans, it had black water, grey water and fresh water tanks, sewer, electrical and water hook-ups, so when you stop at a camp site you are fully self-contained. The reason for such a big unit was to provide accommodation to anyone who wanted to come along and help. This was to be headquarters of the 'global movement'. Klaas, as chef, had free rein to stock the kitchen. That was his domain.

Applying the stickers

Fitting the fly kayak sail with Nick

The rig (Texas)

As we left Austin and set off for New Orleans, the state of Texas opened up before us. Texas is pretty flat, so they build road interchanges the size of hills which allows you a good look at the countryside. Well, that's what it seems like anyway. You ain't seen roads until you've been to Texas. And then, you ain't seen bridges until you get to Louisiana. Mile after mile, as far as the eye can see, there are double bridges across the swamps with at least two lanes each way.

The weather into Louisiana and New Orleans was dreadful. The day before we arrived the authorities closed schools just up the river because of ice on the roads. Our entry was better, but cold, overcast and miserable. The Mississippi was grey and rough, and about as attractive as lumpy gravy on ice-cream, but we didn't come here to be sooky about it. We needed to explore and find where best to get in and out of the river.

The temperature rose slowly to 8°C, where it maxed out for the day, and I realised I would be wearing gloves. On earlier Australian kayaking trips, as in Victoria during August, and the same near Bourke in July, my hands used to ache until 10.00am until they thawed out and would then be fine for the rest of the day. Around New Orleans, there are whole days that hovered below 5°C, so I reckoned that without decent gloves they would ache all day. At the time, the eastern states in the US were copping really cold weather. Because polar areas are heating much more than those nearer the equator, partly due to the loss of Arctic ice, the northern hemisphere jet stream wanders much more than it has in the past. Known as the Polar Vortex, this brings really warm air to places like Alaska and really cold air to the eastern United States. Of course, the deniers use this as evidence that global warming is a hoax, but a paradox is not evidence that the scientific experts are wrong. This is just an example of wishful thinkers grasping at any excuse to deny the major body of evidence. It is like a smoker denying that smoking causes lung cancer because there is one healthy ninety year-old who smokes.

Climate change means climate chaos. With 7% more energy in the atmosphere we are already experiencing extreme events that reflect that. Maybe even if the deniers don't accept the science, one day they will work out why insurance costs keep rising. Then again, maybe they won't. Many have already altered their argument to "Yes the climate is changing, but that's natural. It is not man-made." There is always something else to blame.

We were ready for action. The logistical nightmares were over. Anne would arrive in a couple of weeks to help Klaas support me on the river.

The North American leg was about to start and we were excited. Connor arrived Friday, 27 March, ready to start contacting media. It was an entirely new situation for him, but that's what he does for a living and he just got stuck in. He was a bit miffed that Menatwork had insisted that he take the two weeks as annual leave, and I should have taken that as a warning sign about his level of commitment, but it went right over my head. Impressively, media aside, he reckoned he had a date lined up for the following week. Quick work or what!

CHAPTER 5

THE GULF AND THE LAKE

The team was excited. At last, whatever doubts we had, whatever troubles might lie ahead, we were ready to go. Because the mouth of the Mississippi is nearly 200 kilometres downstream from New Orleans, I studied the maps to find a departure point on the Gulf as close as possible to New Orleans. The Silver Slipper Casino Hotel was the closest landmark, so we headed off around Lake Ponchartrain to explore the area. Behind the casino we found a fishing business near a beach where we met the very friendly Nicole and Mike. We told them our plans of paddling across the lake to New Orleans and then up the Mississippi to Canada.

"It is easy, just head west from here, go under the big railway bridge and keep going until you hit the next big bridge. Can't go wrong really," opined Mike. Nicole advised that whatever happened, river people are very friendly and will always help if they can. That was reassuring.

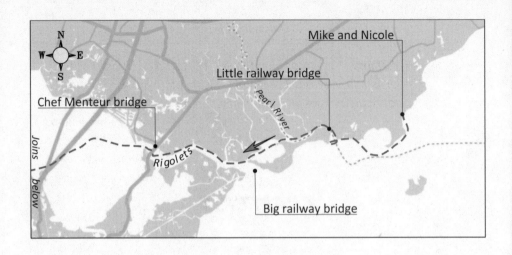

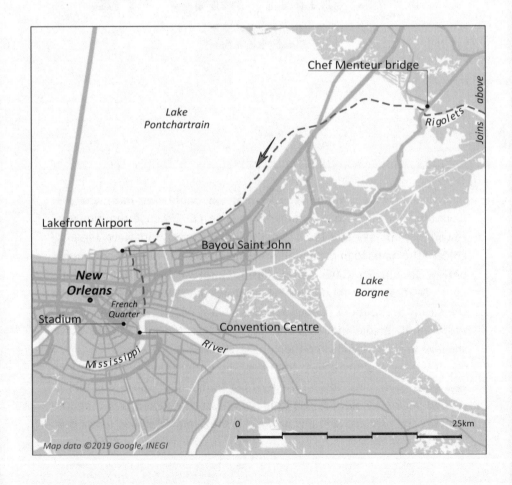

Maybe my experiences with the friendliness of boaties in Australia would translate to the United States.

> ***Klaas' blog:*** *Hi. Greetings from the great Satan. New Orleans' French Quarter is still very much alive and swinging, with narrow streets and clapboard houses all painted in different colours, and bars every 10 metres with jazz being played everywhere. Just as I remember when I first visited in 1948 as a sailor. The city is modern but the suburbs vary greatly. Lots of beggars on the streets and slums with dead cars and rubbish everywhere. The houses are totally different to what we know. Yesterday we went down to the Gulf of Mexico to investigate the site for launching the great paddler and had a nice time seeing how the other half lives. Huge mansions, all new or built during the last 10 years, because hurricane Katrina flattened the lot. Literally blew them away. A lot of roads are still looking like a war zone, with pot-holes and debris in various parts of New Orleans. The place we picked to launch is called Pass Christian and is in the state of Mississippi. After we launch the great master, Connor and I are taking a boat trip through the mighty bayou to see some alligators that inhabit this place. 'Gators', as the locals call them. I hope Steve can paddle fast.*

We awoke for our early morning start to a 'pea souper'. There was no chance of paddling in that sort of fog, so we fixed our leaky taps in the van and explored the route that I would take through the city on the third day, when I arrived in New Orleans. The Bayou St John is a narrow finger of water from Lake Pontchartrain almost to the French Quarter in New Orleans on the bank of the Mississippi River. It seemed to be the best route between the lake and the river with only about six kilometres of walking. There isn't kayak access from the lake to the bayou, but wheeled kayaks are made for minor obstacles like that. I wrote down the streets at the closest intersection to the bayou entrance and Klaas put the directions in the glove box. We then explored the crowded French Quarter with its myriad of bars and eateries, before crossing a railway line beside the Mississippi riverbank. The river was grey and bleak with sheer walls from where we stood on the concrete footpath. Eventually, we found a set of wooden steps down the bank which would make an ideal entry point. Despite the setback of a day we were on the edge of something really epic.

Many people had advised us of the dangers of the Mississippi, that it was impossible to paddle up it, but I had heard that sort of thing before.

We called Mike down at the beach on the Gulf. He was confident the fog would clear during the night, so we made plans to launch the next morning. We managed to get a new GoPro® to mount on my chest, after we decided the equipment I had originally bought in Lismore was simply no good. A cheap waterproof camera from Walmart would be the backup. From my diary:

> "Did I say I am paddling tomorrow? Yee haa, about bloody time. Man, am I fat! The photos are so embarrassing I censor them. Klaas is more suited to when I am piling up the kilometres. He is a bloody good cook. Will send Conner home a wee bit heavier – sorry."

I kept up the emails with Lea. Admittedly, I may not be the world's best communicator but hey, anyone can beat a 21-year-old bloke at that game. Connor could fill in the details when he got home. Lea was up and down. We both missed each other's company. I wanted to be mates while I got on with my adventure, and she wanted the adventure over and me to come back, something I could not promise. If I am honest, the seeds of destruction were sown when she decided not to come on the trip. Despite living for the moment, as she had suggested, deep down I probably knew that my life would be more than simply living for the moment. I had no idea how the trip might change me, my life, or my perspective, but I did know that something this big would have some sort of lasting effect.

It was a foggy morning again, so we squeezed in an interview with a local Republican radio station before starting. My point to the audience was that, as an engineer, I thought it very risky to ignore everything NASA and the rest – I won't bore you with the list again – are saying about how we have a serious problem, but we hang our hats on the advice of politicians who have no training whatsoever in the area. Bear in mind here that Al Gore, Democrat, brought us An Inconvenient Truth. The issue then became political in the US. Politics seems to be a belief, rather than rational analysis, for many people. If you are a Republican and a Democrat tells you something, it must be wrong. Sometimes I wish that a Republican like John McCain had done the job of promoting awareness of the dangers of climate change because I think Democrat supporters might have still accepted the science. Given the role of money from fossil fuel companies in politics, though, that might be wishful thinking.

The fog cleared on the way to the Gulf, came back with a vengeance when we were on the Chef Meneur Bridge near Lake Pontchartrain, disappeared again and reappeared at the beach. On the way we passed the pick-up point at a marina next to the Chef Menteur Bridge. By any standards this is a big bridge. It is easily seen from a long distance away and climbs in a high arch to allow ships underneath. The bridge marks the entrance to Lake Pontchartrain and is just over a kilometre long. Big as the Chef Menteur is, the next one on Highway 10 is nearly nine kilometres long and the one across the lake is more than 38 kilometres long. That's right, it is not a typo, a bridge nearly 40 kilometres long. We were to find this was not exceptional. The bridges and elevated motorways cover hundreds of kilometres. My route would take me to the first bridge on day one, then under the Highway 10 bridge and along the southern side of the lake on day two.

At the beach, we spoke with Nicole, who also reckoned the fog would clear, so we prepared to go. It wasn't until 1.00pm that the fog lifted, allowing us to see along the coast more than a couple of hundred metres, and I wasn't about to set off from a strange shore with no vision. We were about to embark on something quite unknown in an unfamiliar world. I may have looked reasonably nonchalant, but I was far from it. I was excited, proud and maybe a bit apprehensive, but this was the start of something I had dreamed about for a long time. There was no time for savouring any moments, though. To get to the pick-up point I would need to cover 43 kilometres. That would be a huge task but the Chef Menteur was a big bridge with lots of lights, so coming in after dark should not be a problem.

Paddling out from the white, sandy beach and across the estuary where the fishing boats go in and out of the Gulf of Mexico, I was about to enter gator country. The shore on the opposite side of the estuary was flat marshland, which extended all the way to the pick-up point. The land rose out of the grey sea in vertical banks only about half a metre high, with grey grass at my eye height disappearing into the distance. There isn't a lot to look at there, just the flat delta with hardly any bird life and, hopefully, no gators. The wind was light and then picked up to about 20 knots when I passed an inlet with a railway bridge that I thought might be where Mike had said to make a turn. I was of two minds. Do I keep going to the big railway bridge that crosses the main entrance from the Gulf or accept this as where Mike meant? I kept going but it didn't feel right, so I turned around and paddled back upwind half a kilometre to head into the bayou, hoping that was what Mike had meant. It was getting rough, I wasn't exactly sure of where I was, the wind was cold and I hadn't seen a soul.

Chef Menteur bridge (Bayou Savage National Park)

Starting at the Gulf of Mexico

Luckily I had fitted the Fly Kayak sail, because I needed to cover more than 40 kilometres before dark. Kayaks don't sail like sailing boats because they don't have a keel to keep them straight, but under the right conditions they can scoot along at twice normal paddling speed. With paddle in hand, instinct will prevent any capsize. Although the wind was gusty, the water beside the bank was smooth and we flew under the railway bridge and along the Pearl River. There were no trees to break the wind, just dead flat land with swamp grasses, so the sailing was about as good as it gets on a river. I was very glad my instincts had brought me onto the inland route running parallel to the Gulf where it was much more sheltered. I guess in summer there are boats about and people fishing, but on this winter day with a cold wind blowing, grey water and flat land about the same colour, and no sign of any humans, I was glad to just be going from point A to point B as fast as possible.

The Pearl went off to the right, but my path was straight ahead across Little Lake. Way over to the left was the railway line which eventually provided a train for my amusement. Trains here are kilometres long and they go really slowly, like at jogging pace, and they blow their horns every few minutes. I have no idea why. Perhaps it is to scare wildlife but I doubt there would have been anything on the tracks out there by the alligator marshes.

This was all very strange to me. I was out in the middle of nowhere in a strange country. The only people aware of my location were finding it equally strange. It wasn't until later that I understood just how confused they were. My yellow kayak had been my partner for over 6,000 kilometres in some very challenging conditions back home, so I wasn't worried, but I did feel very isolated.

About 5.00pm we made cell phone contact. Connor advised that they were before the bridge and on my left, rather than at the marina where we had agreed.

"It's easy to see us and easy to get out of the water," he advised.

On reaching the bridge, I had not seen them, because they were nowhere near my route. I have no idea where they thought I would be coming from and we both had the same maps. Thinking back on it as I write, I guess they expected me to paddle along the shore until I found them. They probably thought of the whole thing as a bit of a jaunt, rather than as a seriously challenging physical activity that involved planning, coordination and the careful reading of maps. Luckily, Connor figured out that might be the case and came over to the bridge to hail me in. They were about half a kilometre before the bridge and in a bay that I had no hope of seeing. It was a good enough spot to organize a pick up, but it was not the pick-up point we had arranged and it meant back tracking and taking longer than if they had been at the marina. Perspectives on the water are very different to those on the land, especially if those on the land are not used to being on the water. After some discussion, we all agreed that it was advisable to stick to the original pick-up point if at all possible. I got some great shots on the GoPro, trust me, but it died when I tried to extract the footage. The good news was that the sail had worked a treat and saved my bacon. Paddling through a gator-filled waterway in the cold and dark would not have been fun.

The next day's paddle was a cold, windy and sometimes wet slog along the exposed edge of Lake Ponchartrain and around the airport to Bayou Saint John. Near the protected bank of the lake, with the wind offshore, conditions got much better and I cruised around to the rendezvous point past a few walkers and even the odd person sitting on stone steps on the shore, all rugged up and looking out over the vast lake that stretched past their horizon. Again, it felt like an adventure: the strange country, the excitement of discovery, the paddle around the airport that is all on reclaimed land jutting over two kilometres into the lake, and the battle against the wind and waves to get back to the shore. It was tough, but I had done tough before.

When I arrived at the pick-up point the sun was going down and the entrance to the bayou looked different to what I expected. I rang Connor to say that I wasn't 100% sure where I was. After all, my map was not very detailed, just a blue line along with other blue lines to indicate bayous into the lake. Connor replied that they had just decided they were in the wrong location too. I dragged the kayak up the concrete steps that formed the bank, climbed over the levee and confirmed that in fact I had got it right. Phew! Connor said he and Klaas would be there soon. God knows where they were. Given that they had all day to get to the pick-up point and that I had found it under much more difficult circumstances, it concerned me that they could get it so wrong. I asked why they hadn't initially put the street names from the list in the glove box into the GPS. Although we had been there two days previously to scout my route, Klaas hadn't seen the importance of the street names and hadn't told Connor. He was just along to drive where Connor told him. Unfortunately I hadn't made sure that Connor knew that Klaas had the street names in the glove box, assuming that he was watching what was happening when we had been there to check out the bayou. As a consequence, I was frozen stiff from sitting in the wind, in the dark, by the time they arrived. Once again, their complete misunderstanding about the nature of their job had caused me serious discomfort after a huge physical effort on the water. I was a little worried about how this was going to work out on the difficult parts of the river in the wilderness, rather than in a huge city with road signs and detailed maps.

After only two days, we were ready to go through New Orleans to the Mississippi, which I thought was not bad progress, given the adverse winds I'd encountered most of the day. We planned a shopping, scouting and media day the next day with just a short paddle up the Bayou St John, then the following day the walking leg through New Orleans with the launch into the Mississippi River around 2pm. I'm sure Klaas gave me an extra heavy spoon to eat my soup that night. I could hardly pick it up.

We awoke to very different weather. Klaas and Conner were shocked by the temperature change. It was 21°C lower, raining and gusting to about 35 knots.

We had some chores to do, like get some bits to fix the taps in the van, check out the first pick-up point further up the Mississippi River, have a good lunch for the old guy's 83rd birthday, and buy a new GoPro and GPS.

At 1pm, at the edge of the Mississippi River, my next launching point, we turned up with a banner to advertise the trip, but the only media was Julia, a radio producer. Who would want to be out in that weather anyway? She did a great interview that was circulated on the web.

After our frozen stint at the river's edge, I went back to yesterday's finish point and did a quick spin along the length of the bayou heading towards the French Quarter. I kept my trousers on and swapped my shoes for booties, and set off with the vow to stay dry. One bridge later, after about only half a kilometre, I had to advise Connor that my nuts were wet. But with my arctic gloves on I was fine, particularly as the kayak nearly planed with 35-knot wind gusts up its clacker.

I encountered lots of bridges where I had to haul down the sail. The run covered only 6.4 kilometres, but I had fun and we got a few pictures.

Jacqueline had been in contact with environmental groups in Louisiana and put me onto Renate (pronounced 'Renata'), who had invited us to a 350.org meeting that evening. The meeting was held at the Louisiana Bucket Brigade house. Jenna, who chaired the meeting, also runs the Bucket Brigade. The name makes sense when you understand the group's mission is to end petrochemical pollution in Louisiana, and they use a special bucket to sample air. The 350.org organization was set up by Bill McKibben, an American author, to convince the world of the necessity to adopt 350 parts per million of CO_2 as the safe level to avoid catastrophic climate change. This number was based on a paper by James Hansen of the NASA Goddard Institute for Space Studies. We have now exceeded 400ppm and climbing. 350.org has grown to be a global organization and continues to grow rapidly. I was at the inaugural Brisbane meeting a few years previously. Lynette Smith, one of this trip's valiant supporters, joined the Eurobodalla Group on the south coast of NSW when she had finished helping out for the English leg of my trip, and can attest to the strong growth of the movement in Australia. The meeting in New Orleans was attended by about twenty enthusiastic members who displayed discipline, resolve and courage. That doesn't sound like many people, but even major political parties struggle with low numbers at grass roots local meetings. It was just the sort of networking that we had been looking forward to.

Connor came into town with us for the start of the meeting but disappeared after half an hour to go on his date. We didn't see him again until we were at the French Quarter halfway through the next morning. Told you he was impressive.

I really enjoyed the discussions. It was pretty much like an Aussie meeting, same sort of people, same sort of issues. In every group there are a couple of standout doers and they were evident there. Renate was studiously taking notes and helping Jenna, the organizer. She was fascinated with our trip and we somehow clicked. I had thought there might be an informal get together after the meeting but everyone drifted away. Renate and I talked for a while after the meeting but it was freezing cold outside, and Klaas had gone off to sit in the car. We resolved to stay in touch by email and she set off home on her bike.

I wondered at the people in power who have destroyed so many lives in Louisiana all for money. Did the film Erin Brockovich make a difference? Why did the Bucket Brigade have to fight so hard? These people I had met were all labelled as environmentalists. Many times the media have called me an environmentalist. I don't see why it has become a derogatory term to many, especially on the 'right'? Maybe we should start from the other foot and call it what it is. You are either in favour of destroying the environment or you are in favour of preserving as much as we can. I see myself and the people at this meeting simply as people who want to preserve the future. That means the people who sneer at environmentalists are actually destroyers of the future; thieves really, robbing from our children.

Many call themselves conservatives, but I can't really think of a more inappropriate term. A conservative should conserve, not destroy. I think that a false division comes about when people see the environment as something external to human activity instead of something that supports life on earth. The classic mistake is when someone says we cannot allow the environment to get in the way of the economy. Without a healthy environment there can be no economic activity. The problem is that we won't pay the price of environmental damage, our children and grandchildren will.

The crisp, clear morning promised to warm up to 13°C. What a relief, a fine morning for walking through New Orleans. First there was a quick

Crossing Bourbon St (New Orleans)

Skype interview with Bud Ward, the editor of Yale Climate Connections, which broadcasts on climate change issues for 90 seconds per day on 210 public, university, community and alternative radio stations across the United States. Then it was time to walk down Conti Street from the end of the Bayou St John into the French Quarter. Klaas drove the car using the same system as in Australia, leapfrogging me and parking where he could find a spot so that he could take photos, check if I needed anything and talk to people who noticed me dragging a kayak through the streets. It appeared, though, that a guy dragging a kayak through the French Quarter in New Orleans was no big deal. Nobody seemed to think it was unusual, they just politely made way where necessary. I wasn't the only one being politely ignored. Even the bloke balancing halfway up a ladder that was in mid-air didn't rate more than a second glance. A jazz group was popular, as was a comedian and juggler.

Connor turned up looking fresh as a daisy just as we crossed the famous Bourbon Street through the throngs of people. We pressed on to the walkway at the riverbank and the big timber steps leading into the water.

CHAPTER 6

MEETING THE RIVER

Embarking on the Mississippi River from New Orleans was nothing like the grand departure that Hoody thought we would have. There were some casual onlookers, so we handed out some business cards and told our story.

"I am just going to hop in the river and paddle up to the top of Canada. No worries."

Short and sweet and a bit more flippant than I really felt, as I did expect some worries, but I was actually excited and confident: here we were at the big river and about to do our stuff. I was getting used to the paucity of media in big cities and we had made grass roots connections while learning just how hard the locals had to struggle.

To set out on the great river was a significant moment, but it was nothing like the day I paddled onto the Gulf of Mexico and headed into the unknown. This was just a river, big as it was. Maybe I was just getting used to it. Planning a trip for three years then travelling halfway round the world to paddle in a strange environment with strange animals, like

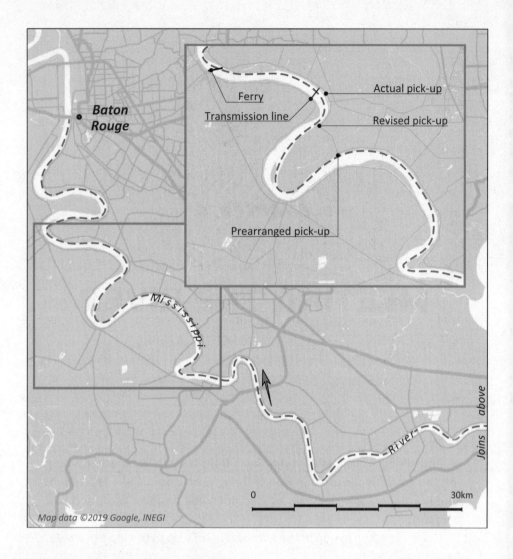

Ferry

Transmission line

Actual pick-up

Revised pick-up

Prearranged pick-up

Baton Rouge

Mississippi

River

Joins above

0   30km

Map data ©2019 Google, INEGI

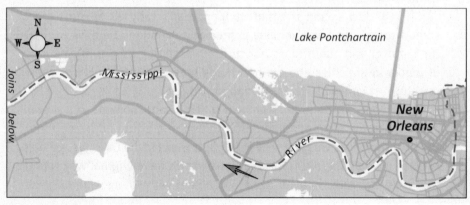

Lake Pontchartrain

Mississippi

River

Joins below

New Orleans

Levees make it impossible to see the river.

alligators, had really been a big deal. I had put myself out there, cut myself off from normal life for a year. The Gulf waters were the start, the launch into the unknown. This felt like getting down to business.

The Energy Patriot, an empty oil tanker, pushed its way upstream. It was my first taste of a bow wave from a ship that big and, despite all the dire warnings I had received, its wash was of no concern at all. The first set of barges I saw was huge, one big tug pushing 18 barges in a configuration six barges long and three barges wide. It took more than 20 minutes for it

With Julia, ready to take on the big river (New Orleans)

to pass me. The wake behind the pusher tug is serious, but if you stay far enough away its wash is no problem. I had been told that the river traffic would get worse, but at that stage I was pretty comfortable and made it 15 kilometres to our prearranged pick-up point at a suburban park, 102 miles from the mouth of the river, according to the milestone there. I had a problem using the sail to get some help against the current, though. I had to get away from the bank to catch the wind to use the sail, but that was the area of strongest current. It was only possible to use the sail once, when I paddled around a kilometre or so of barges. Regretfully, the sail was stowed in the van, to be brought out somewhere past the rivers, perhaps on the Great Lakes.

We had taken some video with the new GoPro but, after uploading the footage to my computer that night, the image had lines on it, making the whole lot useless. I was quite frustrated. Video is a major part of modern communication and here I was on a major trip with absolutely no reliable video component. All my attempts to date had been little more than a waste of time and energy. Connor offered to exchange the camera at Walmart the next day while I paddled. What I really needed was a support person to troubleshoot technology problems for me. I could paddle, I could do the logistics to get us there, I could post my blogs every day, but that was my limit.

After two prior pick ups that had not gone to plan, we were all pleased with this one. "Not a bad start," we thought.

From mile marker 102 to mile marker 122, a distance of 33 kilometres, my understanding of the Mississippi matured. Now I knew! It is possible to paddle up that river, but it is very, very hard. Where you can get to the bank, it is fine. Not easy, but fine. The problem is that there were thousands of barges along the banks. To go round them you are out in the current again where it takes full strength to inch forwards. It is a bit dangerous as well. After you go round a string of barges, maybe four or five side by side, you need to get back to the bank. The easy way is to ride the pressure wave about five metres in front of the upstream barge. I stayed about 10 metres in front but still benefited from the effects of the wave. The thing is not to tip over. That would be certain death. You would be dragged back under the barges. That said, if a wheel fell off your motorbike at highway speed you would probably die. It is somewhat of a calculated risk, I guess, and

I accepted it without concern. Perhaps if someone was monitoring my adrenalin levels, some major spikes might have been evident.

Everyone I met that day, all ten of them, was friendly and supportive, although they thought I was mad. One bloke wanted me to come onto his tug and have a drink. Another bloke even backed his tug out of the way. We had been told by Nicole at the Gulf that river people are great. They certainly are, Nicole.

My hands suffered with blisters under the tape and the gloves. It was just a result of prolonged, full-strength paddling. I assumed they would toughen up eventually, so I just had to put up with it. Squeezing the pus out in the mornings and then wrapping tape over the raw skin wasn't something new, but it was never what I would call fun.

> *Klaas' blog:* Hi all. Still in New Orleans running around like the proverbial blue-arsed flies getting replacements for either lost, misplaced or broken bits and pieces. The great master in the meantime has been paddling up the mighty Mississippi. And mighty is an apt description, the traffic is unbelievable. Hundreds of barges, locked together in four or fives, 80 footers pushed along with huge tug boats. Very similar to Europe on the Rhine. Big passenger vessels, steam paddle wheelers, container ships, etc. Stevie boy has to dodge all that, as well as deal with the current, but he is doing all that and his twenty-odd miles a day. Picking him up this afternoon and waiting for him, I sat on an old log washed up near the shore and put my cap on the ground so I could remove my jumper, as the weather was lovely and warm. Putting the cap back on my balding noggin, I started screaming. Hundreds of fire ants had invaded my head piece and were now frantically biting my eyelids, arms and legs, as well as my feet inside my crocs (shoes). I now know why they are called 'fire ants'. I needed the fire brigade. But, as usual, I survived and, after half an hour, the fire burned itself out. Tomorrow we are shifting the caravan closer to the next town, which is Baton Rouge. That's all for now. Be good or if you can't be good, be careful.

> *Connor's blog:* Having been in the thick of things here in sunny New Orleans for a week now, the boss has asked me to offer you, the valued readers, an insight into how the mission has unfolded so far. In a word; bloody-well. In a few words; not without its challenges.
>
> We've been greeted with Southern hospitality beyond what I expected. Americans, in my experience so far, are helpful, warm people. We've met some serious characters. Sean, the cleaner in our

trailer park, has face tattoos and gold grills on his bottom teeth, is a Clan Leader on the Facebook game 'Clash of Clans', and is concerned about what rising sea levels might mean for New Orleans, which is situated a few metres below sea level.

Jeff Crouere hosts a highly conservative republican radio show, however he's invited Steve back on the show to discuss his trip on a fortnightly basis.

Buck, a man with NRA bumper stickers on his truck, stood around our rig and discussed Steve's motivations and the adventure for a decent 20 minutes.

People are consistently not what I expect them to be in Louisiana. It has been a hard slog getting the public to take notice of what we're doing, but with each day comes a new, albeit small win. These wins are great paddlin' fuel and I think that the next few months will see Steve's fuel tank full to the brim.

Again we were all pleased with the day, as the distance paddled was exactly what we wanted to achieve. After a day and a half on the Mississippi everyone was confident and we headed back to the van, ready to move it up river the next day. The Mississippi was causing two problems that we just had to put up with. The first was paddling around barges. It slowed me down a lot and caused the damage to my hands. The second was finding access points in and out of the river. Up to 30-plus kilometres between two possible river access points was common.

The bends on the river are impressive. Whereas I had been underwhelmed on my first day, the opposite was now becoming true. Some bends are long enough that they extend nearly to the horizon. They are bloody huge and it can take hours to get around just one bend. Looking at it on the map doesn't convey the correct impression at all. Despite our confidence the day before, I became dissatisfied with progress and was determined to go as far as possible the next day. It looked like we would reach Chicago mid-July, which wasn't good enough, but surely the barges would not line the banks all the way.

When we set the van up, I constructed a work table inside the wardrobe, complete with a power outlet. In that space I could use my computer, printer and laminator. Each day I would use Google Earth to figure out where to go using the 'path' feature to measure the distance. I would then

This lot could be three kilometres long

switch to Google Maps and print out the route in colour. Any notes that I needed to make would be written on the map and then I would laminate it. The support crew would get the same map but not laminated.

With our maps for the day we returned to the river behind the huge levee that extended all the way downstream to the other side of New Orleans. Visibility in the fog was a few hundred metres. Behind the levee is a road and behind that are houses, shops and all sorts of life that has nothing to do with the river. It is urban living beside a six metre high hill. I'm sure a lot of people hardly even know or care that there is a river over the other side. Others, like the bloke who served us at the supermarket, talk about how dangerous it is, and how people have lost their lives there.

"Be careful," he advised solemnly, "someone died on the river just last week. It is treacherous."

Talk about a disconnection.

Over the levee and onto the river, the fog was heavy, with visibility less than 30 metres at times. At other times it would clear enough to see refineries on the opposite bank floating above the mist, but such moments were few and far between. In such conditions everything looms out of the fog, slowly taking shape as you approach. It is an eerie feeling and takes some getting used to, and I was never actually comfortable with it.

There were not many barges for the first 16 kilometres and I was able to paddle very close to the bank where the current is slowest. This was what I had expected to do before seeing the river, but it very rarely happened. That section slipped by in two hours, fifteen minutes. The second 16 kilometres took nearly four hours. When the difference in paddling times can almost double depending on the conditions, it makes it very difficult to determine when the end of the day's paddle will be. Whatever the conditions, this was a busy, industrial river with many different activities to ponder.

A long wharf lay about 25 metres out from the bank, running parallel to the river with a connecting bridge to the bank. On the wharf, a large grab crane was lifting scrap metal out of the barges into trucks parked on the wharf. Paddling between the two was easy, as the current was quite slow. After the wharf, a set of posts held barges about five metres away from the shore. The barges were stacked about six wide extending into the fog, but paddling in a five metre wide area next to the bank with hardly any flow, I scooted along for a few hundred metres. The water became shallow and there were many burrs growing. They would cling to my sleeves, somehow find their way inside my lifejacket and generally make life uncomfortable, but they were just a minor discomfort compared to the real obstacles. These were the small log jams that I had to crash through. Finally I came upon a big one with no way through. When this happens, it is often possible to force the kayak over the logs using my knuckles and jerking with my bum, but in this case there was no chance. The log jam was too big. The only option was to turn around, go back to the start of the raft of barges and go out into the river. I set off with visibility now at about half a barge length and no idea how long the raft of barges was, except that it was more than the half a kilometre I had already paddled. I slogged away, inch by bloody inch, up the side of the barges. At full power I could make less than two kilometres per hour and, as it turned out, the string of barges was more than a kilometre long. It was a boring slog for more than half an hour.

Barges vary in size, some being twice the standard size, but in the main they are about 60 metres long by ten metres wide with about a three metre draft giving a capacity of about 1500 tonnes. If you take a common barge set of six long by four wide, that is like a big tug pushing four football fields. Fully laden, the set is 36,000 tonnes. This is staggeringly huge. On a bend where I had the inside running I would be out of the current, they would be in the current, and I could just beat their speed, so we could be side by side for a couple of hours. Racing something for hours on end really helps with average speed. Back in Australia, I would race the houseboats on the Murray River for four hours at a time so this was very familiar.

The big problem is when the barges are moored along the banks. There are thousands of them, some pushed right onto the bank, some moored a little way out. This can be a single barge but usually at least six long by six wide. When empty, they draw less than half a metre, but when full they can draw 3.5 metres. Some have a vertical box front, some curve upwards. The ones curving upwards would certainly suck a kayak under them if caught. If an empty one with a curved front is pushed hard onto the trees on the bank it is often impossible to get past.

I came to understand the river a bit more. Its moods were mostly bleak with rising waters, rain, heavy fog and more and more debris. Sometimes I would race barge sets that I could hear thumping away in the gloom out there in the wide river. Sometimes I would paddle for long distances under wharves, hoping that there was not a steam pipe among the liquids that sprayed down towards me.

Small islands rose out of the river about 50 metres apart. They were the tops of sand heaps. It was a sand quarry that was all but submerged by rising water. Loaders and excavators worked the new shoreline which was still about two metres above water. This was my first real indication that the river was rising. Just upstream a pipe gushed water. As a sewage and water engineer, this was my business: it was undoubtedly a sewage outfall. My guess was that it was from an old-style trickling filter plant with what we call a 20:30 effluent. That is 20 parts per million of BOD (biological oxygen demand) and 30 parts per million suspended solids. It had the usual musty smell of that treatment process but quite strong. Further up the river I met a fellow engineer who told me that the effluent standard was 30:50, something that I had not heard of and much stronger than we would allow to be released in Australia. It might reflect the fact that there is a lot more water in the United States to dilute things than there is at home.

I called Connor at our scheduled time of 2.00pm. We had arranged to meet on the southern side of a big bend. On our maps, a major road crossed the bend from north to south, so we had agreed to meet where that road met the river as it was an easy point to put into the Ford's GPS. Because I had made better-than-expected time I was already there. I explained this to Connor, who was still back at the van with Klaas, and suggested that I meet him at the opposite end of the road, on the north side of the bend, at about 5.00pm. This seemed simple enough. The river headed west for six kilometres, took a sharp right turn of only three kilometres and then back east for six kilometres to the other end of the road. I set off paddling west along a shoreline that rapidly became deserted. It was raining heavily but the fog had thinned enough to see a barge set plodding up the river behind me. It slowly gained despite my advantage of being close to the shore with less current. After about 20 minutes the pusher tug was just over my left shoulder, but I reckoned on beating him round the bend.

The fog closed in and we arrived together as the river turned sharply. The big unit had a lot further to go because there was an island, about three kilometres long, that he had to go around, whereas I could hug the inside. The rain pelted down, my companion disappeared into a fading throb and then the island disappeared in the fog too. The bank became steep with lots of sections falling into the water. The current became fierce as the river straightened out. Back behind the bank I could see the big levee. It was 4.00pm so I had some concerns about reaching the pick-up point on time, but to stop paddling and make a call would have invited disaster. Between the levee and the collapsing cliffs was impenetrable jungle. The rain pelted down and the fog covered everything with its insidious blanket. "This is adventuring," I thought. "Who'd have thought it could be like this on the Mississippi."

At 5.00pm it seemed by dead reckoning that I was somewhere near the pick-up point. The river had calmed and the thinning fog allowed glimpses of the other bank. Over the phone, Connor and I tried to explain to each other what we could see, but nothing made sense because he kept talking about a ferry. There was no ferry on my map, nor on the one I had given him, so I battled on. Just before dark a major transmission line crossed the river with lights on the towers on each side. Because of the very thick fog I wasn't sure what direction I was headed, but I was almost certain I had passed the next bend and had started to turn north. Connor and Klaas reckoned they could see a ferry, which was very confusing because as I said, there was no ferry on my map and there was none in sight. I pulled out of the water, hid the kayak in brambles and stinging nettles near the tower, and climbed up to the top of the levee bank. Any bare skin was bleeding from bramble scratches and stinging nettles, and boy, do they sting. With a good view of the road I waited in the cold twilight talking to Connor on the phone as Klaas drove, but I had no idea whether they were upstream or downstream. The levee was about six metres high with the road running parallel but set back about 20 metres, and they were nowhere to be seen.

Eventually I saw them coming in the gloom. Waving my arms frantically from the top of the levee worked and they stopped just below me. Phew! I was tired, cold and wet. Connor looked at the tower and said that it was obvious when you see it but somehow it had eluded them. The kayak could stay where it was. We headed off for a hot meal and a shower. The distance for the day was 56 kilometres, about four kilometres past where I had been aiming, and indeed almost around the next bend.

I was tired, cold and wet but I had done something that many said was impossible. That day I had paddled over 50 kilometres up the swollen Mississippi. Sure we had yet another pickup problem, but we had got through it. The battle was on and we would win. There was no point worrying about the pick-up issues. It was frustrating and I had some concerns that it might get worse, but I had no other answer.

That night I got to see what 'The Farm' had been up to. A digital marketing and development company, The Farm had heard about Connecting Climate Chaos and wanted to get involved. I had left it with Connor to deal with them and they had taken over the Facebook posts. It was very impressive and they invoiced me monthly just for the cash they outlaid to boost posts. I was so pleased firstly that they noticed, secondly that they thought enough about our efforts to want to help, and thirdly to make the commitment.

Let's take some time out now, and think about what happened with the problem of meeting at the pick-up point. The pre-arranged meeting point was marked in the Ford's GPS. The map quite clearly shows the road across the bend. (page 68) Follow the road across the bend, simple yes? Well no.

Years later, going through the map of that section of the river with other people, I have realised that they were not reading the maps at all. They simply got on the road and drove until they saw the river again and then stopped. Because the levee had hidden the river from them, they had driven for 16 kilometres instead of the three kilometres across the peninsula. I had never thought for a minute that there are some people who simply do not understand the idea of a map, or how to use one to arrange to meet someone at a particular place. I'm not sure how I would have responded if I had understood that at the time. Perhaps I would have taken a couple of days off to deliver a course in Map Reading 101. My life was literally in the hands of people who had no idea what they were doing.

Chef (that's Klaas) chose lunch again: a salmon and mayonnaise sandwich, ham and mustard sandwich, and selection of fruit salad in a separate bowl with a jar of the chef's special dressing. He was doing a mighty job of keeping me fed. Evening meals were delicious and, while I sorted out the maps in the morning, Klaas would prepare and pack my lunch. Breakfast consisted of muesli, if we could get it, otherwise the most solid cereal that we could find. That was not always easy here. Sugar-coated air bubbles were mostly all that was on offer. In fact, if you are not into copious quantities of sugar and fat, there is not a lot to eat in this part of the world. On the other hand, booze was plentiful. I had one or two beers every night, Klaas likes his whiskey and it was less than 20 bucks a bottle.

Walking to the kayak, the stinging nettles attacked once again through my trousers. "Impressive," I thought, but it would take more than vicious stinging nettles to curb my elation at finding the kayak right where I had left it. All night I had worried that the river might rise and sweep it away. The river did rise about 30 centimetres, but the kayak was placed well above that.

The opposite bank was in view and there was a wharf on our side of the river, about 50 metres out from the bank with a connecting bridge. Neither had been visible the previous evening. A lot of debris floated down the river, just like after any flood in any part of the world. With a clear bank, I battled on until I reached a cross-river ferry. This was the first one I had seen. It was marked on my map for the day and was four hours from where I started in the morning, about 13 kilometres, around a huge bend off the top of yesterday's map (see page 68). That was where Klaas and Connor had been waiting for me the previous day.

The bank stretched out before me, curving around to the left with waves of fog rolling in like giant Pacific rollers breaking on a headland. I half expected to see ghosts on surfboards. Perhaps another day as hard as yesterday and I might have seen them. Mind you, I was not in the best of condition. My diary notes say that I felt like crying for the first four or five hours. This is my gauge of stress. When I was younger I got that feeling when I pushed my heart rate over 200. Other people react in different ways, but mine was always to feel like crying. That was a long time ago I have to admit, and 200 beats per minute is way outside my capacity now, but it has been a useful gauge for about 40 years. The feeling passed, especially towards the end of the day when I could see where I was going again.

About 300 metres up the inside of a set of barges – that is, between the barges and the bank – my way was blocked. This necessitated backing out, turning around and retreating to the start; then a paddle out around the back of four barges and bursting out into the current, followed by a long slog to get up to the front and then, finally, a dangerous cut back into the bank. After that the day brightened, there were no more barges to navigate around, industrial wharves started to appear and I could see the bridge at Baton Rouge way up ahead. Klaas and Connor were waiting for me at a boat ramp after 38.4 kilometres for the day. No more rain, a clean pick up, even a glint of sunlight, with Baton Rouge ahead. Connor had been busy during the day and had arranged a television cameraman to film my arrival, and we were on the evening news. All I needed was a beer, and that would come in half an hour when we got back to the van.

Klaas had blogged that I needed some encouragement and lots of emails were waiting on my computer. What a difference the evening was compared with the tough slog that morning.

I was having an adventure while all the people back home were dealing with life.

> **From Amanda:** *"Everyone is still trying to kill each other here. With the change from daylight savings we're all now up at four-fucking-am! It's currently 6:15 and I'm on my fourth coffee, two loads of washing done, built three Lego® trucks, and made breakfast and morning tea for the boys. I wish I was by myself, in a kayak, on a river … that wasn't in flood."*

I think at that time I considered myself lucky.

We took Connor to the bus stop where he headed back down to New Orleans for some more time with his new girlfriend before flying out the following evening. Little did we know at the time, but that was the last effective work we did with Connor. He went back to the other side of the world and I guess life caught up with him. He'd had the excitement of being involved in the start of the North American leg, but now it was back to the life that he had been building with Menatwork and a new stage in his career. Contact would only be intermittent from then on, and only when I sent him something. It took me a long time to understand that he was not as committed to the project as I thought. It was my mission. I was starting to identify the gap between my commitment and everyone else's.

Anne arrived from Australia just in time to enjoy the St Patrick's Day parade in Baton Rouge, so we took a day off. Jacqueline had been in touch with environmental groups in New Orleans and they had passed us onto groups in Baton Rouge. She had said that she would probably come over to the United States to help as support crew, but I had no idea whether that would eventuate. It was a pleasant surprise to receive her help with the introductions.

It resulted in two long interviews with a local radio station WHYR. Doug Daigle was the interviewer and the sound man was Bruce Morgan. It was recorded in Bruce's home. Both are lovely blokes. Bruce learned his skills doing books for the blind. He is a fair bit older than me, so obviously retired, and coincidentally we both have five grandchildren. Despite his modest means he gave me $100 for the trip, which was very touching.

> **Klaas' blog:** Hi all. It is Friday 'blurb time'. Now there are good blurbs and bad blurbs and half-way in between blurbs. This one is short, now that Steve has reached the heart of Baton Rouge. The media has been conspicuous by their absence. At least there was one TV channel there to meet him and not before time. Up till now, he has done some interviews for radio, but these have been few and far between. Tonight Anne joins the crew, and tomorrow we have been invited to the Saint Patrick's Day parade, which is a big deal apparently in these parts. So, don't expect a blurb from me tomorrow as I will be busy entertaining Anne and drinking green beer (hic). Cheers!

A bloke called Steve Poss – yep that's right, just a cut-down version of my name – had invited us, and all the people on the email list that I was to meet, to his first Parade Party. Only one person came, apart from us – another example of people having their own lives. It is a big day in the city and everyone would have made their own arrangements. It was a fun day, though. A giant line of floats all seemed to throw strings of coloured beads to the crowd, adding even more colour to the noisy pageant. We were certainly impressed with the huge mess of beads in the streets after the parade, but we were on a mission and Natchez was the next city up the river. It hadn't been easy so far, but I had the bit between my teeth and I was going for it; focused, strong, unflinching in the relentless push up the river.

CHAPTER 7

TESTING TIMES

It was time to cross the river. There were access points on the west bank, crucial for successful pick- up points that did not exist on the eastern side. The rain and fog had gone, the sun was shining and the Baton Rouge skyline stood crisp and clear against an azure sky streaked at the edges by high, white clouds. USS Kidd, a museum ship, stood out about 50 metres from the grassy bank that dipped into the grey floodwater. About a kilometre upstream, a set of barges was anchored a third of the way across the river. Perfect, a resting place. It was an easy paddle along the shore to the midpoint of the barges and then it was time to turn left and take on the current.

The paddle to the barges was no problem, the eddy behind them was fine for a rest and then the mighty Mississippi could show me what she was made of. A barge set headed upstream, so I waited for it to pass. The tail from the 3000 horsepower motors in the pusher tug was about two metres high, a mountain to a kayak. Crossing about a 100 metres behind this tail I was able to use the waves for assistance without being in danger.

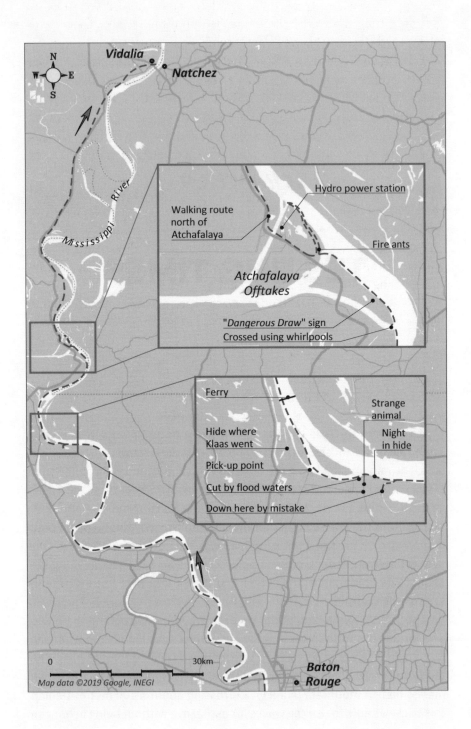

The journey was less than 20 minutes from bank to bank and I lost no ground, hitting the calmer water on the opposite side about level with where I had started. This was a great confidence booster.

Looking back at the city, I wondered what this opposite side of the river would bring. My luck ran out within a few kilometres. Three pusher tugs had a large set of barges pushed at about 45 degrees into the trees on the bank. It would have been a real bummer to go round them, especially with the propeller wash as well as the current, so I paddled along the inside looking for somewhere to get the kayak to the bank. The pilot of one of the tugs was yelling at me to get out of there, but I ignored him and found an exit point about halfway along and dragged the kayak onto the bank to evaluate the situation. The trees gave way to grassy weeds about 30 centimetres high for about 10 metres and then the levee started. It had a 15-degree concrete face which was fine for towing the kayak along. After a few hundred metres the top-side rear wheel fell off and the kayak came to a grinding halt. "Not good," I thought.

The shafts for the wheel nuts are 16 millimetres, which is not the same as 5/8 inches and I was not in a metric country. Like most blokes, I have been accused a few times of having a 'man look', so I was not confident of finding the wheel nut. Luck goes up and down, though, and I did find it about 15 metres back along the concrete. It had rolled down slightly but had not reached the weeds at the bottom. Phew! I put it back on, tightening it with a shifting spanner and continued. Just after the barges, access back to the river was possible through grey bracken and vines. I lifted the wheels up and pushed and pulled the kayak through the mess of brambles. Brambles. They must have been here a while, given the Johnny Horton song that played in my head:

> *"They ran through the briars and they ran through the brambles*
> *And they ran through the bushes where a rabbit couldn't go*
> *They ran so fast that the hounds couldn't catch 'em On down the*
> *Mississippi to the Gulf of Mexico"*

Ten minutes later I reached the water, ready to continue on my way, but that bloody song wouldn't go away. I wasn't running from the British to save my life, but I was paddling to do my bit to save the world as we know it.

The pick-up point was only 17 kilometres from the start, but it was the only one in the area. At about 14 kilometres an opening in the treetops, maybe with a road hidden down below the murky river, led to a calm stretch of water about 25 metres wide between the trees and the grassy levee. The trees had no foliage, but the water level was about halfway up the canopy with no possibility of getting through unless it was above a road or track. Klaas and Anne were waiting at the water's edge where a gravel road ran from the bitumen on the other side. No doubt it continued to where the river would normally be, but today it met the water halfway down the levee. Klaas was excited.

Klaas' blog: *Hurrah. Saw my first 'gator'. Then, waiting for the Master to arrive at designated pick-up point, some hillbillies arrived in an old pick-up truck. She was rather plump, about 20 stone with no teeth and he resembled a match with all the wood scraped off. They were delightful and told us all about the river and bayou. She wanted to buy my book, Past My Use By Date. They could not come up with the $20 for it but would order one from Amazon.*

We are now travelling in lonely rural areas and access to the river is highly restricted. The levies are fenced off and leased to farmers who run cattle on it. Interspersed are huge oil refineries and electricity power stations with 'No admission' signs and guards. Waiting to pick Steve up, I drove the car and kayak box onto the top of the levy wall so Steve could see me easily from the water. Next thing a police car came up and the sheriff came out looking like John Wayne. Two revolvers, one on each hip. "Private property this here," he drawled. I explained to him I was extracting a mad Australian kayaker and he would be coming any minute. "Alright," he replied, "I won't book ya, seeing it is Sunday, a nice day and I hate the paperwork."

These are the hazards of pick ups.

Bridges are good. They make it easy for the support crew and the paddler to meet. We had been able to use them to good effect with Connor and Klaas on a number of occasions by paddling bridge to bridge from the Gulf to New Orleans. This day would require paddling alongside the levee bank until I could get into the main river and then to a spot we had selected just before the bridge at Highway 10. That's the other Highway 10, not to be confused with the one down south.

Bridges don't always make it easy, though. Paddling on a river in Australia in 2009 my support crew set off up the highway one morning. I set off up the river. We were to meet at the bridge three hours later. One highway, one bridge, one river, what could go wrong?

After waiting at the bridge until the agreed time, I phoned them.

They weren't sure how to get there. Could I give them another half hour? WTF! So I said as politely as I could that I would keep paddling.

This was gator country according to Klaas and the locals backed him. Gators are pretty tame, most people advised. "Just poke at 'em with your paddle and they will move away. Course the big bloke, about 16 foot, is a bit more stubborn, but y'all be fine." They must be different to crocs. The Australian saltwater crocodile is a dangerous animal. I don't paddle where there are crocodiles, period! I have seen a few sharks in my travels but I'm used to them. Crocs are another story.

We were down in Louisiana where the alligators grow so mean – "… polk salad Annie, gator's got your granny." How did that get in my head? They might not be mean, but apparently they like grannies.

The mist on the river probably hid any sign of alligators, but I had decided they would be asleep because the water was too cold. I didn't see any, so all I had was hearsay about their existence, which I found comforting. "Gator's got your granny." It was still in my bloody head. Inside the trees the current was slow and things went well, until I came to a log jam. It was about 50 metres long and right across the bayou. With my new troubles, the song finally disappeared. The tops of the trees were thin, like saplings, and they hooked onto the wheels as I tried to negotiate my way through the floating timber. It was not a lot of fun, but the alternative was a return of about 10 kilometres to the last pathway through the tree-tops to the river. Even big log jams have an end to them, so eventually I was free. The bayou finished and I was back to the main river.

Occasionally I would paddle past a small sand cliff. This was the top two metres or so of an eight metre high hill. The cliffs would collapse with a big splash. Nothing unusual about that except for one big factor: they were on the inside of bends. River banks do not usually collapse on the inside of bends. The insides have beaches that gradually grow, whereas the outside of bends wear away until finally the river cuts through and forms an oxbow lake. This river was straightening, no doubt about it. That was the work of the US Army Corps of Engineers. The Mississippi is vital as a transport corridor and it is a highly efficient means of transportation. It needs to be kept within the gargantuan levee systems and it has to run deep enough, even during low flows, for the pusher tugs and barges to operate.

Even just inside the tree line, the current against me was quite strong. A log trapped crossways between two trees had water 10 centimetres higher on the upstream than the downstream side. This is called velocity head and, with a bit of concentrated mental arithmetic, I reckoned that equated to about 5km/hr. River folk did say that the flow would be about 3mph, so I guess I just confirmed their advice. I love being an engineer, even if we cop some occasional flack for our insensitivity and focus.

Nothing is easy paddling up a swollen river, but the day had been relatively pleasant with no real issues. The crew arrived on time, so we made a flawless pick up, and we went back to the van for the last time at Baton Rouge.

We moved the van up to Vidalia, across the river from Natchez, and scouted the river in the Ford. According to a local bloke who spends every hour he can fishing, the river was flowing 20 feet (six metres) above normal, which made some potential pick-up points submerged. We eventually found a suitable extraction point for the next day, but not without difficulty. I checked everything on Google Earth first and then tried to drive there. It was off the Mississippi River Trail, along a gravel road called Raccoci Hunting Club Road and then we had to find a track to the river. The road was noted in the GPS database, but not the tracks. If you look it up on Google Maps you will see it is in the middle of nowhere. Our first attempt, about one kilometre along the road, turned us west, away from the river, through two wheel ruts filled with water and ending in a clearing. The clearing had a hunters' blind, or as the Aussies among us call it, a hide. This is a square box about 1.2 x 1.2 metres set on stilts about four metres above the ground. I guess you hide in there with your gun pointing out and blast away at whatever comes to the clearing to feed on the grass.

"Well, there is no bloody river here," I complained and headed back to the gravel.

About 300 metres further on, the gravel road turned sharply to the right with a 50-metre long track heading left to the river. Klaas stayed in the car in a small clearing at the edge of the road while Anne and I battled the mud, but at least confirmed that river access was indeed fine. As we were walking back to the car I spoke with Anne.

"Don't let him try to drive in here," I advised. "I will be bloody tired by the time I get here and if he gets bogged we will be in trouble. Just park in the clearing at the bend where he is now."

This was not a place to drive, particularly in the dark, and as I had already proved if both front and back wheels on one side start spinning, you are stuck.

Access points were few and far between, making the next day's paddle to get to that point longer than the longest day so far, 60 kilometres, the absolute limit that I could do in a day, but only four kilometres more than I had already done. With the crew having seen the pick-up point and with the road in the car's GPS I was reasonably comfortable there would not be a problem.

> ***Klaas' blog:*** *Last Friday I needed to obtain some money, so drove to the nearest ATM and inserted my Visa card. The next thing that happened was that the uncouth bastard-machine spat out a piece of paper informing me that my bank had requested the machine to swallow it. No warning, no sorry Sir, no I beg your pardon; Vamoose, gone, lost. Here I am, a traveling man in a foreign country needing urgent funds to buy the necessities of life (such as booze and some tucker) and one is left stranded. So I ring the Visa people and some idiot in Calcutta or somewhere far away who spoke a very broken English listened to my tale of woe and after several hours it was established my account in Australia had been compromised and the fraud squad was investigating. I talked to my bank and they are now issuing a new card, which I should have tomorrow. Wow, what a relief.*
>
> *We shifted the caravan yesterday to the nicest place we have so far been, right on the river near Vidalia. It is getting very difficult to find places to launch and retrieve the kayak, as we are in very lonely territory.*
>
> *Yesterday, while looking for a site, the Master managed to drop the car into a hole which had no bottom and buried itself to the floor boards. We finally managed to stop a 4WD ute with recovery gear which pulled us out. (The joys of motoring.)*

We learned that night that six blokes in canoes were about two months ahead of us. They were heading up the Mississippi as far as possible and then up through Canada to the Beaufort Sea near Alaska. Being locals, they knew to get up the river before it rose. I had strong doubts they could

Better to go under the wharf:
Slow current and dry

Battling up the outside.
Strong current, no end in sight.

Sometimes the inside
is completely blocked

The bank or the current?

I complain a lot about the barges. Many of my trials and tribulations were deleted during the editing process. "Boring," everyone cried. Yes they were. They were a boring, annoying problem that maybe I fixated on, but the fact is they were the bane of my life. When they are tied up along the bank there can be a run of them for up to three kilometres. Because they could be up to six barges wide, to go around them put me out into the current where I could not even get to 2km/hr forward speed. To go inside, between the bank and the barge, was much easier but was fraught with difficulty in that I could encounter all sorts of things that stopped my progress and I would have to retreat. Imagine paddling along for a kilometre only to have to turn around, go back and start again out in the current with no idea how far it would be. These pictures are an attempt to give you some idea of what it was like. For more images see www.kayak4earth.com

Go around, or under the wharf?

make it in canoes in the conditions that I was encountering, but bloody good luck to them for being smarter than me. The flood peak was still 10 days or so away and there was debris all over the river, with locals warning about the danger of logs.

With a bit of trepidation we set off early for my big 60-kilometre paddle day and I was out onto the river and into the mist just before 8.00am. I climbed out of the kayak to cross the smaller levee closer to the river, not as high as when I had finished two days before because the river was up some more. Back on board and looking at the main river, I remembered that my sunglasses and jacket were still in the car. Too bad, time was tight and I was on a mission. At least the crew had an extra map as well as the road we visited yesterday programmed into the GPS. I had especially drawn it to show the gravel road and the tracks.

First obstacle was a log jam on a wharf, so I had to battle the fierce eddies around a set of petroleum storage tanks that actually stood on the underwater river bank. Then I had to struggle back into the tree line: slipping backwards, inching forwards, but inexorably heading towards the bank.

At 9.00am, I received a call from Jeff Crouere at radio WGSO990, the bloke Connor had organized back in New Orleans, who we had previously confirmed for an 8.30am phone interview. "Better late than never," I thought. Luckily I was able to pull into the tops of some small trees and the interview was fine. The rest of the morning was pretty straightforward but slow. Flow came through the trees making serious log jams, so the number of rests and eddies had reduced dramatically compared to previous days. The river roared and gurgled to the right. To the left it gurgled through the trees, while logs and sticks did their twisting, swirling dances towards the kayak. It was challenging work and needed concentration.

After 27 kilometres there was a route to get to the levee through the trees. The underbrush was way below the water, so the levee was visible and I could hear the cars behind it. "Do I stop?" was the burning question. Given the problems we had previously encountered when changing pick-up points I decided that the only thing to do was push on to the point the crew knew of and had actually seen, and it was just near the GPS-marked road with a detailed map. Better to push on to where we had decided to meet.

At this stage I knew timing would be tricky because the going was slow, but that was the call I made. About 4.00pm I called the crew and suggested they leave in time to get to the pick-up point about 6.15pm. Sunset was an hour after that, plenty of time.

With darkness looming and me still about three kilometres short of the target point, Klaas called to say they were at the hide, but there was no sign of the river, so maybe they should shoot a flare for me to see. Remember, that was the first place we went to yesterday where we could not find the river.

"That is not where you are supposed to be," I advised. "Go back down the track to the gravel road, turn left and stop at the right-hand bend we finished up at yesterday. I will be coming in after dark, so it would be good if you have a torch to guide me to you."

Twenty minutes later Klaas called, "We are tired and angry and lost," he moaned.

Shit!

"Stay where you are and we will try to work it out later," I advised. "In the meantime I will try to get to the pick-up point and then find you."

This was worrying. I did not want to spend any significant time on the river after dark.

Sunset was gone and darkness was closing in, reducing visibility and turning the river into a malevolent dark torrent. I thought I had found a nice eddy to ride but within minutes I was half a kilometre down a river about 100 metres wide racing to who knows where. The flooded Mississippi was flowing over its normal banks and away, into the swampy landscape. I could have ended up kilometres from the map we were working with that day. The tree canopy almost touched overhead, forming a tunnel. It was isolated, dark and threatening. With trepidation, I wheeled the kayak around and headed back out of there with all my strength. At the main river I turned left to follow the bank again. A part of me had just wanted to go with the flow, but I knew the danger in that. This was probably a life or death decision.

Fifteen minutes later, with 59.7 kilometres on the GPS log, and the pick-up crew lost, I decided it was too dangerous to stay on the river and pulled in near a hide on the bank. I had to bash through three metres of floating logs and another five metres of brambles before I could call the crew. My intention was to walk along the track heading upstream from the hide, until I reached the gravel road. After a few hundred metres the track dipped into the dark floodwater racing away from the Mississippi to some unseen destiny. Retreating, I followed another path away from the river.

After about 10 minutes I thought I saw lights from a house but no, it was bright fireflies high in the trees. And then, a pair of eyes appeared on the track. My headlamp showed a strange animal indeed. It was a bit like a Tasmanian tiger/devil cross, about the size of a bull terrier, mangy colours; long, strong snout and a thick tail: horizontal, rigid and pointed at the tip. It stared at me but did not move. As it was in the centre of the track, I had to go close to get past; my only potential means of protection being a plastic water container. Rabies was on my mind as I crept past, but it just stood there and watched me. Another 10 minutes and the track dipped into the floodwaters. There was no way out. I called the crew and sent them home while I made my way back to the kayak that was firmly lodged in the brambles and then climbed up into the hide.

There was carpet on the floor of the hide so I used my life jacket as a pillow and was able to get my arms into the top of the paddling skirt like a straight jacket. In a tight foetal position I was able to spend some periods during the night without shivering violently. About midnight it poured with rain so I was very grateful to the blokes who built the hide. The temperature was about 8°C. Of course, a jacket would have been very welcome, but I had made that call to leave it behind at the start of the day.

Klaas' blog: *Remember the ATM that swallowed my Visa card? I arranged for a replacement card which came but can't be used on an ATM. Only for shopping, petrol, etc. I also arranged for a cash advance which only took three days, answering the same questions 27 times and voila, this morning they (The Visa people) told me I could pick it up from any Western Union office. Looked up the nearest one and off I went. Filled in several forms, was photographed, showed passport, questioned, and finger printed. With great reluctance they finally parted with the AU$1000 and gave me US$725. Bloody ripper, mate, we can buy some Budweiser with that.*

The Master in the mean-time is paddling his ... off doing something ridiculous like 78 kilometres or thereabouts and the pick up will be done in the dark with torches, something I don't look forward to. Too many hazards, alligators besides, the country is full of fire ants and it's impossible to see in the dark. Oh, how we suffer.

The crew called before daylight and then a number of times until they were in position. They were still very confused, so I had to do a lot of talking to guide them. Their first call was from the ferry point three kilometres upstream from the pre-arranged pick-up point, about six kilometres from where I was. When I was comfortable that they were where they should be, I set off to meet them. It was three kilometres in thick fog but, about halfway, they heard my shout. Klaas has a deep, booming voice so we were finally in direct communication. Eventually we extracted the kayak through the brambles, loaded up at the gravel road and headed off for a shower and bacon and eggs from Le Chef.

Klaas's blog: You have no doubt heard about the trials and tribulations of the Master yesterday. No one in his/her right mind would attempt 78 kilometres in one day paddling upstream. Stevie, the 'Wonder Boy', of course, is like the Lord, is omnipotent and thinks he can float over the currents. In the meantime, his ever faithful crew was instructed to retrieve him at around 6pm.

It was a 58-mile drive and we were finally in position and found no Master. At 7pm night closed in. It is dark and the place is isolated in the middle of 'No Where'. We had to leave the car up the track and were armed with torches and my flare gun. The place is boggy and we wait. Another hour goes by and he rings that he is in total mist and can't find us, so instructs us to go home and try at first light next morning.

I notice on starting the car that the petrol gauge is on red and we would not make it home. I Google up the nearest outlet and go some 20 miles the wrong way home to fill up and head for home. Two hours later I am totally stuffed, driving through fog, and we are home. We fall into bed and are back up at 4.30am, make some sandwiches, grab a bottle of orange juice and get on the road again.

We are there in position by daylight and the mist is impenetrable. We shout and cooee and finally he answers and we were united. The crazy bastard did the distance but was defeated by a total white-out to rendezvous.

From the swirling gloom, beyond the light, goading, taunting, looms Stevie boy, and Satan is his shadow.

Then the shit hit the fan.

I was writing an email to Warren, but went outside for a beer with Klaas. Anne decided to read what was on my laptop. In the email, I asked Warren how I was going to deal with the rest of the trip given I had a support crew that needed the same sort of care as children. She took offense and suggested she go home; at my expense, of course. Klaas was upset but very magnanimous. He suggested I was under a lot of stress and that we all cool down. I had written another email to friends and family back home, which I had copied Klaas in. This caused more angst. In that email, I explained the problem with Klaas' mind. He knew he did not have dementia but, whatever he had, he did not appear to be aware of it. The symptoms are hard to explain, but it was definitely a shutting down of some functions as a result of his grief.

It was my fault that I was in this situation. I had opted to make sure Klaas stayed with me for the trip, no matter what. I had flown Anne over to help him without ascertaining what she could do. I had given her detailed maps and instructions for a pick-up point without understanding that she could not read a map or remember where she had been the previous day.

Besides, no other options had presented themselves, despite many false starts. My only other option would have been to cancel the trip and that was never going to happen. I had said I was paddling to Paris. Maybe luck just wasn't on my side, but adventuring means you take the bad with the good. You suck it up and get on with it.

This was a very low point. Support from friends, apart from Warren, was pretty thin on the ground. The mighty Hood advised me to "Sort things out and get on with it," which was not very helpful.

"Get on with what?" I asked myself. "How can I possibly do this journey in the way that it was envisaged?"

An email each from daughters Amanda and Heidi were of great comfort, but I was in a bad way. My ex-wife, Carol, whom I had not really spoken to since the divorce, sent me this message:

"Sometimes the hardest thing and the right thing are the same. The kids are proud of you, and I'm sure Billy, Max, Joshua, Ayla and Lachlan will be when they grow up and understand what you have done."

The messages from the girls and Carol hit the spot. They broke through the gloom, the disappointment, the frustration. They knew me best, understood that I was on a mission, even though they were not there to help me. The problem was there was no-one to help me.

Renate down in New Orleans said, "My God, you really are alone."

That is exactly how I felt, despite the wonderful emails from family. Feeling utterly alone, I jumped in the car and headed off to see Renate. It was three hours' drive, but I needed it. I needed to talk to someone but, even more, I needed to think things through away from the pressure of the situation. I needed Renate's companionship.

We met outside the church hall where Gulf South Rising (GSR) was holding a meeting. We didn't talk too much about my troubles, but it was good to disengage from the immediacy of them and to embrace the issues of the meeting. The group's motto is 'The sea is rising and so are we'. GSR is a *coordinated regional movement* created to highlight the impact of the global climate crisis on the Gulf South region (Texas, Louisiana, Mississippi, Alabama and Florida). Through collaborative actions and events around strategic dates, like the five-year commemoration of the BP Oil Crisis and the 10-year commemoration of Hurricanes Katrina and Rita, GSR demands a just transition away from extractive industries, discriminatory policies, and unjust practices that hinder equitable disaster recovery and impede the development of sustainable communities.

It was a special meeting in that some of the commercial fishers had been invited and spoke about their hardship and the catastrophic results of the BP failure. It was chaired by a very formidable but lovely lady called Collette. The commitment to respect, even when opinions are divided, is a salutary lesson to anyone who has watched debate in any organization, let alone the unseemly confrontations in our parliaments. The stories from the fishers stirred up a lot of anger in me, but it was not my fight. It is just another example of the total failure of our political system, bought and paid for by anyone with enough money.

After a couple of hours, I was no longer feeling sorry for myself. Renate and I chatted about her coming along to help during the school holidays in a couple of months' time. We said goodbye and I headed back to Vidalia with a clear head, determined to find a solution. The immediate future, the section up to Vidalia, was not a problem. The journey was downstream of the camp site so, every morning, we could go past the pick-up point for the day. Anne had told me that if I had tied a piece of yellow rope around the tree at the pick-up point corner, she would have been fine. I could see the sense in that. They had driven countless times past the one that caused the major blow-up, but still had no idea where they were. I would fix it. I would tie the yellow rope around a tree with them watching and then continue downriver to where I would start paddling for the day. Oh no, 'Tie a yellow ribbon round the old oak tree'. If only there was an easy way to clear a song out of one's head.

Back to business. The space of a couple of hours between us seemed to have put the pick-up disaster to rest. We arrived back at the infamous corner and, on the short walk through the brambles to the river, the fog was doing its best to cover the landscape without quite succeeding. On the water, visibility was still about 100 metres, considerably better than expected. The current wasn't too bad as I threaded along through tree tops slowly unfurling their small bright-green messages that spring was arriving. Some nasty-looking branches had thorns about three centimetres long on them which necessitated a bit of caution. That sort of thing is not life threatening, but can be painful. Rafts of logs forced me into the main current occasionally, but there were no really strong sections to make forward progress doubtful.

Loaded gravel barges passed by. Plastic bottles tied to trees indicated locals reckoned on a feed of fish from their traps – unless it was their version of the yellow ribbon. Oh no. There's the song again. Lunchtime came and went. It was just another day, until the first branch of the Atchafalaya River. The Atchafalaya is only one river but there are three offtakes, like a reverse delta, that branch from the Mississippi and to the Gulf. These offtakes form a distributary so big, they take about a third of the Mississippi's flow. The dam and the huge gates could be seen as I approached this first offtake channel. In itself, the channel – one of three, remember – was big enough to be called a big river in my terms.

The current bounced off the corner where the offtake channel started. It rushed down the river too fast to paddle against. In the offtake channel it raced towards the big gates and certain death. First impressions were not that great but, like all first impressions, they turned out to not represent the total situation. As the great river hurtled towards the sea with its branch bleeding off some of its energy, giant whirlpools about 20 metres across formed. They didn't seem very friendly, but in a practical sense they could be useful. It looked like it might be possible to ride the edge of these whirlpools across the channel all the way to the other side. It wasn't the whirlpools per se that worried me. It was what I later came to call 'the mouths of the Mississippi'. These are the breaking waves near the edge of whirlpools where the water is going down, just like the plug hole

Lucky that's feet and not metres. Only 15.8 metres sounds better.

in a bath tub. The good thing was that I could see all the way across the offtake channel. If it didn't work and I was losing ground, I could head into the main river and come back to the start point again.

The idea was fine. In 10 minutes I was on the other bank drifting 10km/hr upstream in an eddy. A horn blared a warning to boats in the area and after about two kilometres there was a sign that said, 'WARNING DANGEROUS DRAW, Old River Control Structure, US ARMY CORPS OF ENGINEERS, New Orleans District'. There was no sign below the draw-off, so I guess they don't get many people heading up-stream. In fact, I didn't actually find anyone who had heard of someone paddling up the Mississippi in a flood.

The next channel, second of the three, was very tame. The amount of water being released through this one was not enough to cause any concern at all. Klaas and Anne were parked on the control structure and, as I paddled towards the upstream bank, they drove down a gravel access road that disappeared into the water. The kayak slipped up onto the grass but, when I stood up, I needed the paddle for support because my right leg had decided it wasn't going to work properly. It must have been a bit more of an effort crossing with the eddies than I thought.

The distance was only 27.5 kilometres for the day but I had learned my lesson, don't push too hard. That said, sometimes there is just no other option when there are such limited extraction points on the river.

We headed back to the van to meet Adam, a 'River Angel'. These guys live for paddling and are always there for paddlers. Adam lives on the east side of the river at Natchez. The town of just 15,000 people is perched on a bluff overlooking the Mississippi. The fact that it is a popular destination for heritage tourism indicates its historic charm. With so many beautiful buildings it is hard to believe the population is so small, until you realise that it has been in decline since steam trains took over from river traffic as the main form of transport. Tall, slim, easy going, Adam's dream is to make a living from his river ventures but in the foreseeable future he probably needs to stick to his day job. Like all the river people we met, his generosity was unbounded.

We shared many a story, had a look around Natchez where he worked and observed his pride and joy where he kept his river toys. There were many different canoes and paddles that he uses to take people on river trips. All good things come to an end, though, and it was time to prepare to do battle with the river again.

Arriving just after sunrise, the area where we parked the previous day was underwater because the river had risen another 30 centimetres. What we didn't realise is that fire ants' nests float and when they brush against your leg, the ants invade. On the kayak, having just secured the spray skirt on the cockpit, they attacked around my ankles. As that little problem was unfolding, Kyle from the US Army Corps of Engineers, who control the structures along the river, came to tell me that it was too dangerous to paddle there. He was concerned about me being sucked into the dam gates and wanted me to start downstream in the river near where I had seen the DANGEROUS DRAW sign. That wasn't smart, so I said I was going anyway. He then requested I stay inside the willow trees for a few hundred metres, which I did, but only to please him. After all, I had easily paddled in the area the day before.

He reckoned they let 200cfs (500ML/day) into the Atchafalaya system and that is about one third of the Mississippi flow. I did a quick calculation to work out he meant 200,000cfs (500,000ML/day). In 2007 when I paddled the Darling River in drought, I could keep going as long as I had about 100ML/ day. With these flows 5,000 times bigger, it was a very different ball game. The height difference dropping into the Atchafalaya system is significant, so they run a hydro power station at the offtake furthest upstream, which I was yet to cross. Kyle said to cross the river before I got there, because the draw into the hydro power station was severe. I noted to be careful and set off, knowing that crossing the river in 20-metre visibility would not be on.

Back to the fire ants. Having undone the spray skirt and rubbed my ankles enough to kill the ants, I pushed off into the backwater behind the willow trees. After two paddles an ant bit me on the left calf. Bugger. Off with the skirt and kill it. Back on went the skirt. Then it was my right calf. Same procedure. Then it was my left knee, then my right knee, then my thigh. Each time necessitated the tedious job of pulling the skirt off the cockpit surround and attacking the ant problem. When one bit my upper-middle thigh I started to become concerned. Above that were regions that I didn't dare even think about. Luckily that was the last bite and I began to relax.

Fire ants aside, the first three kilometres of paddling were fine. A fallen tree seemed to indicate something different in the river. Its base was towards me with fast-flowing current streaming around it. The only thing to do in this situation is to get 'a run up' from behind the tree and burst into the flow. Power on, swishing into the maelstrom, the kayak was thrust 20 metres off the bank. I sat stationary paddling with all my strength. Bit by bit we inched forward enough to creep back towards the bank. The current roared, the whirlpools had me doing a merry dance on the rudder pedals, but I beat it. After five minutes I had won. Victory was fleeting, though. I had reached the offtake and was now in a stronger current, being swept into the hydro station river. There was no other option but to get to the bank, fast.

Visibility was now only about 10 metres and I had to turn round. What to do? The only sensible thing was to keep the nose on the bank, easing the back into the flow and allow the kayak to spin around facing back against the current. Then I stopped to regroup.

Luckily, it was just possible to paddle against the flow with one blade hitting the rocky bank and the other just inside the racing current. In a few minutes, in which I made about 20 metres' progress, I was back around the corner into the main river next to the fallen tree. I stopped paddling and watched the GPS. The flow that I had paddled against was 10km/hr. That is about the limit of a heavy, plastic sea kayak. The flow into the hydro power station river was significantly greater than that. Dodged another bullet there.

With my tail between my legs and a little dejected, I headed back to where I had started.

Klaas' blog: What a horrible day so far. Up at 5am, the usual routine; teeth, pills, ablutions, coffee, make Steve's lunch. Away by 6.30 and drive 36 miles, unload kayak, forced to walk through floodwaters and get soaking wet. Step on fire ants nest – the floodwaters have driven them out of their nests and they are all over the roadway and climb on board. Over feet, into socks, up legs and certain private parts you only tell your mother about. Drive back 36 miles, arrive outside caravan and phone rings, Steve has aborted due to total white out and very dangerous conditions. Drive back 36 miles. Pick up Steve and kayak, drive back 36 miles, clean shoes of mud, put in oven to dry. How was your day?

Of course, I could have waited a day or two until the fog cleared enough to get across but, once I am going, I stubbornly go at full speed. It is a drive that consumes me. I put the wheels back on and walked up the road to Vidalia. Anne knew the silos just outside town, so I said that I would call when I got there so they could get ready to take a triumphant photo as I dragged the kayak into camp at the RV park.

Just before 3.00pm I called in to say that I was near the silos. Five minutes later Klaas and Anne turned up in the car.

"What are you doing? Why have you come here?"

"To pick you up."

"But I don't need to be picked up. I'm nearly there. I just need you to take some photos of me arriving in camp. Maybe one could be of Klaas giving me a beer." Hint, hint.

Confusion seemed to reign. They were unsure what to do, so I explained again.

In the end, they seemed to understand and headed off to set up near the sign at the entrance to the RV park. Anne took photos as I passed and I suggested they get down to the caravan and snap one with me coming up to the van and Klaas handing me a beer.

Once more into the car, they set off to the van to await my arrival.

Again confusion reigned.

I wanted a photo in the RV park with the van in the background, not some nondescript photo that could have been taken anywhere. They had no idea what I was talking about.

I was starting to accept that I could not rely on the support crew to support me with the most basic of tasks. Three years later, I finally understand. When I assumed the support had heard what I said, I was wrong. Instead, they had a low level of awareness. This is the same with climate change communication; much of what is said or written just does not sink in. This happens for many reasons.

As luck would have it, a guy from the local paper arrived and we were able to get a shot of Klaas handing me a beer near the van with the bloke taking a photo. I told my story to the reporter and drank my beer thinking, "All's well that ends well."

The truth was, I had formulated a new plan over a few emails with Warren. I was only a bit over 500 kilometres from the Gulf of Mexico but it had been a taxing trip so far. The next leg would be back on the river with a loaded kayak so I could support myself on the river without worrying about the support crew. That way, all I had to do was to paddle myself between major towns and then hitchhike back to pick up the crew, a bit like the leapfrog plan in Australia, only on a grand scale. I would be on my own for about five days at a time, and even less further up the river where there were more towns. Blogs would be reduced, of course, but we could live with that. In effect, I was supporting the support crew. I was hauling myself up the Mississippi as well as guiding two seniors in a caravan along a land route as close to my kayak journey as possible. It would be hard work, but it would give me a rest every few days or so, and a chance to blog and record the journey.

Unfortunately, with this method, there was no way I could make it to Hudson Bay, my original destination in North America, through the wilds of Canada. Warren would formulate a new route and a new plan while I continued the push up-river. I was frustrated but resigned. Even if I had to support the support crew, somehow I would do it. We were going up this bloody river! The only person to blame for my predicament was me, so I had to get us through it. Apart from the stress of the pick ups, Klaas and Anne were having a ball, so at least I didn't have to worry about that. I did suggest to Anne that she try to tame Klaas' enthusiasm with the cheap whiskey. Without the obligation of looking after the paddler, lunch time drinks were likely to begin at morning tea time.

Klaas' blog: *Today was a lot better than yesterday. Steve decided to walk rather than kayak the distance and so we had no trouble locating him, as there is no other road. I decided to start making my own bread as all the loaves here are loaded with sugar. [We met a guy called] Adam, a wonderful bloke and a tremendous help to Steve, as he is a kayaker and knows the river back to front. Not only did he buy my book, today he came and presented me with a beautiful Delft Blue Jar filled with Bols Genever. The elixir of life to a Dutchman. Great gift, mate, and very much appreciated. Went swimming today and had a hot spa. Wonderful.*

CHAPTER 8

ALONE ON THE RIVER

Warren, perhaps because of his engineering background, is very methodical and analytical. Via email and phone calls we tried to figure out an alternative route, something possible I could tackle but still embracing the Connecting Climate Chaos theme. In our original plans, we had figured on a side journey across to New York. That now became the journey. Rather than continue northwards on the Mississippi River and head to Chicago, I would head east, probably along the Missouri River, add a little bit of overland walking and slide down into New York. Warren was investigating likely routes, cognizant of the fact that I wanted to keep walking over mountains to a minimum.

The change in route was a big deal, a very big deal to me. Since 2007 I had wanted to journey between the Gulf of Mexico and the waters north of Canada. That was just a personal goal. This trip was not about personal goals, it was about the bigger picture, the threat global warming poses to the existence of humanity. At a personal level it was about my grandchildren. Maybe one day I could do an adventure just for me, just

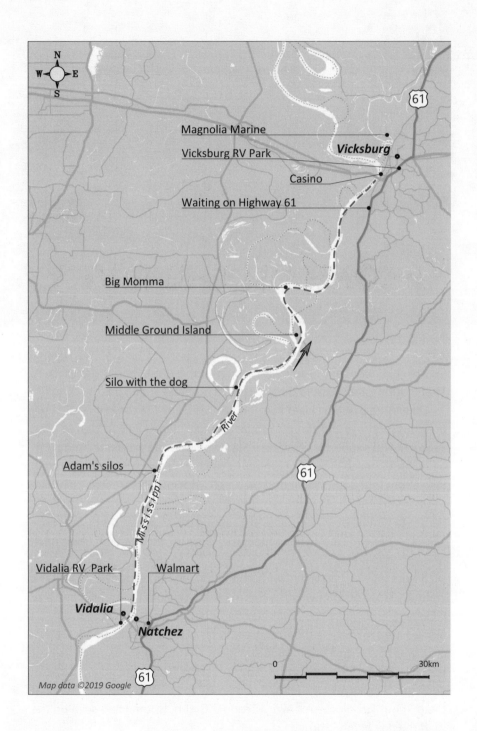

Trooper powered entry (with hat on)

for the enjoyment of the adventure, but not this time. I had to get to Paris. That is what I said I would do and so that is what I would do.

On a more practical level, I would be sacrificing the pattern of all of my previous journeys and this one so far, the daily blog I had written to keep in touch with supporters. The new plan would have me off line for days at a time. Natchez to Vicksburg is about 130 kilometres by river. That should take about four days. We loaded the kayak with enough provisions for five days. It was heavy. At well over 100 kilograms it would be significantly harder to handle in whirlpools and paddling up strong currents, but there was no other choice. I would paddle to Vicksburg and then hitchhike back to Natchez to collect the crew.

Before leaving I arranged with Anne that I would hitchhike back to the Walmart store on Highway 61, the main highway between Natchez and Vicksburg and where she and Klaas had often journeyed by themselves. I also advised in my blog that there would be nothing posted for a few days.

It was cool with a bright blue sky, clear air and sunshine doing its best to warm the sodden landscape. Chef cooked a hearty breakfast of bacon and eggs. The kayak was loaded and ready to go. We walked to the boat ramp about 1.5 kilometres away. Trooper Green, whom I had seen on the road the day before, turned up.

"Did you have those beers for me?" he asked.

"One for you," I replied, "the rest were for me. Thought one was enough for ya."

Seems like the humor translated, because we had a merry chat before he grabbed his hat out of the patrol car ready to push me into the water.

"Need to do the job proper," he reckoned.

Into the kayak, and I was propelled by a trooper-powered slide down the ramp into the water, where I grabbed a wheel and pulled it up. Klunk. Both rear wheels sat behind me in the raised position.

Klaas' blog: *We launched Steve on his way to Vicksburg in style. Trooper Green drove his squad car down to the ramp and wanted to know all about it. Steve had forgotten something back at the caravan, so the Louisiana state trooper drove him there and back and helped launch Steve with a mighty shove. The kayak felt unstable with all the extra weight of food and water for three or four days, so Steve came back and we removed the front wheel and off he went. Anne picked up the front wheel and its solid aluminium frame, but Trooper Green would have none of that and put her and the wheel in the squad car and drove her to the trailer park. What a nice man. He wistfully said he wanted to arrest me for being "Past my use by date" but could not be bothered as the paperwork would be too much. Master Steve in the meantime is still paddling towards Vicksburg, overnighting wherever he can find a spot.*

Passing under the bridge I could see the last of the Vidalia buildings on the left and the town of Natchez over on the right bank. The current was not too bad, a few people were out walking and the kayak was slipping through the water okay, if slightly slower because of the weight. All in all a pretty good start to what was likely to be a four-day trip.

Just before 3.00pm a movement in the water caught my eye. It was heading towards the bank quite quickly. Powering up the kayak for a couple of hundred metres I got close enough to see that it was a deer. They are powerful swimmers and it outpaced me in the kayak. I had to be quick to get a photo of it before slipping too far behind. It found the bank, climbed out over logs and bounded off up the river bank in search of its mates. I pulled into the bank on some grass near a set of silos that Adam, the River Angel, had highlighted.

Within an hour I had everything ship shape with the tent up and a fire going. The wind was from the south east and quite gentle. Making the fire was a challenge until I realised that, unlike back in Australia, I needed dry grass and not leaves to start the small twigs. A beer was in one hand, a bag of crisps in the other and I was about to cook dinner. Not much more a bloke could ask for really.

Whoosh! The wind came howling across the river from the north east and blew the billyo out of the fire. The smoke took off across the ground, not rising much more than a metre all the way to the backwater on the other side of my little paddock.

In my kit was a small stove with a wick coming out of it. I lit it in the lee of an old cupboard that had floated down the river. Fair dinkum, if I had two candles it would have been better. The stove was cheap and might boil water for a cup of coffee in about an hour or so. That's what you get for cheap, I suppose. The fire was still burning, even if horizontally, so I took the top off a can of stew and shoved it into the logs.

Before dark I crawled into my sleeping bag, read my book for a bit, and fell asleep. The river was close but there was a mound about 100 metres away that I could retreat to if necessary, albeit that there were lots of fire ants about, and they like the high ground. Waking about every hour I kept a watch on the situation but all was well. Note to self: bring long johns camping next time. Brrrr.

Again it was a crisp morning, but clear and bright. As the sun rose over the Mississippi, its warmth penetrated my body and started to dry the dew from the tent before I packed it away in the kayak. Stripping off my jacket, I rolled the kayak into the water for another slog up beside the tree tops.

The current was unforgiving and constantly dragging me towards the trees and thousands of logs jammed up against them. A piece of high ground appeared. It stood out of the water by about half a metre, but it was back about 20 metres inside the tree line. Picking my way inside the trees a huge log barred my way, creating a flow that might have been possible to paddle against, but probably not. With dry ground available, I took the option of walking around the log. Stepping out of the kayak I was careful not to disturb a cluster of fire ants floating on their nest. Wheels down and dragging the kayak along the grassy shore to the other side of the log, the fire ants had their fun with my left ankle. Must have missed seeing that lot. I reckon the blighters come back from the dead and have another go. Despite washing all of them off it took an hour before the last one was finally gone.

The next section of water was very fast, so I paddled furiously then took a selfie video after I had made it through. Because of my earlier GoPro® failures and complications, I was using a simple, tough, waterproof camera that I had bought for $150 and wore around my neck. The section wasn't the hardest or most dangerous that I had been through, but the footage reveals how much effort it takes. No wonder a few minutes' recovery is necessary before moving on, after something like that.

The reward at the end was worth it, though. My first raccoon was going about its business on a log jam near the bank, watching with passing interest this funny yellow thing coming by. Its eyes reminded me of the strange animal I had seen that desolate night when Klaas and Anne got lost, which seemed so long ago. That animal was bigger than a raccoon and, to this day, I have no idea what it might have been.

More land came into view and an eddy allowed the kayak to be towed up the river again without much more than guidance from me. This came to an end with the usual rush of water but, popping out into the flow, I easily made it past the point to find another set of silos around the corner. Adam had not told me about them, but they had to mean dry ground. The land around the silos gradually formed into a clear picture. A gravel parking area and maybe the top of a boat ramp just before the silos offered a clean exit from the river, but I paddled past and onto a concrete apron near the silos. "No fire ants on the concrete here," I thought as I stepped onto dry ground.

The lawn had just been mowed and there was some sort of elevated office about 100 metres away. A dog spotted me and started barking. Guard dog maybe? A bit small, I thought and, by the way it was carrying on, I reckoned its position would be low down in the pack, just the one to sound the alarm and let the others fix it. Within a couple of minutes we were mates and set off together to explore.

The wind was from the west and quite strong so the area behind the silos, right beside the river with the fire set up where the silos joined together, was ideal for camping. Being the weekend there was no-one there and I figured any security would not come around that side anyway. With my new friend the camp was set up, wood found, fire lit, beer in hand and crisps opened. My new mate didn't drink beer but she liked the crisps.

I hadn't seen my mate for a few minutes after the crisps were finished and wondered where she could be. Uh oh, there she was on the other side of the kayak. She had put her head inside the hatch and taken out the plastic container which included my muesli that Anne had made. With a gaping hole now in the side of the plastic container, more than half of the muesli was on the ground. I'm not too proud to share with a dog, so I grabbed what was left and put the container in the hatch with the cover securely fastened. A repeat of that would not have been good, so I locked everything away and just brought out the essentials for dinner.

The fire was very welcome as the sun went down behind the silos and a chilling north wind blew. My mate insisted that she sleep in the tent with me, but I was even more insistent that she didn't. She slept all night beside the kayak. I was cold in my sleeping bag so I guess she was too, but she had survived colder nights without me.

While I had breakfast, my mate took advantage of my carelessness and sneaked inside the tent. She was curled up and sound asleep just inside the door when I found her 20 minutes later. Unfortunately I had to pack up and get going, but I left moving her until the last minute. Paddling away I immediately encountered a difficult section. It took almost all of my concentration, but I could see my mate watching from as close as she could get, probably sad that food, shelter and company were on their way again.

Late morning brought a large island into view, a major landmark, instrumental in my plan to cross the mighty Mississippi. Adam reckoned Middle Ground Island had high ground on the far side but mid-day was too early to stop. The plan was to use the island as a crossover point. Vicksburg is on the east side, so it had to be done some time. The trick was to paddle far enough up the left bank of the river before launching into the flow to paddle across and make it to the downstream tip of the island. Too early and I would be swept too far downstream, miss the island all together and have to start the process again. Too late and valuable energy would be wasted flogging upstream.

The moment came.

"Let's do this," I thought. It was only about 400 metres away. Lining up trees on the island, I could tell that I was crabbing across nicely, almost holding my position. Whoops, lack of concentration and 100 metres was lost. About two thirds of the way across I was going hard, losing ground, and hoping that when I got behind the tops of the trees at the bottom of the island the flow would drop enough for me to catch up. The current

Like the one I spent the night in except water is 4m deep under this one

Cockpit map

started to slow a bit, I held my ground and made it, with over 100 metres to spare.

Starting for the other side of the island there was no current. None at all. That didn't last, of course. Pretty soon it was just the general slog beside the tree tops. The other bank of the Mississippi was a long way off but I could see a house on a hill. That had to mean there was land somewhere over there. I was next to the island's high ground Adam had referred to and, when I thought I could reach the other side of the river just downstream of the house, I set off.

Slipping, slipping I crabbed across the wide expanse. A white strip of sand appeared up ahead on the island. Now that would have been a nice place to stop. No time for those thoughts, so battling on, I made it about two thirds of the way towards the other side of the river when things changed. The great mouths of the Mississippi were appearing. This is the name I have given to the whitewater standing-wave that is about three metres wide and 10 centimetres high that comes out from the centre of the whirlpool. You don't want to be in the centre of these big ones. Crash, splash, I slipped through the outside edge of one. A merry dance on the rudder pedals followed as I tried to miss the next one. Crash, splash, again and then a rapid pirouette, followed by a right turn towards the bank, and I was in big upflows. Water welled up in whorls about 30 metres across. Using the edge of these, I could easily gain on the river and I made my way into the trees just upstream of the house. I had crossed the Mississippi in a flood unscathed. A doddle really, compared to what came next.

The next few kilometres were a battle against a great rush of water heading through the trees, presumably into some sort of wetland area. Back on the western side of the river was where Adam had marked a section as tricky. He said he had come through that bit with river levels up near this height and clocked 11.1mph (18km/hr), so it goes without saying that I was not keen to go there.

The wind started to build from the west and things got wet. By things, I really mean me. Waves hit the wheel supports and splashed up to my armpits, which is where the top of the spray skirt sits. The current was not too bad and I made good time, especially when some land appeared about 10 metres in from the tree line, on my right side. I even got an eddy, but conditions stayed wet and messy and then turned nasty.

The mouths of the Mississippi were smaller here, just licking their foaming lips, but they were there alright and not at all friendly. A big log jam jutted out into the river. White water rushed past. Not wanting to think about it, I paddled hard towards the edge of the log. Crashing into the white water, I was thrust 20 metres into the river in one second. Two seconds and it was 30 metres as the rudder responded. Paddling desperately, I had held my ground, but only just. I edged back towards the log jam, just holding on. About three metres out from the logs was a standing wave that gave me enough relief from the current to inch forwards. Go, go, go! With every ounce of strength I had, the kayak inched forward. The top of a small tree was 30 metres ahead and just inside the line of logs.

Got to make that…

Got to make that …

Got to make that …

My words echoed around my head. The carbon wing blade flexed in the water as I thrust like a man possessed. Past the point of no return, I was above the log jam. A broken blade, maybe even a missed stroke and that could be my last. The river was rough, it was ugly and I was bouncing like a cork.

This was committed. No way back.

A tree just under the water started to break the flow ahead; I was winning. Thirty seconds later it was all over, I was through.

Tricky was not the word I would have used, Adam. It was a bastard! Never, ever again did I want to flex a carbon fibre wing paddle.

There is something about the limit of physical exertion that impacts on the mind. Half an hour later I was recalling an email from my daughter Heidi. She had reckoned there was still time to do my Canada paddle in a few years. After all, I would live forever. I guess children are inclined to think like that. This dredged up the reasons for the trip and thoughts of my kids and their kids, and I was a blubbering mess until I straightened myself out.

Heidi had nailed it. She had forced me to face how far I was from my personal goal of crossing Canada. In the absence of any interest by anyone in my climate mission, and with a support crew that couldn't provide real support, I was really up the creek with a very small paddle and I had just pushed that to its limit. Of course, there were plenty of physical issues to deal with as well. Really hard and prolonged paddling makes a mess of your hands, no matter what gloves and tape you use. The big worry, though, was my shoulder, still dislocated from the bike accident in 2006 in the central Australian desert. It was screaming at me to back off a bit.

I had crossed the river, but was still navigating tree tops submerged in the swirling flood. It took another two hours before land appeared again. Although the map indicated a boat ramp up ahead, I pulled in to the first land I saw at 4.15pm. With nothing really to gauge against, I didn't realise how fatigued I was. Setting up camp, lighting the fire, washing and drying clothes, and a quick wash in the cold, brown Mississippi settled me down nicely.

That night was warm. The air was still warm in the morning when I headed upstream on the eastern side of the river. By 2.30pm, with the GPS registering 131.9 kilometres from Vidalia, I pulled in to Vicksburg and stowed the kayak behind a wall next to the casino. This was just off the property of the casino whose security guards had insisted I could not stay on their land.

I then walked a road towards Highway 61 that runs down to Natchez without the single offer of a lift. I had the green and yellow kangaroo flag out for all to see. Some people tooted and waved, even a truck driver; fat lot of good that was when I wanted a ride. Perhaps Highway 61 would be different, but after an hour on Highway 61 it didn't seem so. People just didn't seem to hitch there anymore. In desperation I called Anne.

"Hi Anne, Steve here. I got here but this hitchhiking is not going to work. Seems like they just won't pick people up."

"What are you going to do?"

"Well, you are going to have to pick me up."

"How do we do that?"

"Walmart is on the 61. I am now on the 61, so all you have to do is drive to Walmart, and then about an hour up the 61 you will see me on the side of the road."

"Okay."

I waited about 40 minutes, figuring they would need time to get ready, plus it was 10 minutes or so to Natchez's Walmart from their camp. If I knew what time they left I could figure out how long they might be.

"G'day Anne, how are you doing?"

"We're fine, but you aren't here."

"Where?"

"Walmart."

"No, I am about an hour up the road from there, where I tried to hitch from."

"Oh, okay."

"Just go across the road and head north for about an hour and you will see me."

"Okay."

I then waited 15 minutes and called again.

"Steve here, how's it going Anne?"

"No good, we can't find a Walmart in Vicksburg." They were studying the GPS in the carpark at the Walmart in Natchez.

"You don't need to find a Walmart in Vicksburg, just go across the road, turn left and drive for an hour until you see me."

"Okay."

Another 15 minutes went past before I called again.

"How's it going, Anne?"

"No good. We have tried over and over and there is no Walmart in this GPS thing."

"Anne, turn the GPS off. Do not look at it. You see the big road in front of you?"

"Yes."

"Go out of the carpark, across the road and turn left. Drive for about an hour until you see me. Do you understand?"

"Yes."

"Bloody hell," I thought. "What the fuck am I going to do now?"

To avoid thinking about the situation anymore, I just sat down on the grass and read my book.

Yet another 15 minutes later I called again. This time the response was angry. "We are on our way now."

I have since learned that just because you say something doesn't mean that what is received is what you said. Studying this in detail with friends, I finally understood how strongly Walmart in Natchez was implanted in Anne's mind and how my communication actually confirmed that. If she missed the detail about going an hour up the highway, I had just confirmed the earlier instructions about going to Walmart. Details like that can easily get lost in many minds. I really had not put myself in their position and worked out how to communicate in terms that they would understand.

The similarities in talking to people who don't want to hear the message about climate change was becoming clearer to me. We all know that to say the same thing over and over again, only a bit louder and more forcefully, will not work. That doesn't mean that because we understand, we will stop doing it. Human nature is, after all, human nature.

The day began to fade. I was worried but I was powerless. About an hour later, I spotted the Ford with its huge kayak box on the roof. It was a couple of kilometres away and going fast in the centre lane. Darkness loomed, but there was still a good amount of light. Standing beside the road I waved my arms above my head. They hurtled along, still in the fast lane with two cars in the lane next to me. About 200 metres away, they slowed.

"Phew, they saw me," I thought gratefully. At last, things were falling into place.

"Uh oh, Klaas is about to pull right, into the car beside him."

He figured it out in time and pulled left, onto the grassy median in the middle of the highway. What a relief. I was about to cross the road to climb into the car, when the Ford started again. Klaas had spotted a service station about 100 metres ahead. He pulled out onto the road. There was a car coming up in the slow lane. Surely he had seen it. Nope. As he crossed into the slow lane, the car headed into the service station. It was going slightly faster than Klaas and seemed to think it was out of danger, so it veered left, back onto the highway. Bang! The front of our Ford and the back left corner of the car collided. The other car continued, albeit with a few wobbles, Klaas entered the service station driveway and drove back down the grass beside the highway to where I was. He was in shock. I was flabbergasted. I jumped in the driver's seat and we drove home with muted conversation, arriving at 8.45pm.

A few days before, I had sent an email to Heidi to read to her kids:

Dear Max Batista and Ayla Batista,

I miss you a lot.

Lots of love, from Pa

An email was waiting for me:

Dear Pa,

Thank you. I can't believe you said what I said. I wish you could come back.

Love Max

Apparently Max had been thinking about me when I had sent my email. And then there was this one from Amanda.

You're probably feeling pretty alone at the moment and wondering what your next move will be. But, you've been here before, you know that you just have to keep moving. From what I can gather, Klaas is a big boy and can handle a lot (Anne, probably not so much). Don't sacrifice your mental health for keeping the peace. Whatever happens, you'll figure it out, there's always a way. Probably not the way you would like it to be but, nevertheless you will get to Paris one way or another. Perseverance is your mantra. Apply it not just on the river or road but in everything.

We love you.

Amanda, Matt, Billy, Josh and Lachy

CHAPTER 9

HITCHING A RIDE

The RV Park at Vidalia had been like a holiday camp and we were not sure what future parks might be like, but this Vicksburg one was just as good, and reasonably priced. Buses regularly shuttled people to and from the casino just down the hill. The kayak was now safely back in the roof box on the Ford, which was a great relief. I was resting and frantically sending emails. Publicity for the trip had been declining to just above zero. The number of Climate Reality Leaders I had met through Al Gore's group was zero. The interest that I had from meeting environmental groups was zero. Nothing was as I had anticipated.

I'm not sure I was entirely well, mentally, at this stage. It wasn't just that I was physically tired. Almost every expectation about the trip had been dashed. It had been going on long enough that most friends back home had drifted back into their lives and would await my return. I wanted to fight, but fight what? The river? I was doing that and it didn't seem like I was winning. I wanted to fight the apathy. I wanted the world to wake up to itself. I wanted to talk to someone, but there was no-one except Renate, a day's drive south, and I had only met her a couple of times.

In that state of mind, I emailed Lea. To be fair, despite our emails I don't think she had any idea of what I was going through. She reckoned I should be grateful to Klaas and Anne who had given up their lives to support my dream. Given up their lives? I was supporting them on a trip around the world.

I was never going back to that relationship. Lea and I were too different. This trip would change me forever. We could be friends if she wanted, but any hope of future romance was dashed.

I knew the whole venture was in danger of failing and just hoped it was at its lowest point. I knew that somehow I would figure out something, but at this stage I didn't know what. If I couldn't move ahead and hitchhike back for the crew on the next leg, perhaps it would have to be by public transport. It all seemed insurmountable and I needed a respite from worrying, so I concentrated on local engineering for a day, trusting that something would turn up. Even half an idea would be good.

Klaas' blog: *I'm taking a PhD in parking big rigs, and I mean BIG RIGS. In our present park there are 67 spaces and we have a lot of fun every afternoon watching new ones come in. Without exception they drive their 50-foot monolith units, often towing a small 4WD car, up onto their allotted concrete slab and stop. The passenger door opens and the wife gets out and walks to the back and starts gesticulating with arms and hands. They all have different ways to tell their beloved ones, who are driving, how to back or drive to the left or right and invariably the communication is not understood by hubby, who then puts on the parking brake and gets out, with great difficulty for a number of octogenarians, and the arguments start, sometimes heatedly with language like, "I told you a thousand times, you stupid cow." Some drivers are so pedantic about parking they insist it has to be parked right down to millimetres. Then the ritual of 'hooking up'. First of all the electricity, then the water supply, then the sewer outlet, then the levelling, then unhooking the tow, then the making up (not always, and I expect a number finish up in the divorce court.), and then, operating the slide-outs, finally 'drinky poohs', but always inside their rigs with the blinds down (what would the neighbours think). Every site has a table with bench seats, but less than 5% use them. They lock themselves in their mobile castles and hide, coming*

Brian Anderson – US Army Corps of Engineers (Vicksburg)

*out briefly to let their poodle wee. Next day the whole process starts
in reverse order.*

The river is unlike anything I had ever seen. It is contained within
levees but there are large wilderness areas within those levees. The Corps
of Engineers has to keep the river functional for the huge volume of traffic,
and they now need to provide sediment to the delta area below New
Orleans to stop it disappearing below the waters of the Gulf.

All Australian engineers know and respect the US Army Corps of
Engineers, but it was interesting to actually visit and learn a little about
the organization. Unlike Australian organizations, they seem to think
that people qualified in the field are best to run the organization. As a
result, you will find an engineer, hydrologist or someone used to doing
calculations actually on the river in the top job. You will also find decisions
being made by engineers. The building work is like stepping back in time,
but to a good era, before the nonsense started about engineers not being
managers. Books and maps abound. Technical discussions with managers
are easy.

Brian Anderson, a very senior manager, took me through some of what the organization was doing. His office had a huge map on the wall and his bookshelves were full. He was excellent technically and agreed wholeheartedly with my observations about rivers in general and the Mississippi. Maybe it speaks of a bygone era, but I was very comfortable there and certain that good engineering was practised without any of the smartarsery that we see in many of our Australian institutions.

At the time, a huge hydrological study was underway to determine whether the parameters used by the Corps are still valid and what the effects of climate change might be. My belief is that the engineering has reached a zenith. Massive structures, massive control and engineering might have all been well and good, and allowed the river to function as required, but the approach seems to be softening. Environmental concerns are now being addressed with care.

The United States, just like Australia, is turning its rivers into drains to speed everything up. Farmers on the Upper Mississippi tributaries are even tiling parts of their fields to drain water more quickly. As a result, the river has a lot more water flowing down it during floods than 200 years ago. We saw in Toowoomba and Grantham (in Queensland, Australia) in 2011 what these drastically more intense flows (known to engineers as reduced time of concentration) can do in an abnormal event. The 'inland tsunami' claimed lives and caused untold damage, but nobody blamed the real culprit: modifying the landscape, streamlining creeks, channelling flows. The hydraulic equations are well known: speed up the flow and you increase the volume and power of the water; every event becomes shorter and more powerful. Interestingly, 2011 also was the biggest flood they had on the Mississippi – a bad year in Queensland and a bad year in North America.

With the river contained within levees, the term 'flood' is not normally used. That is reserved for when levels are extreme and the river breaches some low levees. When I paddled into Vicksburg, the river was up 43 feet, about 13 metres, and that is just at the start of flood level. Society has learned to live with river levels moving up and down more than 10 metres. Fishermen can be seen prowling the treetops in their tinnies on the weekends. Low, medium and high-water levels are talked about with the river being vastly different at all stages.

There are many groins, or dykes as they are called there, on the banks that direct flow into the centre of the river to keep it scouring. The effect of these at high flows can be quite alarming to a kayaker trying to battle up-river, even though they are submerged under many metres of water. I discovered that I had been right over a 'big momma' of a groin when I did the paddle-flexing exercise near that island.

What to do? If it were just me to think about, the river was still there and needed paddling. This wasn't about me, though. I could not support the support crew and paddle the river. Besides, the trip was about more than an adventure. It was about my grandchildren and it wouldn't do much good to die.

From my diary at the time:

> It is Easter Sunday and we are in limbo. Tomorrow I can try to get on a barge to Memphis. The river beckons. Although Klaas looked at it from the top of the hill and counselled against getting back on it, I have no issue with the stretch that I can see. It is the really bad bits out in the wilderness that are the worry. The lack of land is also a concern and I won't try spending the night in a hammock in the trees as one group did coming down the river a few years ago. If I can't get a barge I will walk the next 350 kilometres up the highway. After all, the goal is to get to Paris.
>
> Interesting the effects grandchildren have on me. When each of them was born I felt as protective as I did when my children were born. This feeling consolidated my actions around climate change, especially as it was on top of my vow to make a difference every day after I didn't die in Central Australia in 2006. Their faces now stare at me when I think of the river. What that means, I have no idea, but it is useful to remind me that getting to Paris is the goal and winning against a river is not important. It is just a river.

Monday morning 7.30am found me at Magnolia Marine. After a brief wait, senior VP Roger Harris came out to talk about my predicament. He was not confident his company could give me a lift on a tug because they transport fuel, which has higher safety restrictions, but he reckoned that he would find something via the supply store in town. Before lunch, true to his word, Roger rang me saying, "Be at the store at 4.00pm. We should have one of our boats coming through about 5.30pm." He told me what my restrictions would be, which were fine. Yee haa! I had a ride on the *Emily Davis* to Memphis.

At 3.30pm, after packing my bag and making sure the site was ship shape, it was time to go. Klaas seemed to be in one of his more muddled stages. Maybe it related to how much he was thinking about his son's death, I don't know.

We arrived at the ship store where I settled down for a long but interesting wait. The radio and screen, sort of like an air traffic control room, was manned by people that the river boat companies paid for. There doesn't seem to be an organization controlling how it works, just goodwill between the companies. I wasn't sure who did what, but there were no crew changes to be made, just me, so everyone there had a task once the tug arrived.

The *Emily Davis* is a 3000hp twin-screw pusher tug built in 2013. These boats typically haul around 21,000 barrels of petroleum and run all over the inland waterway system. That is the equivalent of 76 of the biggest road tankers on our highways. (Tugs have big square fronts and push things, hence they are called pusher tugs. The barges that are being pushed, together with the pusher tug, are called a tow.) The *Emily Davis* is captained by Beau Cummins, but more about him later. A crew boat runs out to the tugs with personnel and a few pallets of supplies. To load the crew boat, a ramp leads from the land to a barge, which is exactly the same height above the water as the crew boat deck, allowing easy forklift access. The forklift drops the pallets onto the boat then backs up and pushes them further in with its tynes. My job was just to get into the truck driving onto the barge and then after that to hop onto the crew boat.

The *Emily Davis* had pulled into a tributary with lower flow so that it could drop off a fully fuelled barge. Coming alongside, our crew boat was firmly tied to the tug and four of us offloaded the pallets of food, paint, electrical and mechanical spares.

"You've got the cook's room," I was told, so I deposited my bag there and headed out to watch the machinations of giving another tug our full barge and re-securing the remaining two empties. Fuel barges are bigger than other barges, about twice as big at 90 metres long and 6.5 metres wide. When I enquired with Rob, the engineer, I guessed a water depth of about 10 feet, but he told me with, I forget with what liquid exactly, that it was 9.5 feet. Sorry. There are, of course, two types of people in the world, engineers and others. For all our faults, and the jokes about our thinking that is simply logical, we do have a practical way of understanding the world. Well, that's the way we look at it, even though we have to accept there might be other views.

The bridge on the Emily Davis

180m of barges in front of the Emily Davis

My accommodation was a whole lot better than expected. The cook's room was small but not pokey, and it had its own toilet and shower. On the same level is the mess which seats nine; the galley which is like a large kitchen, but with a bit more storage area and very large fridges and freezers; and the engineer's room opposite the cook's room. One level up is accommodation for crew, captain and pilot. Two levels up is the crew lounge with comfortable seats and a TV. Right at the top is the bridge, with all the latest in electronics, commanding an uninterrupted view of the barges, the river and its banks.

I spent many hours on the bridge absolutely fascinated by the skill of the captain and pilot. The captain, Beau Cummins, is a big man with a ponytail to the bottom of his back. Turning 60, he had spent his life on the water and he loves his work. We watched sunrises and sunsets together, shared yarns, talked BS, and agreed on what is wrong with the world. From another country, maybe very different to each other, but with the common thread of loving the water, we both enjoyed our hours together.

The captain is the boss. Under him is the pilot, Larry, aged 53 and also with huge experience. Then there is the relief mate, Matt. After a day Matt left to go and witness the birth of his first child. Rob, as I said, is the engineer. Billy, the tankerer, came on when Matt left. Shay and Jason are deckhands. That's the crew, but for two thirds of the time there is also a cook. My timing was perfect because she was on her time off so I could have her room. This boat works its crews 30 days on and 15 days off. There are other boats in the fleet that work 30:30.

The boat is dry, as I suspect are all boats. Thirty days straight with the same people would be hard if there was conflict. Couple that with six hours on, six hours off and it is a lifestyle completely different to what most would call normal. What probably binds everyone together is the love of what they do. Most times it is a quiet life: not a lot of pressure, not even much to do. Then it is action stations: hard, fast, careful, skilled, until the action is over again. If something goes wrong, it goes wrong fast. Shit happens sometimes. That's why it is called shit. It is unexpected, it happens despite all safety procedures and must be dealt with.

Just before the *Emily Davis* picked me up, she caught a tug that had lost its steering and was spinning like a top down the river. No safety manual, no safety inspector, no words will be able to fix a situation like that. Experienced people will achieve extraordinary things calling on decades of knowledge and intuition, and they will sort it out when shit happens. It's a bit like that on a kayak adventure too.

Australia has become so ridiculous with its safety rules and regulations that individuals now are not allowed to be responsible for their own safety. These guys were allowed to think for themselves. I heard Beau speak to the guys. He wants them to be safe. They want to be safe. They also want to get the job done and be allowed to think. At the top, the company wants them to be safe. In what is supposed to be the most litigious country in the world, they still know how to work and have not been reduced to the rule-abiding robots most Australian workers are told to be by CEOs scared of their own shadow.

Travelling upstream, the 'mouths of the Mississippi' could be seen in the context of the groins or dykes. From three stories up and with the map on the large screen in front of you, the huge lines of vortices and upwellings can be seen starting at the groins and spiralling downstream. The boats can often be seen in what appears to be a bad part of the river, where you would expect the current to be fastest. In effect, though, they are riding the swirls and whorls and actually pick up speed. It is sort of counter intuitive, but it is exactly what I had done to get across the large flooded offtake to the Atchafalaya, and would have used at the power station had it not been so foggy.

In the afternoon we were running close to the left bank. Beau pointed out rough water about a kilometre ahead and slowed down to hold position.

"There's a current running off that point," he advised. "There's a boat coming down and I don't want to have that water push me out into him."

After a few minutes the boat came into view. It was another big tow. Rather than push sideways across the river, though, it continued towards us until less than two kilometres away before slowly turning to its left. It came right through the area that we would have been in, only missing us by about 200 metres. That was not right, it should have been much further out in the river. The helmsman on the oncoming boat apologized and Beau took it with good grace. That's what 60 years of living can do, I suppose, or maybe it is just the way with these guys. The bloke knew he had stuffed up and our man just let him wear that for himself. With a few thousand tonnes at risk, it was just as well that Beau had been cautious. Was it just good luck that we were cautious? I don't think so. It is instinct, borne out of years of experience, perhaps a really close one in a similar situation, perhaps a story about that bend. It doesn't matter what it was but it is all about feel: what feels right, what feels necessary. That's what experience is.

The crew changed at Memphis. My new mates had finished their 30-day shift. With their cars back at Vicksburg I had a free ride with them back to pick up Klaas and Anne, and move camp to Memphis – the RV park at Gracelands. I felt okay again.

CHAPTER 10

BEATEN

Memphis started so right. We spent the afternoon investigating up river for a place where I could be picked up and that had cell phone coverage. It was 100 kilometres away, three days' paddle and all phones worked.

Hallelujah.

I had hit rock bottom in Vicksburg, but with the generosity of the river people I was rejuvenated, all the way to Memphis and ready to deal with anything again.

Although keen for an early start next morning, Sunday, we had to cool our heels waiting for the TV people that Anne had contacted. By 9.15am we established they were not coming so it was time to paddle. About a kilometre upstream some sort of outfall was bubbling below the surface. That explained the sign at the boat ramp warning people not to eat the fish. Shame really, seeing as the city is bike friendly and had impressed me until then.

At the 25 kilometre point, a boat ramp came into view and being a Sunday there were people all over the place. People are probably the

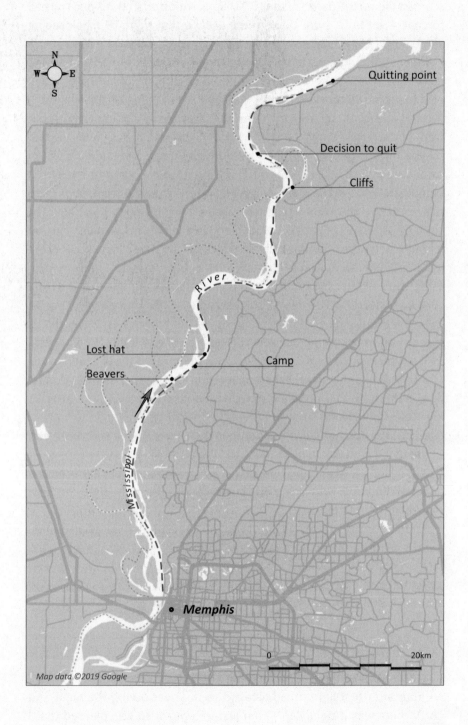

scarcest life on the banks of the Mississippi. Unfortunately no-one wanted to chat. I got little more than grunts. Maybe they were in shock seeing some nutter clawing his way up the river.

About 1.00pm many small islands were dotted over the river and the current seemed to be evenly distributed at about 3.5km/hr, so I took advantage of the peaceful scene to move over to one of the islands. A brown head swam off from the bank at 45 degrees to a point 20 metres in front of the kayak. Whack! A big hit from the tail and it was gone. "Beaver maybe," I thought, so I stopped for a few minutes, just paddling at the same rate as the current. Whack! This time it was about 20 metres from behind and next to the bank. In the meantime up in the sand, about two metres above the waterline, there was a constant sound like a kitten crying. "Some sort of baby," I decided and headed off, not wishing to upset its mum anymore. About a kilometre further on, a grey furry body dived just beside me. All I saw was its back. but it was wide, wider I think than an otter. There was always birdlife around, but animals were scarce. Did I just see two beavers? Who knows, but it was nothing like I have seen at home. Over the thousands of kilometres in my kayak I have seen many things that will sit in my memories forever. This was one of them. Who needs a TV if all you need to do is to sit, reflect, and call up all of those experiences.

About 5.30pm a sandy area appeared in the trees. "This will do just fine," I thought. Pity a million mozzies thought so as well, but after 35 kilometres on a warm sunny day I was in fine spirits. Lighting the fire was easy, but the mozzies were tougher than the smoke. In the end I retreated to the tent, killed the 50 or so that had slipped in when I had left the front unzipped for a few minutes, opened a beer and ate some of Klaas' chicken and cauliflower. It was delicious, but I wasn't all that hungry and kept most of it for the next night.

It isn't normal to work your guts out all day and then not want dinner, but the significance escaped me at the time. This time I was confident the pick-up point in a couple of days would be okay. The river was big and powerful with a new flood peak coming down, but I was making good ground, better than our budgeted 32 kilometres per day.

Next morning rain was threatening and I was on the water at 7.30am, an hour after first light. I had listened to the river during the night and knew there was a significant groin just up ahead, so was pleased that I

*Typical decision
– around the log
into the current
or inside through
the tree tops*

*Beside the cliffs
for 2km*

would be fresh to tackle it. It appeared after just 10 minutes. The approach was tight with little room for a run up, but it didn't look too bad. I hit it hard, moving half a boat length into the torrent. Every ounce of strength didn't help, though, I was slipping backwards. "Can't give up," I thought, so I moved out into the main flow of the river. Behind me was mayhem with whirlpools and roaring water, but I started to win. Inching forwards I crept back towards the bank just 10 metres above the jet that had thrust me backwards. Phew, it was over as fast as it had begun. I was safe.

Holey dooly, not yet. There was an eddy here and I was being carried into trees at 6km/hr going upstream. Steering left and paddling at full power half helped. I got halfway past a tree when my hat was torn off and then I side slipped into the next treetop. No chance for the hat; it swirled a bit and was sucked under. I was very pleased my head wasn't in it as it went down. Stuck sideways in a treetop is not a lot of fun, but with only a 6km/hr current it was just manageable and I eventually extricated myself.

"Well. that was an interesting start to the day," I thought. Having no hat wasn't the end of the world, but the mozzies thought it was pretty good. There was no bank I could put into and get something out of the bulkhead in the kayak to fashion a hat with, so I just put up with it until a flash came to me and I reached around for the plastic container just behind me. Inside was the pressure bandage for snakebites that I wrapped around my head, but it didn't cover the bald bit on top. My handkerchief soon fixed that and my head was protected again.

A groin at a different depth, probably shallower than the others I had crossed, offered a smooth crest of water over it with a drop towards me of about 15 centimetres. It looked confronting, but there was no way of avoiding it as it was right next to the shore. I thrust the kayak forward. Surprisingly the kayak burst right over the top into water that I could paddle against. It wasn't easy but it was not insanely hard either, so it was a huge morale booster. Something that had looked almost impossible had been conquered. Maybe I could paddle this river.

Good thoughts like that don't last long on the Mississippi, and with rain falling and fog moving in I found myself in a narrow area with large grey rock cliffs that channelled strong currents, and swirls and eddies in the water. The first outcrop was tough. For a while I slowly went backwards until there was enough of a swirl that I could beat. Backwards again, then another swirl. Hard as you can, mate… pull hard, do not slacken off. My legs were quivering as I tried to control the rudder. The spindly little things were trembling right up to where my backside used to be before it disappeared a month or so ago. But I made it. And I made it past the next one. For over a kilometre I fought that water beside those enormous grey cliffs. I did not let it beat me, but I was concerned about the toll it was taking on me.

The cliffs disappeared and were replaced with trees. There was no land here. None turned up until 5.30pm when I found some sand in the trees, just a narrow strip maybe 200 metres from the real bank, which was impossible to get to through the treetops. Was it high enough? It seemed

A little hill on the river bank

so and I was tired. Being so tired is of concern because you need all of your wits about you to stay alive. There was a lull in the rain and I decided this would have to do.

I pulled the kayak up as far as I could, which was about a metre above the waterline, and tied it to a tree just as I do every night. The previous night a lot of water had entered the rear bulkhead. I'm not sure where it came in, but I needed to check it before the next leg.

With mozzies everywhere and stupid me without any repellent, I settled into the tent with the new stove as rain started tumbling down again. I opened some barbeque crisps but wasn't keen on them because they are so sweet in the US. The beer was good and gave me enough energy to start heating Chef's chicken cauliflower dish. This I forced down because, tasty as it was, I could not get my stomach to want it. That was serious, I reckoned. Maybe 10 hours paddling, including a few life-threatening bursts and the rest just slogging on, was a bit too much. But as I was 77 kilometres up river from the previous morning, the next day would be shorter and better, I figured.

Lying on the small self-inflating mattress, about 20-millimetres thick, water started dripping on my right arm. It was entering through a seam and then running down along the floor to the corner near my feet. The rain was teeming down and a fine mist was coming in from just above my head. My plan was to lie on the mattress with the sleeping bag covering me to keep it dry. Good plan in theory, but I got wet anyway. The rain poured until 4.00am when a big wind gust rushed down from the north, shaking the trees and cooling the air. The waves crashed on the sand and I was pretty sure the water was rising.

Daylight showed I was correct. Having risen over half a metre, the water was lapping the kayak wheels. Sure, it had just been a wet night camping, but I wondered about my reserves. Most importantly, my thought processes did not seem as they should be. I enjoyed my muesli, drank two coffees, lay down for half an hour, and then was up and at it. At 8.00am I was on the water but felt drained. From the river I took one last look back at my camp and I saw my life jacket. There it was, hanging on the tree where I had hung it to dry in the cool northerly. That was the moment I decided to get off the river. Having suspected I wasn't the full bottle, here was the proof. If I wanted to live, I had to let it go.

I paddled back to get the life jacket. Maybe I was just arrogant. Maybe when I was down and feeling sorry for myself in Vicksburg, I should have been smart enough to quit the river. There were many maybes but, the fact was, I had pushed to the limit and I had not been good enough: better to acknowledge that and live to fight another day.

The north wind blew fiercely, just like it does when paddling the great straights of the Murray River, only this time I had to deal with a 4km/hr adverse current as well. I was wet from the waves, the sky was an angry grey and purple, and the bank was about 10 metres behind the trees, thus keeping me in the current.

A big groin lay underwater at 30 degrees into the river. Its whirlpools were murderous. Although there was no way around on the bank, there was a narrow path through the treetops. The flow was fast, but possible to manage. Bursting into the trees, the right back wheel snagged a branch. Dancing on the pedals I freed it, only to have the branch catch on the stove lashed across the rear deck. Great, now I had a tree branch between the wheel and the stove. Think. Think! Gradually, just keeping pace with the current using close to full power, but not flat out, I managed to move the kayak to the left. Phew. Easing off the power I slowly drifted back to safe waters.

Next shot at the treetops, I steered about 30 centimetres wider. I was surging ahead when a vortex swirled down from a large tree ahead. Left rudder. No, right rudder. No, left rudder. Into the treetop on the left now. The bow danced from side to side, but the left wheel was snagged on another branch. "Please, not here," I thought. What a stupid thing to think. Why was here any better or worse than the other places? Only this time, it was after I had already decided to call it quits.

Snagged, I was in a life threatening position. If the kayak spun sideways I would be caught between the two treetops and, with this water velocity, highly likely to be turned over. I backed off just enough to drift out of the snag. The tree to the right was still there but, under full power and dancing rudder pedals, I inched forwards. Another 20 metres and it was all behind me. Yet again I had made it.

The river was not finished with me, though: another groin, another fight, trembling legs, burning arms, sick stomach. Please, I don't want to spew in the middle of this, I thought. It might make me break my stroke, which would be a very bad thing.

Then it was over: the river straightened with just the tops of trees to paddle beside and only a 4km/hr current if I could keep really close to the trees. When I arrived at the pick-up point, Anne took a photo of me sitting on the kayak. Klaas and I dragged it to the vehicle and we set off back to Memphis. I had covered just under 100 kilometres over the three days.

The river had won.

I wasn't as despondent as I expected, but respectful of the river and the fight I had been waging.

Maybe I was secretly pleased that it had taken the best I could give and spat me back out still alive. I really just wanted to be a grandfather. Shattered, deflated, tired, emotional, and downright buggered really, I conceded defeat. That was two losses. First time was in the Southern Ocean off South Australia in 2007, then this mighty Mississippi River. Ah well, better to have tried and lost than never to have tried at all. At least the fight was good and long before I conceded this time. Better than being bashed up by a huge wave after about 10 minutes and then getting hypothermia, as had happened in the Southern Ocean.

PART 3

PLAYING TOURIST

CHAPTER 11

DOWN BUT NOT OUT

The goal was to get to Paris, so another plan was required. With a few hours' sleep to recover from the river ordeals, I woke at 2.00am with the answer. I would stow the kayak in the Ford's roof box and get a bicycle and pedal across from Memphis to the east coast, about 1,600 kilometres away.

An internet search showed Bikes Plus had many awards for service, so we tried there first. All I can say is that the business' web site had to be written by them. Service? Advice? The guy wasn't even going to lower the seat so I could try it for size. What a waste of time, and although it's probably unfair of me to not try another bike shop, I went to Walmart next. It cost $150 all up: with helmet, spare tubes, tyre levers and a new seat. The custom seat was designed to cradle just your backside's cheeks, rather than the regular nose-shaped seat that at the first opportunity inflicts pain on your tender regions, in my case, the testicles.

For decades I had thought bike seats were a crazy design and here was one exactly as I had designed in my mind, and it was only US$16. Back at

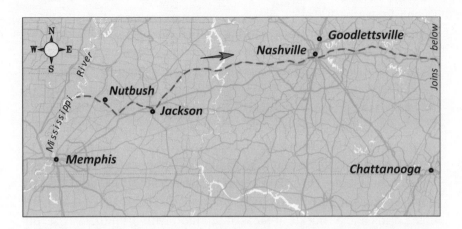

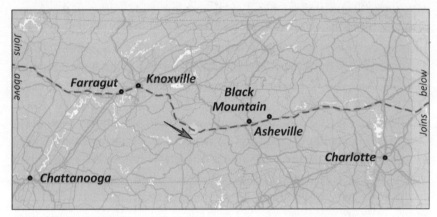

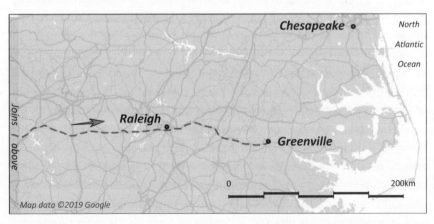

the RV park, the test ride was less than perfect. The bike was too short and the seat was uncomfortable but the gears were good. Oh well, I thought, it's only for a month.

Klaas and I set off next morning to the departure point from the Mississippi River. The first 13 kilometres of riding were on the river flat, followed by a climb onto the bluffs for a last look at the great river system. The climb off the Mississippi floodplain and past the grey kudzu covering the hills wasn't as hard as expected because the bike's gears worked so well. Green patches were appearing in the acres of grey, heralding the coming of spring and with it the mosquitoes. Klaas had stopped halfway up the hill ready to take a photo, so I grabbed a spanner and fixed the seat that had come loose. For 10 kilometres I had been able to experiment with the seat's angle so I could sit more comfortably, so at least I got that right. After a drink and a chuckle at Klaas' discomfort with the mozzies, I set off with a new attitude to the bike. It was starting to grow on me, plus I was getting a handle on what my speed would be. Unfortunately, this was a big disappointment. My average speed was not even quite 15km/hr. What possessed me to think it would be about 25km/hr? I might have done that when I was 40, but I probably didn't and I had just forgotten. The older we get, the better we were.

The area on the hills was much wealthier and more populated. Churches, mainly Baptist, popped up with monotonous regularity. Pretty soon we reached the town of Ripley, where Le Chef issued sandwiches which we both devoured in seconds. There were roadworks blocking our route, but I sort of worked out where to go until I came to a stop sign and wasn't sure whether to go left or straight ahead. After unsuccessfully trying to flag down cars and ask, I chose straight ahead. About six cars made sure their windows were up and just drove around me. It is so sad to see this in the United States. People are so fearful. As I had found out earlier, hitchhiking in the US is a thing of the past. Americans are now too scared for that to work. It is not a reflection of their generosity, just a result of their media, especially that belonging to a certain ex-Australian.

Having made the decision to go straight ahead, Le Chef himself went whizzing across from right to left at the traffic lights a few hundred metres ahead. He had the GPS, so he had to be right. Turning left I rode for a couple of kilometres and spotted an old bloke standing in his driveway about 30 metres off the road. I called out to him a number of times, but it took a while to get his attention. This sort of behaviour must be foreign. Strangers don't talk. Eventually he came towards me and he could not

Kayak stowed, bike ready (Memphis)

have been nicer. Together we figured out what I needed to do, so I set off in pursuit of Klaas. Luckily he had stopped about another kilometre on. He reckoned he got there by guesswork, just like me, because he had tried to put something in the GPS and it hadn't worked. I re-entered the destination as I had done at the river and it came up with the route that the old guy and I had figured out. Back on track.

As the road wound through the rolling hills, a sign proclaimed it a bikeway. It wasn't the sort of bikeway I was used to, though, just an ordinary bitumen road with only about 30 centimetres of riding space outside the white line at the edge. There was a green crop in most of the fields. It looked like grass about 45 centimetres high, but no doubt would mature into something with a head. Pity I am so ignorant of these things. I am not ignorant about water and found it interesting to note the lengths that the farmers had gone to direct the water off their fields as quickly as possible. It was yet another example of how we each contribute to speeding up the flow of water across the landscape. This is why most rivers in the world have to cope with more water and thus more power, which means more destruction every time there is a significant rainfall event. The other huge impact of this is there is much less moisture in the soil, so droughts take hold much quicker. We seem hell bent on exacerbating climate change, not mitigating it.

The next town on the map was Nutbush. "How many Nutbushes can there be?" I thought, but this one wasn't even a town really, just a name on the map. The sign coming into town said it is unincorporated, which basically means it is very small. Klaas had stopped at a dilapidated building up ahead. The sign on the building boasted 'Birthplace of Tina Turner' and the road out of town was named Tina Turner Highway. All in all it was pretty unimpressive. Apparently there is a Tina Turner museum south of Nutbush itself, which is more accessible to the I-40, the main interstate highway, but that's not where we were headed.

My backside was getting sore and my legs were complaining. Although bike riding is a great way to quickly get across the country, there are limits to what one should do on the first day, so we called it quits at 64 kilometres. It was time to move base camp, so we went back to Memphis and next day took the van to Goodlettsville just north of Nashville. It took half a day to get there, so there was no riding that day.

The weather report for the next few days was mixed, but Klaas and I set out in the Ford leaving Anne at Goodlettsville to fend for herself. Good weather or bad weather, kayakers and bike riders eat it up. Some may say that I am biased, but unless paddling up a flooded river, give me kayaking in the wind and rain any day. That said, screaming down the other side of a hill that you have just conquered on a bike on a pleasant day … well, you could get to like that too, I guess.

Oh, and another thing. If the kayak leaks a bit, you just sponge it out every now and again. Maintenance is minimal. Bikes have tyres though, and tyres have air in them. When you run over something sharp, the air comes out and you have to stop and fix it. The good thing is that the front one seems to be the one that goes down most, maybe because the back one is just running behind a wheel that has already 'cleaned' the road.

The first puncture happened on the second day of riding. I had asked Klaas to keep behind me and every 10 kilometres or so he could catch up, where we could have a rest and maybe eat and drink. That didn't suit his plans, though, and after about five kilometres he whizzed past. A kilometre later my front tyre went down. There was nothing on the bike

This was a surprise (Nutbush)

Legends Corner (Nashville)

to fix it. The gear was in the Ford, which was supposed to be behind me. There was no mobile phone coverage, so I propped the bike against the Armco, took the wheel off and tried hitching again. Surely holding a wheel next to a bike would be enough for someone to stop. It took over an hour. Young dudes sped past in their trucks, but finally an old couple stopped. That was when another older couple, who had driven past, turned around and came back to see if they could help. Both couples were lovely. One pair agreed to drive ahead until they found Klaas when I advised them that he was in a Ford Explorer with a huge crate on the roof. It turned out that Klaas had been waiting only a kilometre ahead. He was waiting in a park near an old cannon which he reckoned would make a great photo with me in the background. Time didn't seem to matter. It didn't seem to register to him that he had driven only two kilometres since he passed me and that it should not take me over an hour to ride that distance. If I had known he was so close I would have just walked to him, but I didn't know. The poor cell phone system with the independent networks was certainly frustrating. I also made sure I put the repair gear on the bike for next time.

The first thing you do when you change a tyre is to check that there is nothing on the inside. We had done that each time but had found nothing. Eventually I turned the tyre inside out and looked closely in the sunlight. There was a miniscule shiny bit. "That's it," I exclaimed to Klaas. "Mmm," he replied, rubbing his finger on it and immediately drawing blood. It was so small that extraction was difficult, but that puncture repair was the last for the whole journey.

We saw quite a lot of confederate flags on the lawns of rich and poor homes alike. American flags were far more popular and sometimes we would see neighbours flying different flags. It seems that people fly a confederate flag for different reasons. Some fly it because they wish to honour those who died in that bloodiest of wars 150 years ago, some because it is a symbol of rebellion, maybe some because they were born flying it. Even today there is controversy about flying the flag in Virginia. The state touches Washington DC, reaches to within 300 kilometres of New York City and was confederate apart from Fort Monroe at Hampton, which was a union outpost in a confederate state. Feelings run high on both sides. Most of us think that the war was about slavery, but it seems so much deeper than that and the divisions in the United States are still there today.

I was lucky with the weather. It was fine most of the way across, but water could be seen lying in ploughed fields from previous downpours.

This was an important indicator of why farmers want to drain their land. Some fields had big drains down the sides with smaller ones across them. Of course, all were designed to get water away quickly. I didn't see any lined drains that the Vicksburg US Army Corps of Engineers had told me about, but even here you could see what the land use would do to exacerbate flood heights on the Mississippi River.

The US 70, the highway that we followed until the signs disappeared, is known as the Purple Heart Trail to commemorate and honour all men and women who have been wounded or killed in combat while serving in the US armed forces. It covers 20 states right across the country, and the number is growing. Confederate cemeteries were not uncommon on US 70 so, although the countryside is picturesque and peaceful, the warlike predisposition of many of the American people is never far from the surface.

Standard US-style cheap houses were the most prevalent between towns and on the outskirts. These dwellings are basically long boxes, transported by road and placed on the land in what looks like a random fashion, because fences around the properties are practically non-existent. Huge shiny cars are invariably parked next to them and the lawns are always well mown. Ride-on mowers are very cheap, so I guess second-hand ones cost hardly anything, as do old cars that still look good.

I didn't see any other bikes on the road until 20 kilometres from Nashville when I saw an old bloke huffing along the other way. My excited hello was met with a raised finger as he struggled with whatever demons were plaguing him. Then three kilometres later, a couple cycled towards me on a tandem and waved enthusiastically back. That was it, though. Sadly, no more bikes.

The Climate Reality Project, which was set up by Al Gore to train presenters to spread the word as shown on 'An Inconvenient Truth', regularly updates its program and holds seminars around the world. My mate Hoody, a prolific Climate Reality presenter, reckoned the Climate Reality Project was based at Nashville. Wikipedia also says it was set up there in 2006. We had budgeted to fly over before the trip, but in the end decided not to. What a good decision that was. When we approached Nashville I rang our liaison man, Mario. He is based in Boulder, 2,000 kilometres away. Whoops.

I couldn't find a Climate Reality Project number in Nashville, but since I was passing through the city I went to the address shown on the web site. Unfortunately, there was no receptionist, no person who you can talk to unless you know who you want, not even a mention of the Climate Reality Project anywhere. Oh, the joys of a foreign country. In the end I found Al Gore's office, visited his staff, advised them about my trip and heard nothing more. It was all a bit of a wasted day really.

Chestnut Mound rated a dot on our map of the route after Nashville. The climb up was the longest so far, but given that mounds have tops to them I was looking forward to an exhilarating ride down. Just as the Mississippi Delta region is not on a delta, Chestnut Mound was not a mound. What a disappointment, no downhill.

Highway 70 is full of surprises. I was glad of that, sort of pleased that our maps were very limited. Farragut looked like any other small town on the map, but riding along the country road, very wealthy subdivisions began to appear. Huge, expensive houses with large manicured lawns displayed their opulence. One after the other, they appeared. I was in the countryside and here were the arrays of wealth. It seemed odd until it gradually became evident that I wasn't in the middle of nowhere and, in fact, that I wasn't far from somewhere big. Farragut is big, and it is wealthy, with large European car dealerships, huge stores spread out just like in Texas, but with trees everywhere. It exudes affluence.

After another hour of riding, Farragut just seemed to keep going. The wealthy look disappeared and I assumed that was just evidence of which side of town I was on. Eventually a sign declared that I was in Knoxville. Throughout the ride, I had been surprised at how far I had come. A week previously, when I had ridden 130 kilometres in a day, both Klaas and I were both surprised to be just 20 kilometres from Nashville. Likewise, we had slipped into Knoxville, with the poorer area giving way to wealth again, hills and no room for bikes. You just have to take your chance in one of the two lanes, stay off the edge, especially when there is a rock wall beside you with nowhere to go, and trust that drivers obey the one metre rule for cyclists. Luckily they did.

Thinking back to that awful night stuck by the river when Klaas and Anne got lost, gave me an attack of the negatives. Walking three kilometres through a dark-flooded forest and confronting a strange dog-like animal after a giant paddling day, then spending the night in a box that you cannot lie full length in, at a temperature of 8°C with no jacket, would be draining on anyone. When that is over, you have your dreams of the past five years dashed to ribbons. You turn to your team to try to explain what happened and you get silence and criticism for the way you went about it.

Maybe doing something way outside what other people think is normal has its retribution. Bleak, bleak thoughts invaded as I pedalled along: down a bit of a hill, stand up to get up the next one. The bike didn't help my mood in the way that the water and the kayak do. It wasn't therapeutic, like paddling is. Pedal, pedal, pedal, bleak, bleak, bleak thoughts: but then the family emails from the time popped into mind. I saw the kids, the families together, and their love. I missed not being with them, but the images of these emails pulled me through. Family is critical. We stand by each other, we understand each other, even if we seem a bit weird to others. The mind is a powerful friend and a tough foe. It can take you through things that you would think impossible, but it can also bring you down if you let it. Self-pity time was over. The bleakness had been powerful, but it was brief, and it was consigned to the rubbish bin. I did not particularly like being on the bike, it was not the journey I had planned, but it was the only way to finish the job, so I had to do it.

After a good night's sleep, the mountains that I could see ahead in the distance were not so worrying. The road flattened out as it followed the French Broad River. Mountains crowded in on both sides as the road departed from the river for an absolute bitch of a climb up to the state border with North Carolina. With a great sense of achievement, I passed a few signs declaring that this was a bike route, so there are obviously people who ride this for fun. Mad buggers!

I had passed a sign by the highway that read, "Jesus knows your thoughts."One of the advantages of such trips is that you get to have sex in many remote and exotic places whenever you like. It would just be nice to have someone to share it with. I had been quite a while on my own, so to speak. Not a lot of activity in the sleeping bag, but you can't help what your mind does and I really didn't want to share any of those thoughts with Jesus.

Coincidentally, Jacqueline had finally decided to come over from Australia to help with support until Renate arrived in June. Throughout the Mississippi ordeal she had been in the background. She had seen me off at Brisbane Airport saying that at some stage she would come over and help. I didn't know when, or even if, she would come, so I just waited to see what she decided. She arrived in the US at the end of April planning to stay for a month or maybe six weeks. I had no idea of her motives, but celibacy is for monks and I needed support, even though I was terrified of possible romantic complications. I made it very clear that trips and romance are incompatible. She was still studying environmental subjects at university, and reckoned she wanted to write a thesis about the trip. That seemed a great idea, but meant she would have assignment work to do while she was with us.

Jacqueline had been critical of my choices, especially the support-crew selection process. She believed I should have advertised for a support crew and sent Klaas and Anne home. She had not experienced what I had, not tried for two years to find a support crew as I had done, but I reckoned she would figure it out after she arrived. Coinciding with her arrival was a package from The Farm people who had been running the Facebook post. They had put together a 'care package' for me, with mozzie nets, space blankets and anything useful they could think of. This boosted my morale after the disastrous Mississippi tribulations and it sure helped given that my ground-swell support was as thin as air. I wasn't hearing from many people back in Australia. Connor had moved on without taking the GoPro back to Lismore Camera House, so Amanda volunteered to do that. Even Hoody was having a hiatus from contact, for personal reasons which I understood. I felt pretty much out of sight, out of mind with most people, but when special friends, or someone that you have been waiting on for a reply, ignore your emails, you really worry that you might have upset them in some way. Jacqueline had to chase Hoody back in Australia to get him to respond to emails. Mostly there is nothing you can do except suck it up, but it does drain one's spirit.

The good news was that The Farm was boosting Facebook views with great memes, and they were only spending $260 per month, which I hardly noticed compared with the other costs. They were the one bright light in an otherwise gloomy media situation.

Was I wasting my time, squandering money that could be used to set up the property I wanted for the grandkids? Some people thought so, but others seemed to have faith. The trip was not the roaring success that we had all hoped, but I knew that I did touch some people and that their efforts would outweigh anything that I could do. On balance, despite the fact that I would return home broke after giving up quite a good life, and even my motorbike and yacht, I reckoned it was worth it.

It is hard to explain if you are driven to do something. This had been so much a part of my life, my soul maybe, that I was committed to do whatever it took. There just wasn't any doubt in my mind that I would get to Paris in my kayak, but it certainly wasn't going to be easy. If only I had been able to do it as part of a team, all working for the same cause.

We moved the van from Goodlettsville to Asheville. Jacqueline stayed with Anne at the RV park while Klaas and I set off for a day's ride east. Back on the road the weather was a bright and sunny 8°C, but after a couple of days off, my legs reckoned this was a mug's game. The first couple of kilometres were a struggle but my body settled in, just in time to pass through Black Mountain and then head for the summit.

What summit? It was nuthin'. Highway 70 had merged into the Interstate and the grade was not too bad. The distance wasn't much either, so I was at the top, way before I expected. A six degree downhill slope for 10 kilometres followed. This was my best day's riding yet. At the bottom the temperature slowly climbed, the road stayed flattish and I decided that Interstate highways were much easier to ride than the minor roads.

All went well for about 60 kilometres. The shoulder was wide and I felt safer than on the narrow highways. Heading east with the sun to the south meant that a lot of the time the road was shaded by trees. I was actually enjoying myself, thinking maybe this bike-riding stuff wasn't so bad after all.

Then the state trooper arrived.

"How many bikes do you see riding on the Interstate?"

"None," I replied also thinking, "same number as on any bloody road here, mate."

"Well, that should tell you something."

"Yeah, like what," I thought, but actually said, "There are no signs and it is a lot safer than Highway 70."

"Speeds are too high; it is for your safety," was the trooper's comeback.

"Like I said, it is safer here than the 70 where there is no room for bikes."

He mellowed a bit and said that he personally couldn't care where I rode but "do-gooders" ring up and complain and he has to do something about it. He told me to get off immediately at the road crossing where I had stopped. I carried the bike up the hill to the bridge and rode back up to Highway 70 with its narrow edges and hoped that people didn't get too impatient waiting to pass a bicycle. We made 106 kilometres for the day but it would have been more if I had been allowed to stay on the Interstate.

Funny how I had to ride on dangerous roads for my own safety. I was to find out later that my safety was very important to the law, even if they had to put me in danger to enforce that law.

Jacqueline took her first shift at driving for a day while Klaas went fishing. He came back with plenty of stories, but no fish. At the campsite by the water many people were fishing, some in small dams and some in the main creek with pools and rapids. Success seemed to be few and far between but, for fishers, it is not the catching, so I am told, it is just the act of fishing. Next day Klaas would resume driving duties while Anne and Jacqueline took a tour they had booked to get to know the area and meet some of the locals. The bike section was working just fine with Klaas as the support person, so he would keep doing that until it was time for me to get wet again.

My head was clear, my hands were getting soft and my legs were getting fitter, but I was still a long way from being a decent bike rider. When the road started to rise it wasn't long before I got 'dead legs' and had to back off or stand up on the pedals. Mostly I stood up and went up to top gear before gradually changing down as I got slower. This is totally different to paddling, where I can flog my muscles until a tendon pops, which actually happened on the last day on the Mississippi River and had still not healed. Mentally I was healing. Female companionship had certainly helped. I wasn't feeling dreadfully lonely and isolated, but I was starting to learn something more. Sure, I was a fine warrior, but was that the answer? Maybe I was being plain stupid expecting to influence people in this way. Maybe a glimmer of understanding was emerging.

All the trains we saw travelled slowly: 50km/hr and less, with long, macho blasts of the horn. It's fine during the day, but a bit over the top at midnight. The Asheville RV park was adjacent to the train line and it carried quite a few coal trains. They were the only evidence we saw of destruction in the region. All the images we posted on the web site were of picturesque scenes, but the trains take coal from areas where whole mountains have been removed. Imagine the mentality of the people who raze these beautiful mountains. The destruction is almost unimaginable.

This was some of the most spectacular country I have seen: lush, green, productive, scenic. It is vast. Mankind destroys it to get at a poisonous material that is changing the earth to a state that is unliveable for mankind. It is understandable that we used coal before we had cheaper alternatives and understood the damage it causes, but to continue mining it in the 21st century is simply insane.

The hills flattened out to gently undulating country and I went flat strap, with the old fella following, to finish the ride. With the temperature climbing to 28°C, everything started to feel different. Throughout the ride, there had been strong contrast in the houses. The distinction between rich and poor areas is not so obvious in Australia, but every day along this route I had passed through both. Covering 100 kilometres per day on the bike took us through vastly different landscapes, from leafy country roads to crowded cities, sometimes picturesque lakes and mountains, sometimes flat farmland, but always changing.

We finished the last day at lunch time, after another roadside discussion with some nice policemen in an unmarked car. I think they were checking our sanity. When they heard our accents and saw the two litre vodka bottle full of water, their preconceptions, whatever they were, were probably confirmed.

The pedals had started to click and groan, and I think their axles were a wee bit bent, but for a cheap bike from Walmart it had done the job. It had covered 1,400 kilometres over some pretty hilly country. You certainly see the country a lot faster from a bike, but it wasn't for me. I was well and truly ready to hit the Tar River in my kayak the next day at Greenville, back to doing what I am good at.

CHAPTER 12

BACK ON THE WATER

Radio, TV and the internet were full of threats of all sorts of bad weather at Greenville, in North Carolina, but I reckoned it was over-hype, so we were at the Greenville boat ramp at 9.00am, ready to go. None of the media we contacted turned up, but that was pretty much par for the course. It was 34 kilometres down the Tar River from Greenville to the camp site at Tranters Creek against 15–18 knots of headwind. Into the mix throw some heavy showers and high humidity, but none of the wild weather that was forecast eventuated. Forecasts do tend to be on the dramatic side in the United States, and Australia is rapidly catching up.

Grandfather's beard grew in many of the trees. Banks of water lilies lined the shore. Huge trees grew out of the clear, dark water. Moccasins guard the swamps, we were told. "Be very careful," they advised, "a moccasin is a deadly snake." So is an Australian brown, and I had paddled through plenty of these in the water during the floods in Brisbane in 2011, so I wasn't too concerned. Apparently there was a moccasin in the water

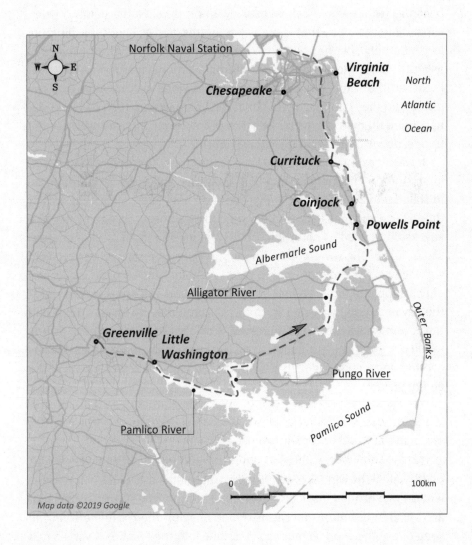

near the pontoon at the caravan park on Tranters Creek, but I didn't see one during the whole trip.

The Tar River was mainly wilderness interspersed with very expensive houses. At Greenville the river is quite narrow and gradually gets wider, as all rivers do. At Washington, near where Tranters Creek flows out, it becomes what I would call an estuary, but it is called the Pamlico River, expanding into a bay that is many kilometres across. That's Washington, North Carolina, by the way, not Washington DC, and it is often referred to as Little Washington to distinguish it from its more famous namesake. As I reached the Pamlico River, a speedboat zoomed over towards me. The driver said they had met a woman at the boat ramp up the creek and she had asked them to tell the bloke in the yellow kayak that she was near the bridge, downstream from the caravan park.

It wasn't easy to find the entrance to the creek. There were islands and inlets and no channel markers. By guesswork and good luck I made no mistakes and arrived at the bridge about an hour later. Jacqueline wasn't there, but I thought I spotted her a kilometre ahead on one of the hire kayaks. After a bit of sprinting, I pulled alongside in an area of smooth water, out of the wind and in bright sunshine. She said that it got cold waiting and she thought I might catch up if she started paddling. It was only a couple of hundred metres to the pontoon and ramp, where I took the kayak out and wheeled it up to our camp site. No snakes there and the severe weather had not appeared. A celebratory beer in the sunshine marked a great start to paddling again. I was back, more or less, in my comfort zone, paddling with a support crew who could pick me up at the end of the day.

The weather wasn't so good the next morning as I wheeled the kayak to the water. The wind was coming from the south east, which was roughly where I was headed. Back down the creek through the swampy areas that are apparently full of moccasins, I was hugging the shoreline trying to keep out of the wind as much as possible. Into the Pamlico River, I could see the freeway bridge crossing the river and the outskirts of Washington.

People had been talking about storms in the morning. They thought I was crazy to be going out when storms were forecast. True, I didn't see too many people about, and one that I did see, walking on Washington boardwalk, told me to be careful of the storms that were coming. I was

Very different to Australia

paddling directly into wind, which was like a 20-knot southerly, so it was a bit of hard work, but not impossible, like it is at sea. I had experienced similar conditions when I paddled across the Myall Lakes into a strong sou'easter on my way to Sydney or when I set off into a sou'wester across Lake Alexandrina down near the mouth of the Murray. Coming into Washington, I noticed that there was an abnormally high tide because the lawns at the houses had about 15 centimetres of water over them. Watching a woman photographing the event, I mused that maybe this was a storm surge so I had better just keep my wits about me.

After paddling under the railway bridge, the sky looked quite ominous to the south east, dead ahead. The land on the other side of the bay disappeared, so it seemed prudent to get ready for a downpour. A bridge was handy and I pulled in a minute or two before it started bucketing down. It was quite cosy, apart from the sand flies, but a few gusts of wind soon got rid of them. As the rain eased, something came round the pylon straight at me. "Bloody hell," I thought, "not a moccasin!" I quickly paddled backwards, only to realise it was just a stick. With that little heart flutter over, I set off again with the wind down to less than 5 knots. It was bouncy but my speed was a good 8km/hr.

All went well for about half an hour, until the land ahead disappeared behind the rain again and I needed shelter. A boat shed was about a kilometre ahead, so I sprinted for that and slipped under the roof, again with a minute or so to spare. The wind blew, the rain bucketed down, but I was snug as a bug in a rug – well more or less anyway. Eventually, after many peals of thunder but no lightning to see, the rain eased and I set off again. After about a kilometre, with the last of the houses on my left, I was about to enter 12 kilometres of wilderness. Unfortunately, the wind had picked up and was around 25–30 knots, and only an idiot paddles against that stuff. I pulled into the bank with waves crashing all around and called it a day. It looked like what I would call cyclone weather, as if I were on the edge of something significant. My confidence in reading northern hemisphere weather, though, was about zero.

The phone coverage was okay, so after standing in the pouring rain for 45 minutes, Jacqueline arrived to drive us to a motel with a bath. The bath was just big enough to lie down in and luxuriate in its warmth. The weather channel had a map with what looked like a cyclone on it. They were calling it Tropical Storm Ana, with wind gusts at the centre of 100km/hr – that's about a category one (Cat1) cyclone. Seems like it passed over my route, so indeed, I had been in something significant. Live and learn, I guess. Didn't I say only an idiot would be out in that stuff?

At North Carolina's East Carolina University, in a state that once prided itself in education and democratic ideals, we learned that the politicians have outlawed the use of the words 'Climate Change' and 'Sea Level Rise'. As a result, where there are serious problems on the outer banks, it is called 'Coastal Flooding'. After a Coastal Resources Commission report came out in 2000 allowing for up to one metre sea level rises by 2100, certain science-denying politicians had managed to have that prediction reduced drastically by only looking 20 years ahead. The US General Assembly in 2012 passed a law declaring that rates of sea level rise "shall not include scenarios of accelerated rates.". Although this was great material for local comedians, it is pretty frightening stuff, akin to Book

Burning Bernardi back home in Australia, and his science-resisting mates like our Prime Minister at the time. I hope we won't be burning witches at the stake but, given half a chance, these people would. If you are not scared of these thugs you should be. They have censored government vocabulary. America is a democracy? Pull the other leg. Real democracy died years ago. Money and corporations now make the decisions and if science has to be censored, so be it.

What the scientists would say about the Outer Banks is that sand naturally migrates and that sea levels are rising. These potent forces cannot be resisted by mankind at any reasonable cost and one day the Outer Banks will be abandoned. The big question is when.

When Jacqueline arrived in the US during the cycling leg, she had only tried the support role for one day. Klaas was okay for support on the roads, as there were no pick-up points involved. With the cycling over and only paddling involved during the leg up to New York, we would see if Jacqueline and I could move quickly with minimal equipment while Klaas and Anne looked after the van. With nothing to do, if Anne didn't stay on top of him, Klaas would continue to take advantage of the cheap US alcohol. Anne's attempt to refuse to start drinking with him before lunch lasted a day.

On the opposite side of the Pamlico River there's a huge mine, totally different to the scenic north side. It is the Aurora Phosphate mine and chemical plant, largest of its kind in the world. There were not many birds about, but I did eventually see a few shags and pelicans. Maybe it was coincidence, but when I saw the birds, two dolphins cruised past. Their fins were quite large compared to our Aussie dolphins, and the rolling motion they created as they surfaced was not as pronounced. Still, you couldn't mistake them for a shark.

We had picked a landing spot at Woodstock Point about 10 kilometres up the Pungo River, which was a left turn off the Pamlico. It was also where I joined the Intracoastal Waterway that I was to follow almost to New York, albeit with a couple of deviations. The entire waterfront was private land. Jacqueline had made friends with some locals; Ella Hudson, Billie Mann and Eli Powell, a young lad who was there on school holidays. Ella and Billie had lived there for decades. I asked Ella about the hide that I had seen on the water that morning. She didn't know what a hide was, but said what I saw was a duck blind or bird blind. Dunno whether you sit in there and watch birds or shoot 'em. Can't see that either would be very rewarding. Pelicans and shags were few and far between and there was the odd duck and pair of geese, as well as an occasional osprey, but that was about it.

Osprey is not happy with me

This water looks a bit high (Little Washington)

Jacqueline's friends were back to greet us in the morning and showed us a much easier way into the water than the rock wall I had climbed out on the day before. It was overcast and cool with a good paddling temperature, but the wind was from the north at 12–15 knots, which was the direction I was headed. As I put into the water, Billie commented that when she started coming to this area in the late 1960s the water was much cleaner. That is the same sort of story I have heard everywhere in my travels over the last decade. Perhaps it was no coincidence yesterday when I saw the shags, pelicans and dolphins at the same time. Maybe they were there together because that was where the food was. Certainly most houses had hard shorelines, not beaches, which had been constructed to stop erosion and maybe maximise the size of the lawns. After all, with a flashy mower you need to give it plenty to do and mowing lawns seems to be a popular American hobby. Nice car, flash house, big lawn: it is the American dream, whether or not that fits in with the environment. Even worse, it seems not to matter if it degrades the environment.

After three hours battling against the wind, I entered the canal to the Alligator River by following the line of the boats using the intracoastal route. I did see a few sailing boats, but overwhelmingly the procession was of motor boats – 'stink boats', as they are often called by sailors. In the canal, the wake from a decent-sized stink boat dwarfs that of the barges on the Mississippi River. Most skippers slowed right down, but the odd one didn't really care about a kayaker. This suited me if it was going in the same direction because I could get a bit of a run from the vessel's wake, but it really was a display of arrogance and stupidity.

After seven hours I reached the bridge where Highway 94 crosses. The arrangement with Jacqueline was that I would not, under any circumstances, go past the bridge. The radios were not working, there was no phone reception, I was 1.5 hours late due to the headwinds and there were swamps on both banks. While I tried to figure out what to do, the big yellow sign on the Ford crossed from left to right far above me on the bridge. Jacqueline was tooting the horn. She crossed over and, luckily, I just spotted the top of the sign coming back, so I headed for the north bank, up through the swamp, hoping to find solid ground. After all, roads don't float, so there had to be ground somewhere. I kept trying the radio without response and in the end I tried shouting. She returned the shout,

Tree stumps indicate extensive erosion (Alligator Pungo River Canal)

I found a path through the reeds and there she was, a very welcome sight for a tired and soaking wet kayaker.

The only RV park we could find in the area was North West River park, south of Chesapeake and near Great Dismal Swamp. It was only about 10 kilometres west of my route and it turned out to be a pretty good base camp for Klaas and Anne. The facilities were fine, there were very few people except on weekends, the sites were huge and it was in bushland (forest) among tall trees. The bush meant plenty of wood for Klaas to have a fire and there were bike trails to ride on and canoes for hire. Without the responsibilities of pick ups, Klaas and Anne had settled into enjoying a pretty good holiday.

We had previously discussed ways to get to the United Kingdom, and with New York within our sights it was necessary to formulate a plan. My preference was to go by ship, so I tried Google. Lo and behold there was an answer. The Queen Mary 2 sailed from New York to Southampton on 14 July. We could make that easily. The shipping line, Cunard, took a few days to get back to me, but they were extremely helpful. "Kayak? No problem. We will put it in the hold, but you must present it in New York for checking well before the ship sails."

Phew! What an easy answer. I booked a cabin for Klaas and Anne, and one for me. England worried me, and France too, of course. I had no idea how I was going to provide accommodation for everyone without our big van, but maybe I would figure something out. Perhaps it was like before I left for the trip, like when Lea suggested we 'live for the moment'. I would keep paddling and think about the next step later, maybe on the ship.

Next day Jacqueline and I set off for a serious attack on distance, with the plan to only come back to base camp when we had to move it. We arrived back at the swamp near the canal and the bridge in zero wind, but it picked up a smidgeon once I was back on the canal. I hoisted the sail, but mostly it just sat there; although the wind was behind I was paddling faster than the wind. The occasional gust filled the sail to pick up my pace, and I cleared the canal two hours later.

A couple of real boats (sailing boats, of course) – a 40 foot Beneteau, and another I didn't recognise – went past. The second one hoisted a headsail just after the canal, so I was able to see it ahead for more than an hour. After three hours, I reached the straight on the Alligator River that goes all the way to the bridge at the mouth. The wind was still fickle, but useful. If I paddled hard I went faster than the wind, but I couldn't see much sense in using energy I didn't need to, so I ticked along at about 7km/hr, keeping the sail full.

The intracoastal channel markers run a big zig zag up the river, but kayaks don't draw much so I straight-lined down the middle. The river is about 7 kilometres wide. Australians would call it a bay. On each side are swamps, with alligators, bears and snakes, so the middle seemed just fine. In another two hours I saw a truck driving across the water a very long way ahead. The bridge finally materialized. The wind built to 8–12 knots with the occasional white cap and a few waves. When the kayak picked up a wave, the sail lost all pressure and back luffed. The GPS showed 13km/hr, so that gave me the wind speed. Eventually it built to 12–15 knots, with waves to catch and lots of white caps. With a good runner, I would surge along at 13km/hr and average about 8km/hr, so the distance rolled by quickly.

About 15 minutes before the scheduled pick-up time, I was 200 metres from the bridge. Jacqueline drove across from right to left. I knew she would not see me in the waves so I waited next to the bridge for her to come back. After 20 minutes she wasn't back but the cold was seeping in, so I headed off to the rendezvous point, just after the bridge and around the point to the right. The trip log registered 48 kilometres for the day and the Alligator River was completed. Jacqueline arrived just before me. She had been talking to locals who told her I would be blown over to the other side, so that is where she went until she thought better of it. She realised I would stick to our plan and so crossed back again. False information can be dangerous and, as I was to find many times over, local information is not always reliable.

Next morning brought favourable winds to cross to the other side of the bay, via the shortest crossing, to the bottom of the peninsula and then to run up to Powells Point. The destination was below the horizon but I figured it would come into view soon enough. After two hours on the water I found that I could actually see the Powells Point area, as well as the southern end of the peninsula. Having agreed to meet Jacqueline at the southern tip of the peninsula, though, it was better to be safe than sorry. I did not want to miss a rendezvous for the sake of a couple of hours. The wind was from the south west at 15–18 knots, but gradually died as I came into the bottom of the peninsula. Jacqueline was nowhere to be seen, so I sat under a tree and dozed until she arrived about 90 minutes later. I was never worried that she wouldn't be there. She had proved herself and anyway there was no point worrying, and I had a rule never to go past a pre-arranged meeting point. It transpired she had just lost track of time and had been reading in a coffee shop. I couldn't figure how that could happen, but by the end of this book, you just might.

When I set off again, the wind had picked up from the north west, straight ahead at about eight knots, which was just comfortable. It was all pretty uneventful, but I was surprised by the lack of people about, given the fabulous weather, warm water and the fact it was a weekend. One bloke I did see was doing something to his jetty. He was standing in the water in front of it. The water was below his waist. After that, I checked water depths and discovered that, almost everywhere, I was paddling in water I could stand up in. You can walk out to all the bird blinds that I saw.

When Warren heard this he cracked, "How do you avoid drowning in Chesapeake Bay?"

"Stand up."

Powells Point is on what they call the North River. From there to the other side is about five kilometres. With a flash of brilliance, or that's what I thought anyway, it occurred to me that these big bays that they call rivers are named that because the water is fresh. Maybe that's right, maybe it's not, but it will do me for an explanation.

The Mississippi River was half a continent away: memories were dimmed but not forgotten. I had played tourist on a bike ride across 1,400 kilometres of very scenic country and now I was having an easy paddle up a protected waterway all the way to New York. The problem was that I was really tired at the end of each day. Everything was starting to hurt, even my heels where they touch the bottom of the kayak, despite changing position regularly. On top of that, I wasn't quite sure everything was okay in the waterworks area. Luckily, things improved a bit, but my body was getting tired. This was the longest trip it had been on.

The North River narrowed into what I could now call a river. After a few bends, the canal through Coinjock was marked by boats streaming past me on their intracoastal trek. The canal seemed to be an extension of the river with the natural banks becoming parallel. The current, the first I had seen in ages, was against me, so I paddled close to the shore: through the town, past people drinking at tables on the wharves, where other lives and other perspectives continued so differently to mine. On past the marina, and finally out into Coinjock Bay where, as if to celebrate, the heavens opened. It poured for 15 minutes and then abruptly stopped. I knew where I wanted to go, which was straight across the bay, but why were the intracoastal cruisers going on the other side of the island? When the sea grass enveloped the kayak I figured out that maybe it was a bit shallow for them. I aimed for the point on Bell Island. It was tempting to aim a few kilometres to the west, but even though my map wasn't detailed enough to show it, I thought there would be no way through. I could see houses on the island and guessed that there would be a causeway to it.

The point was guarded from the water by rock walls which were slightly higher than the land behind them. A car parked on the grass gave me the perspective that I needed to see that the grass was about 30 centimetres above the water. A tidal surge of half a metre would certainly cover most of the land and most of the houses were barely above that, so they would be flooded. Quite apart from rising sea levels caused by climate change, such a rise could be caused by a hurricane at any stage. It seemed pretty crazy to me. Around the point, a really good storm threatened. Time to pull out all stops and put the last five kilometres to bed. The storm hit while loading the kayak onto the Ford, but it didn't matter to me. It was just more water on top of another soaking. Jacqueline made it into the car just in time.

Back at the launch for the next day, the freshly washed landscape beckoned the inquisitive adventurer. We made arrangements to meet at Princess Anne Bridge, Virginia Beach. The bay at Currituck was about five kilometres across but, as I headed north, it quickly reduced to about a kilometre and then, into a river about 200 metres wide. With the wind coming from dead ahead, I was pleased to find the shelter of the narrow waterway. Intracoastal boats regularly passed by, crab boats were out and the Coastguard was installing new channel markers from a large flat-bottomed ship with a crane and pile driving gear. I stopped to talk to a couple of crab boaters who had rafted their boats together. Only one person would look me in the eye and chat. The others almost pretended I wasn't there. I'm not sure what they had to hide: maybe illegal workers, but maybe something else. Apparently they catch crabs eight months of the year. Winter is no good at all. That equates to where I am from, where mud crabs are only caught in months with an 'r' in them, thus excluding the Australian winter months of May, June, July and August. The pots in the area are on about a 25-metre grid and a crabber reckoned they get maybe a dozen crabs per pot every day. That is amazing. The bottom must be crawling with crabs. No wonder crab meat is ubiquitous in the restaurants.

Luckily, there is a sign advertising a marina at the branch into the river that runs to the canoe trail, otherwise it would be easy to miss the turn. The river is more like a creek through a swamp, until it becomes a channel through a swamp, and then straightens into a canal through a swamp. You feel like you are in the everglades and very isolated; tentacles of water branch off every hundred metres or so; towering trees grow out of the dark water; alligators and moccasins call it home. It is an eerie yet exciting place. There was no wind in the swamp, so I made good time gliding through the smooth water until there was no way forward. The route was blocked by weeds, rubbish and logs for about 50 metres. Dragging along the land was no option. In a swamp, a kayak with wheels won't fit between the trees.

I had cut my teeth on log jams, though. They were everywhere on the Darling River system in Australia in 2007. On my Don't Murray the Mary trip in 2008, the Brisbane River had long stretches of water hyacinth, so this problem was nothing new, just a real nuisance. After backing up, I crashed full speed into the mess, achieving penetration of a kayak length. Timber spanned the canal just under the water. By pushing on it, I managed to progress until reaching an area where the only obstacle was the weeds that had floated into the blockage. Although slow and tedious, it is possible to paddle and bum-jerk through that stuff, and within about 20 minutes I was through.

Another blockage about two kilometres further on started to test my patience. They advertise a coastal canoe trail and they don't maintain it enough to allow kayakers through? There is no way that inexperienced people could have made it. There is also no way that anyone had been through there in a boat in the last year. Another half hour wrestling with the mess and I was clear again, only to come across a fallen tree. It was in an area with solid banks. Someone had chopped down a large tree to form a bridge to cross the canal. That was no problem: pull up to the tree sideways, climb out, drag the kayak over, put it back in the water and climb in. Still, it would not be an easy thing for an inexperienced person to do while balancing on a log.

It was hot work in the 33°C heat. Princess Anne Bridge appeared ahead, heralding the suburbs of Virginia Beach; from wilderness to civilization in 100 metres. Parked in the shade of a tree on the other side of the bridge was Jacqueline, complete with a cold beer. Bless her.

The narrow waterway eventually gave way to a wide, structured canal beside a timber plantation, then a freeway and finally, the start of Wolfsnare Creek – the estuary to Lynnhaven Bay. A crane (wading bird) watched silently and majestically from a mud bank, but a very noisy goose advised me that this was his estuary and I had better keep going. Huge houses with huge trees and huge lawns lined the banks. Heaven knows how many millions of dollars each of those is worth. One had its own small island proclaiming ownership of the oysters lying on the sand. The estuary had lots of small bays and no long stretches for the wind to gather

Through the swamp

Choked with weeds (Virginia Beach canoe trail)

strength so, although it was from dead ahead, most of the time the wind didn't cause any problems and I made better time than I had allowed.

The big bridge crossing the exit to Chesapeake Bay was being reconstructed on an even bigger scale. They had an area on the western bank for construction gear. Many sand islands provided interesting kayak pathways. On one of these, I met a recently retired couple out on their first kayaking adventure. He was from the US Army Corps of Engineers coastal section and corroborated what I had heard about shifting sands and rising water. In return, I showed them some basic paddling techniques. They indicated that the ramp I wanted to go to was behind the new sand hill created by the bridge constructors. It was hidden up a little bay, around past a small wind turbine, and was big enough for four large boats at a time, complete with timber finger wharves for each one. It wasn't until two days later that I learned the significance of the wind turbine.

Near the entrance to Chesapeake Bay, I wheeled the kayak up the large boat ramp onto the grass and called Jacqueline to ask where she was. She was in traffic and took another hour to arrive, but with large boats going in and out there was plenty to watch while I dried off in the sun.

Memorial Day was fast approaching and we had struggled to book somewhere to stay. The only place we found was at Prince William Forest Park, about 300 kilometres north and 50 kilometres south of Washington DC. That would have to be the next base for Klaas and Anne, while Jacqueline and I covered the lower Chesapeake Bay over the next five days. We dropped Jacqueline off next morning at a Virginia Beach hotel so she could spend the time working on her assignment, while we headed north for 300 kilometres to check out Prince William Forest Park.

The park was well laid out, a bit tighter than most we had experienced, but with lots of trees and fire pits to hire. Klaas and Anne love their fires, as do I and most other people. Attraction to fire and water are quite powerful instincts. Klaas and Anne always make friends with others in the park, so I wasn't worried about leaving them without a vehicle for five days. We stocked up on food, ensuring that beer, wine and whisky would not run out, and I headed back south to pick up Jacqueline at Virginia Beach. With just Jacqueline and me with the Ford we had moved quickly during the previous legs, and I wanted to continue that pace without having to worry about Klaas and Anne.

CHAPTER 13

LOWER CHESAPEAKE

Virginia Beach is home to the Chesapeake Bay Foundation's Brock Environmental Centre. The foundation is about saving the bay through education, litigation and restoration. Carol, an environmental journalist running her own blog, had alerted us to the importance of the Centre and introduced us. Now I knew what the wind turbine behind the sand hill was all about. Many people beaver away, making a difference, countering the degradation of centuries, slowly leading the world back in the right direction. The only reward for them is seeing the difference, the return of species to an area, the gradual improvement in water quality. To them, backward steps in the area are a bit disheartening, but they just push on and take them in their stride.

A good example of a backward step is the huge increase in the number of bay-side properties with vertical walls to the water. These assist landowners with flooding and erosion problems, but rob shore birds of their habitat. The Audubon Society, a non-profit organization dedicated to the conservation of birds, other wildlife and healthy ecosystems, knows

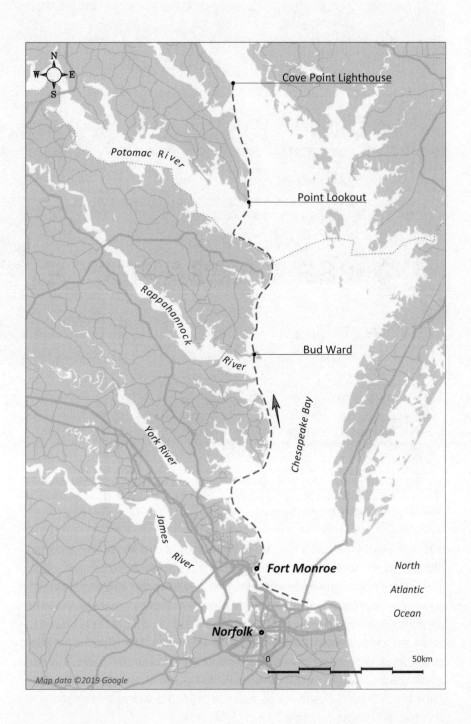

Cove Point Lighthouse

Point Lookout

Potomac River

Rappahannock River

Bud Ward

Chesapeake Bay

York River

James River

Fort Monroe

North Atlantic Ocean

Norfolk

0   50km

Map data ©2019 Google

Soft foreshore – bird friendly habitat

Hard foreshore – bad for birds

this, but what can it do? Not much has happened, but the society does manage to get other areas protected even if the protected areas are small. The society had set up an island just off Roanoke on the outer banks that I remembered clearly. It is teeming with bird life. Hardly a square centimetre remains without some sort of squawking, nesting, or a fight for territory. It is like the most densely populated city in the world. The island is intense and vibrant: very much alive with a cacophony of communication. It is but a few hundred square metres in size. Perhaps that is how the entire earth once was. We have destroyed so much, eliminated so much productivity, that today a desert is normal.

Huge ships ply Chesapeake Bay. To cross from Virginia Beach to either the eastern or western shores you drive about a third of the way by bridge, plunge into a tunnel and resurface onto a bridge that takes you to the opposite bank. The western shore, to Fort Monroe on my route, was just a few kilometres, but most days you can't even see the eastern shore because the tunnels are much longer and the route runs for nearly 30 kilometres. An aircraft carrier, bigger than many islands I had seen, was heading across my course. Even military radar would probably struggle to pick up a plastic kayak, so the best option was to be as far away as possible. I crossed its bow about two kilometres ahead and hastened away.

Its speed was quite slow, probably less than 10 knots and easy to avoid, just like all of the other shipping traffic I had seen.

Fort Monroe, Hampton, is where many slaves used to escape to when fleeing the South. During the American Civil War (1861–1865), the bloodiest war the United States has ever had, most of the state of Virginia became part of the Confederate States of America, but Fort Monroe remained in Union hands. It was finally decommissioned as a fort in 2011. Virginia extends northwards to Washington DC, just 330 kilometres from New York.

We camped near Fort Monroe in a very spacious park. Jacqueline and I had the tent and a paddling job to do, while Klaas and Anne were van-minding 300 kilometres north. The park owners were very friendly and although the RV spaces were all taken, tents were being pitched over an area hundreds of metres long. To get power for the computer, a club room was available in the office and shop area. Jacqueline was working on her university assignment, and I was writing up my blog and posting photographs to the web site when we were interrupted by an excited woman. She had seen the sign on the kayak crate on the Ford and was extremely enthusiastic. Bursting in, she had insisted the park manager find us. Heather worked for the Audubon Society and was there for Memorial Day weekend with her parents. Her parents had completed the Great Loop, a boat circuit of New York to New York via the Mississippi, and could provide valuable information for my route. Heather was going to New York about 10 days later and would talk to her society about our trip. We all chatted on for an hour or so, gleaning as much information as possible. Heather was really excited about the synergy, so we arranged to meet her in Audubon's Lower Manhattan office. All the breaks we got during the journey were from chance meetings like this.

Back on the beach, the holiday had finally brought the crowds I expected. The tide was nearly out and the beach fairly flat, so people could stand in the water about 20 metres off the land. The wind and tide were against me but neither was very strong. One bloke was swimming south. I asked him how far he swam because he had a pretty good stroke. "About 3k's every day," he replied. Now that was impressive! I congratulated him on his use of metrics and his distance, then I was past. A fleeting moment, like two ships passing, but an important contact for both, a link to savour as both parties returned to the task at hand.

My goal was Bud Ward's house on the north side of the Rappahannock River. Bud is an environmental journalist and has been focusing on climate change for about 10 years or so. He had interviewed me when I was in New Orleans. Having checked Google Earth I reckoned that I could pick his house by its significant roof but, to be sure, I aimed slightly to the east; ready to come along the shore where Jacqueline could wave me in. I called her before the crossing and, as I was early, decided to slow down a little and just sailed along with the odd paddle stroke. The crossing is about nine kilometres and about halfway across, the waves got quite big in a wind of around 20 knots. Two sailing boats in the area were struggling with sails for some reason and I really sympathized with the guy whose headsail was in a knot halfway up. There was nothing I, nor anyone else, could do. As he disappeared behind me, his situation did not seem to have improved.

After eating a sandwich, I opened the spray deck again to get out my water bottle. As I unscrewed the cap – cap in one hand, bottle in the other – a wave slewed the kayak to the left. The sail crashed across to the starboard side and over I went. The paddle went to port, I went to starboard: so grabbing the paddle was number one priority and holding the kayak was number two. One minute I was relaxing on cloud nine, a second later inverted. Upside down in a rough bay, it was time to evaluate. I released the line that hauls the sail and mast into position, gathered up what I could find floating around me, stuffed all the bits into the cockpit under the water and, finally, turned the kayak back over. Climbing in from port side, I noticed the sail hanging lazily in the water on the starboard side. A wave came, the sail grabbed the water and out I went on the starboard side again. Bugger. I negotiated my way back to the other side and tried again. This time when I tipped out it was with both feet in the air. If you are going to look like a clown you may as well do it properly, I guess, but experienced kayakers are not supposed to look like clowns.

My next strategy was to get onto the kayak but wait before trying to put my legs in. Timing with the waves was crucial. My previous attempts were marred by impatience and overconfidence. This time, the strategy worked and I was ready to paddle again, albeit with a kayak full of water. My bailing sponge was gone, but I manoeuvred around enough to pick up the remaining gear, which was within about a 10-metre radius. This included my bottles and a container with trail mix in it. The trail mix container was a good bailer and it didn't take long to get the water level low enough to set off.

The GPS was still working fine and it registered 17km/hr as I careened down a wave. With the paddle in my hand there was no chance of tipping over. About a kilometre from shore I dropped the sail, because the wind had increased to the point where the rudder did not provide enough steerage to hold the kayak in line. Even with the sail down it was a wild and twisting ride as I approached the sand bar where I thought Bud's house might be. My phone started vibrating on my chest, so I pulled out its waterproof pouch from under my life jacket. The pouch was full of water. The drowning phone was in its death throes.

There were some figures on the beach but I couldn't recognise them, a man, a dog and … "Ah ha, that looks like Jacqueline," I thought. "The bloke must be Bud." Bud's mooring area was easy to recognise based on what I had remembered from Google Earth. It was a rectangular indentation into a grassed area with trees and houses behind. Firstly, I pulled the kayak onto the sand, then up behind the bushes and left it there. We discussed the crossing and the phone situation. Bud reckoned that heading for a warm shower and a beer should be top priority, and he was right. We had just met for the first time in person and he already felt like an old friend.

The phone pouch was now empty, so the water had obviously drained from it the same way it had made its way in. It was a bit disappointing, really. I would have expected better, but I guess I should have filled the pouch with water to check its effectiveness before relying on it. Anyway I was safe, Bud's place was magnificent and a new phone could wait until tomorrow. I just had to do a quick interview with a reporter from the Rappahannock Times that Bud had organized.

After the obligatory clean-up, Bud and his wife Cathie provided oysters from their own colony. The local method is to get the barbeque hot, put the lid down so it is like an oven and then pop a tray full of oysters in, making sure that there is some water in the tray. They tasted just fine and there was plenty of them, but they weren't as tasty as the Pacific rock oysters that I grew up on. Before we did that, we had a tour of the Ward oystery. Bud explained that you buy the plastic containers and the oyster spats and that's it. You put the spats into the containers, chuck the containers into the water, tie them off with a rope and then wait. We met their friends Karen and Bill, over a beer, of course, and swapped stories. Bill used to have a brick-making business but now concentrates on fishing, crabbing, eating oysters and drinking beer. Karen seems to be in training for all of those activities and is a remarkably talented student.

Bud informed me that there are now only nine science journalists working for the 200 major newspapers. The rest have been dispatched, terminated, got rid of. Without science, anti-science gains ground. On the radio I had heard an interview with a bloke trying to talk about climate science. The host was getting stuck into the climate educator using similar tactics to what I had heard before, first denying it is happening, then claiming it is natural, then attacking at a personal level about someone who is polluting the atmosphere with their own lifestyle. In this instance he was raving about President Obama and how much fuel he used with Airforce One and the cargo plane that transports his security team. He got stuck for a while in the 'naturally occurring' mode, repeating four times that it is a natural phenomenon occurring throughout the solar system; that Pluto, Jupiter and Mars are experiencing the same effects. The educator did not seriously challenge that, so I guess many of the listeners now believe the presenter's rubbish. Did the presenter really believe it, though? Could he have been that stupid? Surely not.

How do you deal with that? Well, there is a course at Queensland University called Climate Denial 101 – in fact, Renate was enrolled in it – but I think it is impossible to deal with such ignorance without a fight. My response to that jerk would have been to question whether he should be allowed onto the radio with such a tiny brain. Pluto is not even rated as a planet these days, despite the recent fly past. Jupiter is probably a big ball of gas, and the Mars atmosphere is nearly all carbon dioxide and is less than one hundredth as dense as that on earth. Believing in fairies at the bottom of the garden seems more logical to me than his rubbish.

Bud and Cathie's place was absolute luxury but there was just one small worry. I had the bottle to pee into when in the kayak, but something didn't feel right. I wasn't sure, but maybe I had been leaking from time to time. It is hard to know when you are wet. "Not to worry," I reasoned, "day after day of clenching stomach muscles every second or so was bound to cause some funny feelings."

From Bud's place on Chesapeake Bay I was headed for the north side of the Potomac River, the one that runs through Washington DC where it is a normal river and you can easily see the other bank. The forecast strong breeze did not eventuate, so it was a very pleasant paddle all the way, although hot enough that I had sweat running down my cheeks. Watching the horizon, I was eventually rewarded with land, but what was it? Could I see right across Chesapeake Bay? I didn't think so, but it was further away than I thought the north side of the Potomac should be. Maybe I could see the other side of the bay on the horizon, but it got closer the further north that I went. Although it seemed too far away, perhaps it was Point Lookout on the far side of the Potomac. The further I paddled the closer it got. My plan was to head across when the distance was about 14 kilometres but you don't just head out to the horizon without being sure that is where you should be heading, so I clung to the shore. Rationally, it had to be the Potomac that I was looking across, but I kept going.

Eventually I found a bloke mowing his lawn, zooming up and down on his ubiquitous ride-on mower. Luckily, there was a small patch of sand below his rock wall so I was able to beach the kayak and climb up to him. We chatted until I started to get concerned about being late to the pick up. Yes, this was the Potomac River. Yes, that was Point Lookout over there and the distance is 11 kilometres, which I could cover in less than two hours. His name was Dan and he is firmly of the opinion that climate change is a manifestation of the imagination of scientists who are using it as a reason to get funding and keep their jobs. Nothing will change his view on that. My protestations that many scientists have actually lost their jobs from speaking out did not seem to get past his ear lobes. He has his beliefs and that was that.

After a paddle in calm seas and little breeze and an uneventful pick up at Point Lookout, Jacqueline and I headed off for New York. We left the Ford with Klaas and Anne after driving to the train station at the end of the Washington DC metro. The train took us to the bus station and the bus to Manhattan. A train to Manhattan was about 10 times the price of the bus and took about the same time, so it was a no brainer, despite both of us preferring to go by train. Jacqueline had discovered an Airbnb but we couldn't get into the apartment she had booked until Jason, the owner, arrived home about 8.00pm, so we headed to our first port of call, The Manhattan Kayak Company.

I had read a book written by Eric Stiller 20 years before this trip called *Keep Australia on Your Left.* Eric's father was running the Klepper kayak shop in New York when Eric teamed up with an Australian bloke called Tony Brown and set out from Sydney to paddle around Australia. I remember being impressed at the time, but as I know the New South Wales coastline quite well I thought they were more than a little crazy at the time, and lucky not to have busted their kayak a few times over. The fascination with their trip remained dormant until I made the decision to paddle into New York. I Googled his name, found that he owned the Manhattan Kayak Company (MKC) on the Hudson River, contacted his deputy director, Jules, and organized to meet.

My impression when I met Eric was that he was a bit shorter than me, looked a bit fitter and had an incredible energy about him that seemed difficult to harness sometimes. The photo of us together, however, shows us as exactly the same height and similar in appearance except, at only 55, he is obviously younger. We discovered we looked at the world through similar lenses. Neither of us is materialistic, we both have similar concerns about the environment, we both want people to be connected to the environment, not to machines or computers, and we are both deeply concerned about the state of the world in general, not just environmental aspects. We arranged for me to paddle into the MKC pontoon on 21 June. All I had to do was to get there on that date.

Next day Jacqueline and I went our separate ways, to meet later at the Audubon Society with Heather and her colleagues. The society is all about birds and the environment. Even though many members are strident deniers of climate science, they manage to reach the deniers among them through birds. It doesn't matter what the reason, the important issue is that it was working. We had a very fruitful meeting. The New York arrival date that I had set with Eric was confirmed as fine, and the Audubon Society agreed to allocate a journalist and a photographer to do a story for their 450,000 members. "Good on you Heather," I thought. Like so

Bud and Charlie

many achievements of the trip, a chance sighting of our kayak crate with its huge sticker had brought totally unexpected outcomes.

After the meeting, Jacqueline and I headed off to see the Ground Zero site and the spectacular new building that had just opened. I was walking towards Ground Zero but not sure how far we had to go. We had just entered a construction site area with a white hoarding and a roof over the pavement. I stopped.

"We are here," I breathed quietly. "This is it."

"How do you know?"

"I feel it. Let's not go there."

However, we continued to the great square holes in the ground with the impressive marble, names of victims around the edge, sheer walls and running water way down below. I was very uncomfortable. I wanted to pay my respects, but I felt like an intruder. I had experienced this once before in 2009. It is a feeling of death, of dread, of indescribable sadness and pain. Then, I had been paddling across Lake Somerset, the reservoir behind Somerset Dam near Brisbane. The feeling was so powerful that I hurriedly paddled away as fast as possible. I had thought I was an atheist but, after that experience in 2009, I admit to something I would call spiritual. How else can I account for what I felt? Only later did I realise that I was above the confluence of two rivers, a place known as Gunundjin to the original inhabitants, meaning 'hollow place'. It had become a place of drowned spirits – 50,000 years of settlement in Australia has produced plenty of evidence that science does not understand everything.

Obviously, by the sheer numbers of visitors to Ground Zero, most people probably don't feel as I do. On entering parliament, Australia's immigration minister visited the site. He came home invigorated and set to preside over cruel policies that have caused the deaths of many people and destroyed thousands of lives, all in the name of protecting our borders. I guess one man's dread is another man's exaltation.

Our foray into New York, albeit just Manhattan and Harlem, left me with a taste for more. I was surprised by its sheer liveability, its energy and its humanity, but there was other work to do for now. Klaas and Anne's party camp needed to be relocated to a park near Annapolis now that the holiday weekend was over and, of course, there was still a lot of paddling to do. I caught the 12.30am bus to Washington DC. Jacqueline was under pressure to get her university assignment finished, so she stayed in New York another day to work on it and to see a Broadway show.

My plan had been to arrive early enough into Washington DC to allow Klaas to get to the metro station before the traffic started to get heavy. Surprisingly, the plan worked. The bus arrived about 5.00am, I whizzed through the city stations and out to the pick-up point before most of Washington was out of bed. Klaas arrived by himself! Wow, he didn't bring Anne with him. Had I known that, I would have been very concerned about him with no-one to help interpret the GPS and navigate the tricky bits. Luckily, I didn't know, so I didn't worry. He was fine.

Yes, Klaas was fine! This was when I knew he was back. Whatever demons had caused the disconnections in his brain, my mate was back. He had some subsequent problems when disoriented, but he was back on track and he stayed back.

It seemed that while we had been away, every night had been a party. They had made lots of friends and even organized a taxi tour of Washington DC. My boring old paddling stories, or even those of New York and Eric, couldn't compete with theirs.

We moved the van to the RV park near Annapolis. Jacqueline finished her course assignment and arrived the morning after the move and it was time to get back on the water again. It had to be a short day because Renate was flying into Reagan Airport. We decided to run the next leg backwards so there could be no possibility of missing the pick-up time and not get to Renate. That would be a pretty bad start for someone who had given up three weeks to help with the trip, had paid for the airfare herself and had donated a few hundred dollars. I therefore set out from Cove Point and paddled back down to Point Lookout.

The wind was direct on shore and less than 10 knots, just as the forecast said. With the sail set up reasonably tight for the reach, the first eight kilometres flew by. As the wind strengthened and control became impossible, I pulled the sail down and headed across the bay in a direct line for the next point. With waves above head height, I was looking seawards most of the time and concentrating on the swells coming towards me. Occasionally, I would get a good runner and skip along the top of the swell and down the back, but most of the time I was simply trying to keep reasonably straight. That meant a lot of pressure on the pedals as the kayak slewed into the troughs.

The next open stretch across a wide bay between the points was worse, with waves about 1.5 times head height and lots of white water. Still, it was nothing compared to the ride up by the Royal National Park cliffs on my way from Wollongong to Cronulla, way back in January. Up ahead, Point Lookout faded into the rain as it started to bucket down. The pick-up time was 1.00pm and I was going flat out trying to get there by then.

There is a causeway out to Point Lookout and, while I watched the white foam on the rocks with tentacles spitting over the concrete topping wall, Jacqueline drove across the causeway in the wrong direction. Still nearly 300 metres off shore, I knew she would have no chance of seeing me. It was about 12:45 and I reckoned that I could make it by 1:00pm so, if she was off looking for me elsewhere, I would have to go and sit in the toilet block out of the driving rain.

It was raining even harder and the wind was blowing the tops off the waves as I aimed for the small beach about a kilometre away, but still out of sight. The vehicle re-appeared ahead, Jacqueline jumped out and scrambled along the top of the rocks. "Get out of the rain, back in the car," I thought, willing her to take care of herself. She continued her mad scramble until I eventually managed to convey by hand signals to go back to the car. She indicated that she would drive to the small beach at the other end of the rocks, exactly where we had originally agreed.

With that crucial communication successfully conveyed, it was time to think about the landing. I hung back 30 metres from my destination on the sand, watching the waves carefully. Jacqueline bounced the car to the rocks just above the beach. I snapped the rudder up and locked it into place. Three large waves passed underneath and it was time to commit, follow the last wave of the set and ride onto the beach behind it. Bugger! The set was four waves, bad mistake. Up we went, a metre above the sand. "Uh oh, done this before," flashed through my mind. We slewed sideways almost in the air and then crashed unceremoniously onto the sand. Out like a flash, I grabbed the bow and hauled the kayak up the beach and above the waves. The sail was loose where the force had broken the elastic cord strapping it to the deck, but otherwise the only serious damage was to my pride.

Soaking wet, Jacqueline helped me to get the kayak over the rocks and into the roof box. My trip had been a bit of fun for me, but quite worrying for her. She said that she was amazed to see me right on time at the right location. She had been off to talk to the Point Lookout State Park people and had an emergency number to ring. Because she was close to the shore and could see its fury, the sea looked very ominous to her. There was also a small boats warning because of the dangerous weather. To me it was just a bit worse than the day I turned turtle on the Rappahannock: another day at the office, really.

First task was to call into the park station and report all was well. Then we headed for the showers only to find that the park was closed, due to the bad weather. It was what we would call a rain depression in Eastern Australia, not a cyclone, but warming up to one. With no other options, Jacqueline changed in the front seat of the car while I stood out of the wind under the rear lift-up door. Soon we were reasonably dry and warm and set off looking for some hot chips. Camaraderie forms in such circumstances. Jacqueline was relieved that I was okay and I was touched that she was so concerned.

People say that I am extreme, but I don't see it that way. Many men and women do much more extreme sports than I would ever do. Maybe I have just spent all of my life in and around the water and am more comfortable with what is dished up. It took me a long time to realise that most people look at the sea and make a snap judgement. When my kids were little I used to make them watch the surf with me for at least 10 minutes before they were allowed go in. We looked at where the flows were, along the beach and at the rips, where the waves were dumping, the length of time between sets and how many waves in a set. It was basic stuff, but gave them the tools to read the sea: tools that should last for the rest of their lives. As a result, what is comfortable for me is perceived as dangerous by others. On the other hand, often when I perceive a problem, many other people are oblivious.

We found hot chips about an hour up the road to Washington DC, headed for the airport, picked up Renate, and then spent two hours in traffic before reaching Klaas and Anne at the RV park. All in all, a most varied day and, in my mind, very successful with all goals accomplished. That was the last stint with Jacqueline as the pick up. Our last few days had drawn us quite close so I was pleased that she had decided to return for the UK and French legs. Jacqueline had helped me get 550 kilometres up the eastern coast of America and there had been fringe benefits, so it had been like a holiday. Now my friend Renate, a rock of support, and both compassionate and efficient, would make sure we would arrive in New York on time. The end of one era, the start of the next.

CHAPTER 14

INTO THE BIG APPLE

We drove Jacqueline to the airport for her long flight home to Brisbane and Renate and I set off for Cove Point. Although we'd had extensive email contact and a few phone calls, this was only the third time Renate and I had met. She had lived in New Orleans for more than two decades, having emigrated from Germany after being swept off her feet by an American serviceman. Her car has hand-painted signs about climate change all over it: a source of great embarrassment for her son. One day, sitting near the car, he was approached by two lovely young ladies who complimented him on it. They got chatting and he finally realised what an asset it could be, absolutely eclipsing his existing, best pick-up lines.

Renate lived through Hurricane Katrina and what she told me was truly shocking. The stadium that was full of people in appalling conditions during the flooding is a prominent city feature. Surrounded by elevated freeways, you pass it on most journeys around the city. The elevated freeways were way above the floods. They could be used to drive in and out of the city the whole time. The stadium is just 150 metres from a freeway.

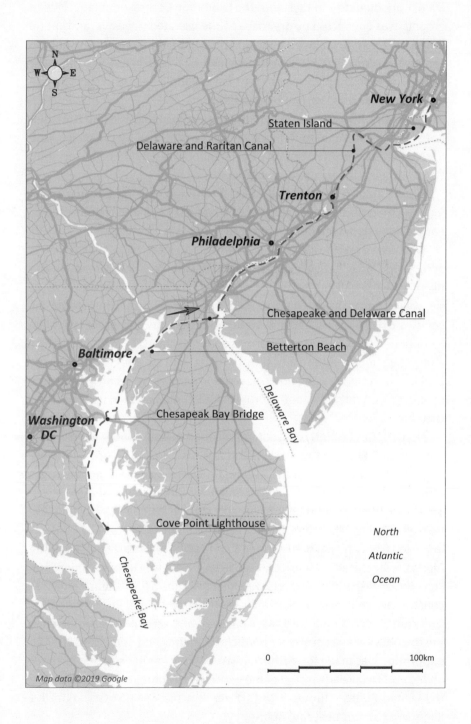

Even more dumbfounding is that the Exhibition Centre, on relatively high ground, was connected by dry roads to the elevated freeways, and yet no buses were sent to collect the crowds that gathered there. In desperation some of the crowd walked up onto the nearby bridge to cross to the other side of the Mississippi, but were sent back. People had been shot, people were scared, and yet no-one helped them.

When the floodwaters receded, Renate's husband returned to their house. While cleaning up the yard he was approached by the police. Had it not been for the intervention of a neighbour he would have been shot. Why? My guess is because he is black.

Renate and her husband split a long time ago. She has a new partner, Rick, with whom she is very happy. She had only a year to retirement and had decided to devote her life to climate activism.

We arrived at the Cove Point lighthouse, next to a beach that is accessible from the lighthouse carpark. Renate was beach-ready in her bikini, which, I must admit, made me think how good she looked and yet she was about to retire. The carpark is large enough to accommodate the vehicles used by guests for the wedding receptions and other functions held there. This is important information for kayakers, as everywhere else along the shore is all private: private roads with no parking and private beaches with signs saying no access. Bloody charming. As an Australian, I couldn't give a rat's arse for their rules, but Renate has been better trained than me.

North of Cove Point, large communication aerials dot the shore. Many of them look like giant drive-in movie screens from a distance. Some are huge domes. They presumably serve a military purpose. There is a gas terminal about a kilometre long, parallel with the shore and quite a way out from where I paddled. Enormous gas storage facilities hide behind the hills adjacent to the beach. Originally commissioned in 1972 to hold gas imported from Algeria, between 1978 and 1980 it fell into disuse when the Algerians increased their prices, then from 1994 it was used to liquefy and store local LNG. In 2003 imports were resumed and a fifth storage tank was constructed, thus making the facility both domestic and import oriented. Unfortunately, the imported gas is different and serious leaks occurred in the distribution system amidst predictable claims and denials. In 2013 an application was made for further construction of gas liquefaction facilities and export to take advantage of the gas fracking contagion that has seized the United States. Thrown into this mix is a nuclear power station five kilometres away. Locals are not happy.

I don't care if it is private property, I'm going in.

Coming up towards the Chesapeake Bay Bridge with so many boats about, I guess it was inevitable that I would see a race, but I didn't expect to be in one. A 40-foot yacht was on a collision course with me. My sail was on the left, meaning the wind was from starboard. The other boat had the sail on the right, meaning I had right of way. My speed was slower but in the mad, frantic race that I was having I was surfing waves at 17km/hr, which is not too shabby. Should I call right of way? Maybe I would have in Australia, but maybe their rules are opposite here? Discretion won and I passed about 10 metres behind their stern. The frenetic pace continued all the way to the Bay Bridge, where I pulled into Mezick Ponds in Sandy Point State Park, just after the bridge and Renate took me back to Klaas and Anne for a shower and a sleep.

The wind blew all night and was a howling 25 knots when we reached the water at 7.30am for my paddle from Sandy Point to Howell Point. Luckily it was from the south east, because one does not paddle against that sort of blow. Keeping to my safety regime, I paddled sideways across the waves towards Love Point on the other side of the bay. After about seven kilometres I reckoned, if the worst happened, I would be blown further up the bay but still on the eastern side where I was headed. That was about 14 kilometres, away but a lot better than about 70 kilometres if I missed it.

With such a strong wind, there was no chance of hoisting a sail. The waves hid the horizon when they rolled past, indicating they were above head height. I tried not to catch a wave, but some of the smaller ones picked me up when I least expected it. Close to the eastern side, one of these shot me along even faster than the day before.

A lone seagull flew against the wind towards me. Feeling the air, it almost touched the waves, drifted up and to my right, only to plunge back towards the water and swoop to my left. Underpowered, it felt its way slowly: threading through the wind, going to who knows where. About five minutes later a shag came along a similar path but with rapid, purposeful flapping about three feet above the water. It powered past. The difference was like a Mack truck compared to a postie bike.

After about 23 kilometres I was safely across, found a small beach and called Renate to let her know all was well. I wanted to take a photo as I came in with the bow of the kayak way above the land behind it, as a wave rolled underneath, but it was out of the question. You can't put the paddle down in conditions like that to take a photo because it is all that keeps you upright. The Rappahannock experience wasn't something I was keen to repeat. The shoreline bent slightly to the right, so the wind came from behind my right shoulder, while the waves refracted towards the shore and came a bit from the left. The balance was perfect and I rocketed along with the sail up.

I discovered a neat little harbour snuggled into the bank providing acres of roofed area for power boats plus moorings for 40 or so sailing boats. I was keen to photograph it, but as I went past the entrance I was doing 13km/hr, just about on the plane and very busy staying upright. It was a screamer of a run up that shore. Many times, the wind tried to knock the kayak flat, but each time, I managed to dig us out. That skill comes from wave skiing, which is like riding the waves with a cork up your bum; and from K1 racing, which takes at least three months before your reactions prevent you from being unexpectedly beside the kayak instead of in it.

I arrived at the pick-up point at Howell Point before time but Renate wasn't there. The message on the phone was that it was all private and she was at Betterton Beach, another four kilometres or so further on. I was getting heartily sick of this private ownership of foreshore so had another pee on their beach, this time with feeling, before setting off again.

For more than half the day, I had heard booming noises every few minutes. Sometimes it was like distant thunder, sometimes it was followed by a sharper sound 20 kilometres further south. Renate heard it as well, so I wasn't dreaming. I guessed it was some sort of military work. For the whole east coast journey the military had been present in some form or another, from the roar of aircraft, to acres of aerials, loud explosions and staccato fire that moved 30 kilometres in a few seconds.

This ever-present military and the war graves I encountered on the bike ride made me think of that day at Ground Zero. America is like a powerful tiger and 9/11 was like poking the tiger in the eye. The War on Terror was simply the tiger lashing out irrationally. My big concern with all this militarism was the division we saw among the people. The biggest war America has ever had, the one with the largest loss of life, was fought among themselves. It seemed to me that, particularly given the conflict that climate change will cause in the next few decades, the United States might not be 'united' for much longer. I suspect we will see serious internal strife within the lifetime of many people alive today.

Next day, my last on Chesapeake Bay, the wind was favourable. Setting out from Betterton Beach, it increased gradually as I came away from the lee shore. I had paddled up the arm, through the palm and was now into the fingers of the mighty Chesapeake. The route was up the little finger, smallest and to the right. My map gave me enough information to know exactly where I was. The thunder from the east bank of the bay started at 9:15am and echoed all the way to the top but, because the distance was getting greater, only the really big rumbles reached me. Renate heard much more down at Betterton where she waited before she set off for our pick-up point at St Georges on the Chesapeake and Delaware (C&D) Canal.

As I paddled the Elk River and reached the start of the canal to the Delaware River, I wondered where the boats were. At previous canal entries, there had been a steady procession showing me the way. As if on cue, a huge stink-boat roared past, trailing a metre-high wake. Two more followed close behind, but both of those slowed down for the kayak. The canal is like a river for the first bit, so I guess that is the natural part and the actual canal structure starts after that. This is where the first bridge crosses and where I encountered a car transport ship coming towards me. It was actually going slower than I can paddle so the wake was negligible.

Nonetheless, it was hugely impressive to have such a behemoth trundle past.

As the shore line had squeezed in on both sides as I paddled up the bay, I had noted a pretty good current in my favour and it increased to about three knots in the canal. With the wind behind me, which built to a gusty 20 knots, I just sat and enjoyed an average speed of 13km/hr while doing nothing except to stay upright. It was by far the easiest ride of the trip and I reckoned about time after nearly 4,000 km.

Nothing lasts forever, though. A speed boat approached as I neared the pick-up point. The person standing near the bow waved me down. I turned around into the wind and dropped the sail. It was a policewoman with a policeman driving the boat.

"You can't kayak on the canal," she yelled.

I drifted closer, "Then how do I get to New York?"

They had no answer and were not very sympathetic. "It's only about a mile to the end so I've nearly finished," I pleaded.

Rules are rules and it seemed a mile, 10 miles, a yard, whatever, broke the rules. After some discussion she suggested that maybe I could get permission to paddle the canal from the US Army Corps of Engineers.

"Sometimes it's better to seek forgiveness than permission," was my response.

Mum used to say, "Steve, nobody likes a smartarse." It's a shame I didn't listen to her.

The safety mantra had been trotted out a number of times. They watched as, for my safety, I paddled over to the rock wall and turned around into the current. Again, for my safety, I clung to a slippery rock with three knots of current trying to grab the kayak, climbed out onto those rocks and dragged my 70-kilogram kayak five metres up the rock wall to the top of the bank. Satisfied, they sped off in the direction I had come, returning about half an hour later after patrolling the whole length of the canal, I guess.

Because I had been so fast, with the current and wind both in my favour, Renate was over half an hour away. I settled down under the bridge to wait. She finally arrived, closely followed by a police car. The boating coppers had seen me sitting there. They really hadn't trusted me, eh? To be honest, I had tossed up what to do. Maybe run the last three kilometres at night, maybe start early just after sunrise? Because I was in a foreign country and on my best behaviour, and because these cops don't

Smooth talkin' Aussie (off the Chesapeake & Delaware canal)

seem to understand the flexibility of rules, I decided to skip that bit of the journey and start again at the northern end of the canal.

Dan, the policeman sent to check on me, was a hoot. His round belly sent peals of laughter out under his huge moustache. We got on like a house on fire. Most contacts we had with police, troopers and sheriffs were a pleasure. The culture in the US is a lot different to what I am used to, though. In Australia, people are allowed to think. It is similar in the UK. Based on my experience, I imagine that the law in Australia, having appraised the situation, would have said something like this:

"You have now been told that you are not allowed on the canal with a kayak. I have to finish my patrol to the end of the canal and back. That will take half an hour and if I catch you here I will have to arrest you."

Having said that, we both would have known that I had half an hour to do whatever I had to do and we all would have been covered. This difference between cultures confronted us many times. Maybe we colonials are still too close to our convict history, but I don't think it is that. Americans are just much more inclined to do as they are told and have a much higher regard for authority than we do. On the other hand, the boat crews on the Mississippi were able to think for themselves in ways that Australians are no longer allowed to do. Society is complicated.

Cutting out a couple of kilometres was a big deal to me, but we did need to keep the local coppers happy. The morning start point was at a narrow cut-through from the canal to the Delaware River. I had forgotten to take the camera. Bugger! The Delaware State Police – Marine Unit must be on Canal Road because I saw the boat that had apprehended me for my own safety yesterday. Near the exit onto the Delaware River, a small barge-type boat with a crane on the front and two guys on board chugged slowly along. They had to travel at zero-wash speed so I managed to catch and then pass them. They reckoned I was a show off and I replied that some Aussies are just like that. Out onto the Delaware River they went past me with the tide against us at less than a knot. The west bank curved off into the distance into the smog with the ubiquitous, oval water reservoirs hovering above the trees. It was almost like the Mississippi: same width, same huge bends but without the huge current. I straight-lined it, heading for the tip of the far bank, which was actually an island. Paddling through the shipping channel on the other side, I had to avoid ships doing 10 times the speed of those in the canal. The island was some sort of hub with birds commuting back and forth: shags, cranes, ducks and some seagulls.

After 10 kilometres, I was confronted with a deeply curved shoreline and had the option of continuing in a straight line or following the edge. The current still wasn't too bad so the decision was to go straight. Not too smart really, as the outgoing tide picked up to nearly three knots. It was a tough battle all the way to the Delaware Memorial Bridge about 16 kilometres from the start. Although I could see the bridge from a long way off, I could see nothing beyond it. Smog blanketed everything else. Way over on the west bank a horn blared a warning about something and staccato barrages of heavy-weapon fire rang out, but I was intent on my struggle with the current. About a kilometre before the bridge I pulled over to the shore to fit the skirt in anticipation of increasing wind and waves.

The bridge came and went, and so did the wind. I hugged the shore, which was a residential area interspersed with patches of trees and grass. A few rock groins jutted out into the river to clean the shipping channel out in flood, just like the Mississippi. They were a bit ragged, with many of the top blocks having been washed off, indicating that the floods must be pretty strong. An abandoned island, with a fallen-down bridge emerging from a street by an abandoned building, completed a picture of decay. A guy in a white T-shirt jumped up from behind a bush and started battling a fish. His rod bent as he struggled and two more guys appeared. A big catfish, well over 60-centimetres long was dragged out of the murky waters amidst cheers from his mates.

Eventually, I made it to the Talen Energy Stadium to meet Renate but, with the skirt on and the temperature at 33°C degrees, I was cooked. Dipping my hat in the water all the way had simply changed the cooking method from roasted to boiled. I was pretty much done-in and needed a rest before loading the kayak into the box. A few beers when we arrived back at the van soon fixed me up. A couple of Western Australians from Bunbury rolled in to the RV park, complete with guitar. With our neighbours, who hailed from Connecticut, we had a party. Klaas has an excellent voice and he often serenaded us with the guitar that Nick had bought him in Austin. He called it a night maybe at about 9.30pm, I can't remember exactly, saying that Stevie Boy needed to go to bed.

Next morning at 3.30am I was glad he had done that. When I had left the C&D Canal and headed up the Delaware River I had departed from the Intracoastal. It went out to sea, but with Warren's assistance I had a plan to paddle an old canal over to the New York system. Now back on the water and up the Delaware towards the next canal, I was close to the end of the tidal zone as evidenced by the lack of tidal flow. I didn't know what that meant, but eventually found out. Renate was at a ramp about five kilometres before the scheduled finish, bearing news that there were rapids up ahead and, also, a small waterfall in the canal that we had thought might provide a continuous water route. I had a cooling swim, shoved the kayak in its box and we set off to explore Trenton and find a walking route that would avoid the maze of freeways. We found one with about nine kilometres of walking to the canal launch site before heading back to the van.

Renate was methodical with pickups and the whole time she was there, everything operated like clockwork. Klaas is Dutch and Renate is German. Klaas is very free spirited, sometimes even a bit of a rogue, whereas Renate is as straight-laced as you get. Occasionally there was a bit of strain in the van, but nothing serious.

Klaas and Anne had been having a ball again, but Klaas was missing his dog, Wolfie. Jacqueline had advised us she was coming back for the UK leg, so Klaas and Anne decided to fly home as soon as they arrived in England. This was a relief, as I could not figure out how to accommodate everyone through England and France, even though my goal had been to get to Paris with Klaas. It was mid-summer and school holidays, but I managed to get a half reasonable price for them, flying Garuda from the UK back to Australia. It would have been a lot cheaper to just fly them from New York, but the Queen Mary had been booked and paid for, and they were really looking forward to the trip.

The morning began with heavy rain but, as we were not dependent on tides, it was a comfortable start time of 6.00am. The rain stopped before we unloaded the kayak. Wondering whether my feet would stay dry, I set off on the walk through the streets of Trenton. Traffic was still light, although many people were out and about. Renate leapfrogged with the car and took some good images. The route was along the Delaware River bank for about a mile, around the edge of the city and then along the canal bank, past beams spanning the canal to support the concrete walls. Along the river bank, signs described how productive the wetland on the opposite bank had been, even as late as 1915. Both Native Americans and European settlers used the Delaware Falls, just upstream of the wetlands, to walk across the river: so it had been a focal point for a very long time.

Dug by Irish immigrants between 1831 and 1834, the canal links the Delaware and Raritan Rivers and thus New York to the Delaware. Starting off noisy from nearby traffic, becoming quiet and serene for many miles past Princeton University, and then noisy again coming into New Brunswick, it is such a notable journey that I was surprised to be the only paddler. Not that I am competitive (ha ha), but I wanted to finish the canal in a day. For the record, in case anyone wants to beat it, from the Delaware to the end of the canal at the Raritan River it is 62 kilometres and it took 11hrs 10mins. That's nine kilometres walking and 53 paddling, not counting the portages around the locks, of which I think there were five, but maybe it was six. Whatever, there are enough to make a paddler well and truly over them by the end of the day.

Next day was an easy paddle from New Brunswick to Staten Island, but bleak with lots of smog. The river is brown and murky until you get towards the mouth and then becomes much clearer. Around Staten Island it was salty and a very slight swell rolled in from the Atlantic.

The landing point was at Great Kills State Park on Staten Island. Renate arrived early and had a very memorable experience taking pictures of hundreds of horseshoe crabs which mate for only about a week each year.

Renate's blog: *The landing is perfect and will be easy for Steve to spot. I have several hours at the beach, but it's foggy, windy and cool. I decide to walk down the beach, collecting shells, taking pictures of heaps of plastic trash – washed up or left behind? Around the corner and into the calmer bay I run into a green horseshoe crab on the water's edge. It's not moving; is it alive? I grab a stick to gently move it. It feels like it's suctioned to the ground. Here comes another one. Wow, three in a row in the sand, like a choo-choo train! Over there are five in a heap. Way up on the beach a horseshoe crab on its back. Not moving, but all organs still look intact. Must have just died.*

I'm standing in the water, utterly amazed. Horseshoe crabs following each other, some heading straight for me like little slow-moving puppies, turning around – wrong mate. Haha, those two are using a condom! A large plastic bag got in between them. The one out there in the water sticking up its tail must be a water acrobat. Horseshoe crabs are everywhere on this beach, clinging to each other, digging into the sand or crawling around. I'm utterly fascinated.

When loading up the kayak we talk to a guy who is familiar with the wildlife in this area. The horseshoe crabs mate for only about one week each year. They are a 4–5 days late this year, because the water has been slightly cooler. (Due to this year's cold winter, or the slowing Gulf Stream?) Horseshoe crabs are 450-million-year-old living fossils. Their blue blood is used to test medical equipment for bacteria. Numbers on the US East Coast have declined because crabs die if they experience too much stress.

Overnight, my strange feelings of achievement that I had experienced way back on the Gulf of Mexico were building. I felt anticipation that I was close to something monumental. I was about to paddle into New York! Me, an Aussie: a long way from home but with countless tales to tell.

Passing under the Verrazano-Narrows Bridge (the longest bridge in the world from 1964 until 1981 and 3.5 times as long as the Sydney Harbour Bridge) the Manhattan skyline was straight ahead with the Statue of Liberty just visible.

The Statue of Liberty!

Should I pinch myself to make sure I wasn't dreaming?

Nope, too busy.

The wind blew directly towards the statue, so I straight-lined across the harbour. It was necessary to keep my wits about me with so much shipping traffic, but it was quite manageable. The route was across the line of the Staten Island ferries. A pusher tug with a large barge came out fast from the left and after making some rough waves, flattening the seas behind it for a few minutes. A large container ship controlled by three tugs crossed my line, going slowly to stern. After they reached a buoy in the harbour, the two tugs at the stern pushed the ship around 90 degrees, pointing it towards the bridge and the open sea.

Finally, I was near the Statue. Three groups of barges, about a kilometre apart and filled with rocks and gravel, provided a bit of a wind break for me to take photos. Holding the camera at arm's length, I recorded my thoughts with the Statue of Liberty in the background. Hoody complained that he could hardly see the statue, but it was the best I could do with what I had.

It was pretty rough and I didn't have the spray skirt on, but I did soak up the scene. Here was I, at the Big Apple after coming all the way from the Gulf of Mexico and probably being the only person to have paddled up a flooded Lower Mississippi. There was still a long way to go, but this was a big, big milestone. I think we all felt it as I sailed in to Liberty Park behind Liberty Island.

*It feels great
(New York)*

My diary from around that time says: "I miss Australia. I miss my family. I miss home."

I was a very long way from home, on a global journey about a global problem. I had made a major milestone, New York, but did not feel like I was succeeding on my mission. This email from Harriet who organized a group meeting in Central Park helped a lot and boosted me along. I'm not sure Harriet or any of the others who have sent me inspirational messages understand just how much it means, but they are everything, especially when you are lonely, feeling down and not confident that what you are doing is worthwhile.

Thanks Steve,

So glad you could be our reason to get together! Your journey is so inspiring. One of my 'climate heroes' is a Canadian artist and climate activist, Franke James. She likes to say we must "do the hardest thing first" if we are going to work to solve this. Thanks for leading the way. Wishing you much success, good adventures and a positive spirit. We must keep going and we must win. We have no other choice. With much respect and admiration.

Harriet

I'm guessing that Harriet is about 25 years younger than me, a generation that will pick up after we die. If only there were more Harriets in the world.

That connection with the Central Park crew and the exhilaration at reaching New York contrasted markedly with the separation from my family and the sense that I was terribly alone on this journey. I did not dwell on that contrast, but those feelings – at such a significant milestone – are an important part of my eventual understanding about the journey we must take as climate activists.

We sold the van and the Ford as a package. The loss, counting a replacement fridge in New Orleans, was $16,000. That was over a five-month period and both did their jobs admirably. The upside was that they went to a couple with young children, so I was glad that someone good was to benefit from our loss.

Renate flew to Germany to see her family. What a find she had been. She was super organised and helpful and very reliable. Although she usually hangs in the background just doing the work that an organization needs, she is strong willed and very determined. The climate movement needs her.

We contacted Connor who tried to get our story into a newspaper in Australia, but the feedback I received was the story was already covered. There had been ten words written in The Fitz Files, a very popular column by Peter Fitzsimons, a legendary raconteur. Popular as Peter's column is, it is hardly the kind of coverage I had hoped to achieve. Kirsten from The Farm Digital advised that they could no longer afford to promote the trip. The mayor of New York had not been interested in meeting us. All of these were disappointing but we were inured now. What was of utmost importance to us was of little interest to others. Individuals that we thought were totally on board to spread the climate emergency message were only there as part of their jobs and when push came to shove they had other things to do.

At least Harriet and Renate gave me faith that I was part of something and not completely alone.

PART 4

ENGLAND AND FRANCE

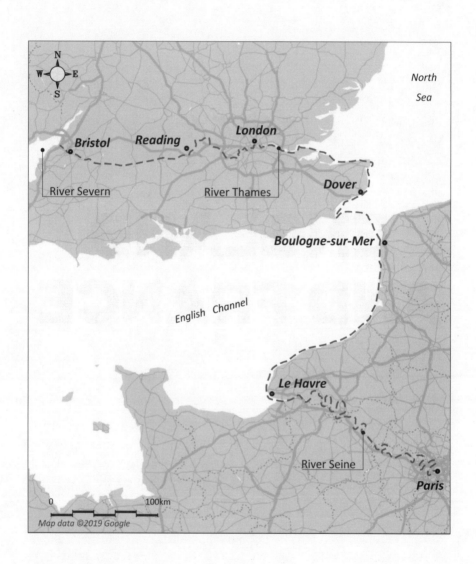

CHAPTER 15

DIFFERENT PERSPECTIVES

When we boarded the Queen Mary 2 in New York, my kayak was the last item loaded onto the ship. I had waited hours, looking over the railing, watching for something to happen on the dock five floors below me. It was an anxious time, but I need not have worried. Although it was the very last item to be loaded, the Cunard staff handled it perfectly. It was also at no cost, just baggage as part of my ticket.

This was my first cruise and the Queen Mary 2 is magnificent. To me life on board was opulent and I soaked up all the information about the ship that I could. We had five metre following seas one day and the great ship hardly moved. I didn't mind that my cabin was on the inside, it was just for sleeping anyway. This was far better than any aeroplane ride. Anne and Klaas enjoyed the seven days to London. It was a trip to remember and I did meet some lovely people but, driven as I was to paddle to Paris, I couldn't really relax and appreciate it. Maybe another time, another

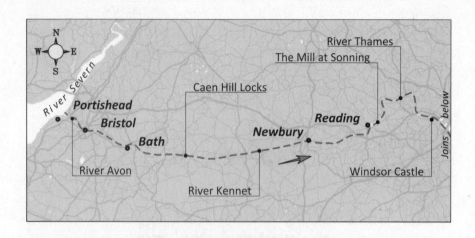

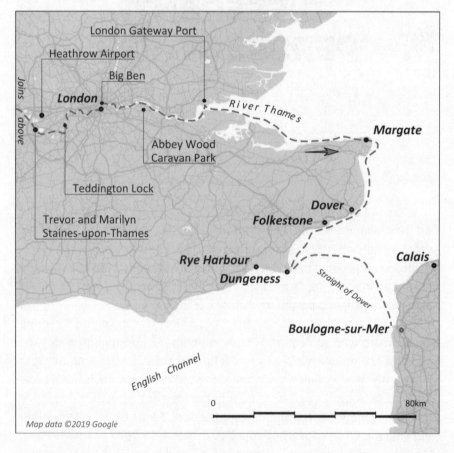

*Old Yella lines up beside
Queen Mary 2 (New York)*

place, with someone to share it with. Again, that nagging desire for companionship.

Arriving at Southampton in the United Kingdom early Wednesday 22nd July, the anxiety about the kayak returned. You have to wait your turn to get off the ship, and our turn was towards the end, so I spent quite a while trying not to worry. Eventually, we were allowed down the gangplank and into the baggage pick-up area. The kayak was there, on its wheels over against the wall. Phew! All I had to do was wheel it out the door, albeit struggling through some tight bends, where I found Klaas and Anne waiting with their baggage.

In England, with a six metre kayak weighing over 100 kilograms, two friends booked to fly to Australia the next day, and nothing organized whatsoever – no worries! There are lots of cars, buses, taxis and huge throngs of people around when the Queen Mary 2 docks. I threaded my way through the mayhem, parked the kayak in a bus parking space and headed off to see what I could find. The security guys at the gate told me about a long-term car park back near the terminal and within half an hour that problem was solved. The kayak was snuggled in behind the car park's office and could stay there until it opened again the following Tuesday.

Next problem was to find a car – I had given up trying to do that on board with the slow internet. In great hope I set off walking to an area where there were a couple of hire car businesses. They were all very busy and I was last in line at the last place. They had one car left, a Mercedes. It was a lot of money for a three-day hire and drop off at Heathrow airport, but there was no other option. With a big number now weighing on my credit card, I drove back to the terminal, picked up Klaas and Anne, and delivered them in style to their hotel at Heathrow. They flew home to Australia the next day and I started the next chapter of the voyage.

My base was in Staines, next to Heathrow, at Trevor and Marilyn's house. Staying there is more like staying with family than friends. Trevor was my boss in Libya in 1977, which doesn't seem that long ago really. He is a great engineer who had been retired for seven years and was now doing other fun stuff. The day of the week he likes most is when he puts on his Concorde uniform with a British Airways tie. That is the day he shows people through the Concorde at the Brooklands Museum. He helps in the workshop for another day, is an assistant lock-keeper on the Thames one day per week, and a volunteer boat builder on Saturdays. Volunteer work is popular in the UK and seems to be a very important part of society, as it is in Australia. Some of the engineering things Trevor taught me have never left me. He was my first and best mentor.

Klaas and Anne confirmed they had arrived home okay.

Klaas said he was 10 kilograms heavier and his dog Wolfie was 5 kilograms heavier. Klaas reckoned it wouldn't be a problem to fix either

The rig for England and France (Southampton)

of them. Anne didn't advise me what had happened to her, but I thought she might be in for the same diet and exercise regime about to beset Klaas and Wolfie. With nothing to worry about there, my process of establishing myself in a new country started again: a phone, an internet connection, a car, insurance, a caravan.

By Sunday, having arrived the previous Thursday, I had a 2002 Audi A6 Quattro, complete with a rack for the kayak and a towbar for a caravan. The rack was a timber construction built on Trevor's driveway, fastened to the roof bars and designed to support the kayak along its length. If you are happy with high mileage, an old car like the 2002 Audi is cheap in the UK and does the job just fine as long as nothing serious goes wrong.

Telephone and portable wifi were sorted out with Trevor's help. I really needed him for this, because the UK is problematic for overseas credit cards. Many organizations, for services like topping up phone credit or paying vehicle tax, will only take UK cards. Jacqueline was coming over to the UK but had not yet committed to a date, so I just busied myself setting up the caravan, hoping she wouldn't take too long. Ably assisted by Trevor, I got a reasonable deal on the van, but it came with no accessories. As in any new country it was difficult to find where to get things, and I was learning how the British do it, which is vastly different from the US and Australia. The local Homebase hardware shop is what I would call 'boutique'. They have lots of different products, even some bedding and electrical goods, but it is about a quarter the size of a decent Bunnings store in Australia. When you travel, you miss your familiar brands and the ways things work. I had the same issue buying car parts. I didn't find anything like a decent Supercheap Auto store. Most things – like tools, adhesives, timber, hinges, screws, rope and so on – cost more in pounds than Australian prices are in dollars. At £1 = $2.20, that meant they were more than twice the price. That is the case until you work out where to go. Shop right and you can halve the price, but it takes ages to learn.

Because I had time to spare, I decided to pay some 'rent' and help Trevor and his son Simon cut the back garden hedge. The hedge runs around four properties and is about six metres high. The first half of the first day was easy. You can actually stand on the top to cut that, although it gradually sinks below you. Round the corner was a bit different. The trunks were up to 15 centimetres thick, another four metres higher than the rest of the hedge, and had a rose vine growing through the lot of it. I was the one on the top at the time, so drew the sawing duty. To be safe, we had a rope fastened up the trunk that Trevor and Simon pulled from the ground. One particular top had too much vegetation on the wrong side, so I cut it as the guys pulled. Slowly but surely they pulled it on top of me, rose thorns and all. I emerged a bleeding mess, and Trevor suggested that I go and wash off because I looked awful.

Next day we went in the other direction. Trevor was like a man possessed as he ploughed along the face, swinging the electric trimmer up and down. At first he had it tied to the top of the ladder, but the process of moving along with it tethered to the ladder was a bit slow. I was underneath, picking up his mess, when the cutter smashed into my arm, hit the ground and broke the handle. "Thought you might have caught that mate," shouted Trevor from the top of the ladder.

We fixed the trimmer, finished the last house, congratulated ourselves on what a fine job we had done and wondered just how many trips we'd have to make to the local recycling depot to get rid of the vast amount of waste trimmings. Apparently this hedge trimming is an annual event and I was lucky enough to share the 2015 occasion with them. I did hope that I might be lucky enough not to share 2016 as well.

After the hedge trimming, I fitted out the caravan, and established it at Devizes. That is a picturesque town near the famous Caen Hill Flight of 29 locks on the Kennet and Avon canal that I would use to get across the hills to the Thames River. It would stay there, as the base camp, until we were about halfway across England. It was August school holidays and finding a camp site had been difficult, so we needed to hold onto this one as long as practicable.

My public message for this leg of the journey would be different. For the US it had been about the folly of disregarding the advice of the scientific agencies, such as NASA, in favour of what politicians had to say. In the UK, both sides of politics accept climate change science as a reality. The challenge here is about energy policy. The UK campaign would be about coal, and Australia's role in increasing greenhouse gases whatever efforts the UK makes. If you circled the earth with Australia's annual coal exports the pile would be higher than you and 4.5 metres wide. Australia is intent on doubling this in the next 10 years. This is morally wrong, dangerous and pretty stupid. No other country in the world emits more CO_2 per capita than Australia and on top of that Australia is the largest exporter of coal – that's not per capita, it is absolutely the largest. To do this, we destroy our own country, including the iconic Great Barrier Reef. When we dig a hole it is big. The proposed Carmichael coal mine in Central Queensland will create a hole in which all of the City of London would fit. That is just one of the mines proposed in the Galilee Basin. In 2000, a group of eight people bought Bimblebox, an 80,000 hectare property in this Basin, with the aid of the federal government, and established an iconic nature reserve. Despite this being held in perpetuity with the strongest laws in Queensland, it is now under threat because 'King Coal' wants it and that subjugates all other laws. How moral is that?

Eventually, Jacqueline managed to get her affairs in order and flew over, albeit later than I had hoped, putting pressure on the Channel crossing. She is frugal, though, so the fare was as cheap as possible, for which I was grateful. We needed to be at Dungeness by 6 September because I had booked a spot with Full Throttle to get across the English Channel in the week of 7 September. That made the crossing legal, taking a load off my mind. Full Throttle provides an escort to take the kayak across the French shipping lanes before sending the kayaker on his way again on the French side. It isn't what I wanted and I didn't want to spend the $2,700 but, c'est la vie, if the French would not allow a kayak in their shipping lanes, there wasn't much else I could do.

I have lots of ideas, some really good, some really dumb, but there had been one rattling around in my head since arriving in the UK. Jacqueline was not enthusiastic and I wondered if it was just an indulgence. Julian Assange was holed up in the Ecuadorian Embassy, less than two kilometres from Chelsea Bridge which I would be passing underneath. He is an Australian and I thought a visit from a fellow Australian paddling halfway round the world might be a boost for him. Besides, it would be interesting to see the man and just say that personally I was grateful for Wikileaks' exposures that the world would otherwise not know about. Although exposed digitally rather than in print, I felt it not dissimilar to the Pentagon Papers in 1971. Then, the US Supreme Court allowed damning reports to be published after a tense court hearing. Not today though, the US is after Mr Assange's hide.

It still plays on my mind that it was a lost opportunity, but England was full of those. I was tired, our publicity efforts had fallen on deaf ears and I wasn't getting any support from Jaqueline. Time was also a pressure, but whatever excuses I make for myself now, the fact is I didn't do it and I regret it. There is always the relentless push to the finish, no matter what. It is the drive that makes for success but it also means that some things are lost on the way.

We launched at Portishead at 9:15am, ready to ride the tide up the Severn River and then the River Avon to Bristol. It was a bleak day – grey water, grey sky and grey mud – with a south easterly wind blowing at 15–18 knots. The air temperature was about 18°C and the water temperature perhaps a bit cooler but it wasn't too bad. It took some skill to find the mouth of the Avon River, but you could say that I have had a bit of practice. It was still pretty muddy with the tide about two thirds of the way in. The wind now came from head on, which was a bit of a problem. It wasn't the wind itself that caused the problem, it was the waves. Because the kayak has wheels, waves splash into the cockpit and run down my back. I should have had the skirt on – mistake number one, and on day number one! Disappointingly, there was not much tidal flow. This is because there is very little volume, despite a tidal range of about nine metres that day, because the river is dammed at Bristol and Bristol Harbour is entered via a lock. This is the same phenomenon as the Delaware at Trenton on the way to New York City, although tides at Bristol can range up to 14 metres, which almost beggars belief.

Bristol is a historic city, with the 'floating' harbour opened in 1809. That must have been a pretty substantial engineering feat back then. Maybe the floating harbour is the most used bit of water in the world? Sailing dinghies, canal boats, large boats, kayaks, canoes, rowing boats, water taxis, you name it, they all use the harbour. Without the dam and the lock, none of this would be possible.

My plan was to paddle around the harbour and up the Avon River, but the lock operators, Michael and Ben, said the tide wasn't big enough to flood the dam and there was no way around it. They put me through the lock after two boats came downstream. I waited for Jacqueline to arrive from Portishead and then purchased a one-day permit to allow me to legally paddle on the harbour. It was a surprise to find that I had paddled all that way quicker than she could drive. I had purchased a GPS for the car, but she reckoned a map was better.

Mistake number two for the day was to leave the camera case at Portishead. It had everything in it, including manual, charging gear and a telephoto lens. Bugger! After going back to look for it and then having a meeting with the Bristol mayor, I only covered 15 kilometres that day. Not a great start, really. Jacqueline had unfortunately broken a significant rule: you leave the camera case in the car when you take the camera out. That rule makes it impossible to leave the case behind on a park bench. Rules and logistics are important on adventures, but not to Jaqueline; she would do what she wanted.

The Mayor of Bristol was George Ferguson. His business card is red and so were his pants. None of that suit-and-tie nonsense for George. He doesn't even own a car and came to meet us on his bike. Bristol was the European Green Capital for 2015. George could speak proudly of Bristol's achievements and their advances in renewable energy, but what could Steve speak about? Well, not much really, except to apologise for the crooks running Australia. You know, the ones that took $1,700 that year from every man, woman and child and gave it to their coal mates. I didn't actually say all that, but I did point out that, no matter what Bristol does in a green way, we can offset that with a few more billion tonnes of coal. Makes ya proud, eh?

I liked George. It would be hard not to like and respect someone who just goes about doing his thing and making a difference to the world. He can be very proud of his city.

I was on the water in Bristol at 8.15am the next day while Jacqueline headed for a camera shop to buy a replacement charger for the Canon camera. It was Saturday, so there were lots of rowers, a couple of kayakers and some walkers on the foreshore probably looking for a coffee somewhere. It didn't take long to paddle through Bristol and then it was back into the countryside again and onto the Avon River. That's the Wiltshire one, not Shakespeare's, about 100 kilometres further up the Severn.

It took 2.5 hours to reach the first lock on the Avon. The drop at the weir was only about 60 centimetres, but it was flowing too fast and was too slippery, so I headed over to the lock. The narrow boat coming out closed the lock gate on me, and by the time I parked and ascertained the situation there were two boats coming down, meaning I had just missed the opportunity to float up while they filled the lock. Narrow boats are so named because they are long and narrow, averaging maybe 18 metres long by 1.8 metres wide. There were no more boats in sight, but they motioned me to paddle in before they came out. They lent me their windlass to fill the lock when they moved out, and stayed to close the top gate when I left. Boat people are kind, friendly and helpful it seems, pretty much worldwide.

At the next lock, about halfway to Bath, I met a group of four stand-up paddle boarders paddling down to Bristol for the day. One of the guys looks after the media for the Bloodhound, which at the time was preparing to be the fastest car in the world – at 1000mph, that's right, miles per hour (1,600km/hr). I love that sort of thing, but I can't help thinking that the money might have been better spent trying to ensure the earth would be liveable for humans in 100 years. Not everyone gets how serious the situation is though.

Paddling on through leafy glades, I saw quite a few sets of steps cut into the bank and a couple of groups cutting some more. Apparently at the end of summer they re-cut the steps and get ready for a winter fishing competition. One of the blokes digging had the temerity to mention the Ashes (a famous cricket series), which Australia had just monumentally lost to England with a record woeful performance.

I replied that "I couldn't really worry about the thoughts of some English nutter digging steps in a canal bank in the middle of nowhere."

Discussions with the Poms are always fun; they give as good as they take, and you can take the piss out of them which is a favourite Australian pastime.

It was warm, 28°C, and two lovely young ladies were swimming along the canal between a couple of barges. They reckoned the water had cooled down, and maybe it had, seeing as their summer was way back in June and lasted two days. Sorry, that's a bit harsh – that day made it three days. It was just a wee bit cool for my liking, but they seemed to be enjoying themselves in the water.

This stretch of waterway was my introduction to UK locks and I was already sick of them. The mob with the stand-up paddle boards said there were two, maybe three to go to Bath, and I had just lugged the kayak up the steps of the fourth one. Jacqueline picked me up at that lock and we called it a day just at the edge of the Bath suburbs.

It was raining heavily at the start the next morning, so I put the skirt on and donned my rain jacket before I left the car. Jacqueline had something to say, but I think it might have been derogatory and about my intelligence, so I deleted the conversation from my memory. Unfortunately, the canal splits off from the city before the centre, so I missed the famous view of the Avon River running over the weir in town. The first lock I met was a bit of a chore. I couldn't fit into the lock because two narrow boats filled it.

Into the Bradford lock with the party boat

The bonus was that when I managed to get out, cross over a busy road, and then get back onto the canal path, I had managed to bypass quite a few locks. The narrow boats would have been at least an hour behind.

The canal skirted around Bath and clung onto the side of the hill. Unbelievably, it then crossed the valley to be perched on the opposite side. I'm told that this aqueduct is nothing compared to the big ones, but it impressed this little black duck. At Bradford-on-Avon, I was trying to figure out how to negotiate a beer garden and cross a busy road to get around its first lock. Luckily some kind merrymakers turned up and I raced back to the kayak and paddled furiously into the lock to get a lift up with their boat. They were on a day boat hire from Bath and were travelling between pubs, but drinking in between as well. A bloke from Hobart was in their team, but that is all I learned. Merriment was their prime objective and I wondered what their trip back in the afternoon might be like.

Jacqueline was scheduled to pick me up at Foxhanger Marina, at Devizes and, like an idiot, I asked some boat people how far it was and how many locks were involved. I soon learned: never ask anyone where you are, how far it is to where you are going, or how many locks there are. You will get a different answer from everyone and most probably none will be right! I paddled to where the canal touches the gravel road at Foxhanger and Jacqueline drove alongside within about five minutes.

Again, the start of the next morning was a lovely English summer day, 15°C and raining. Sure, sometimes the rain reduced to just a heavy mist, but it was wet all the time. Foxhanger is at the base of the famous Caen Hill locks that I mentioned earlier. The distance for me to walk around them, up what was probably the old tow path, was just four kilometres. This took about 45 minutes compared to a day which I reckoned it would take a boat to go through the locks. A few hardy souls wandered along the path in their wellies and a couple of boat teams were traversing the locks. During the day I passed maybe a dozen narrow boats, all with people under umbrellas. It was pouring, I was cold and wet, and we called it a day at 1.30pm so that we could do some emailing to contact mayors and media. The forecast was for just showers and a high of 19°C the next day, so that looked brighter.

When Klaas and I had left Lismore – on our way to Dirk's funeral and Canberra – the mayor, Jenny Dowell, had given me a heap of introductory letters to mayors along the route. They weren't much use in the US, with only the mayor of Vicksburg showing interest. They proved very popular in England, though, with about 50% uptake. Unfortunately, London was on a par with New York for disinterest.

I had some maintenance chores to do in the morning, so paddling didn't start until after midday. Everything was on track for a 5.30pm finish until the locks started in earnest. I eventually finished at 6.45pm after portaging around 30 locks over a 32-kilometer distance. The back wheels had worked loose from all the ups and downs and I was grateful to have picked that up before they fell off and added to my woes.

Along the way, I passed the high point of the canal where the locks started going down rather than up. Just before that was a tunnel. Unfortunately, I had forgotten to bring my torch. Luckily it was only 500 metres long and I could see the other end. I'm not sure what would have happened if a narrow boat had come towards me in the tunnel. Maybe I could have shouted loudly enough to be heard. I'm glad it didn't come to that and the worst that happened was a few scrapes along the wall. Although you can see the light at the end of the tunnel and you aim for the centre of it, without a side reference you drift off. Interestingly, each time I hit the wall it was the left side, even though I tried to compensate after the first scrape.

I only saw 18 boats all day and most crews made jovial comments about the weather. The English seem to take perverse pride in their miserable weather. One poor bloke was on his own and had to drive the boat and operate the locks himself because his wife had gone home. Better to not ask about that, I decided. It must take close to half an hour to get through each lock single handed. Multiply that by the number of locks and it is pretty slow progress. Another bloke assured me that it was a "good hour" of paddling to get to the next lock. It took me 10 ten minutes! I decided on a new rule. No matter what advice I received, if I couldn't see the next lock I would paddle, if I could see it, I would walk. Believe nothing, was what I had decided the day before and yet here I was, same old gullible self. Would I never learn?

With all the heaving and dragging on top of paddling hard, my muscles got just a wee bit sore. That's all fine as long as my crook shoulder held up, I decided. I had been getting more pain in the upper arm just below the shoulder, which is the location of my referred pain point for the glenoid. The glenoid is the cup that your shoulder rotates in, but mine has a crack through it and it is pushed out of place so that it is like a saucer with a 10-millimetre high knob pushing the shoulder away. It wasn't too bad, but it was unusual. Normally, paddling helps rather than hinders the injury. Anyway, it all made for going to sleep pretty quickly at night. We got back at 9.00pm after a pub dinner and I reckon at 9.01pm I was pushing up zeds.

We met the mayor of Newbury, Howard Bairstow, the next day along with Lady Mayoress Jo Day. Jo volunteered to fill that role because Howard's wife didn't want it and as ex-mayor Jo was experienced. Newbury is aware of climate change and sustainability but seems to be tinkering around the edges. Howard took me into the chamber with the names of all of the previous mayors. They go back to 1596. Howard wanted to tell me that future generations would see his name on the board and he was very proud of that. I admire him but that wouldn't be for me. I stood for my local council once and the really good news is that I didn't get in. Much of it is a long and thankless task.

The long history of the UK and Europe gives this Australian food for thought. Europeans arrived in Australia just a bit over 200 years ago and displaced a civilization that had existed for over 60,000 years. Since then, we have buggered the world so much that we may well not be around for another 100 years. Our national anthem arrogantly cries that 'we are young and free', yet we live on the oldest continent on earth and could celebrate the oldest continuous civilization if we weren't so busy trashing both. I don't sing the Australian national anthem anymore and I don't display our flag, boasting the Union Jack in the corner. Maybe one day we will have an all-inclusive national anthem and flag, but I'm not holding my breath.

Log jams on the Darling, barges on the Mississippi and locks in England. The locks were nowhere as troublesome as the other two, but after a hundred of them I have to say that I had seen more than enough of these interesting, but sometimes annoying, structures.

A slow moving boat approached on the other side of a bridge. I thought it was a bit odd that there was a rope off to the side. Why would they need a mid-rope, I thought? To my surprise, a horse came into view on the tow path. A bloke walked beside the horse, which was towing a barge. In the barge about 20 tourists sat around, enjoying a moment of history. At one stage, a long time ago admittedly, all of the motive power was by horses.

"Haven't seen many of these," I commented to the bloke with the horse.

"You won't," he replied. "There is only one."

The canal rejoins the River Kennet about 10 kilometres west of Reading, which then runs right through the heart of the city. An amusement park straddles the river in an area that was apparently a bus station just a few years ago. Flowers adorn the bridges and the liquid artery melds with the city, taking you from the country to the city heart and back to the country in a way that no road could ever do.

My goal for the day was not just Reading, though. I had arranged to meet Jacqueline at Sonning Eye at a place called The Mill, which was at the first lock that I would encounter on the Thames. The Thames was huge after the narrow canal.

Two women in wet suits had just finished a swim along the river that they said took two hours. Crazy, huh? The Mill was a bit closer than I thought and I arrived while the sun was still warm. It took a while to figure out how to get out of the river and by the time the kayak was in the car park, the sun was gone. Access into the car park looked a bit tricky for Jacqueline so I waited in the fading light next to the road for 45 minutes until she finally arrived, by which time I was quite cold.

When she parked the car, I changed into dry clothes and suggested she investigate The Mill. Our relationship had changed since the US. There, she managed pick ups while doing her university assignment. Here, she was completely disengaged and demanded my support. That is impossible on top of what is involved on a trip like this, and I was questioning why she had come to England.

The Mill is a theatre restaurant so, tired as I was, I suggested she book us in while I changed out of my wet gear. Arriving in the nick of time, we scoffed our food down before the show. It was about women and clothes, which didn't really grab me until they started talking about what is in women's handbags, which I did find very amusing. To my credit, I dozed off for less than five minutes during the show. Although I was fine driving back to the van, we arrived at 11.30pm and I was asleep before 11.31pm. After 36 kilometres, which included 22 locks, plus staying awake until late, I was happy with my effort.

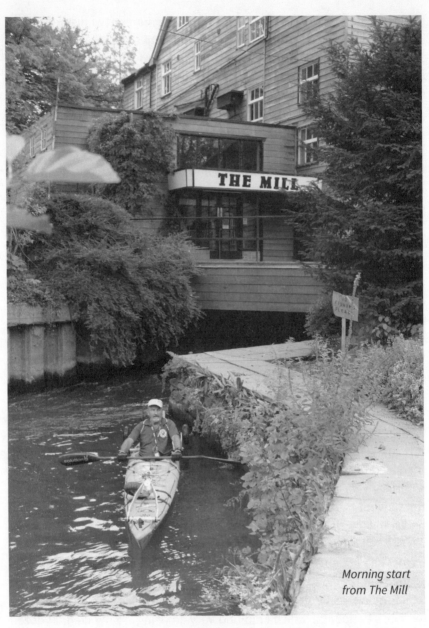

Morning start from The Mill

We had a couple of mayoral responses that needed dealing with, so the next day was a non-paddling day. Jacqueline went to the local farm store to do some decorative painting on tiles while I headed to Reading. She was more interested in taking craft lessons than meeting mayors.

Once again, I wondered at her motives. I really wondered if she had any idea what I expected from the support crew. She seemed to think it was simply a matter of keeping me company while I travelled. The Reading mayor was a young woman called Sarah Hacker. She was the first of a few people to say that she doesn't like the term 'global warming' and gave me the reason why she thinks 'climate change' is better. Her logic is correct in that Britain will be a lot colder if the Gulf Stream loses its power. The country will be a lot more like Siberia, which is quite cool indeed. It's funny how things change. Climate change is a term introduced by the Republicans in the US because they thought it sounded less dramatic than global warming. I guess you could say we had a meeting of the minds, but I did find out that a mayor does not necessarily have a lot of power and is only there for a year, as they take their turn among the elected councillors.

On the way back to the van, a roadside stall was selling flowers. I found one in a pot that would sit nicely in the van near the window and took it back to Jacqueline. She had finished her craft session but, again, wasn't interested in my next assignment, so I set off alone to meet Roger Girraud-Saunders, the mayor of Devizes.

Roger has a mechanical hand on his right arm. He is a mechanical/marine engineer and got stuck in a conveyor when trying to repair it one weekend. Luckily for him, because he had been working alone when the conveyor started and sucked him in, someone came to the site to see why the gate was open. They heard his cries and managed to extricate him, but it was too late for his hand. We bonded and he has stayed in touch, and has even written to the mayor of Lismore, Jenny Dowell. Remember, she was the mayor of Lismore who gave me all the introductory letters. Jenny was a loyal fan who provided valuable support during the trip.

Back at the van, I got stuck into writing my blog, which was a couple of days late due to the extended evening and the mayoral visits. Jacqueline wanted me to take her for a walk but, had I done that, the blog would not have been done. She went by herself but, on her return, gave me a severe lecture about being selfish and not thinking of her needs. I just took it, wondering whether it was something to do with her feeling guilty about being away from her 104-year-old father.

I really had no idea how to bridge the gap between what I needed in a support crew and the sense I got from her that she thought this was a couple negotiating how they travel together. In hindsight it should have been clear. We were on different trips with different objectives. I have no idea what her objectives really were. Mine were simple – get to Paris.

I now understood that she should not have come to England. My desire for human connection had led me to confuse personal relationships with common goals. I needed the Renates of the world, not this emotional blackmail.

Completing the Kennett and Avon canal didn't mean the last of narrow boats; many bigger and wider boats started to appear on the Thames as well. There are still a lot of locks on the Thames but they seem to be spaced about five kilometres apart which, allowing for portage, is roughly an hour for a kayaker. Portage itself is a bit hit and miss on the Thames. The lock keeper at Maidenhead flatly refused to let me through the lock and I finished up dragging the kayak through gardens and down a small waterfall. The next one at Dorney Reach was just the opposite. The guys welcomed me into the lock and when they heard my accent they knew immediately they were onto a winner.

"So how's the cricket going?" asked the lock keeper.

"What's cricket?" I replied. "Is it like rugby?"

With our infamous drubbing in the cricket, I wasn't at all confident for us in the upcoming Rugby World Cup, but hey, may as well lead with the chin. Anything is better than a gloating Pommie when you know they are – heaven forbid – right.

The Upper Thames Rowing Club is on the river at Henley. The river is much wider there than I expected and one side was roped off for a regatta. A pair of singles raced past, not sleek like sculls but, nevertheless, beautifully crafted. I shouted some encouragement before taking my leave downstream.

At Eton, I knew exactly where I was going because I had paddled there previously. Windsor Castle towers over the town and its extensive gardens line the downstream bank for ages. I dragged the kayak out near the railway station and rang Jacqueline. She had parked the car where we had agreed and walked off to see the Castle and would be back in 10 minutes. I put the kayak on the roof and waited. I was cold and wet again, and Jacqueline was lost, again. That wasn't a problem, I just told her to meet me at a nearby pub. The pub was nice and warm and I was careful not to plonk my wet backside on any of the upholstered chairs, as I set about restoring my fluid balance.

With Mayor Derek Cotty and Queen Liz (Runnymede)

Downstream from Eton is the Borough of Runnymede. That is where the Magna Carta was signed and the next day I was lucky enough to paddle through the area exactly 900 years later. Mayor Derek Cotty arrived in his regalia, and we took a photo of us and the kayak under a large statue of Queen Elizabeth II. Derek's team issued a press release in which I had discussed the relationship between the Magna Carta and my trip. The importance of that document is that it was the start of the recognition of rights. It is a charter of liberties, to which the English barons forced King John to give his assent in June 1215. Here we are, 900 years later, jeopardizing the rights of future generations. We knowingly plunder the future wealth of our children, leaving them with a very unsettled future and a much depleted earth. That's 900 years of 'progress', I guess. I wonder if we will even make 1,000.

I met quite a few mayors between Bristol and London. There were no climate deniers. One was a bit clueless. Two very concerned. Two don't like 'global warming' and prefer 'climate change' because of its greater accuracy for the UK. Both were unaware of the history of the terms. Peak oil? What's that? Fracking? Now that is bad! Right up there with the 'swarm' of refugees trying to get through the Channel tunnel at the time. Al Gore has based his approach on the fundamental idea that education is the key. That is the approach we have all been taking unsuccessfully for decades, though. It clearly cannot stop the peddling of anti-science by some politicians and any media associated with Rupert Murdoch. Perhaps the saddest thing about Al Gore is that there is a video of him in 1983 saying pretty much what he is saying now. Despite some successes, he has yet to get the world to make the necessary changes.

Near Twickenham, centre of the Rugby World Cup, is the Teddington lock. This is the last lock on the Thames and has portage to dream about. There is a ramp on the upstream side, with the water level about 30 centimetres below the sill, and on the downstream side there is a ramp and a set of rollers. My exit onto the tidal Thames was timed to take advantage of the tides. It was an hour before high tide when I left and, even then, it had risen to cover the ground under park benches. Had someone told me what was about to happen I would have struggled to believe them. The flow towards me actually got stronger before it turned and as the water rose, the scenes became more bizarre. There was a kayak club on the bank. People were out on the river in racing kayaks and I stopped to talk to a K4 crew. Behind them people sloshed about in shin-deep water over the floor of their boatshed. The crew said this wasn't exactly normal, but it also wasn't unusual. I had heard about Thames flooding and was even offered a job on the design team for the tidal barrage built in the late 1970s, so I had assumed that the problem had been fixed. A few hundred metres further on, a restaurant had the lower half of its door boarded up, with water 30 centimetres above the door sill. A bloke was drinking a beer in a beer garden. No big deal there, you might say, but he was sitting cross legged on the table with water to the level of the stools.

The plan was to paddle to Chelsea where the London Kayak Club has a pontoon. The gate to the pontoon was locked, but it is only a metre high and would therefore present no problem to sliding the kayak over it to get to the car after the paddle. We had tried contacting the club but could only leave recorded messages, and no-one called back. When I was about fives kilometres away, I called Jacqueline but she was struggling to find the spot. Remember, she likes maps and wouldn't trust the GPS. Luckily I found a large ramp at Putney, which had rowing and boating clubs at the top of it. I hauled the kayak out, went to the closest street running down towards the embankment and called Jacqueline, who then put my location into the car GPS. It was supposed to be only a 10 minutes' drive from where she was, but it took her about 40 minutes in the London traffic. It all turned out for the better, with easy access for both car and kayak. I was getting used to shivering.

Next morning, 2 September, we moved the van from Staines to a caravan park at Abbey Wood, downstream of London. It is about 10 minutes from the boat ramp at Erith, which is the next stop for kayakers after Putney. This took all day, but it also allowed more planning and an early start to catch the tide the following day.

I was up at 4.50am and ready to hit Putney at 7.00am. We drove away from the van and got to the park exit. The gate was shut. Padlocked, and three metre-high steel gates barred our exit. It was my fault; I had been told we could not get the car back in between 8.00pm and 8.00am, but I just hadn't thought that we couldn't get out. I just didn't think of giant security gates being locked against someone leaving the park. That's the problem with being in another country, I guess. You just don't understand how it all works until you see it.

With no leeway in the paddling schedule because we were booked to cross to France on 6 September, it was time to re-think. To actually work out the three-day plan for the Thames between Putney and the Channel had taken a lot of work, using tide charts and Google Earth. I could not afford the time it would take against the tide, and I certainly wasn't going to paddle at night. There was only one answer if I had any chance of paddling to Dungeness in time for the Channel crossing: go backwards through London. This was not palatable but, there had been so many trip changes, shattered plans and disappointments, one becomes immune and rolls with the punches. So, the day was to start at Erith, through the Thames barrier backwards, and then paddle back up to Putney.

There was a benefit in this. We had time to go to a Three store and get more data for the portable wifi hot spot – 10 gigabytes per month was obviously not enough. The problem with the plan was that it was not in my name. Not having a UK credit or debit card, the cost would have been $150 per month for 12 gigabytes. We put it in Trevor's name, which cost $25 per month for 10 gigabytes, and I gave him cash for six months after which time he would cancel the plan.

I had tried calling Three, our phone and internet provider, when the data ran out the previous night, but their lines shut at 8.00pm. Phones and internet had been major problems since the start of the trip. So far it had been a lot better in the UK than in the US, but in both places I was amazed at the number of areas where there had been no coverage. We do pretty well in Australia given our much lower population density.

We set off to the Three store to get more data and that's where, perhaps, the real trouble started for the day. One may think that finding the gate locked until 8.00am when I needed to start at Putney an hour beforehand was trouble enough. It took hours and I simply could not accept what they were saying about my data usage: 10 gigabytes gone in days. It wasn't until the end of the month when I was able to see the data usage that the penny dropped. Huge amounts of data had passed through the account over periods of many hours while I was paddling. No guesses on who did that. I now knew how she spent much of her time while I paddled. And she was upset that I had taken her with me to the Three store because she reckoned it was my problem? It finally clicked that her university assignments had nothing to do with the trip or me. The reason for her involvement was a complete mystery to me. Maybe she was there to keep me company or maybe she was there for me to keep her company. I think now that the latter might be closest to the truth.

The wind was from the north west at about 15 knots when we finally arrived at Erith. This made the water a bit choppy, so I had the skirt on but no jacket. After two hours I rang Jacqueline to say that I was on time and would be at Putney between 4.30 and 5.00pm. It would have been really nice to get some photos of me paddling through London but that was, apparently, out of the question. The support crew wasn't interested in doing anything other than putting me in the water and picking me up at the end of the day. Just after that, the river traffic started to increase markedly and I was barrelling along at 12km/hr when I smacked through a wave that brought the kayak to a juddering halt. The action and excitement of actually paddling through London kept my mind busy, so the negatives slipped into the background.

In the grey water out in the middle of the river, a seal lay on its back enjoying the little bit of sun that had just poked through the clouds. There wasn't much time to watch it, though. On seeing the kayak, it was gone in a flash. It was a bit tricky keeping watch front and behind. Ships, sailing boats, tugs with barges, boats of one form or another kept overtaking my little kayak. My course, as is my wont, was to take the inside line on bends to travel the shortest distance so, after every bend, I crossed the river. Green and red channel markers were on the same sides as Australia, which felt more familiar than the US 'right, red, right'. I much prefer to say red is on the left, because port is left and port is red.

Around Greenwich the traffic increased with high-speed river cats, cross-river car ferries, cocktail cruise boats and fast adventure joyride boats. In the middle of this, the odd tug passed, pulling a couple of barges. Between Tower Bridge and Westminster, the traffic seemed to cover about a quarter of the river surface. At the London Eye a tourist cruiser was about to pull out. I waited for him to go but the skipper waved me across in front of him.

"Thanks mate," I called.

"You need to go to the other side here or they will pull ya," he shouted.

With boats everywhere, I bolted across the river and was about to go behind a ferry coming towards me that suddenly changed direction. Behind me another ferry gave long blasts on the horn, presumably aimed at the one in front that changed direction and hopefully not at me. I slipped under Westminster Bridge, carefully staying near the pylons where only a kayak could fit, just as a police launch passed by.

The traffic thinned and the wind dropped until the next bend. The water felt as warm as a bath. It probably wasn't, though, so that meant the wind chill on my hands was significant. With all of the activity and wave action there had been no chance to eat or drink, and I was still running late. I didn't want to arrive after 5.00pm so I continued my mad sprint to Putney.

Pulling in at 5.05pm the tide was about a metre below the top of the boat ramp. I had sprinted for four hours. Getting out, walking, and loading the kayak were all problematic because my extremities were cold and nothing seemed to work properly. I loaded up while Jacqueline chatted to a French bloke with a young child looking at the water rising. She is good at talking with people and always learns something. We parked the car on the high side of the embankment road and headed to the nearest pub for a meal.

Sitting in the pub a bit later we watched the water come over the embankment and up to the tyres of our car parked on the uphill side of the road. Gregoire the French guy came up to our table advising that he was concerned it was our car that had been left on the top of the ramp and was about to get very wet. We thanked him but said we were fine, it wasn't ours. Never missing an opportunity we told him about the trip and asked him to remember kayak4earth. He asked if we were going to COP21! He was the first person who had mentioned the climate summit's real name.

Next day we received this email from the Frenchman (excuse the broken English):

Dear Steve

I hope you enjoyed your dinner as you must need a lot of energy after all this journey and until its end.

We were sorry to disturb but so glad to meet you.

On the way back home, I explained your project to my son and shown him maps from your blog.

He just say: "I met a hero today." I must agree with this.

All the best

Gregoire (the French guy worrying about the car)

When I read it I was emotionally drained, had damaged muscles around my ribcage that affected my breathing and was getting ready to cross the English Channel. His email almost brought tears to my eyes. This is the sort of reward that comes occasionally and makes it all seem worthwhile. Again, emotions welled up in me because of the contrast between the lack of support on the journey itself and the warmth of those strangers who cared.

Rather than take the most direct route back to Abbey Wood, we drove through the city, past the Houses of Parliament and Big Ben and across Tower Bridge. It was all new to Jacqueline and this was a good chance to show her the sights. After we exited the city, traffic became very heavy, so progress was slow. Jacqueline gazed out the window, sullenly, silently. I asked her what was wrong but she continued to stare away. After a couple of attempts I gave up and concentrated on driving.

Back at the van, I finally said something. This was the fourth time there had been a serious problem, the first being at Devizes when I wrote my blog instead of taking her for a walk. I said it just was not acceptable behaviour to turn hostile and not discuss anything. That triggered the same response as the last three times. I was thinking about the trip in my terms and not catering for her needs. I knew it was close to the end for her 104-year-old father back in Australia and I suspected that was the reason for all of this.

The situation was intolerable. We had very few photos of me paddling in England and none through the centre of London. Jacqueline was the only support person not to have written a blog, not one line. I really could not understand why she had wanted to be the support crew for this leg. It had been a lot easier than the Mississippi, but paddling here was still a fairly tough gig with logistics and blog-writing thrown in. I decided that I would get across the English Channel in the only window we had and then figure out how to finish without her. If people are on different journeys, it is never going to work. Success requires complete unity: same goal, same expectation, same team.

There was no point going through all of the reasons, but I explained that I could not cope with her any more. I could not do what I had to do and be abused regularly about my planning, my motives and my lack of support for her. We worked out a price for her fares, I transferred the money and things became better. With the pressure off, she relaxed somewhat: relief!

It was two days before the scheduled Channel crossing. We decided to head for Rye, Full Throttle headquarters, have a chat with the team, check the weather and so make the crossing happen on time, weather permitting. I would worry later about the leg from Erith to Dungeness. When I had planned the crossing date, it had seemed easy to cover the distance in the time. We had been a week late in starting from Portishead because I couldn't go without Jacqueline, and the journey across England had taken longer than planned. Now the chickens had come home to roost.

With Jacqueline going home, I needed to find support. Both Trevor and Andrew, another mate from Libya, had offered to do what they could. We had met nearly four decades previously and we still shared similar values and trust, so that was surely the best answer if they could spare the time. You will learn more about both of these men in the chapters ahead.

Lynette Smith back in Australia had a neighbour who expressed an interest in coming over as support. She had experience in expedition support and could come at short notice. It was an attractive offer but I had just been badly burnt by someone I thought I knew but didn't. Besides, watching my dwindling funds I wasn't that keen on flying yet another person around the world and contributing greenhouse gases to the atmosphere.

Lynette was a rock, bless her, but when we figured out dates that worked with Trevor and Andrew I was very relieved.

Meeting at Rye Harbour for the Channel crossing, the air was a crisp 8°C and the sun was out. The wind was offshore but the horizon was a bit lumpy. I felt a very long way from home, that I had been away too long, and I missed my kids and grandkids too much. It should have been a grand thing paddling across the English Channel, but it was no big deal. I had paddled up the Mississippi in a flood, paddled into New York and paddled through London. This was just another body of water a long way from home.

The paddle across was a doddle, a walk in the park. It was legal, it was safe and it was easy because I was aided by Full Throttle, that small company specialising in escorting paddlers across the English Channel. I didn't want to use them but, like other kayakers, I had no choice. It just didn't feel right following a boat with two blokes in the boat directing me about the busy shipping. Busy? They had to be joking. Try paddling into New York or London, guys. It wasn't until I spoke to another adventurer who was compelled to use the same escort that I understood how deeply disappointing it was not to be able to just head off across the Channel. Axe, his name is another story, told me it had almost destroyed his sense of achievement traversing from the highest mountain in Britain to the highest mountain in Europe.

The French side was overcast and cool and the water a lot rougher, but it was fine. The big issue was the speed of the current up and down the coast. Seeing it first-hand made me understand that the trip down the French coast needed to be timed with the tides or wind assistance.

Sometimes it's the little things that count. I had a crook stomach for a few days before and after the Channel crossing. It was very lucky the crossing was not difficult. The squitters held off for the duration of the trip, leaving me to deal with a little nausea and stomach cramps. Back in England, the problem intensified, but my friend Warren came up with a solution. He reckoned that if I ate charcoal that would sequester carbon, thus assisting albeit in a small way, with global warming. More importantly, it should prevent localized warming to my lower regions. Brilliant? Maybe. Thanks Warren.

London had been typical, media wise. Here's a bloke who had just paddled up through America, across England and was continuing on his way to Paris and nobody was interested? What does a bloke have to do?

Arriving in France (Boulogne sur Mer)

CHAPTER 16

ANDREW

With the Channel crossing completed, it was now time to go back to the Thames and fill in the bit that was missed out when travelling with Jacqueline. Now that she had flown home, I had to complete the Thames from about half a day past London to the sea and the English Channel coast, from the Thames mouth to Dungeness. I was not looking forward to this bit because it felt like dead time. It would have been done already had we started the UK leg on time. Paddling to France and then coming back to fill in was not my cup of tea, but it had to be done.

There was one major bonus: my mate Andrew from our Libyan days of around 1978, was to be the support crew. Andrew is an ex-Lancashire man, if there is such a thing. He is as subtle as I am. He calls a spade a spade and although there is no bush where he comes from, he wouldn't beat around it under any circumstance. Both of us have mellowed somewhat, I fear, but the residual character is still there. We got on well in Libya and we got on well 40 years later. I did think he was a Yorkshire man, after all they all talk a bit funny up there, but he reminded me of the War of the

Roses: a long battle, not about flowers, but over the English throne and fought between the House of York and the House of Lancaster more than 500 years ago. How could I forget that? Shame on me, especially as it was the inspiration for the Game of Thrones.

Veda, Andrew's wife, seemed pretty much the same as when I last saw her many years ago. The discussions we had now were more philosophical, but they seemed to indicate why we are friends. Veda is disappointed that all the things she saw wrong with the world when she was young – such as growing inequality, environmental destruction and corruption – seem to be worse 50 years later. We are all on the same page there and we all want change. It is not just because of friendship that we worked together for the final UK leg; our mutual goals for our children are a powerful bond.

With the caravan in tow, I arrived at Andrew and Veda's house, ready to load up and head off. This was to be a boys' only adventure now. There was me, of course, and Andrew and Linus, a five-year-old Hungarian Puli. That's a black, curly-haired dog that reflects no light and becomes invisible in the dark. He simply disappears when he crawls under a bed.

We left the house in Cambridge, drove to Maidstone in Kent, established the van and went to the Erith ramp where we launched the kayak at 2.00pm. The tide still had a couple of hours to come in against me but it would turn as I was paddling, after which I could take advantage of the run-out flow. The wind was south westerly, quite strong and gusty, meaning that the sail could probably be used. The route took in the last of the tidal Thames and then the Thames estuary.

A few wind turbines rose above the countryside, but more prominent was the big oil-fired power station at Dartford (1475MW). It was being built in 1977 when I was in the area. Oil-fired stations can be fired up in four hours, which is important strategically and was critical to London power supply after the storms in 1987.

The sail was up to help push against the current but, to counter the gusts and prevent a capsize, my paddle had to be in my hands at all times. With a few ships going up and down the Thames, I thought it best to stay on one side, but my natural inclination came to the fore and I cut the bends to shorten the distance and to dodge the current as much as possible.

After passing ships with huge gaping rear doors, open so that two 40-foot containers on top of each other could be wheeled in at a time, Dartford Bridge, the last bridge I would encounter before the Seine River in France, soared above. All of these big bridges are magnificent from underneath. They are huge, towering monsters – testament to the engineers who design them and the people who build them. Dartford Bridge was no exception, but equally impressive is the fact that the bridge is only for southbound traffic, while two tunnels take the northbound traffic.

Passing Gravesend, a huge cry from the far distant bank stopped me in my tracks. I was sure it formed the word "Steve" so I waved and thought I could make out Andrew, but couldn't see Linus. I don't know whether they heard his cry right up in Lancashire. It is only 300 kilometres, so maybe they did. Who needs a radio when you have Andrew?

Tacking back across the shipping channel, with the wind from the side, I was confused. With no map, I wasn't sure where the river went. Was I going the right way or did it go the other way? This was the bloody Thames River and I couldn't decide which bank to be on. A container ship came around the corner and was lining me up. "Good news and bad news," I thought. I now knew my direction was right, but container ships move quickly and I was unlikely to win a battle with one. With a few hundred metres to spare, I passed the buoy inside which the ship could not come. Good news. All good news.

A ship coming down-river led the rest of the way, so my lines were more confident. I called Andrew on the phone at 5.00pm as per schedule, advised that I would be at the pick-up point at 6.30pm, ate an orange, slurped down a drink and set off eastward along the southern shore, which is on the opposite side to the World London Gateway Port. For the next few kilometres the wind, along with the current, pushed me north off the bank. It was a fight, requiring continual tacking back towards the land. Eventually the current eased and I was close to the bank again.

Weirdly, there were white spots on the water ahead. Water? Nope, the spots were birds standing on mud. I could just make out Allhallows, where Andrew would be. There is a yacht club with two launching ramps that we had seen on Google Earth and had confirmed on the web site that gives boat ramp locations. The shipping channel was two kilometres offshore, but I stopped paddling and let the wind blow me away from the land and mud at about 45 degrees. Progress was quite slow despite the strong wind, so I dipped the paddle to get my speed up again. Mud! Mud at about 20 centimetres deep and a kilometre away from the bank. That was the reason for the slow speed. Shallow water creates a pressure effect that slows boat speed. Then the rudder hit bottom and, finally, the kayak scraped the mud.

A murmuration of swallows dipped and swooped over Allhallows. These are striking, fascinating, mesmerising displays of nature, but I had no time to watch. They were over Andrew, so he could do the looking. He can tell the story while he's at it.

Andrew's blog: *Leave home and take caravan to a site just east of Maidstone near Leeds castle. Leave van and head up to Erith (a few miles west of Dartford). Launch around 2pm, weather sunny and moderate westerly wind in his favour and therefore able to use the small sail he has. I spot him about two hours later at Gravesend.*

I get to the pick-up point at Allhallows (should be Allshallows!) just west of the mouth of the Medway. Linus and I go for a walk along salt marsh as tide recedes, rapidly exposing extensive mud flats. Eventually I spot him about a mile off shore & about four miles before the agreed pick-up point. Apparently, even out there he was only in a foot or so of water, although I could see great container ships passing behind him. I finished up with the car headlights on trying to guide him into what remained of a very shallow channel with mud flats as far as the eye could see. The landing was in a caravan park and others had seen Steve out in the mud and called the coast guard. Steve wasn't too pleased about this when we managed to make phone contact, and by the time they turned up he had dragged the kayak over the deep mud and we were carrying it up the beach.

"A local guy says the mud is too soft to walk on," Andrew yelled into his phone. "Stay afloat. He has called the coast guard."

I tried that but was floating back out with the tide and reckoned that wasn't such a great idea. Within a couple of minutes, I was aground again as the tide receded. "Stuff this," I thought. "What's a bloody coast guard going to do? They can't get up here in a boat." I had prodded the mud with my paddle before I took Andrew's call and it didn't feel life-threatening to me. Another few prods and it didn't feel too bad, so I climbed out and started dragging the kayak. After 50 metres there was a channel to cross with fast-flowing water. Bum back in the kayak, but leaving my feet and their thick coating of ooze outside, I struggled across in a very awkward position.

On the other side a shiny area ran into the water with a slope that I reckoned I could stand on. It worked OK and I was able to move up the slope, onto the flat and then towards the bank, only 300 metres away. It took a few rests and a few loud grunts and when I didn't concentrate properly I had to pull my leg out of mud well above the knee. Andrew came down to the edge of the shingle in his gum boots and waited. I had no shoes which was fine because they would have been sucked off my feet anyway.

Eventually I got to Andrew who took the front of the kayak while I took the back. The beach had small pointy shells on it, about the size of marbles. With cold wet feet these hurt a bit, but then I saw the oysters. Bloody hell! There was still just enough light to see so I made sure that I didn't tread on any. Perhaps it was more good luck than good management, but after two rests we got to the steps at the wall unscathed. The ramp was another hundred metres along the wall but I was buggered if I was walking any further. A couple of locals were there, plus two coast guards. Andrew took the bow up the steps and someone else grabbed the back and hoisted the muddy mess to the top of the wall.

I was pretty tired, definitely very wet and very, very muddy but hey, this was supposed to be an adventure. We chatted with everyone, made a good friend in John from the coastguard, washed off with a hose from a kindly local and headed for Maidstone well after dark. Perhaps everyone thought that the Australian they met was stark raving mad. They did have their day livened up though, and they can probably share their story about the daft bugger over many cups of tea or even a pint or two.

Andrew's blog: Anyway, Steve sweet-talked the coast guard and gave them a copy of his book recounting his earlier Brisbane to Adelaide trip. We hosed him and the boat down and headed back to camp. Up to the last bit it had been a great day!

The next day I was still bemoaning the fact that this was fill-in work and that it felt like we had gone backwards. Nevertheless, it had to be endured. With our new-found knowledge we knew to avoid mud and that the solution is easy. Mud is covered with water at high tide. Low tide is when there is a problem. The other good thing is that shingle beaches, meaning no mud, start at Sheerness on the Isle of Sheppey and, also, the estuary does not have the racing tides that the river does, provided you are a bit wary of the Medway and its strong currents. Anyway, it wasn't too long until I passed the 12th century towers of Reculver Church, which stands amid the remains of a Roman 'Saxon Shore' fort and Saxon monastery, which are even older. The fort would have been used to monitor shipping on the Thames estuary more than a millennium ago.

Thames estuary mud (Allhallows)

It had been pretty slow going to Reculver, but around the corner I managed to slide along just off the shingle beach using the waves as runners and cause Andrew to hurry himself into Margate. The Turner museum, right on the water near the harbour, was the agreed rendezvous point. As I paddled into the harbour, another of those shouts that shook the land all the way to Yorkshire, or was that Lancashire, boomed across the water. "Must be in the right place," I thought.

Linus came to greet me as I sat rocking against the shingle beach eating a banana. He seemed very perplexed about the whole situation. He would leave me in the morning, go on a huge drive that probably necessitated a sleep, and there I would be sitting in this yellow thing on the water. Humans! Funny things, eh?

Turner's colours are very recognisable, even if you don't know the name. As I paddled past the museum, Andrew stood on the harbour wall, so I tried to show him what it was like to catch a wave, but all I did was bounce up and down like a cork as I battled with the paddle.

In surprisingly quick time, I paddled around the end of the estuary and into the English Channel to Broadstairs and Viking Beach. A booming voice announced that Andrew was nearby, so I had made it, despite being mesmerized by the cliffs, castles and sense of history.

We loaded the kayak onto the car, watched by a large group of school children. Eventually we spoke to their teachers. They were from Germany. They got it. They understood the trip, they knew about COP21. I couldn't help but think they were far more advanced about the climate change issue than people in my country. It is the sort of contact that was the big surprise of the trip. People would see the kayak and get drawn into the trip and its purpose. Call it serendipity, maybe, but there was no doubt that more people were being drawn to the trip.

The only real exception was the conventional media. What does that say about our media? You judge for yourself, but for over a decade I have been saying that much of mainstream media does not have a clue. They are so absorbed in whatever little world they live in that they have no idea what interests ordinary people. All they do is shove their ideas, the ideas of their clique, down the throats of audiences. Most just accept it but, it seems to me, social media has broken their grip and that the tide, however slowly, will turn.

Despite being hopeful about breaking up existing monopolies, social media is a two-edged sword. It has polarized society so that opposing views become more entrenched. Rather than communicate with each other, we seek dialogue that confirms our existing beliefs. I was pleasantly surprised by the number of strangers drawn to the messaging on my trip because they 'got' the message instantly. That is not a measure of what percentage of the population get it, just a reminder to me that not everyone opposes it and those who do not oppose it are on side and are impressed by my commitment. Even without trying to change the world, it is difficult to connect with people who care, and even more difficult to find leaders.

We were experiencing mixed days: one day good, the next bad, the next good, the next bad. The places that I paddled past were outstanding images from the history we had been taught, but I just wished that I had paddled past Allhallows and not had to drag in to shore through all that mud. Margate, Ramsgate, Dover, Folkestone, the white cliffs, Dover Castle: all significant names to me and just about everyone else in the English-speaking world. The view from the kayak is unlike any other, and it was a privilege to be able to experience all of this.

As I went past Dover Harbour, where the big ferries come and go to Calais, the waves rolled along the harbour wall. My stomach was a bit queasy because I had been tossed around like a cork with a lot of sloppy waves on what turned out to be a significant swell. Although it didn't manifest itself on the beach, the wall clearly revealed the two metre difference between the crests and the troughs. A two metre swell on the ocean is easy, rolling along until it hits land and makes surf, but this was choppy, bouncy, vomit-making slop.

When you dig a big tunnel a lot of dirt comes out and it has to be placed somewhere. Between Dover and Folkestone is where the English put their share of the spoil from the Channel Tunnel. It is apparently about half of the total, which seems pretty fair really. The spoil is along the shoreline with very expensive containment walls and is now a popular wildlife reserve known as the Samphire Hoe.

As on most days, it wasn't all clear sailing, so to speak. When I surfed down the waves my speed would climb to 8km/hr, but when I slid off the back it would drop down to about 2km/hr. We knew that the currents along the coast don't actually match the tide times and, to the uninitiated, they are a bit strange. However, I could pick what the current was doing by watching the GPS. Unfortunately, Andrew didn't have that ability, being on land and out of sight, so a big problem for him was guessing whether I was fast or slow. It seemed that whatever the situation, I would be slow until I got the hang of the current and then I would speed up. When the current runs up the English Channel, for instance, there is a loop that comes back down, and that can be seen on some tide maps. With the loop coming back down there are big eddies, many kilometres long, caused by promontories or harbour walls. That means, with a bit of experimentation, you can figure out how far to be off the land to make it work. Of course, the wind is another variable and sometimes you can also catch small runners along a shingle beach if you are close enough, just like I did near Reculver.

That night we watched England beat Fiji, immediately after the Rugby World Cup opening ceremony. Four pints, some excellent pub grub, some healthy banter in which a Welsh bloke and I thought we might have to deal with a pub full of Englishmen (that's pretty even odds in my book), and so ended a well-rounded day. The English were all happy. Neither I nor the Welshman cared, except that we were slightly concerned that the

Poms had done pretty well. With Wales and Australia in the same pool as England, this was a serious concern not to be admitted to any Englishman.

Andrew's blog: Steve had a bad night and thought he'd picked up a bug, but I reckoned he'd overdone the last leg yesterday to get in before the storm. Nevertheless there's no stopping him and we were down on the water at Folkestone before 9am ready for the final leg to Dungeness. What a contrast in the weather! Lovely sunshine, off shore wind flattening the sea near the shore. It looked an absolute picture and the end was in sight from the start, i.e. the Dungeness power station. Did my usual attempt to spot him on route at Hythe and Dymchurch; no luck again but I wasn't concerned as the conditions were so good. Having got through Friday this trip must have been like the vicar's tea party.

I headed up to the point at Dungeness to check out where we'd agreed to meet, had great a cup of tea and a chat while waiting, headed down to the beach, and there he was at the edge of the surf about half a mile down the beach. Great, I thought, I'll just drive round to the Lifeboat station. This took about five minutes and, lo and behold, the man was just passing. I grabbed my hi-vis jacket and dashed over the shingle, waving it like mad before he went too far! In he came; fortunately the tide had risen and there was a bit of an inlet to the station, so he was able to float virtually to the edge of the shingle bank. Despite feeling pretty rough all the way, that was it, UK leg done. What a guy!

I had really enjoyed my time with Andrew. It was fantastic to have someone that was keen to help in any way possible, was competent and was a local. I had learned to play rugby and bridge in Libya with Andrew all those years ago. We are both engineers and we were on the same journey, so we had been effective and very quick. Part of the difference was that Trevor and Andrew put up their hands to help me. Their only agenda was to get their mate from A to B, although I suspect a wee bit of English pride was at play. A really important difference, though, is the similarity in our way of thinking. This only became obvious, reflecting on the entire journey, years later. Engineers are people who think logically. They collect the facts and then build things in a logical sequence. I could simply describe a pick-up point, a challenge in navigating time and tides, or a problem in calculating arrival times with unpredictable winds, and these guys would look at the map and work out what to do.

I hadn't had one pick-up problem with Andrew. It was 5 days after a 37-year hiatus, we'd had a fantastic experience that neither of us will forget. Maybe we could later reflect on our achievement, the shared goal, the success, but for now I was happy to hand him back to Veda and go to France.

White cliffs of Dover

Linus and the end of England (Dungeness)

CHAPTER 17

TREVOR'S COAST

There was an old connection between Trevor and Andrew. I first met Trevor in July 1977. Three weeks later we picked Andrew up from the Benghazi airport and introduced him to his new home in Libya. The city is a shambles right now, but back then, although Gadhafi had been in power for nine years, it was a relatively pleasant place for expat workers. We were working either on the town sewers or the new sewage treatment plant. Andrew was not a company man. He was new blood. Because Trevor was company, he had to start Andrew's job until Andrew arrived. Trevor was then my boss at the sewage treatment plant, 10 kilometres out of town in the village of Guachia. He was also captain of our darts team called 'Mugs Away'. For anyone who knows anything about darts, the name is a good indication of our skill, or more precisely, the lack of it. Trevor had a tough job leading the team but, to our credit, we were superb at après darts.

Now in their forties, Simon and Mark (Trevor and Marilyn's two boys) are just like they were as kids way back then in Libya. Marilyn still runs up the stairs in the house, still complains about the English cold, and

232

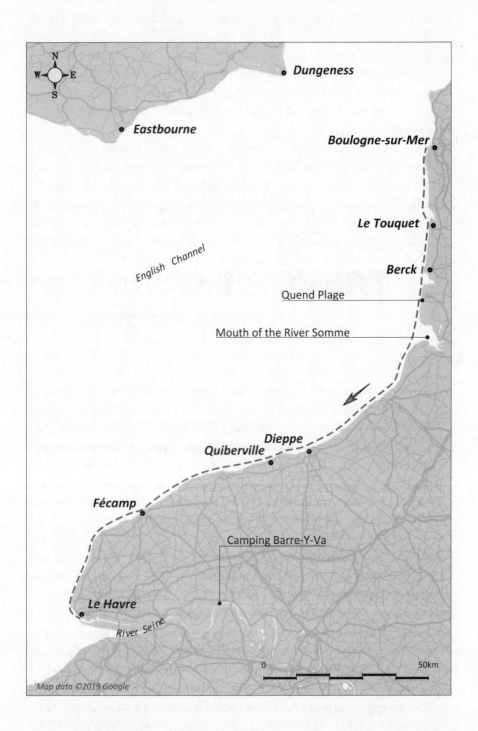

loves their holiday in the sun every year. I reckon she would make a great Australian.

Andrew had emptied his goods and chattels from the van, he and Linus returned to their walks around Cambridgeshire and we had filled the van with Trevor's gear and Marilyn's food gifts. When we climbed into the car at 8.00am on a Sunday, I advised Marilyn that we should be back in three weeks at the latest.

The trip over to France on the P&O ferry was smooth and the day was clear enough to see land most of the way. We arrived on a Sunday afternoon into Calais, scene of all the refugee problems a few months prior where people tried to get into trucks going to the UK. All was quiet, but new, huge, double fences with razor wire on top extended for a couple of kilometres along both sides of the road. No way could anyone get through, or over them. Refugees were out of sight, except for a glimpse of tents and blue tarps behind a hill. A sole gendarme stood at the roadside overlooking the area.

Was this mass of humanity pouring out of Syria related to global warming? To suggest that, even to some Climate Reality Project leaders, is too confronting, but the truth is that Syria had suffered its worst drought ever between 2006 and 2010, turning 60% of its fertile land into desert. By 2010, 80% of its cattle were dead. More than one million people were displaced and living in camps near cities. The Syrian minister of agriculture stated publicly that economic and social fallout from the drought was "beyond our capacity as a country to deal with." Is it any wonder that radicalism fomented in this environment?

Our response in the West was to turn the country into a war zone. My country, Australia, decided to be part of that war and anyone who fled our way was to be stopped, ruthlessly. We don't like desperate people coming to Australia in boats, even though many of us are descendants of desperate people who came here the same way. We put refugees in jail indefinitely, either on Nauru or Papua New Guinea's Manus Island. There, they can be held up as examples to deter others. Tragically, many Australians support this, although the tide of opinion is turning slowly. I genuinely fear the place where my country is headed.

It was quite confronting to be asked in both England and France whether the world had got it wrong about Australians. Rather than being generous, friendly and egalitarian as is our traditional reputation, were we actually over-indulged xenophobic brats? My conclusion is that, overwhelmingly, Australians are not hateful. They have been lied to by both major political parties and have been told that the refugees will take away the privileges we should think of as our rights. There is no-one with the guts to lead the country as Prime Minister Malcolm Fraser did 40 years ago when confronted with a similar influx of Vietnamese refugees. As a result, many Australians are racist. Many find it easier to blame refugees than to address the problem. By his own admission, the then immigration minister was inspired by his visit to Ground Zero to incarcerate innocent people in detention centres specifically designed to kill all hope. Now both major parties in Australia are hell-bent on training the population to be immune to someone else's suffering, because that someone is 'less deserving'. Luckily, not all Australians are that gullible and many good people spend their lives fighting for a fair go for the less fortunate. The perpetrators of the crimes, our own governments, demean us all.

As the French leg would be a serious effort at gaining maximum kilometres, I suggested that we get some paddling in straight away. Trevor was enthusiastic, so we took the van to Le Touquet, set it up and then headed up to Boulogne, where I finished the Channel crossing, and launched across the long beach at about 5.00pm. With the wind behind me, I expected a quick run down the coast to Le Touquet, arriving before sunset at 7.45pm. At a distance of less than 20 kilometres, a following breeze and the fly kayak sail helping progress, what could go wrong, and what a great start to France!

The adverse current was running strongly offshore, so I hugged the coast. Wind turbines broke the horizon, which was to be the case all the way down the coast. A sandy beach ran back to green hills until these were broken by a village, Hardelot Plage. Trevor, the beacon in his yellow hi-vis jacket, was on the beach to greet me and I confirmed all was good to get to Le Touquet just before sundown.

Paddling away from the village, the hills returned and the people disappeared from the beach. After half an hour I came across thousands of sticks about 1.5-metre high, set vertically in the sand, maybe two metres apart. Because the tide was almost low, all of the sticks were exposed. The tide difference for the day was nine metres, so there was a lot of beach. Locals later confirmed my guess that these were for mussel farming.

Just before Le Touquet, a big estuary pushes into the marsh lands. I expected to have already crossed this because the GPS registered 20 kilometres from the start. There was no sign of it, though, and I couldn't see clearly enough to be certain that I was looking at the town of Le Touquet. It wasn't long before the sun slowly sank in the west, as they say. Yes, it was a great picture and it would have been quite romantic under different circumstances. Unfortunately, I was in a strange country (well, off the coast of a strange country, in fact) and it was about to get dark.

What appeared to be the Le Touquet city lights shone up ahead, but there was no estuary. My experience with nine metre tides was increasing; good for future reference but not all that great at the time. We had not looked at the phases of the moon but we should have. It was a full moon. Saved. As the sun headed below the western horizon, the big yellow orb rose in the east, gradually turning white as it gained altitude. It was enough to see the waves and the sand, but still no estuary, just a huge expanse of sand.

Tracking south, it was time to plan an entry into the lights but I was still about two kilometres west of them. How far to go? Where was the channel? A yellow buoy appeared about 300 metres away that I thought might indicate a channel, because the moon was shining off water to the north of the buoy. It didn't look quite right so I discounted it as marking a channel and continued on, albeit a bit more slowly.

A shout from my left, "Steve!" Did I hear that? Another one, and then the yellow buoy moved. I paddled towards it, and it raised its arms. It was Trevor in his jacket. What was he doing way offshore? All the odd features slowly took shape: there he was on a beach, Le Touquet about 1.5 kilometres behind him and a lot of sand in between. What a long drag with the kayak, particularly as the wheels were not on it. Who needs wheels in the sea! Another lesson about the size of the tides.

Between the two of us we hauled it all the way to the car, checked the paddling distance as 27 kilometres for the day, loaded up and headed for the nearest eating house that served beer. Apparently the town is popular with the English and we met quite a few on the streets who told us the best pub to eat at. I saw steak on the menu, actually it said steak tartare, but I thought tartare sauce might be nice on steak. Trevor agreed and ordered the same.

We now know what tartare means. We had raw mince, held together with raw egg. Luckily the dish included chips. Surprisingly, it was quite palatable. By the end of the pile of mince, I was grateful for the experience, but not all that keen to try it again. In fact, Trevor had to make me toughen up and take the last mouthful. He was my boss after all.

Trevor's blog: *We set off from Blackett Close at 08:00 to catch the P&O ferry from Dover to Calais at 12:05 after getting the car and caravan, lovingly termed 'the van', ready for what would be a great trip and a memorable experience. Arrived in Dover early at 10:15 after a clear trip with no problems and was grateful to be put on the next ferry due to depart at 11:05. In fact it departed at bit early and we were off with a very smooth crossing to Calais. Arrived just about 90 minutes later and drove to the first campsite, Stoneham, just south of Le Touquet. Hooked up the van and Steve then decided to give the coast run a bash while there was a bit of time.*

Drive to Boulogne and park just north of the harbour entrance on a sandy beach with the tide going well out. Carry the kayak across the sand to the water's edge and launch at about 17:10. This was a fair distance to carry and I got wet feet and sand in my shoes, knackered even before we started. Drive along the coast to Hardelot Plage, then Le Touquet and wait where we had agreed to meet after about two hours, Steve going about 27 kilometres to get there. Parked up at the top of the beach with what was now an enormous expanse of sand down to the water's edge. Wait there and watch the sun going down with some trepidation. Walked up the sand dunes to try getting a better view up the coast and eventually I could see just the small white sail of the kayak in the distance through the binoculars, and what was to become a very welcome sight throughout the trip. Shouts of joy from me and the pathetic little light on the headband blinking a welcome, in my yellow hi-vis jacket and arms waving like furry, and shouting out to Steve since the sun had gone down by now and it was starting to get somewhat dark. Lug the kayak up the beach and tie it onto the car roof. Off to dinner at a local pub where we met some English guys who said the food was good. Tried the steak tartare without knowing it was raw minced beef. We both eat up but agreed to give that particular delicacy a miss in future!

Next morning, the walk across the beach to the water was just under a kilometre, but with the wheels back on, it was fine. The bounce down the stairs to the sand was no problem but when I got to the water a kilometre away, damn … no lunch box. Off went Trevor at a brisk trot, collected the lunch box back at the stairs, and when he returned he had about 150 metres less to run. The tide was coming in so fast I had followed it 150 metres up the beach in that time. At this rate, Trevor would be as fit as me by the end of the trip.

At first it was a bit tricky to balance the adverse conditions of the opposing tidal current, wind strength and water depth. Whenever I drifted too far off the shore, the penalty would be severe. Luckily, I could monitor my speed closely with the GPS and rectify things whenever I made a mistake.

This seemed to be sea lion coast. A dark shape like a buoy would appear and, as I approached, the head of a sea lion would materialize. Mostly they just watched, not like the shy creatures in England that took off immediately they saw me. The day before there had been a few about, but today they were everywhere. There was even a pair frolicking up ahead and, when they saw me, they swam off to the side and watched me go by.

Although there was an adverse current, with favourable winds starting to pick up and the temperature rising to about 15°C, we had a recipe for some fine gains, if I could just keep out of that current. Hugging the coast closely, I gradually picked up speed during the day with the sail doing a lot of the work. The spray skirt was essential to keep the waves out of the cockpit, but it was all very manageable until the first estuary crossing at Berck. The wind was slightly offshore until I headed out across the bay away from the protection I had been given by the shore. It howled straight onto my left side, making my world very rough, cold, wet and tiring. Relief came when I neared the far bank. I scooted along beside the sand with the tide near full. There were a few people walking along the narrow strip of soft sand left by the high tide, but they were soon left behind and the beach was deserted for a long way.

As the town of Quend slowly came into view, the numbers of people increased again. Some beachgoers lazed in the sun – fully clothed, of course, because it was only about 15°C. Just after I passed a couple who had been taking photos with a mobile phone, the guy shouted and waved. I waved back and thought nothing more of it, but that night I received an email. He signed it "Thierry Huet from Earth," and he congratulated me

1km to water over 1m high undulations (Le Touquet)

about the trip. I don't know for sure that the wave and email were from the same bloke, but he said he saw me from Quend Plage at 1.00pm, the time and the place of the shout from the beach, which is 'plage' in French.

The buildings disappeared behind me, as did most of the people, but a few hardy souls wandered the beach. There was even a bloke swimming in an isolated section. He walked out of the water and up the beach when I was still a few hundred metres away, but as I got closer I could see he was naked. His physique was not a lot different from that of the sea lions, so maybe that was why the cold didn't seem to worry him. With the beach extending a long way ahead I needed to think about the next crossing, which was longer than the last one at Berck. Because the Somme River ran into it, there would probably be a significant current on the falling tide which had already dropped more than a metre.

I rang Trevor to tell him that the wind was strong and the last crossing was a bit tough, so I would head up the estuary a bit before crossing over. That made sense to him so, although he was on the other side and around a curve about 10 kilometres long, he headed inland. The crossing wasn't at all like I expected. Sand pushed due south and eventually turned into rocks. There was no route up the estuary. I was four kilometres from land and still my paddle sometimes hit rocks in the trough between waves.

It was then that I noticed the current was really strong and pushing me towards England. It did not seem to be a great idea to go that way, so I crabbed across the estuary at 45 degrees while sliding inexorably downstream. Near the other side, when I knew I was safe, I turned away from the wind, followed the curve of the land and allowed the sail to fill so that I swept along at about 13km/hr.

Scores of groins poked out from a shingle beach and the waves dropped enough for me to call Trevor. He had driven upstream, reckoned the current was way too strong for a kayak, but waited until I arrived. Unfortunately I had arrived at the point that he had left an hour previously, but neither of us knew that, so confusion reigned. I advised him that I could see cliffs in the distance and they extended as far as the eye could see in a south-westerly direction. That meant nothing to him, but I gave him my co-ordinates, which he put into the car GPS. Problem solved. I was near Ault, at a steep shingle beach with waves just big enough to be annoying, so I landed on the beach as elegantly as I could and headed up to where Trevor was standing. He had just arrived and the car was over the other side of what turned out to be about a five metre levee. It was on a rough road a few kilometres out of town, but seemed to be a popular spot for walkers and fishers.

When we got back to the water the next day, I wasn't entirely comfortable with what I saw. The forecast was for winds almost parallel with the coast but slightly offshore.

"Nope," I said to Trevor, "See how lumpy the sea is. Something is not right here."

As I sailed and paddled down the coast, the wind increased in strength, coming more from the north than the weather report had said, making it onshore rather than offshore. It made for a quicker trip but, when it strengthened to 20 knots later in the day, it certainly was a handful trying to stay as close to the cliffs as possible to avoid the current and also keep out of harm's way.

After setting up camp at a caravan park just inland from Dieppe, and where we first experienced unisex ablutions, Trevor chose a spot close to him and about 10 kilometres north of Quiberville to check my progress. By that time, though, the wind was blowing strongly and I was whooshing along at better than 10km/hr and was already past. It was cold and wet, but good progress was everything. There was no phone conversation between us because the phone had to stay in the dry bag in the small compartment in front of the cockpit. It could only be used when there was no chance of capsize or waves crashing over the kayak.

Peering along the beach at Quiberville I could see no yellow coat. After travelling as far as I thought advisable, I made the decision to land on the downwind side of one of the concrete groins. The waves were about a metre high and smashing onto a steep pebble beach. Paddling in behind the smallest wave I could find, the kayak bounced sideways onto what I would call man-sized pebbles, about 10 centimetres in diameter, slewing into the concrete groin where I bounced out to drag the kayak out of reach of the next wave.

It was a struggle up the shingles, pebbles, bloody rocks – whatever they are called – until I reached a concrete wall about a metre high. Behind it was a concrete path and behind that, another wall and a drop of three metres to the road. Trevor drove over the hill, found me standing on the wall, loaded the kayak and drove us back to the caravan park. As was to be the case until we got to Paris, the caravan park proprietors did not speak English. This is no problem to the intrepid Trevor, though. While one can't say that his French is good, he can make himself understood with his limited vocabulary and gesticulations. He even knows what steak tartare is now.

Sunrise was about 8.00am, so the start time on the water was about 10.00am. By then the sun was warming the 8°C atmosphere, the wind was still relatively gentle and it wasn't too bad putting my wet clothes back on. There wasn't much point wearing dry ones when they would be wet within a few minutes, and there is no-one on the seas to complain about the smell of a bloke with a four-day shirt run.

I was a bit down because I had received an email the previous night from the COP21 Civil Society area rejecting my application to display the kayak. Their reply showed that they had not read what I had said and just treated me as someone who wanted a booth.

> *The General Secretariat for the preparation and organization of COP21/CMP11 regrets to inform you that your proposal for an exhibition has not been accepted.*

This decision is based both on the set of criteria set out in the call for projects and on the great number of projects submitted to the General Secretariat.

The General Secretariat thanks you for supporting the success of COP21/CMP11 and hopes to count you among the visitors to the Climate Generations areas.

My first response was quite negative, I have to say, but it didn't last long and I started to formulate other plans.

While I was enjoying the spectacular scenery on the water, Trevor had his own adventure getting to the caravan park at Caudebec-en-Caux on the Seine, but still very close to the coastal route. Apparently, he mastered the art of a 10-point turn with a caravan in tow before setting the van up, buying some camembert cheese for his lunch and then looking for his kayaking mate.

As usual for 1.00pm, the wind strengthened and I could make up for the slow morning progress, bouncing around the corner into the Fecamp harbour after making 47 kilometres over seven hours. It was a Wednesday afternoon and lots of boats were out racing. Wednesday Afternoon Gentlemen Sailors (WAGS) is a popular past-time on Moreton Bay, Brisbane, where I had done a lot of my sailing, so I presumed the French equivalent was on display here. In the harbour, a concrete boat ramp pointed the way out, a real luxury after the difficult stone beaches. We scurried off to the caravan park, where a warm shower awaited with the bonus of a small restaurant next to the park office. The food was basic but cheap, there was draught beer and also wine at very reasonable prices. Even with my terrible French, I could make myself understood enough to fill my belly.

At dinner, Trevor said how much he admired what I was doing and that he and Marilyn wanted to contribute what I considered to be a large sum of money. I argued that half that would be more than generous, but we did agree to change the subject after I said that I didn't want to cry. It really was an emotional moment for me, to have a mate who had done so much already and then wanted to do more. There is no doubt that I had been through a lot, certainly used up a huge amount of emotional energy to get this far, and it was all there welling below the surface. He almost brought me undone but the conversation moved on and the stiff upper lip survived.

"All done," I thought, but it will never go away entirely. I will never forget how I felt, and how I still feel when I try to talk about it.

Shags cling to the windward face of the pinnacle, held on by the strong winds

I could try analyzing why I felt emotional but didn't want to let it show. The fact that he is an old mate and a Pom is enough of an explanation for me. After all, Englishmen don't cry, so an Aussie wasn't going to let the team down.

> ***Trevor's Blog:*** *Drive to the new campsite, Camping Barre-Y-Va at Caudebec-en-Caux, right on the banks of the River Seine about 30 kilometres west of Rouen, after dropping Steve back into the sea at Quiberville at about 10:00. The campsite sign which I had seen*

Into the harbour (Fecamp)

directed me up a single-lane road where I could see vans, etc, just below me, so thought this was right but which turned into a track leading only to a private residence. Fun doing a 10-point turn on the track with the van in tow. Hook up the van after chatting with the proprietors in a mixture of English and French but gathered that they had a snack bar there and could serve a limited menu, which turned out to be just what we needed. Drive on to the next pick-up point at Fecamp where we had seen what looked like a ramp in the harbour on Google Maps. Get there about 14:00 and suss out the marina/ slipway to get the kayak out. All very good there and a local guy advised that there would be about one metre of water in the marina even at low tide, so should be great. Drive about five kilometres up the coast to Senneville-sur-Fecamp where there was a picnic area on the cliffs with a wooden staircase going down to the beach. Wait there until 15:00 when Steve passed by but too far out to sea to make myself seen or heard, so drive back to Fecamp and get there just about 10 minutes before Steve came into view. Wave like fury in the yellow hi-vis and guide him into the marina and the slipway in the far corner at 15:50, about 10 minutes before the predicted time. Well done, mate – great. Drive back to the campsite for the night with dinner there chez the proprietor.

It was up to 9°C and getting even warmer when we arrived back at the boat ramp the next day. The tide was out another four metres or so, which made the whole floating marina a long way below our feet on the concrete wall. These huge tides still amaze me, having spent all of my life with less than two metre tides. I showed Trevor the rolling start down a boat ramp, flicked the wheels back after crashing into the water and headed around the harbour and out the entrance to the sea. The wind from over my left shoulder blew at less than 10 knots, but the signs were like the last three days, indicating that I could expect it to build.

High cliffs to my left did not seem to deter the wind, as it grew in strength within half an hour. Large white caps appeared 500 metres to my right, indicating favourable wind but adverse current. Rocky outcrops marked a broken shoreline, so it was important to remain vigilant and not be pounded by breaking waves as I hugged the coast to avoid as much current as I could.

It wasn't just the spectacular cliffs here, there were 100-metre high spires that I could paddle between. Shags somehow perched on the windward side in what seemed impossible locations. Between the spires and the cliffs, the wind gusted to maybe 30 knots, so I had a busy time staying upright. An elephant-shaped bluff signalled a slight turn in the coastline. The elephant must have been angry because near where the trunk dipped into the water the currents boiled fiercely. With the wind from behind and the current from the front, the battle raged but, by paddling hard and dancing on the rudder pedals to counter the whirlpools, it wasn't long before I entered calm waters.

There were two guys in a kayak fishing just off the village nestled between the cliffs and a couple of surfers waiting patiently for waves, which presumably did come from time to time. South of the village, the cliffs had huge openings and offshore spires which played havoc with the wind and currents, but certainly provided fantastic views for kayakers.

In the distance I could see a long wall extending about three kilometres out to sea. With the current racing up the coast, this would surely give me a nice eddy, so I aimed for about the middle. The waters slowly calmed and the wind was steady. The eddy pushed me at about 13km/hr towards the end of the wall. I was cold, hungry and thirsty but thought I would get to the other side, pull in out of the wind and fill up.

At such high speed, the area of breaking waves ahead rushed to greet me. This indicated current into the wind, but the distance across was only about 100 metres. It didn't make a lot of sense with the wind behind me, but I soon figured out it was all current related. The other side of the waves was smoother with water welling upwards, the clash of millions of litres of water on collision courses. The end of the wall curved due south for about 500 metres, providing relatively smooth going and giving me a brief period of relaxation. Approaching the southern extremity I could see the current racing straight out to sea at 90 degrees to where I was going.

"No lunch or drink," I thought, "not even a pee."

The nose of the kayak spun to the right as I entered the fray. I slowly turned back to where I wanted to go, which was across the wind that was blowing at something over 20 knots, dropped the sail and set about getting back near land. It was four kilometres of hard yakka. About a kilometre ahead was a green buoy that I aimed for and, after about 15 minutes, I could see the strong current trailing from the buoy straight towards me. It took an hour of bashing along until I could once again head down the coast with the wind astern.

It wasn't possible to paddle as well as sail, because it took most of my strength to hold the kayak from turning sideways into the wind. With a big gust and wave coming together, the kayak would plane at 17km/hr trailing spray. It was exciting stuff and a fitting way to see out the last of the French coastline. The situation stayed like that for 15 kilometres until I rounded the point towards the beach at Le Havre. From the excitement of the rush down the coast, the wind now pushed in my face, the seas flattened to nothing, there were small catamarans and kayaks on the water, people sunbathed and some even swam.

I was guided in by a familiar call from the beach and a yellow jacket waving its arms. The distance on the GPS was about 47 kilometres for the third day in a row. Each day had been characterized by a slow start, adverse currents, and then a wind that threatened to blow me to kingdom come. What a difference a capable support crew made. Trevor looked after all the land details and I paddled. We were doing so well together, a well-oiled machine even if it was a little ancient.

We loaded up and headed back to camp where we had pre-ordered a kilo of mussels each. Moules and frites – mussels and chips – seems to be a French favourite. It is now certainly one of mine.

CHAPTER 18

UP THE SEINE

It was a relatively cool Friday morning at the Le Havre beach for my first day paddling up the Seine River, but a few hardy souls were in the water and two people were walking along waist deep about 50 metres from the sand. After preparing the kayak, dressing it with the skirt, and putting on my lifejacket and other gear, I needed to pee yet again so I headed off to find a toilet. This was starting to become a nuisance, as each morning I would need to go multiple times. I figured it was something to do with what I was putting my body through, but there wasn't much I could do.

The distance around the harbour wall was about six kilometres, making it about an hour before I entered the Seine estuary. We had read about huge flood tides rushing up the estuary, but the conditions weren't like that at all. Sure the tide was favourable, but there was a strong headwind so, again, it was a day of being wet and not very comfortable.

A huge cable-stayed suspension bridge called the Pont de Normandie, about two kilometres long, crosses the Seine 10 kilometres up from where we drew an arbitrary line to represent the entrance to the Seine River.

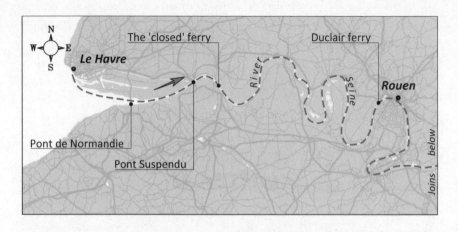

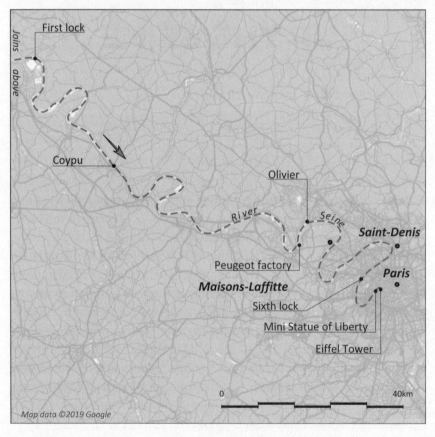

There were a few ships about, but nothing much to see on the flat grassy shore until the next Pont Suspendu at Tancarville, where I was to meet Trevor. After averaging 47km/day down the coast, it seemed to have taken ages to get just 29 kilometres to where he was, under the suspension bridge. He met me with the news that I was to paddle to a slipway a few kilometres upstream.

The bank there was a solid four metre high concrete wall with no break that I could see. Ships were tied next to it and there were a couple of sailing catamarans up on the hard stand. The car arrived in the distance and the familiar yellow jacket got out and walked to the edge of the wall. It wasn't until I was right at the car that the break in the wall appeared, complete with a concrete ramp. Trevor had talked the owners of the yard into letting him in to pick up his mate.

At the office on the way out, we learned that the yard would be closed for the weekend so we discussed plan B. During his investigations into a landing spot Trevor had been told by many that "Le bac ferme." The bac is closed. What's a bloody bac? Anyway, nearby was a ferry ramp and viewing it at high tide it looked perfect for the next day's launch. The caravan park was just a few kilometres up-river by road, about 25 kilometres by river and, with a plan for the morning, we had it all conquered.

The ferry ramp was ideal with but had one slight problem. With the tide now low, mud covered it to a depth of over 15 centimetres. We prepared for the day, towed the kayak on its wheels to the top of the mud, raised the wheels, pushed the kayak so that I could just step onto the back from the clean concrete area and then set about sliding spectacularly down into the water. It was a fine idea, but lacked in one subtle detail. When I sat in the kayak, my weight squeezed the water out of the mud and sucked the kayak down, so that it was nearly impossible to move. I applied my bottom-jerking procedure with a few added sideways rolls and managed to move about 10 metres before I could go no further. Trevor donned his wellies and slid down to give me a push. With the added horsepower we started a mud slide that slowly carried the kayak almost to the bottom of the ramp. Here, the concrete had just a smear of mud on it, the slope was negligible and at the end was a vertical sheet pile wall into the river with the water lapping close to its top. I climbed out, launched the kayak into the water from the top of the sheet piles and then plonked my bum on the seat so that I could wash my feet and prepare to paddle.

The current coming downstream was still pretty strong and we were not sure when it would turn, but the plan was to paddle about two hours against it and then hope it turned to carry me up river at a decent rate. We were near an oil terminal with a few large ships alongside. The first one was on a wharf that I could see through, so I paddled under the wharf, being careful to avoid any areas that might have steam coming down. The next wharf did not have the openings, so that necessitated a trip out into the current to get around the ship tied to it.

"Shades of the Mississippi with its barges," I thought as I battled along at just under 2km/hr. It was only one ship, though. The next wharf had enough gaps to slip through so I paddled underneath it. I started to feel sick where twin pipes about 30 centimetres in diameter discharged some foul-smelling liquid into the mud about 5 metres below top water level and just above where I was. It took an hour or so to shake that off.

Eventually the wharves slipped into history, geese appeared on the water and I was able to paddle along next to the mud with just the occasional clash of the paddle onto a rock. Ships went past in the haze, making waves that seemed to help boost my speed as I lifted gently up and down. After 2.5 hours, the current slowed to almost nothing and I was able to cross to the other side to cut short a bend. After three hours, the incoming tide was making itself known and I was whistling along at 12km/hr. I had averaged just 5km/hr all morning, picking my way along the edge of the river.

Up ahead, a ferry crossed the river. When I got closer I could see BAC written on its side. Bingo, the light came on. Le bac ferme. The ferry is closed. That is what Trevor had been told many times the previous day. They had been trying to tell him to use the ramp where the ferry had stopped operating.

A familiar yellow jacket appeared ahead, signifying the road near the camp site. We discussed the time, my speed and the map, then agreed that Duclair would be the goal for the day.

A phenomenon that I noticed on the canals in England is that, as a boat goes past, it induces a flow going the opposite way due to its displacement of the water. Even on the Seine, a big river, some of the ships were so large that I could see the same effect. Around the bend came a ship. I had seen river cruisers like those you see in the advertisements for Europe, but this one was a full-on ocean liner. The crowd on the foredeck about six stories up waved enthusiastically so I waved back with my paddle. Then they were gone.

I kept a good pace up all the way and pulled into Duclair about 5.00pm, after waiting a few minutes for the ferry to depart the ramp. Trevor grabbed the kayak and set off back to the car at a pace that was way too fast for me. I was a bit weary and the day had exacerbated some aches and pains that were starting to appear more often. "Come on body," I willed, "not far to go now."

A new problem developed in my left buttock. There was no bum left, no padding at all, but the real issue was a twinge from the lower back all the way to the groin. Eric, the mad paddler in New York, said that had become a real issue for him, but after he embraced stand-up paddle boarding (SUP) it slowly went away. I have some great SUP friends, even if a few are a tad crazy. Jules from MKC, where I finished the US leg, was paddling from New York to Florida on a SUP. It does not, at least to me, seem like a sane way to propel oneself across the water, so I really hoped that it would not come to me having to follow in Eric's footsteps.

It wasn't until mid-day that we got back to the Duclair ferry. The plan was to paddle until late and by starting late I would reduce the hours paddling against the current. I crossed the river easily, but still struggled against wind and tide until it went slack at 3.30pm and started to flow in my direction at 4.30pm. Through Rouen, the tide was giving me a boost, but it was cold and windy with small waves slopping onto my life jacket. Across the river someone was playing the bagpipes while another guy stood motionless beside him facing the river. The impressive lift-bridge in the centre of the town signified the last stretch of navigable river for large ships. Just upstream, the first low bridge appeared (less than 10 metres high), so there would be no big boats above Rouen.

Once more in the countryside, with light starting to fade, a single scull approached from upriver. A barge was approaching, coming downstream about 200 metres from the bank. I angled further in towards the left bank to give both of them plenty of room. As I moved over, so did the scull. He came really close and stopped, so I said hello and we had a chat. I tried to explain in French about the trip and where I had been. The discussion was difficult, until he spoke a couple of words in very poor English. It wasn't until I had finished he said, "Thank you, Steve." I was pretty sure I had not told him my name, but it was well after 6.00pm and I was cold and tired. He said my name again and then told me in perfect Cockney he had just met Trevor who was about a kilometre ahead and that he had rowed down to meet me. His name was Jan and was from Putney! Bastard.

The rowing club that we had seen on Google Earth had a floating pontoon which made taking the kayak out very easy. Jan rowed past, but that was the last we would see of him, so he would escape retribution.

There were a number of heavy showers during the next day and it was windy. Paddling against the tide, I managed to average 5.7km/hr, which brought up the first lock in a bit over six hours. No more tides to worry about, just the flow of the Seine. We were making good time, with the blistering charge down the coast and now the tidal slog was just about done. Paris was within our sights. The first of five locks signified only 200 kilometres to the Eiffel Tower and I had just paddled on the last tidal water for the whole trip. Finally, the end was close and I could sense it, feel it all over my body. We were going to do this with a bang, not a whimper. Five days at 40km/day, against the flow, yes!

That night we received an email from Roman Huet. He is Thierry Huet's son. Remember the bloke from 'Earth' who had seen me from the beach at Quend? Roman was studying cinema at a university in Paris. We agreed to meet when I paddled to the Eiffel Tower and he would make a short video about the trip.

The reach between the first lock and the second lock the next day was a good tester for average speed on the non-tidal section, provided the wind did not vary a lot. My speed did improve slightly to 5.8km/hr but was dependent on river velocity, which was dependent on river depth and width. The water was clear, the showers held off most of the day and the scenery was stunning, with white cliffs, a ruined castle, magnificent houses and, at one stage, a conveyor belt right across the river. Viking Line tour boats travelled up and down the Seine, but not many people were on deck. Some of the windows are floor to ceiling and an attractive woman waved enthusiastically from the edge of her bed. I waved back equally enthusiastically, but in half a minute she was gone, ships passing in the night. Well, not really: it was daylight and I was not on a ship, but you know what I mean.

In all it was an uneventful and enjoyable paddle, but when I reached the second lock where Trevor was waiting I had only covered 35 kilometres. That wasn't enough for my 40-kilometre goal, although the midday Sunday finish that I had blogged about would be easily achievable at that pace. There had been just one concern with the big push to the finish. My shoulder was waking me in the night and despite the fact that kayaking is essential to keep it healthy, there was a chance that I had asked too much of it over the past nine months.

We discussed the following day's paddle over dinner and agreed that the wind would be favourable for 20 kilometres along a straight section of river to allow me to get the sail up and rocket along, making a great start to the day and a chance to pick up time.

Our previous night's plans had been great in theory, except that after half a kilometre of fickle winds, sometimes even swinging around to head on, the sail had to come down and it was back to business, hugging the bank and trying to keep my speed above 6km/hr.

A strange animal appeared from behind a boat on a mowed section of the river bank. It looked to me like a beaver. It didn't appear too worried by the kayak as it walked across the grass, slid into the water, swam about two metres and then dived, never to be seen by me again. Apparently it was a coypu, an introduced species from South America and generally regarded as a pest. Known to the French as the 'ragondin', it lives in burrows on river banks, feeds on river plants and is a type of large rodent.

I passed another ruined castle on the top of a northern bend, just like the day before, giving me a sense of déjà vu.

There was one incident that bothered me. When close to the right bank I lost concentration and the paddle hit a rock quite hard, which sent a searing pain through my right shoulder. "Bloody hell," I thought, "a bit over 100 kilometres to go, surely the shoulder will make it." As I explained previously, because my shoulder is permanently dislocated from a motorbike accident in 2006, I have a dull pain all the time and I'm often made very aware of it. For this reason, there is always the worry that it will let me down. I know where the referred pain is from that internal injury and this pain I was now feeling was not in that spot. I just hoped it was a one-off and all would be fine.

The distance from the start of the day to the next lock was 37 kilometres, not enough for one day, so we had decided to finish the day at a pontoon on the river upstream of the lock and near a rowing course. It would have been easy for Trevor to find, until he was redirected by the gendarmes at Rosny-sur-Seine because of some sort of rally, but he got there and I spotted his yellow jacket from a few hundred metres away. The walk to the car was less than half a kilometre, so with an easy departure from the river it was a fine place to stop.

On the way back to the caravan, we pulled into what was described as a pub, but which in fact was a nightclub serving food before the clubbing started. The menu was on a blackboard and none of the staff spoke any English. The only other patron at the time reckoned he knew some English, so between the three of us we managed to figure out what the menu said. We bought the guy a drink for his help and while chatting in broken French at the bar Trevor let slip one of his 'other words'. He has spent so much time working in Middle Eastern countries that in times of confusion an Arabic word, usually Libyan, would pop out.

"You finish when you get to the Eiffel Tower?" the bloke asked in French.

"Oui," replied Trevor, "Halas." (Halas means finish in Arabic)

"Ah ha!" the bloke exclaimed, "I am from Tunisia. My name is Khalil."

With another vocabulary to choose from, the conversation went quite well. I know a lot more Arabic words than French words and even knew how to read the alphabet a few years ago. Quite a mix it was, but a lot of fun.

During dinner a filling dropped out of my tooth. That was the fourth tooth to fail on the trip. "Just another hole," I thought, but no. By the morning the resulting jagged edge had created an ulcer on the bottom of my tongue. It got worse and was painful when I ate, so it was with a conscious effort that I kept my food intake up until the end.

Back in the UK, Marilyn arranged an appointment for 9.30am on the following Monday, my first day back. When I got there, the dentist in Staines explained, after he popped a temporary filling into the hole, what had been going on with my teeth during all of my trips. The reason my teeth often fail on these long trips, he said, is that I must be clamping down or grinding my teeth during exertion. Hallelujah, finally an explanation that made sense. Except, it turned out that wasn't the problem.

Back on the water on Thursday morning, my shoulder was fine and when I managed to keep my mouth shut and my tongue pressed forwards, the pain in my mouth was fine too. I had covered 48 kilometres the previous day and was dead keen to make over 40 again today. I paddled past a power station spewing brown muck into the river, past a few sewage treatment outfalls all of which smelled fine, and past a couple of water treatment plants, all combining to illustrate to an old water engineer just how the river is used. Recycled water? It is everywhere and has been going on for centuries.

The Peugeot factory proudly announced its presence with a huge sign about 10 kilometres short of where we wanted to finish for the day. The factory was opposite a pair of islands splitting the river in two. The channel between the islands, a lock and a weir on the south channel made for some complicated currents and paddling. I made good time up to the wide area near the lock. As I crossed that, a container boat came down the river and turned around into the lock behind me. That was lock number four, the second last one. None had provided suitable portage. In one place, the only exit point from the river was nearly three kilometres downstream. Kayaks are not allowed into the locks so, all in all, they are difficult obstructions for kayakers.

On the gendarmes pontoon with Olivier

The sun was behind me, which made me grateful that the skipper of the container boat had managed to see me with its glare in his eyes. As I rejoiced in this, an official-looking boat sped down the river directly towards me. The spray from the bow dropped as the boat slowed and continued towards me. "Shit, what now," I thought. There was something funny about the boat, though. It looked very official, but the guy in the bow was wearing a yellow jacket. It was Trevor. He had commandeered a fire rescue boat which he then used to escort me a kilometre upriver to the gendarmes' pontoon. That's right, the pontoon with a police boat tied up on it. That's Trevor, though. One never knows what he will come up with next and he is never backward in coming forward.

After we hauled the kayak out and were beside the car, the driver of the boat came over and introduced himself as Olivier. He was the boss of operations and when Trevor had asked if there was anywhere to drag a kayak out he had immediately decided to embrace the trip and help in any way he could. After an enthusiastic conversation in English we arranged to put in at 10.00am the next morning and headed for our caravan.

Trevor had set up the van at Maisons Laffitte, which is 30 minutes by train to the centre of Paris. He advised that everyone spoke excellent English, there was a restaurant and that they played the rugby on a wide-screen TV. It transpired that two staff we met later were from Wales and Essex, so there would have been something wrong if their English was not good.

Looking back, I was falling to bits. Teeth and gums are a telling sign that the body is failing. I know now that the English dentist's very plausible explanation that I was gritting my teeth was wrong. Every long trip that I have done has resulted in poor gums and busted teeth. When you are driven to achieve a certain goal, you resist the signs and plough on. Sure, I was worried about my shoulder, but at the time I had no idea just how stressed my body was. I suspected that I might be losing mental strength but that could just be overall tiredness. With the destination in sight, I was hardly going to stop now and start thinking about the overall state of my health.

Back on the water Friday morning at Olivier's mates' pontoon, it was almost certain that I could make a Saturday afternoon finish at the Eiffel Tower. The water was glassy and just upstream there was a long island with the shipping channel to the north. I paddled on the south side, inside the island where it seemed like the flow was cut off for some reason. Cakes of dark stuff floated on the surface. It looked like cow shit, it smelled like cow shit and the other test didn't matter. I was pretty sure what I was seeing, especially as the land on that bank was farmland.

A sparkle of white spray raced down the river and within seconds a speedboat materialized in front of it. Barefoot skiing. The guy sped past, skiing backwards. It was then that I noticed the lanes marked by yellow buoys. This was some sort of calm area where water skiing was carried out. I guess even at high speed, floating cow pats are no threat to bare feet. He didn't come back, so maybe he was on his way home when he passed me. Who knows? Who cares? My mind was on other things, like keeping my mouth shut to help my tongue, and paddling hard to get distance.

The river stayed glassy until after lunch when a breeze riffled the surface and slowed my paddling speed. More and more houseboats appeared on the banks and the number of fishermen increased. Some of the fishermen had either a tent or a shack set up, where they were living rough. At the fifth and last lock Trevor was waiting patiently to help me with the portage, which went smoothly. At first neither of us was sure what to do when we were putting the kayak back in the water. A fisherman had his gear out on both sides of the only entry point. Luckily the kayak just fitted and we didn't have to ask him to move. We were both relieved to have the last lock behind us.

An elevated roadway, like a bridge, ran along the bank. All the area underneath was concrete where about 20 shacks had been constructed. They looked like they had been there a long time, so I guess the authorities just turn a blind eye, or maybe wait until there is a flood and they all disappear.

We had arranged to meet at a bridge at Saint Denis about 42 kilometres from the day's start. When I arrived the yellow jacket waved me in.

"Go to the eighth houseboat past the bridge," yelled Trevor. "It is maroon. Go inside it and then stop."

No problem. I can count to eight. It was a skill I learned in outrigger canoeing where you have to be able to count to 15 so you know when to change sides. That was a bit challenging at first but I got the hang of it. On the day I paddled an outrigger canoe 93 kilometres I was still counting my steps when I went to the bathroom that night.

"You can tie up here or we can drag you up the bank," advised Trevor.

The bank was six metres high and at least 45 degrees so it was a no brainer: tie up next to the boat. Renaud, the boat owner, helped with the mooring. His English is very good and he is an author. He decided to take his troublesome 17-year-old son out of school, bought a team of horses and a wagon and crossed Bulgaria with him. They then travelled by car to remote Siberia. He had just written a book, Step by Steppe, about their adventures. Unfortunately there are no plans to translate it into English.

That night I was restless. Tomorrow would be a big day. The physical journey would be over.

We were supposed to be at Renaud's boat at 9.30am for the day's launch but were there at 8.45am. The French start the day late, in general, and as it was a Saturday morning we thought it best to wait until 9.00am before pressing the doorbell on the gangway. At 9.00am Renaud came out and helped us depart, wishing me a "bon voyage" and I set off for the last time. Just downstream was a good boat ramp we could have used, but it wasn't visible on Google Earth. Had we done so we would not have met Renaud, and it had been much easier to just tie the kayak up alongside his houseboat.

Most of the houseboats, which are huge steel constructions, are used for living in but they are so big that some businesses are run from them. One large white one was a dental surgery. The windows were large and inside I could see what one normally sees at the dentist. I looked in enviously, though, as I clamped my mouth shut to keep my tongue away from the broken tooth.

Being a weekend, there were lots of rowers on the river. When I came to an island I stayed on the narrow side, where most of the rowers were. They were a mix of singles, doubles and fours. Some had trainers in motor boats alongside, but mainly they were just by themselves. Two young women were stopped near the rowing club, so we had a chat about what I was doing and where I was going. Our conversation was in a mix of French and English, but more English than French luckily.

The girls headed off a bit quicker than me but I managed to keep them in view, so I used them as something to race and thus keep my speed up. The trick had worked in Australia on the Murray and in the US on the Mississippi where I raced much larger boats. Another woman in a single scull was ahead and every time she stopped for a rest I would gain on her.

Two boats to race now and I was hammering along. Unfortunately, the single stopped and turned around. Bugger. Then I saw the weir. A weir! Lock number six, six out of five. How could we have missed that? Since this was entirely unexpected and Trevor and I had not planned to meet up there, I had to manage the exit and entry on my own without the usual help from my mate.

Luckily there were steps out of the river and a muddy path around the weir. Unfortunately, the path went behind the lock keeper's residence with right-angled corners to negotiate and, at the end, a barrier to stop bikes. These barriers also stop kayaks unless you it lift over them, so that's what had to happen. All my sprinting had given me maybe 10 minutes gain and this little detour added over half an hour.

Above the lock, the wind picked up and sailing boats zoomed across the water. A wake-boarder sped past and eventually three kayakers

With Trevor - Job done

… and I could see the Eiffel Tower (Wow)

paddled down towards me. We discussed where I was going but they said it was "forbidden, no kayaks are allowed near the Eiffel Tower section of the river." I told them that I didn't care about rules; I was just going to do it. "Plead ignorance," they recommended. That was my plan.

I paddled on against the wind, hugging the left bank, and then half unexpectedly I could see the Eiffel Tower in the distance with a balloon framed next to it.

"Wow! I am really here. Hard to believe that I have come all this way."

That view will be with me forever, indelibly etched on my mind like the first view from the kayak of the Statue of Liberty in the US, and the Tower Bridge and Big Ben in the UK.

The Eiffel Tower stayed in view and then another surprise. A mini Statue of Liberty appeared on an island in the river about a kilometre from the tower. For a minute or so the statue lined up with the tower behind it.

My job was to get to the bridge near the tower on the right bank and to stop at the steps. I thought every bridge I saw would be the one but no, there was another just ahead. And then a yell from the side. Trevor was on a boat moored on the bank, apparently somewhere he shouldn't be, but that is Trevor. It was before the bridge and just before the steps. A few paddle strokes later and I was nearly there. Trevor ran to welcome me but I stopped paddling.

An emotional moment: everything that had happened in the past nine months seemed to flash through my mind.

"Even if you don't make it ..." Really Bob Brown? Was there any doubt? "I'm here. I'm here!"

It took just a few seconds and then I was back to the reality of the moment. I paddled to the steps where we dragged the kayak out. Trevor had brought a warm can of beer for a toast, Roman was on the bridge filming and his mate was nearby filming as well. I sat on the kayak and said a few words while Trevor took a video with the Eiffel Tower in the background.

"The trip is now very clear to me. It is the same as the fight for climate change resolution, a tough hard slog with huge mental challenges. The fight will be won not by celebrities and not by the rich and famous. There will be no accolades for the warriors. It will be by ordinary people determined that the future of the human race is paramount, and who do whatever they can in their power to bring about the changes in our society that must come if we are to survive."

The video camera did not record that speech. We took no photo of the kayak on the water with the Eiffel Tower in the background because we were on the wrong bank. The car was parked a few hundred metres away so I walked the kayak to it through the crowds. We loaded up, headed to a restaurant near Roman's apartment, about three kilometres away, drank champagne, had a nice meal, answered a lot of questions for Roman's tape, and headed back to the camp site to watch Australia beat Wales in the rugby.

The next morning we were up long before dawn, crossed the English Channel in style (after my indefatigable mate Trevor had wangled us entry into the P&O lounge and free champers) and were in Staines before 3.00pm. The trip was done.

Trevor has written site diaries all his life. Engineers have to do this because mistakes happen and when they do a record is essential. His blogs are great to return to if I have missed a detail because they are like his work diaries.

Trevor's last blog: *Wake up early and push off at about 08:30. [It was a] 20 minute drive back to the boat, great after the time it took last night. Steve did confess that if we were not so close to the finish, he would have had a day's rest, but now was keen to complete and we have arranged with Roman to do the filming today. Steve pushed off at 09:15 after a chat with Renaud, gave him Steve's book since he too has a book being written about his adventures with his son, entitled Step by Steppe.*

Agree that Steve would phone me at 12:00 when he should be about 5 kilometres from the Eiffel Tower. Drive to the Tower and find a vacant parking spot after about 20 minutes driving around the side streets. Phone Roman and agree to meet him about 11:30. He arrived and we spun it out without paying until Steve phoned at 12:00 to say he was all on course for about 13:00. Pay for four hours parking, eight Euros, and walk to river to set up camera, etc. Steve called to say that he had come across another lock which we had not identified previously and had to haul the kayak around it on his own, including negotiating over the fence as well. Steve arrived at about 13:20 and paddled up to the steps from the riverside, although he had met other kayakers downstream who had said that it was forbidden to paddle near the bridge and Tower. Anyway he did it!

Landed safely after an epic journey and took loads of film to record the event before driving to Roman's flat. Treated him to lunch with champagne, but his friend who had also done some filming could only stop for the drink. Good lunch, farewell to Roman and back to Maisons-Laffitte campsite.

Check timing to Calais, four hours and 15 minutes on non-toll motorway, or three hours with toll motorway, so agree on the toll. Realise SatNav would work out timings on maximum speed, which we could not maintain so need to allow, say 3.5 to four hours to Calais and for 11:35 ferry would need to leave at 07:00 latest. Big effort in dark and forfeit tea in bed, but have the tea, tart up and away at 06:30. Exit gate locked so 'negotiate' early opening with the security guard. Drive to Calais doing about 70 mph, all OK. Arrive Calais about 10:15 and manage to get on the 10:45 boat boarding in 5 minutes. What luck. Get on board and have a full English breakfast served by Steph from Melbourne in real luxury. Give her the kayak story and see if we can get on the bridge of the P&O. Boat manager, Bill from Scotland, very apologetic but no way can he get us on the bridge. Try writing to the company and may be more lucky. Anyhow Bill invited us up into the club lounge where he would provide champagne on the company. Very nice way to end the epic journey. Drive home for tea.

And so it was time to await the climax. I had two mates, Trevor and Andrew, who fondly remembered our time four decades previously. Proud Englishmen and proud engineers, they thought that they wouldn't be worth much if they couldn't help an Aussie mate get to Paris. Now all three of us talk about the fun we had, a great addition to those Libyan memories all those decades ago.

Made it (Paris)

CHAPTER 19

A FINAL SHOCK

Back in Staines in the UK, comfortable and normal, the journey to the Eiffel Tower was behind me. All I had to do was wait for the Climate Summit and drag the kayak through the streets of Paris from the Eiffel Tower to the COP21 site.

Trevor went off to his voluntary work the next day and I headed into Staines to treat myself to an English breakfast. Surprisingly, the cheapest and best breakfast was at the pub where I had my coffee amidst many people having their first pint. Climbing back into the car with a full belly, Dire Straits was playing 'Money for Nuthin'. At full volume, windows shut tight, of course, I had my own little dance. "This is life, this is great," I thought.

Wham! My body convulsed and I sobbed out loud. The tears flowed and I was a mess. Two minutes later I collected myself. It took four months for those feelings to stop. I'm still not like I was. Some music can move me to tears, or many events, acts of kindness, or the beauty of nature can touch my heart and the tears will flow. As I've mentioned earlier in this book, my reaction to stress from a super high heart rate is to feel like crying. Maybe there is a clue in that. Maybe I have used physical stress for years as a release from suppressing other emotions. Then again, maybe it is just a physiological reaction in my genes.

I had planned a giant trip for years, reworked it enthusiastically on the advice of special friends, set off to the other side of the world and then crashed hard, learning some valuable lessons about people, about expectations and especially about myself. Despite that, I had stoically continued, made it to New York, made it across England even with a hostile support crew, and then with the aid of long-term friends I had finally made it to Paris.

Yes, I had made it, just like I always expected to: despite Bob Brown's doubts, despite the absence of the friends who had originally encouraged me, despite the support crews who had no idea how to support me. Not getting any attention in Paris was an anticlimax, sure, but most of my adventures finish like that. I'm not Robinson Crusoe in that regard; most adventurers do not have a crowd waiting for them at the finish line. After a couple of years and looking back dispassionately I'm pretty sure that I was just totally drained. I had held it together for 10 months with many more downs than ups. I had come through the Mississippi challenges and I had willed my body to stay together until Paris. The relief of achieving what I set out to do, under enormous pressures and disappointments, just blew the valve on all the pent-up feelings. It was an extreme, slow motion version of my life-long response to high cardio activity.

Waiting for the Climate Summit I settled into writing and watching the quiz shows with Marilyn at 5.00pm each day. She was very impressive and could beat many contestants, whereas I was hopeless. The daily routine provided a sense of normality, but I wasn't anywhere near normal.

I booked a cheap flight to Calgary, Canada, to meet my son Jonathan. Yes, I know that one shouldn't fly, that flying is an important contributor to global warming, but he is my son and I was going to see him. It was the 31 October and the flight was nowhere near full. Being the final of the Rugby World Cup may have had an influence; hence the cheap price just for that day. The flight was through clear skies and I had a window seat. Up through the islands of Scotland, straight over Iceland with lots of grey, bare earth and then over the middle of Greenland. I looked down on this wild, white country with great rocky mountains thrusting through the snow and ice, twisted with great whorls of different seams, defying the mass of white covering them. They would win one day: shake off the snow and ice. The rocks would emerge and the white would become clear blue liquid covering the earth with another six metres of water. My fragile cocoon in the sky keeping me alive at 11,000 metres was nothing compared with what was below.

There was no snow in Banff, too early in the season. Jonathan took me to a bar where most of his mates were having a great time in their Halloween costumes. I'm not big on Halloween, so wasn't aware at first what was happening. I just thought his friends were a bit odd. Nice though.

It snowed that night and I had ordered winter tyres for the small sedan I hired, so I headed for the mountains above Canmore. Two pick-up trucks had been along the road before me so I followed their tracks. All alone, deserted mountain road, lots of snow: it was a great escape. I tore madly along, every now and again coming to snow that flew over the top of the car. The world would go black. The wipers would groan under the load and I would take my foot off the accelerator, holding the car in what I fervently hoped would be a straight line. The adrenaline cleansed my body. I was alive.

All too soon it was time to say goodbye, but not until my son, bless him, had one last crack at his old man. Tunnel Mountain is a feature of Banff with a well-known trail to the top. But we didn't take the trail, not at first. We went straight up from the town, at full pace, both of us pretending to be nonchalant, speaking in very controlled sentences so that the other person could not hear the gasping and wheezing. The view from the top was stunning. We deserved it. I had long since given up hope of thrashing my son at anything, but I sure as hell wasn't going to make it easy for him.

Back in Staines, I planned my COP21 entry. The route through the streets of Paris was quite short compared with everything I had done previously. The venue was actually near Saint-Denis where we had left the kayak tied beside Renaud's houseboat. Accommodation was booked. Renate would be there, friends from 40 years ago now living in France would be there. It was all going fine, except my heart wasn't really in it. I was tired. My body was okay but my mind was exhausted. I wouldn't have my mate Trevor to look after me in Paris this time. It was becoming a chore. Disappointment after disappointment could not be assuaged, even by the wonderful support from my mates at the end. What I fervently hoped for was that the people I knew that I would meet at COP21 would rejuvenate me with a final kick. Four years of planning and serious action was coming to a climax. I would make it work, wouldn't I?

Then everything changed.

The Paris terror attacks charged onto the news.

This was grim, horrible and close to home, having just been there. My friends living in the south of France who I was going to meet at the Summit, decided not to go. I waited, talked to Roman in Paris and vacuumed up every bit of information that I could. After a week, it was clear that the gendarmes would not allow me to drag my kayak along the streets to the Summit under any circumstances. The organizers had already advised me that it would not be allowed inside unless I paid for a stand, which, at many thousands of dollars, was way outside my capacity.

My dreams were shattered, but that was nothing compared with those who had died: families left to suffer for the rest of their lives and people who would carry dreadful injuries until they died. I was disappointed, but also relieved. Secretly, at the same time as I was preparing for the final hurrah, the climax at the Summit, I was full of doubt that I had enough left in the tank to pull it off.

I'm not even sure that I was totally sane at the time. It felt like I had been traumatized and couldn't recover, but there was no way I would admit that to myself. Who in their right mind would have half welcomed the chance not to complete something they had worked so hard to achieve? I think that having given my all, emotionally more than physically, my tank was empty. Despite the magnificent assistance from Trevor and Andrew at the end I had battled disappointment after disappointment. Maybe I was afraid of committing to the final leg. My dreams of arriving at COP21 and being able to say, "Yes, I paddled here," might not be possible anyway. Just about every other dream had been shattered. The only one left in my control had been to get to Paris and I had done that.

Maybe the whole experience was necessary to make the stubborn pragmatist that I am understand that his dreams, his goals, were not necessarily shared in the way that he believed.

I was operating in a haze, numbed by the events, but still able to function efficiently, perhaps like a robot. The kayak was packed and delivered to the shipping agent. I wanted to load a bag of clothes into it that Jacqueline had left behind, but she insisted that I bring it on the plane. The caravan and car were sold, and I booked a flight to Australia arriving 2 December 2015, the final day of the Climate Summit in Paris. I was going home, home to my daughters, my grandchildren whom I had missed so much and home to a world that I was much more familiar with. Some people were disappointed for me, but it was what it was.

My kayak was about to be retired. It had served me well. We had been through a lot. It needed a name so I had to decide, was it male or female? You would not treat a woman the way that I had treated it, so I named him 'Old Yella', which sounded right. We had been on some wild adventures for more than 12,000 kilometres over eight years. Old Yella and I had done a lot. We were both the worse for wear but there was a familiarity, a comfort in knowing what he could and couldn't do.

Old Yella was a bit bent out of shape and showed more than a few scars from the battles over the years. He had never let me down. He did not demand special treatment. He did not complain that he did not get enough attention. He did not have emotions. His plastic body could just take the punishment without complaining, without bursting into tears when a favourite old tune came on the radio. I was shattered, but too stubborn to realise it.

I just wanted to get home.

PART 5

AIN'T OVER YET

CHAPTER 20

REGROUPING

Back home in Australia, the hype around Paris and COP21 confused me. Here we were, excited about promises that, if they all were honoured, might take the earth to about 3°C above pre-industrial levels, but would probably end up in a situation much worse. It was a disaster to me, but only James Hansen, the ex-NASA climate scientist, was saying so. At least, no-one else was getting any publicity for saying so.

I very quickly fell back into the ordinariness of everyday life. Somewhere to live was first priority. Surprisingly, the bank said that I had just enough money for a deposit on the cheapest house in Ballina, the beach-side town near Lismore where I had started my journey. There were three houses available so I made an offer on one. It was exactly what I wanted, land enough to store my kayaks and trailers, and a house that was tiny but liveable and would be much more so once I could afford a new roof. For the first time in 20 years, I had a home mortgage again, a place to call my own and a project that could last as long as I liked. Was this providence?

Had I stayed for COP21 there would have been no money left in the bank. Perhaps it was fortunate that I had come home a bit of a failure.

I thought the right thing to do would be to contact Lea to see how she was, so I emailed her. She reckoned I should not have done so and she never wanted to see me again. That was sad but the door was very firmly closed. Being friends was not an option.

Life was pretty good and I was becoming less emotional, even if I still was a bit delicate. I had been through a lot and needed to recover both mentally and physically. I attended an anti-coal seam gas rally in Lismore where I met a few friends, but I wasn't really comfortable. With tears welling up I excused myself and drove home. This emotional response was foreign territory to me and difficult to understand.

I took Jacqueline's bag of clothes to her. She insisted she take me to lunch, which didn't go too well. She was still angry with me for letting her down, but had no idea that I thought she had let me down by not supporting me on a complex and difficult trip. It took over an hour for her to exhaust her fury. I thought that was the end of it but I was wrong, again. She contacted me a week later for another go. I declined the offer to sit and listen to what a ratbag I was for another couple of hours. I stopped replying to abusive emails, insisting that she drop all contact, but it took a long time before she finally let go.

There was no partner to share my life, a hole that I wanted to fill, so I went back to internet dating. It was a lot of fun meeting people. Mostly the dates would just be swapping life stories over a coffee. Sometimes meeting them was a huge surprise because they had been a little more inclined to present what they hoped to be, rather than who they actually were, but it was always fun. The good thing about internet dating is that you have the chance to filter out the people who oppose your core beliefs. Without that filter I would have met many science deniers or neoliberals, and I doubt such coffee meetings would have gone particularly well.

After a few months, I met Lyn and we clicked. She was passionate about her environmental work and, although a bit older than me, was up to all the adventurous things I liked to do, especially paddling. I thought I had struck gold, but time would tell.

Since the end of the Mississippi River paddling legs, things had not been quite right in my waterworks area, and I was a little concerned. Eventually, I went to my doctor who referred me to a urologist. He booked me into hospital where a brief encounter with a camera inserted through the penis told him what he needed to know. Most blokes my age have

271

enlarged prostates and I was no exception. The difference was that my continual paddling exertions, which involve a lot of core body muscles, had pushed about a third of my prostate into my bladder. That explained the symptoms of intermittent lack of control down there. We had a chat about what to do and I opted to not have surgery unless things got worse.

Every man worries when they get news that affects their very private bits and I was no exception. The operation, if I had it, could leave me with incontinence or erectile dysfunction, but the chances were statistically very low, and much lower if there were no initial problems in that area. Lyn was becoming more important to me. I didn't think it fair to allow a relationship to flourish and then, at a later date, have to disappoint her by becoming a very different man, if it came to that. Most days everything was fine, but one morning I needed to change my underpants three times in the space of an hour. "Shades of some mornings in France," I thought.

I made up my mind. Back at the urologist's I asked if we could do the operation. It was a Tuesday and he operated on Thursdays. He asked when I wanted it done, but with Easter coming up and the fact that he would be going on holidays he gave me limited options. I could have it in a month or so or, alternatively, in two days. I leapt in, "Let's do it," I urged.

That was a good decision: no waiting, no thinking, just commit and go. Lyn was surprised but supportive. If there was a good chance that the relationship would develop, the last thing I wanted was to disappoint her down the track. It was much better to do it now. If the operation didn't work she was not committed and could get out gracefully.

I was nervous. I wasn't even exactly sure where my prostate was. They gave me a nice picture showing a penis and a bladder and the offending organ in the middle. Everyone knows that to check a prostate, the doctor shoves his finger up your bum. Men, think back to your first big kick in the backside. Remember you thought you had cracked your ring gear? That was your prostate complaining. Maybe you don't remember? Maybe you just fell out of a tree, or like me you had done a spectacular ski jump only to find yourself tipping backwards, legs and arms flailing as you sailed out into nowhere, down-ramp receding behind you and fervently hoping for a reasonable landing which was in vain. Or maybe you did the same thing on a trail bike and just about squashed the bike with your bum when you landed. Well, all those painful sensations were your prostate complaining.

After hammering a needle into my back, they then wheeled me into the theatre, where the surgeon performed an astounding feat with a small meat slicer shoved up my dick. There was a green sheet shielding my upper body from the team, but a monitor allowed me to see what the surgeon was seeing. The performance was amazing. The camera and meat slicer gear moved so fast, cutting and washing and sucking. I was transfixed for a few minutes until I lost interest and dozed off because the anesthetist slipped a little more relaxant into the mix.

About 45 minutes or so later, they reckoned it was all over and started to pack up. It was then that I saw my legs. They were suspended at about 45 degrees both horizontally and vertically. That's not where I put them, and I certainly didn't notice them being moved. Everyone seemed happy, though, and off we went to the ward where they fed me for the first time in 24 hours. I ate everything, stopping just short of eating the plates and cutlery, even though I was still starving.

All felt pretty good for a while, with everything still numb. Eventually my toes moved, not in the way they were told, although my feet turned down and jerked a little bit. Things started to wake up, but my feelings were uncertain. Did I want to pee? Can't need to do that: the equipment was looking after that for me. Did I need to have a crap? Probably not: I hadn't eaten for 24 hours. It was all very confusing, so I drifted off to sleep and had nightmares about not being able to find anywhere to have a crap even though I was busting. The staff kept checking me regularly, offering painkillers, but nothing hurt enough to take anything. I just didn't understand what was happening with my body.

The morning came and I learned how to shower with a catheter bag then settled into a relaxing day, with people regularly bringing me food and drink. Late in the day, they pulled the tube out of my dick and I was on my own. That night I peed into a bottle, about 150 millilitres every hour or two and called the nurse each time to measure it, record it and then chuck it out. The fluid was still pretty red, but gradually reduced from a shiraz colour to a rosé. The next day, although I was still feeling a bit weak and a bit tender, I was okay to drive home.

Whatever your fitness, after the surgery I had you have to agree to do almost nothing for four weeks and then take another two to get back to full exertion. For a few days, everything seemed on track with what they told me but, despite best efforts, it all started to go backwards. I developed an infection. It hurt to pee, sometimes the colour was darker, and my dick felt like someone put it on the table and hit it with a hammer. None of this was abnormal, apparently, but I didn't like it. When it was time to pee, there was less than a minute to get to the toilet otherwise it really got hard to hold. If there wasn't an amenity close by, I could push through and hold it, just hoping against hope that it didn't leak, and the urgency would go away. Within a few minutes, though, it would return and I had better have found a toilet by then because it wasn't as forgiving second time round.

Peeing could be an eight-out-of-ten level in pain. I would sweat and shake, especially as I finished. It passed quickly, though, so I could wash up and go back to life as if everything were normal. This probably happens to everyone. There was a nagging question, though. Does everything, you know, work okay? Being curious, I got to day 15 and after a few drinks (not a lot, maybe three wines) decided to give it a shot. Everything was great. Fantastic, really. All of the old skills were working as if heightened by a drug. It was all in harmony, until the very end.

They say it's a fine line between pleasure and pain. Everyone would agree that orgasms are pretty good, but this one was exceptional. The pleasure was intense until someone stuck a napalm bomb up my backside and it went off. How can it hurt so much? Confusion reigned. Was it pleasure? Was it agony? I wasn't the only one confused by it either. Then I felt weak. A triathlon couldn't have left me more drained.

So orgasms were off the menu for a while, but the simple act of peeing was dramatic enough. Urgency became a word to hate. Think back to a time when it took so long to get to a loo that you thought it might be too late. Luckily you made it. Now compress that feeling, that urgency, that panic, into 30 seconds. You can suck air through your teeth, pull your tummy in, flex your arse muscles and even make horrid guttural sounds, but it won't work. You only get the 30 seconds. If you take 28 seconds to get there and you fumble with your zipper for five seconds you are three seconds too late and your underpants will be wet. If it is a public urinal, be very careful as you fling your willie out: the fire hose will have started and you don't want to hit the bloke next to you.

The expression that 'it brought tears to my eyes' is precise and accurate. As you are finishing the stream of pee, a hot flow of energy seeps out of your nuts and all the way down your dick so that your toes tingle, along with the nape of your neck and most places in between. At the end of the four weeks, however, I knew I was not back to normal, but I was feeling positive. The pain in my dick had receded to the tip. The pain when peeing was almost gone. Then it wasn't pain any more, just an awareness and a sensitivity to remind one not to do anything silly.

It took four courses of antibiotics before my infection disappeared. After three months, things improved dramatically. I could pee like a fire-hose. What's more, I could pee when I wanted to and, even more importantly, not pee when I didn't want to. The amount I could hold in my bladder increased daily. I would never ejaculate again but that's no big deal. Life was good.

We remember good things and forget so much about the uncomfortable and painful parts of our lives. That's a good thing. Somehow I found the money for a new roof. Life went on, but a nagging little thought was in the back of my mind, trying to get out. Paris had been disappointing but I was over it, wasn't I?

In July 2016, Ian Dunlop circulated a paper he supported, written by David Spratt. It set out what I had been thinking and did it so unequivocally that there could be no mistake of my support. Ian's history is impressive. You were introduced to him at the Sydney Opera House wharf before I left Australia. His credentials span the coal industry, public sector and academia. He knows his stuff.

The more I read, the more obvious it became that I was not finished. My trip had started in Canberra and I was going back. A few people, including Ian, were promoting a Climate Emergency Declaration. After many months, the signatures collected only totalled 6,000. I offered to help boost that by taking my kayak from Ballina to Canberra, a 1,200-kilometre kayak paddle down the coast and then a couple of hundred kilometres dragging it up the mountain to Canberra.

I was part of a movement. I did not have to pull everything together myself.

The Climate Emergency Declaration people were enthusiastic, Lyn was enthusiastic and Warren was excited. It would happen. Time to get on with it.

CHAPTER 21

LYN

I had some doubts about support for the upcoming trip from Ballina to Canberra, which was unlike me. Was I being egotistical? Was I searching for the finish that had eluded me? Had I just stuffed things up and was looking for redemption? Was I heading for failure again? Was I about to engage in the same grim struggle I had experienced a year ago and had not quite overcome? To test the idea, I bounced it off the local branch of The Greens. Could they help? Their reaction convinced me that I was on the right track, which was all I needed. The Greens didn't cover quite enough bases down the coast but, with their help and encouragement, it was a really great start and we could find more areas of support.

I had three months to organise everything and the trip would only take about two months, so it all seemed quite comfortable. Logistics again: this time to a tight timetable with people arranged to welcome me into their town, some wanting full PowerPoint presentations and others just me saying a few words. The Greens groups, Climate Action Network Australia, Climate for Change groups, 350 Eurobodalla ... anyone we could think of

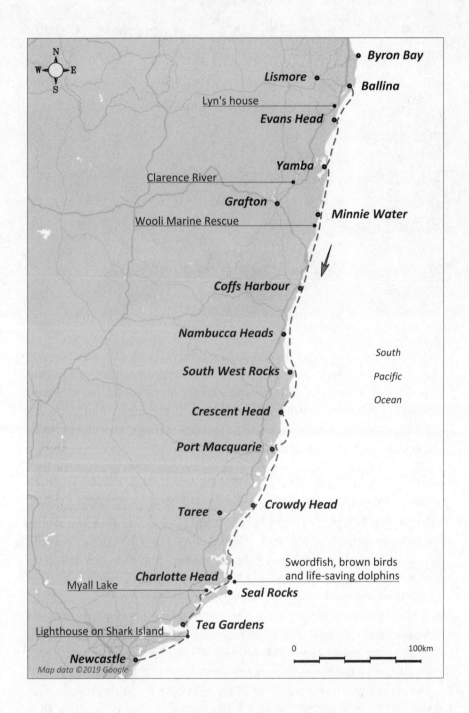

Byron Bay

Lismore • Ballina

Lyn's house

Evans Head

Yamba

Clarence River

Grafton

Wooli Marine Rescue • Minnie Water

Coffs Harbour

Nambucca Heads

South West Rocks

Crescent Head

Port Macquarie

Taree • Crowdy Head

Swordfish, brown birds
and life-saving dolphins

Charlotte Head

Myall Lake • Seal Rocks

Lighthouse on Shark Island • Tea Gardens

Newcastle

South

Pacific

Ocean

0   100km

Map data ©2019 Google

Grandkids say bye to Pa (Ballina)

was roped into helping. Margaret Hender, the stalwart who was running the Climate Emergency Petition, is a brilliant organizer who spent maybe four months almost full-time on the job. She kept control on a shared Google spreadsheet, which some people used but others didn't. During the trip, most big towns and cities I passed through were involved in some sort of activity. Each location had a designated organizer reporting to Margaret and informing either Lyn or Warren, depending on who would be the support crew at the time.

Lyn would be my support crew for the first three weeks before returning to work, Warren the second three weeks and then Lyn would return to go through to the finish. That meant Ballina to Newcastle would be Lyn, Newcastle to Moruya would be Warren, and then Lyn would be able to watch me deteriorate up the hill to Canberra. I knew that section would not be good. Pulling a 70-kilogram kayak over mountains takes its toll. My knees were already worn out, but this time I would have a secret weapon – non-steroidal anti-inflammatories. If things became bad I would take a pill. Old Yella came out of retirement. I dusted him off and promised it would be the last time we would tackle a mountain together.

On New Year's Day, the start of 2017, at 1.00pm it was time to go. I was waved off by a crowd of friends, family and well-wishers, local TV NBN

News filming, and Ballina mayor David Wright, MLC Greens member Dawn Walker and my mate Klaas. They all had great things to say about the cause and my dedication. My words were about what I do and that I do it for my kids and grandkids, as do most of us trying to spread the message of science. Lyn's granddaughter, Tawny, placed a feather from a brahminy kite (sea eagle) into the kayak's hold to keep me safe. One-year-old Lachy was caught on camera running towards the water with the caption "Bye Pa." Corey, Lyn's son, retrieved the newsman's GoPro from three metre deep water after I had knocked it with my paddle. Finally it was time to go.

A small flotilla followed me down the river to the Ballina rescue tower, accompanied by the Marine Rescue boat and a couple of hardy souls who came out into the sea for 15 minutes or so. Many people had driven to the rescue tower and now lined the rock wall. Four climate angels from the group ClimActs, in their white regalia, complete with wings, had been a bit late to get to the start, but now looked down at us.

A gusty nor'easter provided waves with plenty of white caps for the 35-kilometre run down from Ballina, south to Evans Head. The conditions were a great confidence booster. Both sides of the English Channel and Chesapeake Bay had shown me far worse, but this was a good way to get back in the saddle, so to speak. I felt a strong familiarity with the kayak, the wind and the water. Old Yella and I had many adventures behind us, mostly in strange places around the world, and now we were back. Together we were on very familiar territory, which was exciting and fun but, most importantly, we had many supporters to meet on this trip. It was different, more like the way things went back in 2007, a decade earlier. Maybe I could dare to think about success. It certainly felt right.

The Ballina departure had been timed to coincide with high tide and an easy paddle downriver to the entrance to the sea, which meant arriving at the Evans River at low tide. The variables were wind direction and swell but, at that time of year, nor'easterly onshore winds were highly likely and a decent swell would prevail, and they both did. Having left Ballina at 1:15pm, I arrived at Evans Head about 5.30pm and encountered what I had expected. The bar was breaking right across the river mouth, but there was a way through with a dash across the middle between sets. Paddling in, I could figure out what was happening by listening to the roar of breaking waves behind me and make allowances, hopefully, to keep from being engulfed. The crowd on the wall must have been impressed because I saw a few camera flashes go off in the gloom. I was quite proud of how I managed to come through the waves, but to be honest I was a bit buggered by the time I got into the river and ploughed along against the outgoing tide. I thought I heard a yell from the southern bank, but wasn't sure. I thought it might be Lyn and the boys, but the yell I heard came from the opposite side to what I expected.

I spotted the team, Lyn, Corey and her other son, Nathan, about a hundred metres from the boat ramp. It had been Corey who called out and he had been driving along the road next to the river at the time.

"That was pretty spectacular," I called out. "Could be the best photos of the trip."

No reply.

"What did you get?"

"Actually nothing."

They went on to explain that Lyn had been in a bit of a panic. Not being able to see me at sea she had sent Corey and Nathan up the beach to look for me. The trouble was that I do not follow the coast exactly and a little yellow kayak over a kilometre out to sea is impossible to spot in the waves, even with good binoculars. Having failed to get a visual on the kayak they were on their way up to the lookout when I arrived, so they missed the entrance.

"Shit," I thought. "Oh well, tomorrow's another day and paddling out should look good."

Corey and Nathan loaded Old Yella onto the ute, which was good, because I wasn't feeling particularly strong after my sprint through the breakers. It was just a shame that Lyn went through significant anxiety when she was looking at a wild sea and could not find me. I had arrived within five minutes of when I said I would, but trust between the land and water team was yet to build. Because of the number of people on hand and their warmth and enthusiasm, I was not worried by the missed photo opportunity. It reminded me, though, that there is always that gap between the crew on the land and my intentions on the water. It is up to me, as the leader, to explain what I need. There is also a difference in the perception of danger from land and water. I can be quite happy bouncing up and down a long way from shore in the knowledge that the worst that could happen, apart from a highly unlikely encounter with a great white, is a very long swim back to shore. On the other hand, to most people the ocean is a worrying place. It looks dangerous and frightening when it is windy with waves breaking all over the place. Lyn was new to the job, compared to my 12,000-kilometre experience with this stuff. She would gradually learn to trust my advice on timing.

Arriving back at Lyn's house at Broadwater, we found Facebook had gone berserk. Support was astounding, so we all felt like we were doing something worthwhile and were grateful. It was so different to the loneliness and self-doubt I felt all the way to Paris.

Up before the sparrows, I was keen to do battle with the bar at Evans Head before turning south for Yamba. We were at the lookout chatting with the Volunteer Marine Rescue folk before the sun came up. Their post overlooks the bar from way up on the hill, so their view is excellent. I could see where I came in the previous evening, which one of the blokes described as the 'old trawler channel'. He reckoned, "To get out, just stick to the south wall, pick your time and go like blazes for 30 metres and it's all over." Seemed like a good idea to me.

We went back to the boat ramp and I set off. The bar looked like a giant washing machine, but I now had inside information. With the aid of a good run-out tide, Old Yella crashed through one wave, just made it over the next and then I was out. Lyn was on the break wall and took some good photos.

It was a bit bouncy all the way round the Dirrawong headlands, but smoothed out when I got to the long beach that runs to Woody Head. Visibility was poor due to mist, but I eventually saw Woody Head just above the sea and at about 20 degrees to my left. A chord is shorter than the arc it connects, and the shorter the better, so I headed directly for the headland, which took me about five kilometres from the beach.

The usual early trip blisters had appeared on my hands, but physically I was feeling fine and the expected nor'easter pushed from behind. I pulled into Yamba well before the southerly change hit at 4.00pm, an hour before the arranged greeting with Clarence Valley supporters. The southerly brought heavy rain, so it was a rather bedraggled group that greeted us. Councillor Greg Clancy from Grafton was going to say a few words but we just hung around under umbrellas talking about life, the rain (which was very welcome after a long dry spell) and the idea that we probably should get out of it. We moved under a roof with a picnic table, but the wind was blowing the rain in. The kids had the right idea. They stood on the table and were high enough to be relatively dry. Kayakers don't care about rain and it was inspiring to see that this enthusiastic bunch didn't worry about it either. No-one was properly dressed for such inclement weather, so we were all soaked to the skin by the time we decided to call it a day.

Sixty kilometres upstream from Yamba, sitting on the floodplain of the mighty Clarence River, is Grafton. Oh, what memories I have of growing up there. No doubt it was where my affinity with water was incubated.

We were up at 4.00am with the aim of getting from Yamba to Minnie Waters and the hope that the sou'easter wouldn't be too tough. The wind didn't inspire confidence. It had to be dealt with, though, so I wrote some bad poetry in my head as I struggled into it.

The nose climbs towards the sky
We crash down with a thump
And pretend we are a submarine
Dive, dive, dive
Then up we go and power on full throttle
Bloody southerlies
Flap flap flap, my hat slaps my ears
The white water roars
Crash, it hits the boat and drenches even my hat
The noise is incessant
Bloody southerlies

There was more, but it is best I spare you that.

It took five hours to reach Broomes Head and it was a relief to hit the sand and have a feed. I drank deeply and headed back out for another two hours to The Sandon for a scheduled stop. The Sandon was pretty gloomy with grey skies, grey sea and rain blurring the land. It didn't look like there was a way into the small river but, luckily, I knew the entrance; stay close to the break on the south side and you won't get a nasty surprise. Lyn met me there right on time just as she had done at Broomes Head. I was feeling the pressure but Minnie Waters was my goal for the day and that is where I was going to go. Lyn was concerned because she thought I was tired and the weather wasn't good, but I assured her it would be okay. I expected that distance would take bit over three hours but the wind backed off a bit and I made it 10 minutes early. It was 10 hours of very hard slog for the day but my distance was 41.5 kilometres. Very satisfying for a bloke about to turn 65.

Just like Andrew and Trevor, Lyn was astutely organizing herself to be at the prearranged meeting sites. It makes it so much easier when there is no need to worry about the support crew. All I had to do was keep the land on my right and keep paddling south to get where I wanted to go. In fact, it was a lot more difficult for the support crew.

It rained hard all night. With it still teeming down in the morning and visibility at about 200 metres, Lyn put her foot down. No paddling. I wasn't so sure, but acquiesced because the southerly was still blowing. We called into Wooli Marine Rescue (which is the smallest Marine Rescue unit in New South Wales) to let them know our decision; we had been logging in and out with them since Ballina.

Radio operator Jacki said "I think that is wise," adding, "Where are you?"

"In front of the tower," Lyn replied.

She said that seeing we were right there, we should go up and meet Graham and check out the radar. We met Graham, had a chat about his Antarctic trips and thanked him for his help. During the conversation, the phone rang and it was Jacki the radio operator, inviting us around to her home for coffee on this wet, bleak morning.

We turned up at her home, two bedraggled strangers who were made very welcome. It transpired that Jacki's husband, Richard, is the Unit Commander for Wooli Marine Rescue and also a passionate kayaker. We had a very interesting morning with them and Richard makes a great coffee! The weather had not been kind to us in Wooli, but the people certainly had.

Luckily the weather improved and I was back on the water. South of Wooli is Arrawarra Headland, a very special place from my teenage years. This was where I had learned to surf more than 50 years ago, on a surfboard that I could barely carry. Two large Aboriginal fish traps mark the end of the beach and the start of the rocks. A steel post, presumably the same one that was there in the early 1960s, marks the seaward edge of the rocks for the boats that launch off the beach. A turtle floated near the front of the headland but dived as soon as it saw the kayak, unlike the two at The Sandon that ignored me. Lots of people dotted the headlands enjoying their perspective of the Pacific which was on its best behaviour; blue, white foam against the rocks and a 10-knot breeze.

After the big point at Sandy Beach, the wind changed to the north east but, after a half-hour frolic with the sail up, the wind turned on the nose again. Split Solitary Island drifted past on my left, reminding me of a very close encounter with a whale in the same spot in 2008. The whale just rolled over a metre beside me to have a look with its enormous eye at what might be on top of the funny yellow thing. It preceded that with the largest snort I have ever heard. I can report that nonchalantly now but, at the time, it took an hour for my heart to stop racing.

A few patches of bluebottles (Pacific Man o' War) slid underneath. Bluebottles are common on New South Wales beaches, especially when nor'easters blow for a few days. Most Australians know to steer well clear

Uncle Martin

Next to the jetty (Coffs Harbour)

of this infamous hermaphrodite, but sometimes that isn't easy when you are in among them. The sting is painful and the worst thing you can do is to rub the blue line. When I was paddling near New York, a couple of them had arrived on a New Jersey beach causing widespread alarm with numerous media warnings about the dangers. The waitress who served us lunch at the time, reckoned she wasn't going swimming again because of this new and serious danger in their waters.

NBN TV filmed me arriving in Coffs Harbour beside the jetty with the flotilla. The interview as I stepped out of the kayak seemed to go really well. After that, Uncle Martin provided an Indigenous Australian 'welcome to country' and Tu (a Maori koro, or elder) linked Australia and New Zealand with an impressive Maori Haka about bringing the canoes in. The mayor, Denise Knight, arrived right at the end, signed the petition and publicly stated for her first time that climate change is real and serious. That was a big step for Sarah, my friend who had organized everything with her dedicated climate action group. I agreed with Lyn's comment that media had been so helpful and interested. It was a far cry from the United States, and in London when I had the following conversation with the ABC back in Australia.

"Hello, my name is Steve Posselt. I am paddling my kayak to the Paris Climate Summit. I have completed the United States and I'm just about to pass through London before paddling across the English Channel. I wondered if you might be interested."

"Thanks for that Steve, we will alert our people in London."

That was it. They weren't really interested. I tried a few avenues, such as the Adam Hills show, which is made in the UK, but there was zero interest. None of the paddling clubs that we contacted right across England responded. That was then. This was now and my heart was singing.

Just south of Coffs is Sawtell and about four kilometres south of that, on an easy down-winder, a couple of lifesavers came out in their rubber ducky. They had been alerted by someone on the beach that "something was out there". When they caught up, we had a chat and they radioed back to base that I was who they thought. Apparently, Marine Rescue had kept them in the loop about my journey.

Arriving at Nambucca Heads, I prepared for entry into the river in front of the crowds. That involved sitting in the river just inside the heads for an hour or so. A two metre bull shark swam underneath. It didn't worry about me so I didn't worry about it. About 20 minutes later four dolphins decided to fish near the kayak. Life is never boring on the water.

A well-attended event, this time organized by John and Carol Vernon from The Greens, watched me arrive. In attendance were MLC Justin Fields, MLC Jeremy Buckingham, two councillors, local elders and numerous interested attendees. Uncle Martin again performed the welcome to country. As usual, we were astonished by people's generosity. The local Greens convener, Matthew and his wife Carol, offered us the use of their recently vacated house which was on a property 15 minutes out of town. Uncle Martin reckoned bull sharks don't bite black fellas. Put us both in the river with a bull shark, though, and I reckon he might swim faster than me.

Conditions were perfect as I paddled hard down to Scotts Head. This was in contrast to the last trip down the coast when I had walked to Nambucca Head because of strong southerlies. A bluebottle slid underneath Old Yella about every 30 seconds, so I was very pleased not to be in the water. The previous few mornings I had seen a small black helicopter following the coast, which I assumed was on shark patrol. About halfway to Scotts Head, when I was about three kilometres off the coast, it stopped and circled about four times way over near the beach. Presumably they had seen sharks and were having a look, so I just concentrated on putting distance between us.

Morning tea on the water just off Scotts Head was very pleasant and, as I finished, the wind started to pick up. Lyn was about 100 metres above, sitting on the grass overlooking the rocks, so we just chatted on the radio. She seemed to be enjoying her role as she became less anxious and trusted my skills on the sea. She was also meeting many people and feeling justifiably proud of her achievements. Together we really were making a difference.

When I raised the sail, both of the starboard stays had come loose. Luckily, a long piece was still clipped to the mast and trailed back to where I could grab it. With a bit of impromptu engineering, it was nearly as good as new. That was lucky because, as the wind built to about 20 knots, it swung more east and it was busy work trying to stay on course.

With such a strong wind I was early into South West Rocks. The support crew was checking out Trial Bay and I couldn't raise her because it was 45 minutes before the agreed time. I called Channel 16 on VHF and spoke to the Trial Bay Marine Rescue tower who advised that there is a small creek, Back Creek, at South West Rocks that I was not aware of. That sounded fine so I headed where he had said it was. The waves were pretty rough so I watched a set go through, then followed the back of the next wave right into the creek without getting hammered. A strong runout tide twisted Old Yella sideways which threatened to cause problems, but luckily we got sorted before the next set of waves hit and I was organized enough to use them to carry me through the racing tide.

Trying to beat the heat the next morning, I logged on with Trial Bay Marine Rescue at sunrise and raced out of Back Creek: much easier than the trip in. Even at that early hour it was very hot and there was not much wind to cool me off. At 9.00am two dive boats passed me, heading out to some rocks a few kilometres offshore. I passed a couple of rocks, about 150 metres across and maybe a kilometre off the beach, with one bloke in a runabout and another bloke spear fishing. The guy in the boat motored slowly away without acknowledgement, intent on whatever they were doing. It seemed to me that it was going to get bumpy soon, so they had better get on with it. They passed me an hour later as the wind picked up and they headed towards Hat Head, beating me there by about half an hour.

Lyn was up on the headland on the other side of the creek so radio communication went well, but it was more than 20 minutes for her to get back across the footbridge and down to the entrance to the creek. As I approached the creek on the last of a runout tide, a stink boat overtook me and headed into the creek. I backed off, staying less than two metres off the rocks, allowing him plenty of room. He went too far to the right and hit the sand. I thought he would go up onto the beach but no, he was coming up the creek where the tide was running out quite fast and it was a lot less than waist deep. I paddled up, staying well to the left, while about eight people grabbed his boat and walked it up the creek, which was a pretty good effort. Funny how you expect people to know what they are doing and then find out otherwise. I crossed over in front of them, rang Lyn and then lay down in the water to cool off. After 25 kilometres in 40°C heat, I was cooked.

After a feed and lots more to drink, I applied sunscreen liberally and set off for Crescent Head. The nor'easter picked up, which exercised my right toe on the rudder pedal, constantly fighting to keep the boat on track down the waves. Crescent looks a lot different from the water to when I used to surf there 47 years previously, but some things don't change and I knew there had to be a creek in the corner next to the rocks. People were frolicking everywhere. I paddled through small waves and knee-deep water up the creek, with kids and mums in bikinis providing a neat slalom course.

Lyn backed the ute down the boat ramp to just above the water. When I lifted the kayak onto the roof, my shoulder locked. Being permanently out of position from the accident in 2006, it sometimes gets caught. I just relaxed and waited a bit before I moved it. It was the first time someone else had seen it. Lyn said it was obviously out of position with a great hole in the muscles. It was good to know that because I have always felt like a bit of a sook when it happens.

I don't have much contact with people out on the water, but the support crew talk all the time. Lyn's description of my entry to the beach seems to be typical of what she experienced.

Lyn's blog: I walk towards the creek entrance where he will come in. I hear the lifesavers talking while they look through their binoculars.

"What is it?"

"Don't know," says his mate, "It's got a sail but I can see someone paddling."

"I don't want to interrupt but I couldn't help hear your comments, I can explain what it is," I said. Other onlookers also listen in.

People are fascinated on the beaches when they see Steve coming in especially when he has the sail hoisted.

Steve radios in and I quietly tell him of the interest on shore. "I better not stuff up the entrance then," he replies. He doesn't!

When the support crew write daily blogs, the followers get a different perspective, which adds interest. Some people look forward to the daily blog and have their favourite writers: I could see that Lyn was one.

The Crescent Head headland brought back many schoolboy memories. My family had moved to Port Macquarie for my last year of school where I discovered my penchant for surfing, beer and sex. The latter was then very new to me and I do hope that I have improved since then. I had caught many a wave on the point, after driving up the dirt road in my FJ Holden panel van with about six mates. Oh, to still have that 1954 iconic vehicle in my garage. One 10 footer really hurt when I took off too late and the board dropped away underneath me. I landed on my side on the board, which would have snapped a modern surfboard, but in those days the board won and my ribs didn't.

We were expecting 25 knots from the north, but it didn't happen. I had the sail down most of the way and, just north of Racecourse, the wind came from head on. Luckily, it was light but the situation made it difficult to keep to the radio sked. The Racecourse area has a headland with a cut right down the middle and what looks like a sunken headland out to sea with a series of rock islands leading out to it. There is a cliff about halfway out that used to amuse some of the Port Macquarie blokes. Before the wind came up the boys would catch waves and in the afternoon they would swim out to the island and jump off the cliff. I wonder if that still happens.

I knew the beach at Port Macquarie pretty well. When I was in my last year of school it was very difficult to concentrate sitting in English lessons when I could see the waves and figure out where I would be catching them. We planned for Lyn to drive down into the southern corner and me to come in near the big rock. In front of the entrance to the Hastings River, I could see it was much different to what I expected. The fierce runout tide was directed to the south, not far off the Flagstaff rocks and the wind had become a strong nor'easter. That didn't look good.

I called Lyn and advised that I would watch and plan, so not to worry if I was a bit slow. Waves crashed into the water racing out of the river mouth, so I stayed to the north until a set had passed through. With power on and heading towards the rocks, the next decision was where to turn right. A huge wall of white water was coming over my left shoulder, roaring like a freight train, so that made it easy. Go right now, and be bloody quick about it. There were a couple of surfers on my left as I passed to the north of the big rock. The waves threatened to pick Old Yella up and dump us unceremoniously, but with a bit of back paddling and then full power forwards, I was onto the sand. Lyn grabbed the front to make sure I didn't wash sideways. Nice teamwork.

I was pretty pleased with the effort, I must say. We chatted with the lifesavers who helped carry Old Yella up to the carpark and I logged off with Marine Rescue. Lyn kept chatting with the older bloke who had delegated the carrying duties to the young guns. I say older bloke but he was only in his thirties. She seemed to think he was a bit of a hunk but I reckon there's nothing wrong with blokes in their seventh decade of experience. Besides, the young bucks had been quite impressed with the old bloke and his kayak.

The local branch of Climate Change Australia had organized a welcome with media, as well as an evening presentation by me of my paddle to Paris. This was what I had hoped the trip up the Mississippi might have been like. Now I was making a difference, and together we were collecting thousands of signatures for the Declaration.

Axe, an adventurer mate who I met in Ballina on a hiatus in his attempt to row to New Zealand, reckons you can't just be an adventurer, you also need to be a salesperson to sell your story. I'm hopeless at that. Deep down, I guess I feel that selling yourself seems egotistical. It's funny when you consider how much effort I have put into raising awareness of climate change or how aggressive I have been in business, that I should be such a blushing violet about selling myself. I think the difference on this trip is that I am not doing it for myself, I am doing it because I am part of a movement. This time we were selling Climate Emergency and we had a large contingent of salespeople. It is the power of the movement, a group of people all supporting each other, that drives change. We need strong individuals to lead the way and explore the unknown, but the change will not come until groups of people start working together.

> **Lyn's blog:** *"These presentations work two ways. Firstly, Steve inspires people to continue with their climate actions and build on their work. Secondly they inspire Steve to continue spreading his message and his knowledge of the problems that lie ahead if our governments persist on ignoring the emergency that climate change has become."*

We were up at 4.00am for an early start. The forecast on the Meteye weather service was for strong northerlies in the Port Macquarie region. From the launch, the winds were variable and often on the nose at about five knots, so progress was a bit slow. The day warmed up and I cooked again. Then the Thai curry from the previous night wanted to exit, but had to stay there and cause another two hours of discomfort.

Reaching Crowdy Head, with its fabulously easy harbour and ramp, Lyn told me she had arrived early and had been sitting in the shade of the Crowdy Head lighthouse. Two magpies stood at her feet and serenaded her. This was her company for a couple of hours until she had to come down to collect me. Maybe they sensed her tension. I'm happy and at ease out on the water, but Lyn was always a bit anxious. She reckoned that was a highlight of the trip. Unfortunately, though, I had something much more important on my mind and made a hurried trip to the toilet. Back at the ramp, I immersed my whole body and head in the clear, cool waters until my body temperature came back to normal.

With a storm looming, we arrived back to camp to see how everything worked in the rain. All good. The support crew was happy. Last rain, at Wooli, the support crew had actually used a rude word. Sure we had a bit of rain, but it was only between 50 and 70 millimetres. Sure the mattress soaked up the leaks, but I did put a space blanket over it so she didn't have to lie in a puddle. Sure the floor might have been muddy and water was flowing down the sides of the gazebo and across the ground, but my back pack was soaking up most of it. Sure the umbrella blew away and turned upside down, but I did tie it down after that. Yes it might have been a bit inconvenient, but to swear…

The rain continued all night, so we got soaked while packing up, and headed for Taree wringing wet. The following email arrived from a very brave man.

> Dear Steve Posselt and supporters,
>
> I have learned of your Kayak 4 Earth campaign, culminating in delivering a petition in Canberra on the climate emergency. I agree we have a climate emergency, but I do not fully agree with your statement that "for people under 20 now, the effects could be catastrophic, not just the wild weather we are experiencing with just one degree of warming."
>
> Unfortunately, I think catastrophic effects for many are already happening, contributed to by climate change and a range of other 'risk multipliers'. Partly for this reason, I became the first and, to

date, the only Australian IPCC contributor to be arrested for climate disobedience, protesting coal exports at the Maules Creek mine.

I do hope the decision makers in Canberra hear you, but I think real change can only come from enough people recognizing the peril we are in, and changing their behaviour; not just regarding climate change but in a host of other ways. Your unusual mode of reaching Canberra may attract some interest from mainstream as well as social media. I hope it pays off!

Kind Regards and good luck

Colin (Adjunct Professor Colin Butler, Health Research Institute, University of Canberra)

At Port Macquarie, I had spoken about bravery and I have met many brave people. Anyone who confronts their demons, who can recognise they were wrong and change their ways, who can travel a really hard road because they believe it has to be travelled, is brave.

So what is the opposite of this? Someone who will not accept science because it does not accord with their beliefs? Someone who so badly wants to preserve the status quo because they have a comfortable lifestyle supported by corruption and special interest? I had raved about this in my angry phases at the start of the trip. I thought those thoughts had left me but here they were again. This time it wasn't anger but it was cold, uncompromising determination. For all of the neo-liberals and their mates who are prepared to sacrifice the lives of my children and grandchildren I know nothing will change their minds. There will always be a percentage of people who simply don't get it. What we have to do is to remove them from power and replace them with people who understand and who are tough enough to do something about it. That means understanding not just climate change but the accelerating destruction of the environment that sustains us.

I was starting to feel the strain on the paddle from Crowdy Head down to Forster. The distance was 48.5 kilometres and my body hurt and I couldn't walk properly when I got there. Luckily, masseur Lyn found the knot in my back and sorted it out with Deep Heat and a shower. It had been a three shark day. One about 1.5 metres long; one about two metres and one longer than Old Yella that, I have to admit, sent prickles up my back.

The GPS died at 10.00am the next day. Funny how attached one can get to a GPS. It is sort of like a companion. Although I only use speed, average speed and distance travelled, I missed it when it died. That would be nothing compared to missing my support crew when she went back to work, though. Luckily she would be coming to the Opera House.

A kilometre off Charlotte Head, the waves reflected back from the headland, making smooth peaks as they crossed the easterly swell. It was scorching. For relief, I would take my hat off, fill it with Pacific water and tip it on my head. The cool water would run down my back, but in five minutes, my head was baking and my body steaming. The temperature was in the high thirties and vigorous exercise in a shirt, a sheet of plastic (that's the skirt) and a lifejacket makes one think of removing some of it. But you don't. It's not safe. I have been caught before, paddling down the coast, so I make sure that I am always ready.

I paddled on. A big splash of white water materialized ahead. What's that? A swordfish launched into the air ahead of it, and then again and again. Maybe it was enjoying a brief sauna. A large group of brown birds sat on the water to my left. I tried taking photos as some took off and skimmed past me. The group grew to maybe a hundred and then splash, splash. A group of dolphins came toward the kayak. There were about 10 of them swimming beside me, in front of me and rolling sometimes to show their light bellies. I was exhilarated and shouted with joy, racing along with them as fast as I could. Gradually they changed direction. They popped into the air in front of me, steering me to the right. I was forced to change direction. Up ahead, to my left, a great commotion was occurring in the water. When the dolphins were satisfied that I was headed away from it, they disappeared, heading back in the direction of the commotion.

I had just been guided by dolphins. I was more than a bit emotional. It only took a few minutes, but wow!

What had that been about? "Go away, this is ours?" "Keep away, this is dangerous?" I will never know and I will never forget.

The wind came up just enough to raise the sail until I was close to Seal Rocks. This area once had a sustainable fishing industry, but it was destroyed by large trawlers that arrived dragging huge nets across the fragile ocean floor. Pretty soon they had turned the bottom into a desert. Greed prevails. I beat Lyn to the beach, paddled in behind the biggest wave I could find and beached. Gracefully, I stepped out of the kayak, fell over backwards and the kayak washed back down the beach onto me,

Speeding down the lake (Mayall Lakes)

filling with water and sand before I managed to stand and drag it out of the waves.

It was always going to be very hot, with westerly winds predicted, followed by a southerly coming through after lunch. There is nowhere for a pick-up between Seal Rocks and Port Stephens, so I decided to go via the Myall Lakes down to Tea Gardens; same distance but less worry about the late southerly. Things went well at the start, on what is a magnificent waterway, with the westerly just starting to puff a bit. There are a few doglegs to go around and, as I turned east towards the Bombah Point ferry, the wind picked up. Without paddling, Old Yella reached 9km/hr, so I knew it was getting strong. Lyn took some photos as I shot past and turned right towards the entrance to the Myall River that runs to Tea Tree.

A Hobie trimaran scuttled out from the windward shore as I struggled to hold my line while reaching across the wind. Their sail flapped and I wondered how they would get back, but that was their problem. I waved, but they appeared not to see me. The wind grew to more than 30 knots and, despite the heat, I regretted not putting the skirt on, as wave after wave slopped into the cockpit. I just managed to hold the line to my goal, but when I got there I discovered that I was at Mungo Brush, the wrong place. It was a hard 45-minute paddle, straight into the bluster of the westerly wind, to get to the entrance to the Myall River.

As I turned left into the calm waters, the trees roared and danced above, and it was hot; very hot. Morning tea time; I sat in the water beside the kayak and contemplated how to refill my water bottle after it had turned over and emptied in the turmoil. Just down the river, I started calling in to fishing houses, which were mostly deserted. A big black dog started barking and ran towards me just as I spotted a human. When I pulled into the sand, the dog came over to tell me to bugger off. It was close enough that I could smell his breath as he barked into my face, but I figured he was just noisy and climbed out anyway. The young bloke filled the water bottle from the tank and I was away.

The Myall River meanders a lot, but most of the time I seemed to be against the wind and, until it dropped below 30 knots, it was very annoying. At 2.00pm, Lyn and I had a brief communication on the phone while I was blown into the trees. Call over, there was about a 300-metre downwind run before the next bend, so I raised the sail and took off at better than 9km/hr. This was against a significant tidal run, so my speed over water had to be better than 11km/hr. Arriving at Tea Gardens around 3.00pm, the temperature was still well over 40°C. It had sapped my energy, so it took a while to recover before loading up.

Marny, a good friend who runs the Lismore Car Boot Market, met us and took us back to her place where she served a very welcome cold beer. I met Marny in about 2008 when she was running Seabird Rescue and asked me to do my Cry Me a River presentation for their Christmas function. When I was living in Brisbane, I had travelled down to Bangalow for a presentation by Ian Dunlop and Paul Gilding and had learned she had married Gordon, an ecowarrior mate from Lismore. Unfortunately, Gordon was away for work so was not around on this trip, but we had some enjoyable discussions catching up on stories.

We didn't leave the Tea Gardens bridge until 11.30am, after doing a radio interview with 2NURFM. The bloke who did the marine rescue log-on should have been a radio announcer, as he had the smoothest voice and a great presence.

"Are you the skipper of Old Yella? Over."

"That's a bit of a grandiose term for a kayak paddler but yes, I guess so. Over."

"Can you please advise the colour of your vessel? Over."

"It's yellow like a banana. Over."

"OK that stands to reason. Have a good trip. Port Stevens out."

The river heads west after the bridge, so the easterly breeze gave a little help as I sailed across the oyster beds. There is a maze of small islands, so I thought it best to stick with the channel markers, meaning that lots of boats and a ferry went past. The river snaked south and then I was onto the Karuah River bay.

A blissfully cool breeze had replaced yesterday's blistering gale. Within two hours, I was at the heads and into the Pacific Ocean again, enabling me to turn a little to the right and set the sail on a tight reach. It was very bouncy near the cliffs with lots of little peaks on the ocean, but I powered on, thrusting through them. Past Fingal Lighthouse on Shark Island, past Fingal Bay and then One Mile Beach, but I was unsure where I was in relation to Boat Harbour. A discussion with Lyn, who could finally see me, managed to right that situation, although the waves were crashing on the rocks and the entrance looked a bit tricky. Not to worry, there was a big enough gap, so I dropped sail and committed. A powerful current washed me towards the southern rocks, necessitating full power to beat it. A lot of foam on the grey sea made me uncomfortable, but logically there was nothing to worry about. Old Yella slid onto the sand as I said to Lyn, "I didn't like that."

This was the leg into Newcastle. The wind was up early and from the east, supposedly then shifting from the north and building to gale force. Yee haa. Bring it on! Passing round the rocks I took a photo, thinking that it might be my last chance because the wind was only 20 knots. It died a little, so I got another shot of the sand dunes that run for a very long and boring way. They weren't mined for rutile and other heavy metals like a lot of the New South Wales coast, but they are under threat now. As if it matters, the project manager for one proposal said, "In some areas the sand dunes are higher than the existing nine metre-high power cables." Yes, and this means you can remove the dunes? Further south near Williamtown both the local councillors, not the staff, and the NSW government want to extract sand to meet demand in the building and construction markets of Sydney, the Central Coast and the Hunter region. The project has been deemed a 'State Significant Development'. Yep, fuck the sandhills. Fuck the environment. We need development, says government.

We had bought a large bacon, mayo and cheese scroll and I had a piece of that for morning tea at 9.00am. By 10.00am I was really feeling tired. Everything hurt, the wind had stopped blowing and I still couldn't see Newcastle. I thought I knew what the trouble was, so I ate a banana and gulped a sugary drink. Within 10 minutes I was powering on again. So much for white bread and some tasty crap. Next meal would be another banana. Bananas are always my staple on a trip; that is, until I think that I might scream if I have to face another banana. That doesn't happen for at least a month, though. It's not an apple a day keeps the doctor away, it's a banana a day that helps Steve paddle away. Lyn told the Banana Board about the importance of their product to my performance, so they ran a story about my trip and its dependence on bananas in their magazine.

A couple of planes came and went from Williamtown airport. A roar came over my left shoulder. When I looked for the plane I found it already ahead of me and streaking towards its base. Must be fun to fly one of those airforce jets.

With the strong northerly wind forecast and hardly any wind so far at all, I looked at the clouds over Newcastle with a bit of trepidation. Maybe a southerly was coming. The BOM (Bureau of Meteorology web site) had been wrong before, even on this trip, so I hurried to Newcastle as fast as I could. I paddled into Horseshoe Bay, just inside the mouth of the Hunter River, at the very moment the rain started. It bucketed down, so I was very pleased not to be at sea with such low visibility. Weather reports are extremely important, but so too is experience and critical thinking.

The next day was set to be just a staged paddle, where I pretended to arrive into Newcastle. I had to be in position, out of sight down the river, ready to come in with a flotilla in front of the TV cameras. I'm used to just being 'in the zone', so I set off to wait for a couple of hours. There is always plenty to think about and to just observe. In fact I'm quite proud of the ability I have developed to just sit, being comfortable doing nothing. Of course, this is a skill well-known to most Indigenous people, but the trouble is that our society does not see it as a skill. Maybe that is just another reason why we have stuffed things up so badly.

The crowd was impressive (Newcastle)

Most of the two hours was spent paddling around, watching the tide and waves on the rocks and observing people, but during all of this I couldn't help but wonder at the stupidity of governments. A dredge would pass on its way out to sea, return to get another load and then head out again in what seemed a never-ending cycle. It picks up toxic sediment from an expanding coal port facility and dumps it less than two kilometres off shore. Does that get rid of the muck? Years' old scientific advice explained that the best thing to do was to leave the muck in place and not disturb it. Economic advice is that coal exports are unlikely to rise.

Local Knitting Nannas (Newcastle)

Whatever, I wasn't keen on eating the local seafood. The toxins are from a now defunct steel industry.

Finally the call came from Lyn. I paddled up to a flotilla that kept building, as more kayaks came out from the beach. Herding them back in together, so that we could get good footage for the TV, was about as easy as catching flying fish with my teeth, but somehow we managed and it looked great for the cameras.

I hit the beach in front of the NBNTV camera but, as I stepped out of the kayak, a woman ducked under the camera and tried to shake my hand.

"Kerry Arndell," she said.

Wow! In primary school four people vied for top marks. Colleen Eggins, Neil Schafer, Kerry and me. We continued through high school together until I left for Port Macquarie, to finish my last year. I ignored her outstretched hand and gave her a big hug. Speaking duties called, so catching up had to wait a few minutes.

The welcoming crowd stood in a semi-circle and the speeches commenced. Two aspects stood out to me: the large size of the group and the committed nature of the people. It felt like the Climate Emergency Declaration was gaining momentum. The trip was gaining momentum and support was appearing from many different places. Lyn had been busy keeping it all together. Sometimes it was stressful for her, sometimes a bit uncomfortable, especially when the mattress was soaking wet, and sometimes she was anxious because she didn't understand how comfortable I was in wild seas. Some people love the support role, some just can't cope with it. Lyn had measured up in spades. I was going to miss her for many reasons.

> Lyn's blog: For now it's back to work for me for a few weeks. However, I will see you at Moruya for the slog up the hill to Canberra. The journey has at times been full of anxiety, both for Steve and for being there for him, but overwhelmingly there was lots of laughter and most of all it was full of love.

CHAPTER 22

WARREN

Warren's train arrived at Broadmeadow (Newcastle) right on time at 2.05pm, but I was in the carpark, which was the wrong side of the track. His phone wasn't working, but two extremely clever engineers sorted it all out. We turned it off and then on again and it was fine. With no time to waste, I left Horseshoe Beach at 3.10pm against the incoming tide with a good nor'easter blowing. As a result, it wasn't until after 3.30pm that I cleared the breakwall, but that wasn't the end of the struggle. When I wanted to turn right, serious waves were breaking on rocks just to the south. To be sure, to be sure, I battled out to sea for another 500 metres.

Sail up, I was away: slewing down waves and reaching a top speed of 19.3km/hr. Yee haaaa! The radio sked was at 5.00pm. Warren had just arrived at Red Head and could see me straight in front of him. We decided to check in again at 6.00pm and then 6.30pm, but the latter was not needed because I was already there. It took just three hours to cover the 26.5 kilometres to Swansea Heads. Warren seemed to have stepped into

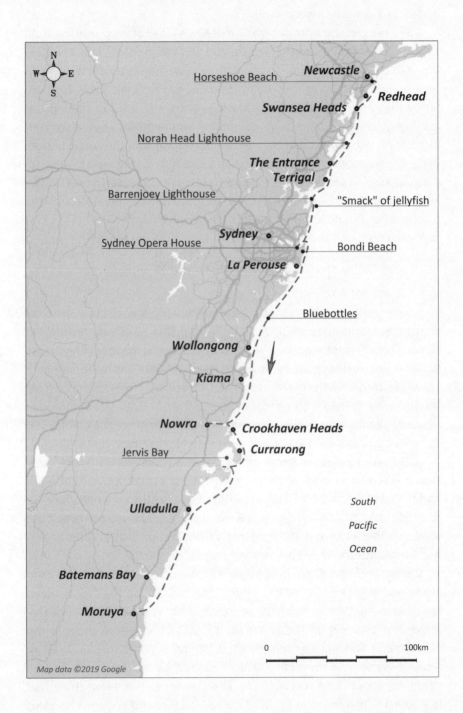

South

Pacific

Ocean

Map data ©2019 Google

the role easily, except for a couple of minor details like changing camera lenses, but hey, he didn't lose any.

Colin Hargreaves from Act on Climate NOW had started sending data applicable to my stops so that I could add them to my blog. For Newcastle he advised that maximum temperatures at Williamtown RAAF, next to Newcastle Airport, have risen nearly two degrees between 1951–2016. He noted that this is mostly over the last 20 years and is faster than global averages. Over the same time, minimum temperatures have also risen more than two degrees, but the rise has been steady for the whole period. Because minimums rose for the first 40 years but not the maximums, the diurnal range in temperature fell and has then risen ever since. This is a fairly standard result. In most places, the minimum temperatures started rising earlier, but now maximums are rising much faster.

Colin continued to email me data all the way to the end of the trip.

A nice gentle nor'easter was blowing when I logged on with Lake Macquarie Marine Rescue at 6.30am, so the first hour was terrific. No slewing down waves, no stress on my toes, no frantic manoeuvring to stay upright: just paddling along at about 8km/hr. Then the wind stopped. Then it started from the north west. Then it stopped. Then it came up from the south west. Then it stopped. I passed Warren at 9.00am, but although he could see me from high up on the cliff I could only see the ute. My last comment on the radio was that I would race him to Norah Head.

At 9.30am I passed a small island and the wind was up again, quite strong, but with enough west in it to allow the sail to work on a tight reach and still aim for Norah Head. As the wind swung further west and gathered strength, a heat haze shimmered on the water just like you see over a hot road. I had never seen that before. Maybe it is standard at 42°C but that is not a temperature that I had seen very often.

Warren and I didn't connect at the 9.30 radio sked, nor at the 10.00am sked, nor 10.30am, by which time I was almost at the Norah Head lighthouse. "Bugger," I thought, and turned right to Norah Head beach. There was a crowd on the beach, so I headed away from them to the western end and slid up onto the sand behind a half-metre wave. When I called Warren on the phone, I learned that he was concerned that I might be ahead and had gone to The Entrance. The same thing had happened with Andrew in England at the Deal Pier and Lyn and I had also experienced that problem, so I really should have briefed Warren. Anyway, like everyone else, he learned from experience that I don't go past the point we last talked about, particularly after three missed radio skeds.

The wind had dropped to nothing, so it was an easy paddle around the lighthouse where I could see The Entrance eight kilometres ahead, but my path was more than a kilometre offshore from there. At 11.30am, Warren and I connected and we had no problems with half hourly skeds for the next four hours, but the wind built up quickly. Coming from dead ahead, it kept progress to about 4km/hr and it was hot. This was a new experience. Westerlies can be hot but southerlies? I arrived behind the point, south of Bateau Bay, still eight kilometres from the Terrigal finish and out of the wind. With no wind, it was really hot and the smell of the land was strong.

Arriving at Terrigal, the GPS showed 51.3 kilometres over a nine-hour day. With seven of these against the wind, I was quite pleased with myself. While being interviewed by Cath from the Central Coast Greens, the phone rang twice, but of course I couldn't answer it because we were live on Facebook. I finally got back to the caller about 4.10pm. It was the Terrigal Marine Rescue checking with me. I had said ETA 16.00hrs. Man, were they on the ball. They were following me all the way down the coast and, although I reckoned I would never need them, they had my back. All volunteers, the Volunteer Marine Rescue are a vital organization doing a terrific job.

After an excellent interview with ABC Central Coast and a big breakfast at the surf club café at Terrigal, we finally managed to hit the water at 10.00am. I advised Warren that I would meet him about 2.00pm at Palm Beach on the Pittwater side of Broken Bay. It took more than 10 minutes on the radio to log on with VMR (that's Volunteer Marine Rescue), as we went over every detail again. The cool southerly was a welcome relief from the heat of the day before. Past a couple of shanties hidden in a valley, I wondered how many people know how to get there, and marvelled that someone could have such a place near a city. It was four kilometres across the mouth of Broken Bay, with Lion Island guarding the entrance. I arrived on the beach behind Barrenjoey lighthouse at 2.02pm with 22.3 kilometres logged. Not bad, I thought. Although Warren had a long drive to get around Broken Bay, he was waiting on the beach. Of course, he's an engineer so I had expected nothing less. Four hours hard work isn't a lot, but we reckoned it still deserved a couple of beers at the Newport Arms.

Between 6:15am and 6:30am, the glassy waters of Pittwater started to ruffle ominously. "Uh Oh," I said to Warren, or words to that effect. Being Australia Day (or Invasion Day), runabouts began to appear everywhere. Many of them passed me on their way out to sea, as I rounded Barrenjoey Head. Invariably, they contained two blokes and a row of fishing rods.

A fluther of jellyfish, or maybe a smack of jellyfish, appeared below me. The pack was so dense they were nearly touching and they weren't all swimming in the same direction. With the tough camera tied around my neck, I tried an underwater photo, which sort of turned out. There are many wasted shots each day because of water on the lens. Wiping it off with a wet finger doesn't really work so well, but it sure beats Warren's efforts of frantic lens changing when it would perhaps have been better to take the lens cap off. Just sayin', ya know.

Another shark made it nine so far for the trip. The wind picked up to about 15 knots from the south as I had feared, but I arrived at Shelley Beach with time to spare. There were crowds on the beach right next to the rocks and Warren tried to let swimmers know I was coming in that way. Five metres out, half a dozen teenage girls appeared over Warren's shoulder and walked ankle deep in water straight in front of me, totally oblivious to anything except looking good. Although it was close, Old Yella didn't hit anyone.

Once on the sand, I dragged the kayak out of the water, the well-wishers shook my hand and, as a special treat for me, a group of kids showed a lot of interest. I wondered if, in time, they will come to hate our current crop of major party pollies.

Janet Ellis, from Ryde Epping Greens and Climate Action Working Group, had organized a welcome group, but they were out on the streets of Manly collecting signatures for the declaration. This was great stuff. Janet called her team in and we got to know each other among the throngs celebrating Australia Day on the sand.

A southerly breeze was blowing at the Shelley Beach start, with a nor'easter predicted. We had started late because I was hoping to struggle the first couple of hours and then be blown down to Cronulla by the predicted nor'easter. Warren was to collect Lyn from the airport and we would radio sked at 11.30am.

He picked her up on time, but I was slowly falling behind schedule because the southerly showed no sign of relenting. Past the cliffs at The Gap, a famous jumping-off place into the afterlife, a tall sewerage vent from the underground Bondi sewage treatment plant rises high above the cliff face. It would be a perfect place for the support crew to view my progress before I rounded the point in front of Bondi Beach. I stopped in the lee of the cliffs for the radio sked. The intrepid pair advised that they were at a café in Maroubra and would be ready for the midday sked. I was pleasantly surprised that the radio worked over that distance, seven kilometres and around a cliff, but felt less enthusiastic that the support crew were enjoying coffee while their mate was sitting in a kayak 50 metres away from a sewage treatment outfall. I found out later that they had forgotten about time and were just lucky the radio worked. It is still a job to get a word in when those two are together. Warren has honey bees, Lyn is into native bees and has roped him into promoting native bees in his area. Just don't let 'em get started, I reckon.

Lyn had advised me that a group of jellyfish is a called 'bloom'. In other words she reckoned that my advice that the collective noun is a 'fluther' was wrong. Wrong? Me? Because Warren is a highly knowledgeable civil engineer I asked his advice. Our code of ethics does not allow us to practise outside our area of expertise so Warren said he was not sure about jellyfish, but that he did know about jelly beans and their collective noun is a packet. My conclusion was that it could also be a jar but that I had work to do, and it was against the wind, not that he cared so long as the coffee was good.

While the two support people got to know each other over their coffee and toasties, I struggled on. They said later that it was a hot day and they appreciated the cool southerly breeze. Apparently, in an effort to maintain radio contact, they wandered through the rifle range at Malabar. Warren, in an astute moment, worked out that there was a mound of dirt quite close and a target that people shoot at, so the neighbouring golf course might be a more appropriate place. We finally made radio and visual contact, when they stood at the third tee which, from my perspective, was on top of a cliff. Apparently, there is another story involving a sewage

Warren helps me drag Old Yella up the beach (La Perouse)

treatment plant and yet another about them pretending to be undercover with the radio but, with apologies to you, the reader, they are for the amusement of the crew.

Turning into Botany Bay, the wind now came over my left shoulder so I could relax and put the sail up. The support crew were in a jovial mood. Lyn was holding her upturned hand at shoulder height while Warren, now master photographer, was trying to use the zoom so that Old Yella looked like it was in Lyn's hand. Lyn then wanted to try her skills with me as close to the camera as possible. Despite the fun they were having with their photo-illusions for beginners, I was tired and cold, in an onshore wind blowing me onto the rocks. We cut the photoshoot short and headed for La Perouse.

We logged off with VMR, using the phone, and the guy said, "I have someone who you might like to talk to."

It was Bernie Ward. Warren and I had started our engineering degree with Bernie. There were about 130 of us in 1971. Bernie and I finished the first five years together. That was when they gave us a diploma. The degree took another year. We were in a group of about four that had started that year. Most had dropped out and others, like Warren, had been delayed on the way. Ordinary Differential Equations were the bane of Warren's life. Why they would call them ordinary, I have no idea. They were bloody hard and I have never used one since. Warren and I still joke about Laplace transforms and Fourier series. Neither of us has a clue what they are now, but the memories they invoke bring shivers to our spines.

We enjoyed talking with Bernie who, as we found out, was new to VMR but just about ready to start his first radio stint. We warned his boss that this could be very risky, promised to meet up with Bernie sometime and headed off to Warren's for the night. We put the kayak on the vehicle, ready for tomorrow's staged paddle on Sydney Harbour.

This was my third and would have to be my last time, but I paddled to the Sydney Opera House for a warm welcome. The wharf was crowded with people holding placards and banners. It was noisy and uplifting to see all of those people. David Bell, an email friend, took a photo as I threw the rope to Warren. Perfect timing. I climbed up the ladder, dragged the kayak onto the wharf and we all trouped off to the park, about 100 metres away.

Perhaps you will recall that Kerry from my school days met me at the beach at Newcastle. Well, the same thing happened in Sydney: Neil Schafer popped out of the crowd. As I said, he and I used to compete with Kerry for top spots all through school. We had seen each other in 2010 at the 40th 1970 Grafton High School reunion, but the three of us go way back to when we started school, which is quite a long time ago seeing as we were all 64 and bemused by the old Beatles song.

The reappearance of all these people from my past added an extra layer of warmth and support to the whole trip. I not only felt that I was part of a movement, that I was inspiring people to make a difference, I felt that the various stages of my life were coming together, that I was doing something I had been building towards my whole life. I didn't reflect on the difference to the trip of 2015, although I do now. At the time it just felt great. My friends appreciated that I was doing something good and came out to support me. It all contributed to the momentum that was building around the trip.

The meeting in the park was superbly organized. Warren, as usual, was meticulous with his note-taking of names. Starting with Uncle Allen, I have to say that the quality of the talks was inspiring. Hoody, now that I was paddling in Australia again, was able to be there and present the case for engineers to do more. Engineers are the professionals who can implement the science. We need to start building the future to mitigate the climate change already built into the system and to reduce emissions that will drive more change into the future. On the other hand, climate activists need to start moving past the presentation of evidence. This is a battle about psychology; facts will not shift the attitude of the majority of Australians who are concerned about their lifestyle and they certainly don't influence the major city media outlets and politicians. We need to keep delivering and promoting the solutions.

Two young and very active engineers made for a very pleasant surprise. I still hold out hope that Engineers Australia can be a major voice for climate action. The only complaint that I had was with the weather gods. Having just paddled four days straight against the wind, it was favourable that day, a lay day, and impossible the next.

A few Knitting Nannas in their trademark yellow and black joined in. Two years previously, one of them gave me a small knitted triangle at

Hoody welcomes me to the Opera House wharf (Sydney)

Capital city crowd (Sydney)

the Sydney Opera House where Bob Brown spoke. I kept it with me all round the world for luck. Unfortunately Baz, a paddling friend in Ballina, has cancer and I gave it to him to see if it would bring him luck. Rosie, a Nanna from Byron Bay gave me a knitted rosette to replace it and I also had Tawny's brahminy kite feather.

We were up at 4.00am to start the day from Warren's house and be on the water at La Perouse by 6.00am. Warren's new buddy was back home, working. With paddling impossible, I had taken her to the airport the previous day. It was now all work for him in temperatures around 40°C.

A light northerly ruffled the water as a sea fog drifted towards the land. Just as I was about to cross the entrance to Botany Bay, an oil tanker loomed out of the fog with two tugs in attendance. It appeared to be going really slowly, but it covered ground quite quickly, so I was pleased that I had seen it before committing to the crossing.

By 7.00am, the wind was strong enough to fill the sail, about 4-6 knots. I didn't go into the bay in front of Cronulla but aimed for the furthermost cliff that I could see in the national park. The line was about four kilometres offshore from the city. As more fog rolled in, the cliffs disappeared but the glow of the sun was still visible, so I used it for direction. When I could see the cliffs again, I was still on course, so dead reckoning had worked fine. The cliffs in the national park were spectacular and picturesque, with the odd isolated beach. What a difference to the horrendous ride the other way, two years previously, when the wind was onshore and the waves crashed over me at chest height.

There were more bluebottles than any other day and, when I didn't concentrate, the right blade would pick one up. The first I would feel would be a tug on my arm from something like a piece of string. Then I would have to unravel the blue line very carefully. This happened half a dozen times, with two getting tangled up and stinging me.

Warren reckoned he was struggling.

> **Warren's blog:** *My first day after Lyn's departure and I was feeling the isolation, nobody to talk to about the excellent coffee, or the passionfruit muffin. Oh well, life's tough, so I enjoyed them and resisted the temptation to do a selfie.*

Coming into Wollongong, many kayaks and other paddle craft arrived to make a colourful flotilla. One arrival was Tom, on his Hobie trimaran

Another warm welcome (Wollongong)

which displayed 'NO MORE FOSSIL FUEL', while we all hovered about outside the harbour. As usual, we hung around out of sight until Warren called. He would know if the dignitaries, or something important like the singing group Ecopella, were ready or not.

When I was waiting with the first bunch of kayakers, I saw a shark and took off to get a photo. It was camera shy, but I did manage to get one image that clearly showed its fin with the city as a backdrop, before it shook me off. Proud of my efforts, I turned to brag to the others, but for some reason they had paddled off in the other direction. Warren reckons I needed deodorant.

The flotilla was well-grouped as we came into the harbour looking like pros. I'm not sure what demand there is for a well-behaved flotilla but there is one in Wollongong if anyone is interested. Flotilla behind me, dignitaries and people with large letters making up 'ILLAWARRA WANTS CLIMATE ACTION' in front of me, singing and chanting. Inspirational!

Just across the road from the beach, we did a full PowerPoint presentation with councillors and politicians present. The applause at the end was thunderous. I was gaining so much energy from all of these people. When it was all over, a few of us gathered at Steelers, the local Leagues Club. We would have starved if it wasn't for Warren, who arranged food 20 minutes after last orders. I am not going to tell you his secret, but it was impressive!

Over a beer after dinner, there were five engineers discussing what the future might hold. Perhaps I am odd, but I don't see any engineers as radical or ratbags, and this was disturbing. The consensus was that because the world is not taking action on what is scientific fact, the future is probably grim. None of us understood why people cannot accept science and facts. We now live in a world of lies camouflaged by the term 'alternative facts'. The way we see it is: we either accept the facts and fix the problem or let the 'alternatives' win. Mankind will fight before he starves and so climate change will lead to wars. The future climate change wars will make Syria, the first one, look like a picnic. Is this radical? I don't think so. The evidence points that way and some of us who have based our whole careers on science think that is the future unless we do something NOW.

During my talks to the welcoming groups on the beaches and rivers I had always mentioned my grandchildren as a motive. Sometimes I would refer to how, surprisingly to me, the timeframe had reduced to be about my kids and finally about me and my generation. Despite that, I had fervently hoped that someone would come along and prove that I was wrong. The content of my flash, bang moment of 2005 had not changed over all of the intervening years, but it had always been future generations that were my concern. For over a decade, my plans had included a refuge, far from large populations, designed and built so that future generations might survive. Instead, it is starting to look like I will see the collapse.

It unnerved me that this gathering of different types of engineers had reached the same conclusion.

A 20-knot southerly was forecast for Kiama between 11.00am and 1.00pm, and you know by now that I don't like southerlies. On the water before sunrise, about 20 racing skis and two six-person outrigger canoes just beat me out of Wollongong harbour. The water was glassy and the sky overcast, so I made good time past five islands and down to Bass Point, which projects a long way out, making the paddle past Windang more than four kilometres off the coast. Windang was the point where I had entered the Pacific on my way from Canberra to Sydney.

Just before the 10.30 radio sked, I saw three mutton birds on the water about 200 metres ahead. They flew off, so I investigated what they seemed to be pecking at. I overshot while trying to take a photo, so had

The welcomes continue (Kiama)

to back paddle and come at it again. Something bumped the rudder three times while I was doing that, so I hastily took a photo of whatever it was and paddled off at speed. It looked like a piece of marine animal, like a one metre long fin. Floating vertically in the water something had taken a 20-centimetre bite out of it. I guessed that something was of a reasonable size and had laid claim to whatever it was. Perhaps it wasn't in my best interests to argue with the claimant.

At 10.30am, Warren said he was on the headland at Kiama and the southerly had just passed over him. That was a bugger, because I was watching clouds that I thought heralded the coming wind, and they were still an hour away. I had banked on making it to Kiama, or at least far enough to shelter behind the headland, before it hit. Kiama was less than five kilometres away and Kiama Downs beach about 3.5 kilometres to my right, but it didn't sound good.

Suddenly all hell broke loose as 40 knots ripped the top off the ocean, turning it a seething white. I couldn't make any headway into the wind at all. Waves about a metre high appeared almost immediately. Turning towards land, it was all I could do to maintain a line perpendicular to the wind and that was paddling at 45 degrees into it. Left full rudder, many more right strokes than left and 45 minutes of full strength paddling before I made it to the beach. By then, the wind had ripped up a messy lot of waves but I managed to land on the sand without disgracing myself, not that anyone was there to see, and dragged the kayak up the path to the surf club. The sand stung my legs in the howling wind, even there, which was sheltered to some extent behind Bombo Headland and Cathedral Rocks.

So near and yet so far. Another 20 minutes and I would have been able to get into Kiama, but it wasn't to be. Might just be a bit more wary next time; 40 knots on the nose is a bitch.

Channel Nine Wollongong rang and arranged for an interview and shoot at 11.00am. The Illawarra Mercury rang for an interview. Warren was becoming a dab hand at being the 'talent'. He had learned to answer questions when asked, lift the kayak when they said lift, and walk when they said walk. He's got it all, eh? He even seemed to have the lens cap issue under control. Media interest had stopped at Gosford, was non-existent all through Sydney and perked up when we reached Wollongong.

The Channel Nine cameraman shocked the rest of his team and Warren by announcing he did not believe in climate change. I have some thoughts on that and how to deal with it, but felt they wouldn't be popular. I think it is time to call out resisters for what they are, too scared or greedy to acknowledge the truth. The challenge is that they do not accept the evidence; they just see it as proof that there is a conspiracy to undermine their lifestyle, individual freedom and human progress. We have to start building a future that leaves them out, so they recognise they are being left behind and change their point of view.

The paddle into Kiama was short, just covering the distance that should have been done two days before but wasn't because of the incredible force of the southerly buster that hit. While Warren waited, he managed to get a photo of his new mate George, a whopping great stingray that slowly prowled the harbour. A couple in separate single kayaks, Anne and Kim, paddled out and we came in together to a rowdy crowd on the wharf. Warren had worked for one of the Sydney councils and had met Anne when she was a councillor there. They had wanted to catch us in Sydney but couldn't, so they came all the way to Kiama. Although there were only three kayaks in the flotilla, the enthusiastic crowd made up for it. Many of the people had seen the event advertised, constructed signs, turned up early and cheered loudly as we paddled in.

A scout hall, less than 100 metres from the boat ramp, was the venue for our evening talks and presentation. It filled quickly and we got underway to a strict schedule so that we could get out of the way for the regular meeting of the scouts. With the introductory dignitary talks completed, I had an hour left and managed to finish in 62 minutes, although the last 10 minutes were done at a gallop. Enthusiasm from the kids was fantastic. They almost stampeded to get to the information table at the end. Again, applause was deafening and prolonged.

We took a photo of a lad using his mum's phone and, after he ran off, she told me, "He said 'thanks for bringing me mum. That was so inspiring and interesting.' How about that," she said. "I did something right for a 13 year old." The energy in the crowd was palpable, so inspiring for Warren and me.

We awoke to a gentle northerly, packed the tent and had a leisurely start at 9.00am, with the northerly wind building. South of Kiama feels different to the north coast of New South Wales, although both are beautiful in their own ways. I tried in vain to figure out the reasons. There are the same number of trees, same amount of open space, similar number of towns and villages. It was even hot like up north, but for some reason it just feels entirely different. Maybe the trees come closer to the water down south; maybe it's the sand hills and progression of vegetation that protects itself from southerlies up north. Maybe, because I grew up on the north coast, that area feels like home and the south coast doesn't. What makes familiarity? I could not put my finger on it before the demands of paddling distracted me.

By the time I arrived at Crookhaven Heads just 30.5 kilometres away, a nor'easter was blowing 20 knots, so the trip was fast. An old fisherman noticed our rig and came over to talk.

"Don't talk to me about climate change," he menaced with an aggravated voice.

"Whoa," thought Warren and I collectively. We hadn't expected that.

"Been fishin' 'ere all me life," he went on, "No bloody winter fish. All gone. Now only summer fish. Don't tell me about climate change. I seen it. Seen the changes."

That took us by surprise but, thinking about it later, it shouldn't have. All the way down the coast we had seen country people who had noticed the changes. Most were interested. Most were concerned. Most would do anything for their kids. That wasn't Sydney, though. It seemed to us that with a few very notable exceptions, Sydneysiders have too much on their plate to be aware of the changes in the natural environment. Just living in the concrete and glass, traffic, bitumen, air-conditioned shopping malls, travelled to in an air-conditioned car from an air-conditioned house, shelters them from the change occurring in the natural environment. For some, listening to the rantings of a shock jock probably doesn't encourage deeper environmental reflection.

It was a short paddle up the Shoalhaven River to Nowra, where an enthusiastic welcoming crowd waited. Some of the crowd ventured onto the water. David was an experienced surfer using his wife's SUP, others were experienced and some were just keen. The welcome included an acknowledgement of country; a speech by The Mayor, Amanda Findley; and a speech by Trish Kahler, the event organizer. Amanda is a formidable mayor and leads a council way ahead of most in terms of their understanding of sustainability and climate change. After the speeches we had 'award winning' snags that, I have to say, were very good. Everywhere we went, we were impressed with the enthusiasm and humbled by the efforts of many people.

The BOM said north-to-north-easterly winds building in strength, but the wind came from the south east, all the way to Currarong. As I approached Currarong, quite a few boats passed me on their way in, confirming that it was getting choppy out to sea and thus time to retire. Warren lined up at the boat ramp because that was the only suitable place to exit, but had to defend his right to do that. Someone thought that a kayak didn't count. Luckily, nothing came of it because neither of us are turn-the-other-cheek-type blokes. Warren was always better than me at karate. Even though I got top marks for trying, I still carry an injury that proves I was second best there.

Warren blogged glowingly about Currarong and the rock pools on the shore, and I totally agree. It is a magnificent place. A southerly was still forecast, but a northerly wind was in my face as I headed out. The rocky shore runs north for a kilometre and a half, before turning east for two kilometres before, finally, running south. Plenty of fishermen were trying their luck and I am not sure how some of them got to where they were. It must have involved quite a bit of walking and climbing down rocky cliffs.

As I have said, the water was magnificent: crystal clear, reflecting the deep blue sky, with deep shades of green from the rocks and kelps below. I passed the cliffs and headed south across the bay. About a kilometre off Gum Getters Point, at what is known as The Drum and Drum Sticks – gotta love the names – something a long way ahead caught my eye. At first it looked like a floating shipwreck, but it was moving and changing shape. The wind was light but I stopped paddling and drifted slowly towards whatever it was.

It looked like sticks poking out of the water, but as I got closer it looked like little black sails, about half a metre high. Some disappeared and then popped up again and others just seemed to sail slowly around. It wasn't until I was nearly on top of them that I could see grey-brown bodies underneath. With my camera trained on the group Old Yella drifted closer, aiming about 5 metres to the right. Suddenly with a huge swirl the whole lot disappeared. Probably one of them had seen the kayak. They could not have all seen us at once but their communication was instantaneous.

The group, or bob, of sea lions numbered about a dozen. They had been regulating their body temperature. With the unprecedented warm weather, presumably they were exposing the area under their fins to the breeze. This was different to what I had seen in the Gulf St Vincent in 2007. There a seal was doing the same thing, but using the warmth of the morning sun on a cool September morning. That encounter had been a little scarier because I thought, at first, that I was paddling towards a great white. It was a relief to see that it was just a seal, I can tell you.

It is about 20 kilometres to Jervis Bay from Currarong, all of it along exposed cliffs with no villages or even houses. Sea caves tunnel below the cliffs for almost the whole distance. Exploring some of those would be great fun, but another time. The entrance to Jervis Bay is guarded by a lighthouse at the aptly named Point Perpendicular.

We had agreed with Trish Kahler, the organizer for this area, to come into Hyams Beach. This was a strip of brilliant white sand inside Jervis Bay. In the morning we'd had a welcome to country at Culburra from

Delia Lowe, a Miga Balaang, or Authoritative Woman of the Jerrinja Clan Group. Delia spoke of her childhood memories growing up on that peninsula, learning from her parents and grandparents of the traditional ways, and of the mission which was set up and where she received her Western education. Delia explained how so much had changed in the physical environment in her lifetime, as well as culturally. She lamented the loss of many fish species, reminding us that her people were water and land-based, and said the spirits of her ancestors would ensure me a safe passage through their waters. We all listened to her story, and were moved by the dramatic and wide-ranging changes, all taking place within a single lifetime.

The next to speak was Frances Bray, President of the Lake Wollumboola Protection Association Inc, and she too lamented the effects of climate change, and wished us well. We were meeting so many wonderful people, trying not to disappoint anyone and yet paddle to a schedule. What a difference that was to the lonely, isolated journey up the flooded Mississippi, doing its best to claim my life. The depth and breadth of people who had shown their support here was truly remarkable.

It had been a hot paddle to Hyams Beach and it was the weekend, so the crowds were huge. Some people even stopped to listen to our group and, with the energy of Judie Dean and her supporters, we garnered a lot of signatures.

Kaye and Jeremy Gartner kindly offered Warren and me a billet for the night and, after a much appreciated hot shower, a little alcohol and an excellent barbeque dinner, we all enjoyed a great conversation and lots of laughs well into the evening. Kaye's sister Dale was also there and added to the occasion. This was what we had anticipated in the United States but never got. This was what I had hoped for in England but knew wouldn't happen. Now the dreams had come true. Warren pointed out that despite our revelry there was a job to do in the morning. Thanks Dad.

The sou'easter blew in about 1.30pm, when I was off what I thought was Manyana, so I headed into the beach to see how serious it would get. I asked some people on the beach where I was and, after they told me, I called Warren with my mobile phone. He arrived 10 minutes later, we discussed the situation and agreed to meet at Lake Conjola. I beat him to the boat ramp by about 10 minutes after sneaking inside Green Island, which is connected to the mainland by sand that is only exposed at very low tide. The island has a very rare, left-hand point break, meaning that the waves are on the southern side of the rocks. In 1972 I had surfed there, but that wasn't my only memory. I had also invited my new girlfriend to come camping for the weekend. The weather was lousy, raining continually and blowing a gale. Our bed was inside the FB Holden wagon but I needed a fire to cook on. Not to worry, I dug into the sand under the lip of a tree-covered sand dune, collected wood from dead limbs high up in the wind and pretty soon had a lovely warm fire. The bigger the better with a fire in winter, I reckoned, and enthusiastically topped up my pride and joy with more semi-dry wood. It was about then that I realised I had set fire to the tree roots growing in the air after the sand had been blown away from underneath. The cave-like area was fine for my pride and joy but, I can tell you, it was quite spectacular as a crescent of fire when all those tree roots caught alight.

Carol later agreed to marry me, so it can't have been that bad, but it was a bit difficult to be nonchalant when it was all ablaze. That was a very long time ago. I was 19, she was 17. We married two years later. A lot has happened since then. Personally, I feel that is what I expect of life: many changes, many experiences, many different people. What worries me, though, is the rapid change mankind makes to the earth: covering it with our cities, eating it up, destroying its natural productivity. The sand dunes of my crescent fire area have long since disappeared under houses. Human population and economic growth are exponential and there are some laws that can't be changed. Exponential growth will stop when the supporting systems collapse.

Lake Conjola is only half a kilometre from the sand near Green Island, that's why I beat Warren despite the southerly that had started to build. It was significant that we had made it that far because, with only 12 kilometres to go, we could make Ulladulla for the greeting the following evening, even against a southerly. We were both relieved to be within striking distance.

I reckoned that the wind was not from the south east as the BOM site claimed. We had learned many times that the BOM is not infallible. It is a valuable tool to be used in conjunction with personal observation and experience. It transpired that the wind was from the south west, but I had to get out on the sea and use the compass to be sure.

I stayed close to the coast because, with the wind from the south west, it was not as strong close to the shore. Behind the headlands it was almost calm. Passing the headlands, I wondered where Ulladulla harbour might be. Tucked well back, giving what looked like perfect shelter, it didn't appear until I was almost there. As the wind gathered strength, I paddled in past trawlers, fishing boats, work boats and all the paraphernalia that goes with a busy little port.

Getting in before the wind strengthened and turned from the south, was a stroke of luck. We went to the local Milton & Ulladulla Times for an interview. The wind was blowing the rain horizontal and all I could think about was my good fortune not to be out at sea at the time.

There was supposed to be a welcome at the harbour, but no-one was coming out in that weather so we had dinner at the pub with Justin Field, Amanda Finley and a few other Greens members. Warren and I really enjoyed the conversation. In fact, conversations had been an important part of the trip – meeting people, finding out how they cope, learning of their experiences. We had met many brave, intelligent people who simply accept what the science is saying, but form different opinions on what the implications will be. Everyone knows that the writing is on the wall. The end of civilization as we know it may happen even in my lifetime, but opinions vary on what that means. None of it is good, but everyone hopes that mankind will survive in what might even be better, more compassionate societies.

I woke to the realization that it was possible to finish the ocean leg in one day. The last stop was to be Moruya Heads, 80 kilometres south of Ulladulla. The wind was forecast to be a strong northerly, which would blow me down the coast and make it possible. We had planned to stop at Malua Bay, 67 kilometres south, on the southern entrance to Batemans Bay, where we would make a decision on whether to make the run to Moruya Heads and finish the ocean that day. It promised to be a big day.

We arrived at the harbour, a few hundred metres from our motel, before dawn. A few cars were in the carpark and a women's surfboat crew was preparing to start training. The sweep, that is the person who stands at the back and steers with a big oar, was a bloke of about 45 or so. The rowers were young women, all looking pretty fit. They did what all lifesavers do before they get into a surf boat to start rowing. You pull your bathers up high and roll what's left into the crack of your bum so that it is only bare skin on the seat. The surf boat then headed out through the opening in the wall only to return five minutes later. It pulled into the beach where all the paddlers took off their track suit tops and headed back out to sea again. Back in they came and took off their shirts, so they only had their bikini tops. Warren is from the Western suburbs of Sydney where there is no surf, so this was all very new to him. He handled it all manfully, such that an onlooker might have thought him disinterested. He couldn't fool his mate, though.

I asked the sweep what it was like outside. "Pretty bumpy still," he reckoned. When I told him that I might go to Moruya he thought I was a nut case. He was right … about the ocean, it was a bit bumpy but smoothed out on the open sea after the headland.

Warren and I were in communication until Depot Beach, almost 40 kilometres south of Ulladulla, where we agreed to talk again at Malua Bay on the other side of Batemans Bay. By then, the wind was over 20 knots from the north and I was covering ground fast, even if it was taking its toll on the paddler. Old Yella is not good on waves because he is too deep in the bow and constantly slews around, necessitating a full-strength battle with the paddle.

We screamed past the Tollgates, a set of islands at the entrance to Batemans Bay, and I reckoned it would be better to keep going straight to the headland at Guerilla Bay. Warren agreed and headed to Moruya Heads for a 3.00pm sked. From the Guerilla Bay headland, I could see where Moruya Heads would be, but not any detail at all.

It was a very quick sprint across the bay with top speed 20.7km/hr, a record for the trip. I also saw a shark that I nearly hit with my paddle as I planed past on a wave. That was number 12 for the trip and another spine-tingling shark moment. That's really a little closer than you want to be.

Eventually, I could see the wall at Moruya Heads and confirmed that it went back to the beach on the north side, meaning that the entrance was on the south side. Warren was up on the headland overlooking the entrance, but he is not a beach person and would not have been able to tell me what I needed to know.

Dropping the sail about a kilometre out, I edged in, trying to pick the channel. Try as I might, I could not see it. There were breaking waves all across the entrance. Surely a channel would open up. I was inside an

Old Yella tows me through the break (Moyura Heads)

area where waves had been breaking, but I still couldn't find it. I decided to treat it as a beach break, pick a wave and paddle like blazes behind it. A six footer loomed behind me. "Back-paddle then go!" was the plan. Hold water, back one stroke, then ... I'm lifted two metres high, spun 270 degrees and dumped in a fraction of a second. The paddler and everything else was violently plucked out of the kayak but, like a true wave-ski rider, I clung grimly to my paddle and let Old Yella tow me towards the river as he surfed the white water. After a few waves passed, we were out of the breaking wave zone enough to get back in the boat. I climbed in the easy way – that is, facing backwards, feet into the cockpit and then roll over to face up and then sit. The first bit worked fine but then I was out again. Righto, try the old way. I got to a sitting position behind the cockpit, one leg in, then I was out again. After another attempt, I thought I might just tow Old Yella to some calm water, so I set off towards a beach on the south side of the river entrance.

After about 20 minutes I tried to get in again and almost made it, but a wave came through and out I went again. This was becoming tiresome, so I gave up. The issue was compounded by the fact that the front bulkhead had been knocked out to put the paddle inside when I packed up Old Yella to bring him home from England. Also, the seal under the seat and the seal to the rear bulkhead were buggered, and the new buoyancy that I had put into the bow had moved to one side.

It was good that the tide was coming in, but I had known that. If it had been going out Old Yella would have been doomed because I probably could not have pulled him around the wall to the northern beach. The beach on the south side of the river constituted two sandy sections with a section of rocks in the middle. Unfortunately, with the incoming tide an eddy came off the beach pushing me back out to sea.

Warren was pacing up and down on the beach, but I couldn't signal where I would come in because I had no bloody idea. Forwards a bit on the waves, wash back a bit, pull Old Yella upstream a bit, inexorably making it closer until my feet touched the sand. Then there were the rocks sticking out of the water. Old Yella went one side and I went the other. The paddle rope got tangled, but I wasn't cold like the time when I was in the Southern Ocean, and my brain still worked. I freed it and finally made the western beach where a relieved Warren helped me tip him over and empty the water.

I had been swimming for 45 minutes but still felt fine, until Warren told me how far it was to the car. It was about 400 metres. I nearly cried. No way was I going to carry a kayak that distance so we agreed to proceed separately to the first boat ramp we could find upstream. After two kilometres I could see a pontoon and aimed for that. Warren arrived just as I climbed onto it and told me the boat ramp was 20 metres away, behind the wall. Climbing back in, paddling around to the ramp and that was me done for the day. I knew it would have been worrying for Warren when I went over and was among a lot of white water, but there was nothing I could do. I just hoped he had captured it on camera.

Warren was apparently very worried. He had seen it happen and it took a long time for him to find me in the water. He didn't understand that I was just doing what I have done thousands of times on my wave ski. I had traumatized another support crew member.

After calling Lynette Smith and logging off with Marine Rescue, we headed to the IGA supermarket in Moruya where we met Lynette before going to her place at Congo. I couldn't walk properly and was very concerned about my leg, until I decided it was just bruised. The last thing I needed was ligament damage before a 180-kilometre walk. That night I was asleep just after 8.00pm. Everything hurt, even my fingernails, but we had finished the ocean leg even if the ending was a bit undignified.

As I have said, there are many people who do not understand the sea. The point that I try to reinforce with all paddling groups is that shit happens when you least expect it. I don't care if you find a life jacket restrictive or hot. If you are placing yourself in a position where it is possible, just possible, that you may need a life jacket, then wear one. To people who think that a bum pack with an inflatable life vest is adequate I say, "Good luck, you will need a lot of it." How you are going to make that work when you are in deep shit, I have no idea. The only thing that I would recommend for paddlers is a well-fitted life jacket that doesn't float up around your face and that has plenty of room for arm rotation without chafing. For me, a couple of big pockets for radio, spare sunnies and so on are also essential. Communication is to be carried on the person, not on the kayak or canoe. It is not much good if they can find your kayak, but not you. My radio is always in the life jacket and the life jacket has been of great assistance every time things have gone wrong. That was probably only about four times I was thrown in the water in 12,000 kilometres but, even if it saves your life once, it is worth it.

Warren's blog: Up at 5am, saw Steve off in Ulladulla Harbour at 6:05am, planning to head south, and stay at Lyn Smith's place at Congo, which is on the coast near Moruya.

Steve was excited about the north easterly, which I now comprehend to be good for sailing south along the Australian East Coast. We did our normal radio skeds, which again took me to some beautiful spots. While Steve was having a great time paddling, I had to content myself with things like a drive through Murramarang National Park, watch a couple of dozen dolphins playing at Pebbly Beach, admire a two-metre monitor and watch lyrebirds scurry out of sight. A tough day at the office. The stop point at Batemans Bay was changed to "I'm gonna keep going to Moruya" by the man in charge.

For no reason that I can understand, Steve got out of his kayak and tipped it upside down for his entry into the river at Moruya. Maybe he was sick of paddling and wanted to practice dragging the kayak despite the deep water, maybe he was showing off, maybe he was celebrating the finish of the ocean paddle, or maybe he is just barking mad, I still don't know for sure, but he seemed to be happy dragging it to shore. I do know that there were two sail boarders nearby, and I waved one in, and asked him if he could check if Steve was okay. I was stunned beyond belief, and livid that he chose to hide, rather than do this.

323

Today included a chat with two people who embraced the petition, and one who said he isn't interested because Australia is only a small contributor, and anyway, he is a bachelor, between him and his siblings there is one child, and because his nephew will inherit four or five houses, he will be okay. Marvellous attitude, really.

Our stay at Lyn's beautiful house in a stunning location was a wonderful way to end my part of the journey. Lyn's hospitality is second to none, and we had a perfect evening together.

Engineers like numbers, and apropos of nothing, while driving I pondered how many paddle strokes Steve did to get there from Ballina. A bit of rough calculating, and the answer is about 750,000. That's a lot, folks!

Well, faithful readers, it is with a heavy heart I say adieu, my stint with Steve is over, until we all converge on Canberra. My nearly three weeks with my mate has been great fun, inspiring, and at times challenging. It is a busy role, and quite intense at times but I would not have missed it for anything. We met lots of people, many passionate about the cause, many who were inspired by Steve's trip and his talks, and a few who don't get it. To everybody who contributed to Steve's trip, hosted of helped with welcome events, the petition and all other matters, thank you. This is the most important issue we face, and there are a lot of great people working to address it, so congratulations to you all, especially to Steve for his Herculean effort.

I woke at 3.00am, waited 10 minutes, then woke Warren for the drive home. When I turned the light on he asked,

"Is it morning?"

Then, "What time is it?

"Time to go, don't look," I advised.

As usual, he didn't listen to helpful advice and said, "I have," as he registered that it was 3.10am.

We arrived at his house at Arcadia at 8.30am, where we said goodbye, and I was at Lyn's at Broadwater about 4.30pm. After an early night and 10 hours sleep, I was nearly as good as new and ready for a 60th birthday party for Fran, our Ballina neighbour.

Warren was a mate in 1972. It was now 2017. That's 45 years. We had a great time together on this journey and we both felt the energy from people we met. It is called living, and we experienced a lot of that together. As with Lyn and I, we had been very successful building momentum for the petition, had made some great friends and were both proud of our achievements.

It was a really hot night when I arrived at Lyn's, so she turned the fan on full blast while I was sleeping my exhausted sleep. I was dreaming. "Oh no," I yelled. "Another bloody southerly!"

CHAPTER 23

REACH FOR THE SKY

Lyn and I arrived at Lynette Smith's around 6.30pm, having left Ballina at 5.00am, and we all agreed to put the kayak preparations off until the next morning. First we needed a bit of a celebration with some champers and Lynette's magnificent dinner. A huge welcome had been organized at Moruya the following day. It would be at the boat ramp near the centre of town at noon, coinciding with high tide. From the boat ramp where Warren had collected me when I was totally exhausted, it was less than five kilometres. The right turn towards Canberra had been a lot trickier than I would have liked, but I was glad that such a major stuff-up was at the end of the last day. We had taken on the mighty Pacific Ocean and had done okay. Now it was time for the next phase of the adventure.

At 11:45am Lyn advised me on the radio to head in with the flotilla that had paddled to meet me. This lot was well disciplined and we came in together. It was the biggest flotilla by far and the most people at the welcome group where the speeches were held. Two councillors had escaped from the council meeting and addressed us. They had just helped

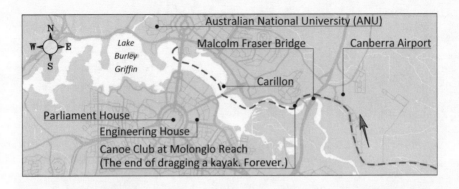

- Australian National University (ANU)
- Malcolm Fraser Bridge
- Canberra Airport
- Lake Burley Griffin
- Carillon
- Parliament House
- Engineering House
- Canoe Club at Molonglo Reach
  (The end of dragging a kayak. Forever.)

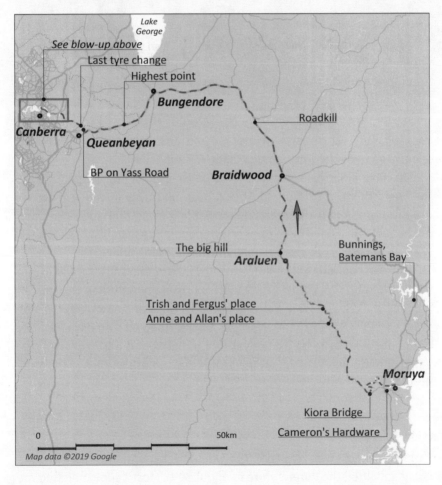

- Lake George
- See blow-up above
- Last tyre change
- Highest point
- Bungendore
- Roadkill
- Canberra
- Queanbeyan
- BP on Yass Road
- Braidwood
- The big hill
- Araluen
- Bunnings, Batemans Bay
- Trish and Fergus' place
- Anne and Allan's place
- Moruya
- Kiora Bridge
- Cameron's Hardware
- 0
- 50km
- Map data ©2019 Google

A welcome on land and sea (Moruya)

pass a fossil fuel divestment motion and advised that our effort had stimulated the vote. Wow, what a team, Eurobodalla!

The most amazing aspect of the welcome was the list of organizations that were thanked at the end. It was huge and truly inspiring. There is usually a problem with organizations wanting to do their own thing and not help others. I have been promoting cooperation like this for as long as I can remember, so to see it happening here was inspiring.

After the euphoria of the welcome, it was back to business paddling up to the Kiora bridge, about 11 kilometres upstream, and then the start of the long walk. It was a big day and I called it quits at 6.00pm after having dragged Old Yella out of the river flats, over a steep hill and onto the start of the dirt road heading up the valley. Lyn had found a friendly farm, so all I had to do was walk in, unhitch from the harness and leave Old Yella for the night.

Next morning was very cool. Lyn wore a jacket until the sun really got going and lifted the temperature to about 30°C. Most people had told me that the area was pretty flat with a few small hills. I would hate to see what they call a big hill. We did four kilometre stints that started at 50 minutes each and ended up at well over an hour. I walked until I could walk no more, which was just 22 kilometres, left the kayak at Fergus and Trish's place and returned to Anne and Allan Rault's place down the valley a few kilometres away. Anne and Allan provided dinner and a little cottage for Lyn and me, complete with beautiful gardens and kangaroos grazing on their lawn.

The following day didn't start well, with the discovery of a collapsed bearing on the front wheel, followed six kilometres later by the bolts holding the wheel halves falling off the replacement wheel. Lyn tells the story below. I felt a bit stupid, but it cemented our relationship even though she reckons she would have felt better if I was angry.

Anyway, it all turned out for the best and I must say that walking into the Araluen pub was one of the best endings to a walk that I can remember. The beer was heaven.

Lyn's blog: We left Anne and Allan Rault's property 'Round River' at 7am and travelled back to Trish and Fergus' place to pick up the kayak, and Steve was ready to recommence the Araluen walk at 7.45am. I asked him were the wheels okay as the front one looked a little crooked?

"No, they're fine," he replied, and off he went.

Just outside the gate he turned onto the road and then stopped.

"All okay?" I asked.

"No. The front wheel's buggered."

Out came the tools and a spare wheel, and he changed the tyre.

"I'm a bit worried about these wheels, the other spares aren't much good," he said.

We decided that I would drive back to Bunnings at Batemans Bay, as Steve said they were the only store to stock these particular wheels (they are wheelbarrow wheels). Steve gave me strict instructions to only get 16mm ones, not 5/8 inch ones, as they wouldn't fit. So, with the old wheel in hand, I headed off for the two-hour round trip. What can I say here but "I messed up."

When I returned, Steve said, "They're not 16mm."

I replied, "They told me these were the right tires as the numbers on the rubber of our tyre was the same as the number on their box.

But are they 16mm? I asked the salesman, and to assure me he called another attendant to make sure. And he also confirmed it was the correct number."

"But that's not the axle, that's just the tyre number" Steve said.

"Oh, what's the axle?" I asked.

Ask me about bees, or birds or frogs and I would know, but axles ….

The other problem was that while I was away, the wheel Steve changed before I left had also fallen to bits after another six kilometres or so. He had been sitting beside the road waiting for his new tyre for about an hour.

I apologized profusely and Steve said "It's okay, don't worry. I'll go back and change them."

I offered to go back but he said he couldn't walk anyway with no wheels. I suggested he try Moruya on the way, just in case their hardware store had one, instead of going all the way to Batemans Bay. Steve dropped me back at Anne and Allan's so I could catch up on some of my other business work load.

As a great believer in Fate, my mistake didn't turn out too bad. (Well that's what I tell myself and Steve was very understanding). He did get three new tyres at Cameron's Hardware Moruya and reckoned, "These are the best tyres I've seen. They are solid and don't need any air in them." Also, as it was a very hot day when he came back to pick me up he decided to have an hour's rest and walk later when it was cooler.

In the cool of the afternoon, Steve got walking. He walked all the way to the Araluen Pub, at the base of the Araluen Mountain. After having a couple of coldies with the locals, Steve stored the kayak behind the pub and we returned to Anne and Allan's.

How could I be angry? Lyn had done her best. I had assumed she knew what an axle was. I reckoned that it was my fault that I had put her through two hours of wasted time. However, it is probably a classic example of how an assumption can cause miscommunication. As we all know, one should not assume. Anyway, we were a bloody good team with just one mountain to cross.

Waiting for me to climb the mountain, Lyn takes a selfie

The big hill had been worrying me since I said that I would do this trip, so it was with a mixture of trepidation and enthusiasm that I set off from the Araluen pub. The hill turned out to be a real bastard. On and on, up and bloody up it went – relentlessly. After half an hour I was walking 20 metres and then resting for 30 seconds or so before moving on. We had been told that there was a lookout about halfway up and that's where I reckoned on meeting up with Lyn. There were a number of places on the way up where she could have stopped, but she thought I'd be fine. I wasn't, but I was bloody well going to beat this sucker. The valley dropped away, the view became spectacular, as I struggled forever upwards. This was going to be my last drag over a mountain. Last one ever.

Where was this bloody lookout? I reckoned I could see the top, but maybe the mountains were hidden behind that. I knew that I would get there, but it would be nice to do it without injury. My legs were complaining, as were my arms from pulling the frame with them. One more very steep bend and there was Lyn. I was at the lookout, not the top, but if I could make it this far, the rest would be okay. We had a bit to eat, a drink and a rest, then I continued to the top, where the road started going down. That was it for me for the day. It was only lunch time but I'd had enough.

We loaded Old Yella onto the ute and headed to Moruya for my talk. It was at SAGE (Sustainable Agriculture and Gardening Eurobodalla), a community garden just outside town. The building only had one wall but there was a small stage and some tables. Of course, the power was solar with a couple of car batteries. People brought chairs and picnic dinners and got stuck into a Friday evening of enjoyment. What a night it was, with about 120 people crammed in. Go Eurobodalla!

Jenny Goldie, like David Bell (who was at the Opera House in Sydney), is an email friend. We met as part of an ASPO (Australian Association for the Study of Peak Oil and Gas) group. Jenny is a tireless campaigner for many environmental issues and anything to do with sustainability. She lives 60 kilometres south of Canberra but had come down to SAGE to meet me and walk into Braidwood.

We picked her up at Moruya Heads before 7.00am on the way back to the mountain top. Unfortunately, the down part after starting out at Sawyers Ridge Road was only about 500 metres long and the next uphill section was about three kilometres long, but it only had one steep bit so it was nothing compared with the previous day.

After six kilometres, the land became pretty flat and Jenny and I strolled into Braidwood about 1.30pm with 19.7 kilometres on the log. Jenny was collected by her friend to drive to Canberra, while Lyn and I had 45-minute interview with Radio Braidwood. This was followed by a beer and a sleep. To be honest, I should have had a day off after the hill but I have never said that I'm smart in that regard. My left Achilles tendon was swollen as were both knees but I had my secret weapon, Mobic. That's the non-steroidal anti-inflammatory that I mentioned in an earlier chapter. They were prescribed by Dr Ross Stinton, my doctor over more decades than either of us would want to count.

I gave in and took a Mobic that night.

Again, it was a very cool start, with Lyn complaining about 'icy' winds. My mood was buoyant because I was able to walk almost normally after the drugs. Yes! For a few kilometres after the bridge over the Shoalhaven, the roadside was littered with the most road-kill I have ever seen. Many kangaroos, lots of wombats, a fox and a turtle: all dead on the side of the road within the space of maybe three kilometres.

It was a very busy day at the office. Larry O'Loughlin, executive director from the ACT Conservation Council, waited beside the road to take a photo. Jeremy, a contact from years ago in Townsville, pulled up with his son to say hello. I didn't remember where I knew him from at the time, but after he drove away the pieces came together. A couple of ladies pulled up for a quick chat and to take a photo, but they really should have been at the Westpac protest about their support of fossil fuels, so off they went. I did feel sorry for the woman who added to the road-kill. She had hit a kangaroo and was trying to get a tow sorted out. The bit she was worried about was just a plastic guard, but when I asked her to start the car I could see the bottom of the radiator housing was busted, so with no joy there, I had to leave her to wait.

Before lunch I had passed a paddock of goats. It is fun when I talk to kids about my trips and ask them to guess what the animals do when they see the kayak. Horses get all excited. They can spot me from over a kilometre away. They stare, then gallop around, buck and then come back to stare again. Sheep and goats are boring. Just like city media, they show no interest whatsoever.

Lyn had arranged with a farmer to park the kayak. Allan has lived in the area many decades. Most importantly, he has noticed the gradual change in the climate. Like most rural people, he gets it. From Allan's farm, my entry to the Molonglo River was only 50 kilometres away. Only 50 kilometres more and that would be it for dragging kayaks. Forever. I was enjoying ticking off these 'last ever' moments.

It was just under two kilometres from Allan's place to the top of the Great Dividing Range nearly a kilometre (well, 850 metres anyway) above the ocean that I had left down at Moruya. Lyn and Warren had been playing with numbers like how many paddle strokes, or bends, or steps have been in the trip while I pondered questions like how much energy is required to lift 70 kilograms 850 metres up in the air, or even how many end-of-day beers it required.

Around lunch time, we were met at the outskirts of Bungendore by Mel, a truly remarkable woman with stories about all sorts of environmental jobs she has had in Australia. After Mel bought us lunch, I was feeling pretty good and set a good pace until Constable Tim caught me.

About a kilometre out of Bungendore a large herd of cows grazed in a paddock beside the road. They were split into three groups totalling maybe a hundred head. A couple in the first group spotted the kayak and raised their heads. The whole group then trotted along about 100 metres back from the fence. This spread to the other groups and pretty soon a hundred cows were following me along the fence line. When they got to the corner of the paddock they just stood there watching. Interestingly, while this was happening I was surrounded by a cloud of grasshoppers. That's the correct collective noun, by the way.

Half an hour later the police turned up. People had seen me on the road and contacted Constable Tim to investigate, as they were worried I might be killed. Bloody 'do gooders' as the highway patrol guy in Tennessee had called them. Tim did his job, but he was intrigued by the trip, so we chatted for a while before he had to get back to work.

The hills to the Australian Capital Territory (ACT) border had been visible since Bungendore. As I climbed up a long hill there were many more trees than down on the flat. Someone, or some people, had placed teddy bears in many of the trees. They must have been breeding because they went on for a long way. This is the sort of thing that you just won't see whizzing by in a car at 100km/hr.

We made it to the top of the hill where a large sign announced the ACT border. A free bed and feed was on offer at Tim and Roz's place just down the road. I had a quick snooze before an entertaining and very informative evening. Their place is my idea of heaven, except it is too far from the beach. They have a hundred acres with mixed farming: lucerne, Christmas trees, native grasses for seed harvesting, olives, and tourists in the cabin Tim built.

After another cool night, the morning warmed up quickly as we departed from the ACT border sign: Lyn to do some food shopping and me to walk, just like every day. The Mobic tablets that I had been taking each night really did the trick.

Police officer Tim turned up twice during the morning, to make sure I was okay. People continued to call to tell him about the bloke on the road who might get himself run over. He reckoned I wasn't really his problem anymore – having crossed from NSW to the ACT, but he seemed to enjoy checking on me. I love the attitude of these guys: helpful, friendly and doing a great job.

From the top of one big hill I could see Lake George far off to the north. Two years prior, there had been no water in Lake George next to the Federal Highway where I walked. As I said then, the water comes and goes, so maybe it was filling again. A wind farm broke the skyline on the hills near the lake. I had paddled 1,200 kilometres down the coast and walked 150 kilometres inland before seeing the first wind turbine. What a contrast to England and France where I saw them on the first day and many days afterwards.

After the regular radio interview for the Sustainability Hour with Mik and Tony in Geelong, it wasn't long before I reached the steep hill down into Queanbeyan. A big surprise was waiting near the bottom: Brian and Fran, our neighbours from Ballina, had arrived.

Fran drove their car and Brian walked with me to the BP servo on Yass Road where we loaded Old Yella onto the ute and adjourned to the Royal Hotel for a couple of cold mid-strengths. No more big hills for Old Yella … or this fella. Ever!

There was no doubt that it was going to be a hot day. Fran and Brian came out to meet us again, but they were a bit late so I flattened two tyres to give Brian something to do. That's not quite right, but they did turn up when I was climbing the rise from the bridge over the Molonglo River. The kayak was too wide for what may have been a footpath. The traffic was heavy and there wasn't much room, so I was in the grass both sides of the bridge. That's when the prickles went through the tyres. As they slowly deflated, I thought the hill was just getting steeper, so it was a relief to realise it wasn't me.

Following a quick wheel change, we walked past Canberra airport and into the Canoe Club area ready for the final, short paddle on Saturday. Old Yella now had three of the super duper wheels with solid tyres that Lyn had found in Moruya. No more flats again. Ever. After a celebratory drink we loaded Old Yella onto the car only to have him slowly sag at the

With Lyn, Fran and Brian – end of walking

front. We pushed him back into shape but had to take him off later, to sit on the ground and straighten out. I knew it was warm but I didn't realise he would start to melt.

The walk was over. I think Lyn was as relieved as me. I knew it would be tough and it was, but there was no doubt in my mind that when I said I would paddle/walk to Canberra that I would do it. The trip had strengthened our relationship. Lyn was proud of what we had done, so we could savour that together.

The little celebration between the four of us was like the one with Trevor at the Eiffel Tower. The memories flooded back. "We made it," doesn't seem to do justice to the feeling, but that is what it was. All of the troubles, all of the hardships, were subjugated by the great feelings of warmth to everyone we met and by enormous satisfaction.

Two years and six weeks after leaving Canberra, Old Yella and I were back. Yes, we had made it. It was a grand feeling.

The weekend would be full.

Hoody was coming down for three days. My daughter Heidi and her family would be at the welcome flotilla. Anne and Kim would drive down from Sydney as would Warren and Kay. The list goes on, but the big one was Klaas. He had missed the start but he would be there at the finish. There was no way I could not fly him down for this. Still bragging, he told everyone he was 85 but I knew better. His 85th birthday was still a week away.

Klaas helped launch at the Molonglo Reach. Tim and Roz brought a couple of mates with kayaks, so we had a flotilla of five before meeting another group near the Carillon on the opposite side of Lake Burley Griffin to Parliament House. More kayakers arrived, including a Hobie tri with a Climate Warrior sail. There was no media, but while we waited for the word to paddle in, ABC radio fitted in an impromptu interview that was encouraging.

The two support crew, now firm buddies, were coordinating the event. Eventually, Lyn advised that it was time for the flotilla to paddle in so we came around the corner, under the bridge and slowly made our way to the group at the boat ramp. As we approached, I raced up to full speed and slid Old Yella up the ramp. Kamilaroi man, Greg, played the digeridoo while Heidi's kids, Max and Ayla, raced down and hugged their Pa. I had seen their faces so many times in so many dangerous places. Everything I had done was for them, their cousins and ultimately for all kids. I was so grateful that Heidi and Carlos had driven a day and a half each way to share this moment.

A public address system had been set up with Hoody and Jenny Goldie sharing MC duties. Greg delivered the acknowledgement of country and then it was time for speeches. Hoody made one, of course. You can't hold the bloke back and he is always passionate and motivating. Two ACT politicians, Chris Steel and Caroline Le Couter, spoke about what a climate emergency means to them. Phillip Sutton spoke about the importance of local government. John McIntosh, president of Engineers Australia, talked about the 'wicked problem' of climate change and accepted the box of petitions from me for safe keeping at Engineering House until delivery to Parliament House on the Monday. Then it was my turn. With Greg and Daniel there to represent the indigenous community I told the same story that I did at many of these welcomes.

On my trips I have learned to feel the land and so have possibly gained a small insight into the relationship between the land and indigenous groups. My belief is that the closer the bond to the land, the better our chance of survival. This is especially true as the earth convulses from having its insides ripped out and burned. The converse is also true. It seemed to me that most big cities, certainly Brisbane and Sydney, would really struggle, and quite possibly explode, in the face of environmental collapse, and the collapse of society that will follow. For me, the key to survival is to listen to cultures that have existed for millennia, about 60,000 years in the case of the First Nations' people on this big brown continent. How we build this into a practical plan is the real challenge.

Daniel and Greg (Canberra)

Ayla and Max welcome Pa (Canberra)

I had a few precious minutes with Heidi, husband Carlos, six-year-old Max and three-year-old Ayla, but we all had to rush over to the Australian National University for the seminar arranged by Engineers Australia. Hoody was the MC, John McIntosh spoke again about the role of engineers, Graham Davies from the Sustainable Engineering Society managed to keep everyone entertained while the gremlins in the audio visual equipment were being tamed, and Klaas delivered a poem about me and the trip, finishing just as the AV gear started to work.

I did my usual presentation with a familiar, enthusiastic response, but it was the first time any of my family had seen it. The two grandkids were delightful, just taking everything in. Max will remember the day but at three I think Ayla might be a bit young. They headed off just after I finished. Driving from Newcastle and back in a day, on top of the trip down and back from the Gold Coast, it was a huge journey, but both Carlos and Heidi reckoned it was worth it.

The seminar after my presentation included Hoody, Will Steffen, a prominent climate scientist in Australia, Ian Dunlop, the ex-coal industry executive trying to convey the facts behind the Climate Emergency, and Phillip Sutton from the welcome group. All the presentations were powerful and, for anyone capable of logical thought, quite alarming.

The following day, Ian screened Age of Consequences at Engineering House. This is a documentary put together mainly by retired US military hierarchy which brings the issue of conflict into the equation. It is sobering and, to me, terrifying. Unfortunately, it does not contradict any of the conclusions I have already come to. Going back to that discussion with the old engineers at the Steelers club in Wollongong, I hope against hope to be proved wrong and yet, time and again, my worst fears are confirmed by people far smarter than me.

We presented our petitions at Parliament House on the Monday. No media attended, but we had representatives from major parties, The Greens, Labor and the Liberals, as well as Engineers Australia. The token Liberal, John Hewson, is not prominent in the party anymore but was Leader of the Opposition from 1990 until 1993 when he proposed a brave rethink of policy in a document called Fightback. He was demolished at the 1993 election by Paul Keating, who probably agreed with Fightback but considered politics a blood sport that he had to win. John came all the way from Sydney just for the handover event.

With so many important people there, I felt that the trip had been worthwhile. Countless people had been motivated both in Australia and

Handing over the petitions (Parliament House, Canberra)

overseas. The Climate Emergency Petition had 6,000 signatures when I started. We now had over 18,000, a good start. Standing in the foyer at Parliament House I was immensely proud to have completed the journey, to have inspired so many people, to have the wonderful people there make great speeches about the undoubted Climate Emergency. Enough people to make a difference? Maybe. The numbers are growing.

This time my job was done. We could go home.

EPILOGUE

That was some journey. I hope you enjoyed it, but I also hope you were challenged at times. It all finally fits, at least to me. Lyn and I are now married. I am very comfortable in myself and we are both very happy. I know what's coming for the world and I can accept it.

There were many downs on the journey. I was ploughing up the Mississippi River against the current and in the end it didn't work. When I gave in, I found another way but that, too, had some trials and tribulations as I tried to work with others. Only when all members of the team were on the same journey with the same objectives did I get anywhere.

When Hoody dropped out, when Geoff Ebbs dropped out, maybe even when Lea told me she wasn't coming, I should have done a better job of reassessing. I am a stubborn bastard, though, and I had said I was going to make the journey. When I say something, I do it.

That being said, the failures on the Mississippi versus the successes in Australia are simply manifestations of what should have been obvious. You can't do something like this on your own. It is so much easier to join inspired people and work with them towards a common goal. You need a team.

Sure, Paris was disappointing. My journey was disappointing to me but, in hindsight, the world will see the whole COP21 conference as deeply disappointing once the horrifying facts sink in. Sure I might have had some relationship problems, but I'm not the only one to have had these. The important thing is that I do my best. Lyn feels the same way, as does Warren. We have all done our best and been rewarded 10 times over.

I have spoken about wearing a life jacket for those occasions when shit happens, but what about when the shit hits the fan for the whole world? When is this likely? In 1972 a think tank called The Club of Rome published Limits to Growth. Basically it said that:

> If the present growth trends in world population, industrialisation, pollution, food production, and resource depletion continue unchanged, the limits to growth on this planet will be reached sometime within the next one hundred years. The most probable result will be a rather sudden and uncontrollable decline in both population and industrial capacity.

Thirty years later, the findings were checked by the CSIRO which found that this sudden and uncontrollable decline could be expected around 2035. I was at university in 1972 and 2035 was so far into the future as to be inconceivable. Now it is just around the corner.

We could be seeing the start of that decline even now. The Global Financial Crisis may well have been the start. Climate change, as dire as it is, comprises just one aspect of mankind's inability to live sustainably. Most of our unsustainable lifestyle stems from releasing energy trapped in the earth for millennia. This stored energy, in what we call fossil fuels, has allowed us to go on a growth binge without precedent. We now inhabit an earth that is out of balance, releasing energy equivalent to exploding 400,000 Hiroshima bombs per day, every day. That is what we have created. It takes that much energy to maintain our current lifestyle.

Do I think a rapid decline will happen to our civilization? Most definitely. When do I think it will happen? The Club of Rome and the CSIRO seem to suggest sometime around 2035. I will be 81 that year. This collapse might happen in my life time, but probably not. It will probably happen in my children's life time, but maybe not. If it hasn't happened by then it will definitely happen in my grandchildren's life time.

I have carried the burden of this knowledge for well over a decade. Sometimes I have been in despair. It is a phase that most people will go through once they understand the awful reality. I chose to act, to do my trips to raise awareness, to do my best to motivate organizations and individuals. The reward has been an interesting life, making fantastic friends, motivating people that I can see now have new purpose in life.

You don't have to do what I have done, but you do have to acknowledge the truth and change the conversations around that truth. You have to engage with people to help everyone understand that the world as we know it is ending. The dream of endless growth is over.

More than anything else, I have learned that there are many perceptions of an issue. Despite clear evidence to one person, another person's perspective may be entirely different. This is very challenging and very frustrating. It can lead, as it did for me while paddling up the Mississippi, to almost total dysfunction. If what is in your head, like "I am stuck on the highway near Vicksburg, please come and get me," translates to the receiver as, "He's stuck so let's go and get him at Walmart," you have a problem. You have to try to figure out what might be in the other person's mind. You have to carefully examine the messages you have been sending in case they have some potential for confusion.

Maybe it would have been better to say, "You know how I told you to go to Walmart? That's no good. I can't get there so that's just the start now. I want you to go to Walmart and then drive for another hour north." Recognizing the possibility that people hear different messages for different reasons is a big start, working with that to achieve better outcomes is something that I still struggle with.

Maybe even that wouldn't work. Maybe Walmart needed to be totally dropped from the conversation. I don't know. What I do know is that if you watch for miscommunications such as this you will see the process many times in a week. Watch how people like to give a bit of praise first, instead of cutting to the chase. The praise message is heard but the real message may well be buried.

Australians have been accused in the past of their brutal honesty. We think we are getting more sophisticated when we soften the message, cover it with sugar. If the message is bitter, then it has to be bitter. That is communication. I have tried simplifying the message and it has been noted that my emails sound like I am shouting, but the recipient at least got what I wanted them to. It was not hidden in any fluff.

When it comes to climate change, you have to work especially hard with those people who do not yet accept the evidence for this. Respect their right to hold their own point of view, but challenge them to identify some event they would accept as evidence: when there is no ice in the Arctic, when sea levels rise by 100 centimetres, when we can no longer farm across inland Australia. If none of that works, just forget them.

Move on. They will come round one day and blame someone else for not informing them.

More importantly, get on with creating a lifestyle that can survive in a post-carbon world. For lots of reasons that lifestyle will become more desirable as things get harder. Environmentally friendly products are becoming much more popular. We cannot consume our way out of this crisis, but we can change people's mindsets by becoming examples of what a future society might look like. Understand that flying to Bali for a wedding, flying to Europe for a sporting event, jetting around the world for business, or even flying somewhere for a holiday, are incompatible with future life on this planet.

Two degrees' warming may well be the tipping point past which the earth goes into runaway temperature rise that mankind cannot control. According to the IPCC, in 2014 to have a 90% chance of staying under two degrees the world needed to stop burning all fossil fuels then. We didn't. The chance of a soft landing is now more like 80%. That is a 1 in 5 chance of failure. Engineers work with numbers like 1 in 10,000 or 1 in 1,000,000. 1 in 5 is unthinkable unless, it seems, when applied to the failure of the human race.

I'm hoping for a more compassionate society, one that is in tune with the earth in the same way as most indigenous groups. There is a lot to learn from a culture that survived in Australia for 50 millennia. Only now are we finding out how robust and sophisticated that culture was. It just didn't have the resources to combat the warlike invaders with their culture of exploitation. That invading culture looks like it will not make it in this country for just a third of a millennium.

I have learned a couple of important lessons the hard way. Firstly, being tough is not enough. We cannot lead by simply setting out to do the impossible. Yes, we need adventurers and explorers, but we also need pioneers who build and lead and support. We need organizers and supporters and we have to accept that most people are none of those things. Secondly, most people are not actively listening and logically analyzing the evidence. Preaching by presenting evidence will not lead people to change their beliefs. We need to listen actively and understand people's emotional framework and then discuss how they might face their fears in the face of the evidence.

To make the change we believe is necessary, we have to lead by example. This also means embracing and working with those people ready to understand. The 10 or 15% of intransigent doubters will be left behind. Some will die out. Some will beg to catch up.

What you do is up to you. If you embrace the issue and help work towards solutions, even when it challenges the status quo, you will receive the same rewards as I have. I can promise you, that is a good feeling. There is also the added benefit that you will develop a network. You will be like those river people who share and help each other. That might just be your life jacket when the shit hits the fan.

LYN'S EPILOGUE

My journey with Steve started a few years ago. My first impression was, wow he doesn't waste any time, next thing I knew my whirlwind life with Steve had begun. We started out with a lot in common, both our working lives and personal lives revolved around the importance of the environment. We also shared a love for water, not just improving the quality of it, but also water sports. Steve introduced me to outrigger paddling, and we both love sailing. Our other shared passion was for our families and their future in a changing world.

Steve is logical; however, he is also impulsive. In saying this he always takes the time to weigh up the consequences of his actions, and any risks involved, it's just that he does it at hyper-speed compared to most people. Before I know it, we are in the midst of a new adventure. I still laugh at how much we pack into a day, every day.

In the story of Steve's journey, it became evident how important a good team was to the trip's success. This was equally important in putting this book together.

Steve was adamant that he did not want to hurt anyone in writing his story, so he was quite reticent to reveal too much of himself. Thanks to Geoff Ebbs, the editorial journey has been filled with many introspective episodes, often quite humorous (at Steve's expense) and then that instant when we realise that Steve has exposed some of those hidden feelings and Geoff and I exchange a knowing look and say, "That has to go in the book."

Both Steve and I are still working in the environmental field. Some projects we work on together and then we have our own areas of interest. I work with Australian Native Bees; they play an important role in Australia's biodiversity, especially with the global threat to Honey Bees. Steve is the Chair of Australia's Sustainable Engineering Society (SENG), and like everything he does he puts his heart and soul into the role.

Steve is a practical-visionary. I know this is a contradictory term, but it really does suit who he is.

Geoff explained at the start of this book that Steve has given so much of himself; now it's up to you, the reader, to make his sacrifices worthwhile.

The world is changing, we are changing. Let's turn the tide on climate change and make the politicians hear the conversations for what they are, not what they want to hear.

DONATIONS

Lea

Trevor and Marilyn

Tony Margan

Mum

Carol & Russell Forsythe

Phil Bradley & Annie Nielsen

Renate Heurich

Mike Drake

Peter McCrossin

Mary Maher

Bruce Morgan

Richard Palmer

Merrilyn Eyre

Barry Lennon

Tony Guilding

Kara de los Reyes

Robyn/Heather Marshall

Bronwyn Fackender

Red Pig

Brian McMillan

Tony Gilding

David Hood

Hamish Wiggens

Fiona Gordon